MW00531883

ROGUE FAMILIAR

BY
JEFFE KENNEDY

Copyright © 2023 by Jennifer M. Kennedy
Print Edition

All rights reserved. Except as permitted under the U.S. Copyright Act of 1976, no part of this publication may be reproduced, distributed, or transmitted in any form or by any means, or stored in a database or retrieval system, without the prior written permission of the author.

This is a work of fiction. Names, characters, places, and incidents are either the products of the author's imagination or used fictitiously, and any resemblance to actual persons, living or dead, or business establishments, organizations or locales is completely coincidental.

Thank you for reading!

Credits
Cover: Ravven (www.ravven.com)

He left to save her from herself… But who will save him from her?

When Lady Seliah Phel wakes from a drugged sleep to find herself abandoned by her newly bonded wizard, she vows revenge—and to hunt him down. Tracking him through the familiar wilds of the marshlands of her home is the easy part; learning to use her nascent magical skills is something else entirely. So is facing the vast, uncaring society of the Convocation in a time of brewing war.

Jadren El-Adrel is not known for doing the right thing, but getting as far away from Seliah as possible before he drains her dry will be his one noble gesture. So what if she weeps a few tears. Better than her dying in his service—or enabling him to become the ravenous beast that crawls beneath his skin. Unfortunately, in his self-imposed exile, and without the power of his familiar, Jadren quickly runs afoul of the enemy.

As her vengeful quest for recapture becomes a rescue mission, Selly faces all she still doesn't know about the greater world of wizards and familiars. And Jadren, once determined to walk his own path and stay far, far away from the idealistic fools of House Phel, finds himself aligning with them against the house of his birth. War is coming to the Convocation, which means a clever wizard should pick the side most likely to win.

Sadly, Jadren has never been all that clever…

DEDICATION

To Robin Perini,
prolific, talented author and generous friend,
lost to us tragically too young.
We all miss you, Robin.

ACKNOWLEDGMENTS

Thanks, as always, to my wonderful friends, writers and otherwise, who held my hand and fed me drinks and comforting words as I thrashed over how long this book took to write:

- Kelly Robson who is endlessly supportive about *everything*. You are the sun who lights my days and the world is a better place that you're in it.
- Darynda Jones, sister in slogging. We'll get there!
- Grace Draven, who was dealing with cancer as I wrote this and thus was *no help at all*. What about *my* needs, Grace?? Love you always.
- Jennifer Estep, always willing to offer her sterling insights. You're the best!
- Megan Mulry, for emergency drinks and reminding me of what's important. I can never pick up the tab enough times.
- Alex Gurevich, for catching the (very occasional) error in my worldbuilding logic and for offering timely advice on what Jadren would or wouldn't do.
- Minerva Spencer, for the blazingly fast proofread and for all her savvy insights on the business.
- Carien Ubink, who says I think every book will be terrible and virtually pats my hand. She's also the one who looks everything up, my walking world bible. If there are errors, blame her. (Just kidding.) (Not really.)

My Writer Coffee peeps keep me sane and connected. Thanks to Emily Mah, Jim Sorenson, and J. Barton Mitchell for everything.

Special thanks to John Murphy, who is not only my SFWA vice-president and doing amazing work to take things off my plate, but also contributed his considerable electrical engineering expertise to the question of magically electrocuting someone.

Shoutout to the staff, board, and key volunteers of SFWA. It's amazing to work with all of you who make my job so easy. Particular gratitude to Kate Baker and Terra LeMay for patience and tolerance—and for being so amazing at all they do.

My cover-designer, Ravven, never misses—but this cover in particular kept me inspired and influenced so much about this story. You are truly incredible.

Because she does her work later in the publishing process, in the past I've missed acknowledging my audiobook narrator, Deborah Balm. She brings these characters to life in delightful ways and I'm so grateful to work with her.

Thanks and appreciation to my agent, Sarah Younger, who wholeheartedly supports my self-published projects and is happy to hustle on the subsidiary rights. She is truly the best.

As always, love to David who has been there from the beginning.

ROGUE FAMILIAR

BY
JEFFE KENNEDY

~ 1 ~

"**D**ID YOU KNOW about this?" Selly shouted, striding into the House Phel library without knocking—the doors hadn't been warded or magically locked—and shocking her brother by smacking the letter onto his desk.

"And good morning to you, too, Seliah," Nic said drily, sitting back from whatever she'd been working on and looking her over. As Lady Phel, Nic had a desk near her husband's. They almost always—unless one of them was unconscious or had been abducted, which was admittedly a fair chunk of their marriage so far—convened in the library after breakfast to handle house business together. They'd been easy to find.

"Hi, Nic," Selly said, searching her heart for some polite chagrin. Nope, none to be found. She was too pissed. "Apologies for the intrusion," she said anyway.

"You're family, not an intrusion," Nic replied easily, her brilliant emerald gaze going to Gabriel consideringly as he read the letter, measuring her wizard, no doubt, with her acutely attuned familiar's senses.

Selly didn't need any magical help assessing Gabriel's emotional state. Not that she had any clue how to be a familiar of Nic's education and caliber. She did know her brother, though.

1

JEFFE KENNEDY

The flush on his dusky skin revealed his embarrassment at the contents of the note she'd slapped on his desk, while his snapping wizard-black eyes showed growing annoyance. "What's the meaning of this?" he demanded in turn.

With an exasperated sigh, Selly snatched the fine paper from his loose grasp. "Here, let me help you." For Nic's benefit, she read aloud Jadren's crisply inked, meticulous handwriting. Even while ruthlessly jilting her, he hadn't betrayed the slightest emotional tremor in a single stroke of his pen. *"No, I didn't fuck you senseless. That was the potion I put in your wine. I said as soon as you're safe, I'd take you to bed. You'll never be safe while you're with me, so... I'm gone. Don't bother looking as I won't be found. Don't shed any girlish tears over me. Just go on with your life. It's the best revenge and you deserve that much. ~J"*

She flung down the sheet of paper again and Nic rose, gracefully retrieving it to read herself with pursed lips while Selly glared at Gabriel. "I ask you again—did you know about this?"

"Which part?" he snapped back, rising from his chair and steepling his fingers on the desk, looming over her. Selly was tall, but her brother was taller. Plus his potent wizard-magic intimidated her now far more than she liked. Spending time with Jadren—also a wizard—had increased her sensitivity to magic, especially since he'd bonded her as his familiar. Gabriel's felt like a gathering storm, prickling her with the animal urge to take shelter. She overrode it and stood firm.

"The part where," Gabriel continued on a low growl, "Jadren—I assume that's the 'J' of this missive—references

2

fucking my baby sister senseless? Or the part where he confesses to *drugging* you? Or..." His voice rose to a near shout. "Or the part where—"

"Gabriel!" Nic said sharply.

He whirled on her, magic crackling silver in the air, a boom of thunder echoing in the distance. Selly had never been afraid of her gentle big brother, not even when the magic had come upon him so suddenly, turning his hair white and his eyes blacker than blackest night. But then, she also hadn't been in her right mind for most of that time. Since her adventures with Jadren, particularly due to the time she'd spent captive with him in House Sammael and House El-Adrel, she'd developed a healthy respect for the immense power wizards wielded. And Gabriel was more powerful than most.

Possibly Selly shouldn't have allowed her temper to goad her into confronting Gabriel with Jadren's goodbye note.

"You need to keep your calm," Nic was saying to Gabriel, approaching him as one might a frightened horse, if that horse was a battle-trained stallion as like to bite your face off as anything else. Completely unafraid and unflustered—how Selly admired Nic's unflappable poise—Nic laid a palm on Gabriel's chest, a slim figure compared to his broad-shouldered one. "Pull the magic back, Wizard," she murmured.

He laid a hand over hers, several expressions chasing across his face before it settled into a heated and tender affection. The sense of danger and lethal silver in the air receded, and Selly found herself envying that, too. Even if—no, *when*—she managed to chase Jadren down, he'd never look at her that way, never treat her as more than his familiar and a necessary burden. She was realist enough to accept that about him. Jadren had his heart locked behind layers of clockwork metal. Having witnessed his vile mother and how he'd grown up, Selly didn't blame him.

Probably she should just let him go, but she'd never been one to back down from a fight. Including this one.

"The part I mean, Lord Phel," Selly said in a sharp tone, cutting into the moment between her brother and sister-in-law, and earning a black glance of renewed ire from Gabriel, "is did you know your minion Jadren planned to leave? Perhaps you gave him permission." Jadren might flaunt many rules, but even he would hesitate before violating a contractual obligation. As a minion of House Phel, Jadren wouldn't have departed without the senior wizard's knowledge and permission. Probably. Selly could hope her brother hadn't colluded in breaking her heart.

Gabriel paused, not meeting her challenging glare, confirming her supposition. The way Nic looked between Gabriel and Selly, an expression of dawning comprehension on her face, gave the answer to another of Selly's questions. Yes, Gabriel had known, but Nic hadn't. Obscurely, that made Selly feel better. She hadn't liked thinking that Nic had conspired to ruin Selly's life this way. Of all people in House Phel, Nic would know the pain of being a familiar whose wizard was moving ever farther away, the wizard–familiar bond growing attenuated, like a strained tendon threatening to snap with every tiny increase in tension.

Gabriel withdrew from Nic's light embrace and sat heavily at his desk, finally meeting Selly's gaze. Hands folded, back straight, wizard-black gaze firmly neutral, Gabriel was all Lord Phel in that moment. Selly rather hated him for it.

"Yes, I knew," he said. "I gave Jadren permission to depart."

Though this wasn't exactly a surprise, the acknowledgment hit her hard and painfully. "And you didn't tell me." Her voice came out a strained whisper.

"Nic, love, would you leave us?" Gabriel asked without looking at his wife.

"No, I want Nic here, as witness to what you've done to me."

Gabriel looked mildly taken aback at Selly's demand, or perhaps at her phrasing. Nic, who'd gathered her skirts to obey her wizard, instead returned to sit on her desk, slippered feet swinging. Gabriel frowned at her and she beamed back with faux innocence. "You can make it an order," she suggested sweetly, "but failing that, I'll abide by Seliah's request. I am, after all, the one ally she has who understands the implications of this for her."

"I wasn't aware we were forming camps," he replied in a low tone.

"Wizards and familiars are, by their very nature and by centuries of Convocation politics, on opposite sides of the table," Nic said without rancor.

"I thought you agreed we're partners," he retorted, unfolding his hands to tap his fingers restlessly on the desk.

"We are. It's possible to be both. Now, Gabriel, my only love, let's discuss Seliah's relationship with *her* wizard instead of mine."

"This conversation isn't over," he warned her.

"It never is," she agreed, sounding ruefully amused. "Back to the subject at hand, I believe Seliah asked you why you didn't warn her of Jadren's plans to desert her."

"It was better for her not to know," he answered wearily.

"What?" Selly screeched, gratified that Nic echoed it, though less strenuously. "My wizard told you he planned to leave me, which goes against all Convocation custom and laws, which *you*, as the lord of my House, are supposed to enforce with your minions, and you decided it was better that I not know?"

Gabriel gazed at her sourly. "Since when did you begin studying up on Convocation law?"

"Since I spent time being mired in those laws as the property of first House Sammael and then House El-Adrel. I figured I'd do better armed with knowledge."

"Don't be ridiculous," he spat. "You were *never* their property."

"Technically—" Nic began, and Gabriel thrust a finger at her.

"Don't you start. I don't need to be lectured on the second-class citizen status—at *best*—of familiars in the Convocation," he snarled.

"Apparently you do," she fired back, "if Seliah already understands more than you do. That is…" She sent Selly an apologetic look. "I take back the 'already.' I didn't mean to call attention to your recent difficulties."

As Nic was the primary reason Selly no longer suffered from those "difficulties," Selly didn't hold the remark against her. Instead, she shrugged, as if it didn't bother her anymore, which it didn't. Mostly. She had Jadren to thank for being able to regard her years-long battle with insanity with a measure of fortitude. Thinking of how compassionate he'd been, how frankly *kind* to her, in helping her face what the magic-induced toxicity had done to her mind, coaching her in how she could emerge from that, only made her angrier that he'd then callously abandoned her.

The coward.

It was especially annoying that she, in turn, could sympathize with the fear and insecurity that had driven Jadren to believe he could only keep her safe by leaving her. At the same time, she fervently wished she could pay him back for jilting her in such a humiliating fashion by putting an arrow through him. Again.

She wrung out a thin smile for Nic. "We don't need to tiptoe around it. Now that I'm in my right mind again, I can acknowledge just how bad off I was for many years. But I'm fully recovered now and ready to—"

"You are still fragile," Gabriel interrupted. "You weren't in any condition to come on the mission to rescue Nic in the first place—I kick myself for allowing it—then, considering what you experienced afterward... Well, no one would blame you for needing peaceful time for rest and recovery. Jadren understood that, too, Selly. We all want only the best for you."

Nic winced at his words and scrubbed a hand over her face, while Selly stared at her big brother in incredulity and building rage. "Don't you patronize me," she said softly.

"I'm not," Gabriel returned, far too swiftly, then held up

7

his hands in a pacifying gesture. "Do you deny that your sojourns in Houses Sammael and El-Adrel, where you were imprisoned and *tortured*, were traumatizing?"

"I don't feel traumatized," she returned evenly.

Gabriel smacked a hand on his desk. "Torture is, by definition, traumatizing. That's what it's designed to do!"

"They barely tortured me. Jadren took the brunt of it and suffered far more than I did. He protected me."

"He bonded you as his familiar. Against your will," Gabriel thundered, a rumble outside echoing him.

Nic cast her gaze at the rapidly clouding sky outside the tall glass windows, shook her head, and opened her mouth.

"*Don't*, Nic," Gabriel practically snarled. "Don't tell me either to calm down or that a wizard bonding a familiar has nothing to do with the familiar's free choice. You and Seliah are as human as anyone and you deserve the freedom to choose a bonding that affects you on the deepest levels for the rest of your lives."

"It's because of that deep-level effect that *you* should not have given Jadren permission to leave!" Selly said. "Jadren bonded me because *he* had no choice either. It was that or I'd have been bonded to one of his siblings, which he assured me would have been much worse, and I believe him. He did it to save me, as we've already explained, more than once. But all of that is immaterial, however, because we *are* bonded and one inescapable truth is that the wizard–familiar bond, once forged, cannot be broken. That's in the past. He's my wizard and I'm going after him."

"You're *what*?" Gabriel's magic flared again. "No, you are

not. I forbid it."

Oh, he did not just try to forbid her. "You're my brother, not my keeper. And unless I'm to be Lyndella to Jadren's Sylus, going insane from the attenuation of the bond, I need to find Jadren before I lose my mind for a second time. A prospect I promise you I do not relish."

"Dark arts save me." Gabriel ground out in appalled astonishment. "Tell me you did not read that melodramatic pile of crap."

"Hey!" Nic protested. "I love that book. So did everyone, which is why it's famous. You read it yourself."

"So that I could understand the influences that warped your young mind, my love," he retorted, then returned his attention to Selly. "The pap that is the supposedly romantic tale of Sylus and Lyndella is Convocation propaganda aimed at familiars to make you believe that the slavery of your relationship to your wizard is not only palatable, but desirable."

"*Slavery?*" Nic echoed with an arched brow and fire in her eyes.

"Don't talk to me like I'm a child, Gabriel," Selly said at the same time.

"You *are* a child," Gabriel shot back, ignoring Nic and glaring silver daggers at Selly. At least he wasn't manifesting real silver daggers out of moon magic. Not yet, anyway. "The madness took you when you were barely an adolescent. *Ten years* you spent barely knowing your own name, let alone anything else of the world. No one expects you to—"

"*I* expect it, Gabriel! I expect it of myself," Selly practically shouted in his face. She didn't add that Jadren had expected it,

JEFFE KENNEDY

too, had taunted, teased, and jibed at her so that she'd stepped up to the challenge, discovering depths of fortitude and courage she'd never dreamed she'd have. Of course, he'd also called her a child in a woman's body, one of his misconceptions that lay at the root of why he'd refused to follow through with taking her to bed. "Is there some measure in the world that tells us when our minds have caught up to our bodies?" she demanded. "If there is, I don't know what it is. There are certainly people out there walking around being treated like adults when they behave like toddlers."

"An oracle head might be able to make that assessment," Nic said with a serious expression, though mischief danced in her eyes.

Gabriel continued to ignore her. "All of this argument is pointless," he said, focusing on Selly. "The reason I didn't stop Jadren was that he *wanted* to leave. He was determined, which is why you should respect his wishes. He asked my permission. I had no basis to tell him no."

"You could have—"

"Hear me out, please," Gabriel interrupted, waiting until she subsided. "You, both of you, know that I don't love being in the position of telling people what they can and can't do with their lives. Yes, I know that's part of heading House Phel, and I'm resigned to that necessity, but I don't have to like it. Jadren made a perfectly reasonable request and I agreed to it. Would you have had me say that no, he couldn't leave because my baby sister has a crush on him?"

Selly flushed, the skin of her face hot and tight. "That's dramatically unfair."

"Is it?" Gabriel studied her knowingly. "I've learned a great deal about Wizard–familiar bonds and how they affect familiars emotionally. What you think you feel for him isn't real."

How crushing to have her feelings for Jadren exposed and pronounced questionable in one blow.

"Gabriel," Nic said, "recall our conversations about you deciding that you know how other people feel better than they do."

"Seliah knows I'm right," he replied to Nic, black gaze still on Selly. "Don't you?"

She didn't know. She wished she did. More, she wished she knew what was going on in Jadren's mind and heart. "How can I find out when he's not even here?" she pointed out, trying to sound as rational as possible. "Besides, we're bonded. There's no changing that, so we have to work this out somehow."

"Actually," Gabriel said, "there is a way. And it's the answer to your problem. Alise has discovered how to sever the wizard–familiar bond."

Nic made a sound and raised her eyes to the ceiling, as if praying for patience, while Selly stood there, mind and body numb with astonishment. And incipient panic. "But that's not possible," she managed to say. If she had any hope of holding onto Jadren, it was this one thing, that they were bonded. She might not be able to escape him, but neither could he escape her. She'd counted on that.

"I thought we'd agreed to keep this information secret," Nic was saying to Gabriel in a very dry tone. "Given what a political powder-keg it is and the precarious situation of our house."

"Seliah is family," Gabriel replied, clearly throwing Nic's words back at her. "And it's important for her to know, especially now."

"I don't understand," Selly said faintly, mostly as a stalling tactic. "It's really possible to sever the bond?"

"It's not only possible, it's a *fait accompli*," Nic told her, sympathy in her gaze. Yes, Nic might understand all too well how she felt.

"*Fait accompli?*" Selly repeated, still not quite able to grapple the implications.

"That means it's been done already," Nic answered gently. "Alise severed the bond between Asa and Laryn, and also between my parents."

If Selly had been thinking clearly, she'd have realized before this moment that something had happened there. Of course they'd had to do something about Nic's maman, rescued from her abusive wizard and recuperating at House Phel. And the healer-wizard Asa's familiar, Laryn, had betrayed Nic and House Phel in the worst possible way, so naturally Gabriel had been obliged as Lord Phel to deal justice. Selly hadn't given a thought to either situation.

No, she'd been intent on Jadren, on his recovery. On wanting him so much and scheming how she'd seduce him once Asa released him from the infirmary. She'd been like a giddy teenager, redecorating her bedroom instead of paying attention to important developments, for the love of the dark arts. Now she'd not only lost that opportunity to be with Jadren that night, she stood to lose him forever.

She felt like she could cry, like the silly girl everyone seemed to think she was. That maybe she was in truth.

Gabriel came around his desk, taking Selly's hands in his. Hers must be clammy because his skin felt hot and dry to the touch. "Don't fret," he said soothingly. "Did you hear me? Alise can sever your bond and you'll be free of Jadren El-Adrel, forever. This is a good thing."

"What if I don't want it?" she made herself ask him, meeting his wizard-black gaze. She'd never found his magic-changed eyes distressing or intimidating the way her family and friends had, but now she found it ever so slightly difficult to face him. Not the eyes themselves, but the look of incredulous condemnation in them.

"Don't be ridiculous," Gabriel said, squeezing her hands just a bit too hard. "Of course you don't want to be mentally enslaved to someone."

"Gabriel," Nic put in, "that's not how—"

"I know how it works," he spat at her. "You told me. You would follow me to the ends of the world whether you wanted to or not, because the bonding, or the Fascination, or both, would compel you to."

Selly hadn't known that part—at least, not the extent of it—and Nic met her questioning gaze with a shrug of rueful acknowledgment. Now Selly didn't know what to think. Did she only want to chase after Jadren because of the bonding? That couldn't be, because she'd had feelings for Jadren well before he'd bonded her. She frowned, trying to trace back the evolution of her relationship with Jadren. He'd irritated her to begin with, annoyed her with all his relentless teasing and jibing. Then she'd seen beneath that prickly armor. And he'd been kind to her. Understanding in a way no one else had ever been.

And he'd sacrificed for her.

And he'd left her.

And everything in her screamed to go after him, to follow the ever-attenuating bond until she could feel the richness of him on the other side of it again. Until she could touch his skin, breathe in his scent, and experience his ardent caresses. She *wanted* him as she'd never wanted anyone.

But was it real?

"How do I know if it's real?" she asked Nic, hearing the plaintiveness in her own voice, her hands limp in Gabriel's grasp.

"Trust me, it isn't—" Gabriel began, cut off when Nic let out a small screech of frustration and hopped off the desk, her sea-green skirts swishing and falling perfectly into place, flattering her voluptuous figure as only an Ophiel gown could do. Something else to envy/admire in Nic. Perhaps if Selly weren't quite so tall, bony, and angular, Jadren would have wanted her more. *I'm not interested in acquiring a stick-insect of an untrained, feral marsh-cat of a familiar,* he'd said. *A scrawny, unattractive little thing.* Oh, he'd tried to walk it back later, but… Maybe the truth had been in those initial, scathing assessments. She didn't know what to think.

"Gabriel, love, would you leave us?" Nic asked with a sweet smile, her emerald eyes jewel hard.

"After *you* refused to leave?" he demanded, dropping Selly's hands and turning on his wife.

14

"Yes. This is a conversation between familiars. We don't need you muddying the waters."

He took a breath to argue and she held up a hand to stop him. "Either you trust me or you don't," she added implacably, some deeper meaning to the words. "Besides, you promised to do the final vetting on the ever-replenishing water flasks that are ready to be shipped out. If we don't start providing a return on our end of numerous financial agreements, we're going to lose the few allies we do have."

"Do they count as allies if they're only our friends for financial benefit?" he asked darkly.

"Yes," she answered firmly. "A contract fulfilled outpaces anything so flimsy as a handshake and ostensibly friendly conversation."

He eyed her. "Sometimes I worry about your cynicism."

She smiled sunnily. "A good balance for your idealism."

Gabriel took a breath to say something more, then bit down on it. "Fine. I'll be in the minions' workshop then."

"Have a nice day at work, dear!" Nic called after him cheerfully as he stalked out of the room, slamming the library doors shut behind him. Instead of wincing as Selly expected, Nic rolled her eyes dramatically. "Wizards."

"Just tell it to me straight," Selly begged. "What didn't you want to say in front of Gabriel?"

With a sigh, Nic gave Selly a rueful smile. "How do you know it's real, how you feel? The short answer is that you don't. That maybe you never will."

"Even if I agree to have the bond severed?"

Nic grimaced. "Maybe? Probably not. I wish I could tell

you otherwise."

Selly wished it, too.

"But I have a question for you in turn," Nic said, canting her head and watching Selly with keen attention. "Does it matter?"

Does it matter? "Of course it matters," she protested.

"Does it though?" Nic persisted. "Don't knee-jerk. Don't say so because Gabriel believes that. *Think.* Feeling how you feel, even if you didn't have a name or reason for it, would you go after Jadren anyway?"

Oh. Selly wasn't much given to introspection. Or maybe she could be, given the opportunity. She'd had precious little time with a mind clear enough for self-examination. One thing stood out clearly, however: She didn't care why she wanted to go after Jadren; only that she did. That she had to. "I can't do anything else."

Nic's full lips curved in understanding. "There's your answer. The only answer that matters."

~ 2 ~

"I SHOULD LEAVE immediately," Selly told Nic, who cocked her head in question instead of giving the affirming nod she'd expected. Maybe hoped for. If Gabriel was firm on forbidding Selly to go, she'd need Nic's help.

"Should you, though?" Nic asked, disappointing her.

"The longer I delay, the farther he'll get," Selly argued, then frowned. "He's truly inadequate at surviving on the land, away from civilization. I hate to think what trouble he'll get himself into."

"Seliah, sweetheart," Nic said gently. "Jadren is a powerful El-Adrel wizard. He's hardly a babe in the woods."

"That analogy is far too apt." *You have no idea,* she almost added, hearing Jadren's favorite phrase of defensiveness and denial in her head all too clearly. "What good are his skills at making gadgets against the predators and other dangers lurking in the marshes?"

"Let's take a moment." Nic held up a hand. "A few minutes more won't make that much difference." She went to pour them both some cold tea. Spring had given way to full summer in Meresin and the heat was beginning to build, layering in thick, languid layers over the ripening landscape.

She handed Selly a glass clinking with ice cubes.

"Ice?" Selly swirled the cubes so they chimed musically.

"A new experimental collaboration with House Ishim," Nic explained. "They're a third-tier house with wizards who mainly work on snow-removal in regions without elementally-heated roads. No imagination, really, or much ambition, which is why they've remained third tier for so long. But what they do have is wizards with water magic and an affinity for cold. We're showing them how to purify water to create ice." She frowned. "Shipping and distribution is still a problem, but the timing is good with summer already in this region and spring coming on in the bulk of the Convocation. I understand it will get even hotter here."

"Oh yes," Selly agreed, sipping the tea. It was delightfully chill and minty. As the cooling, calming elixir settled into her stomach, she realized how agitated she'd been since she woke and saw Jadren's note. And hurt. And betrayed. And furious. And sexually frustrated.

With all that going on, taking a moment as Nic suggested wasn't actually a bad idea. It wouldn't take all that long to find Jadren, not with her tracking skills and the bond between them. Selly sat on the cushioned window seat and took a deep breath. The tall glass windows stood open to the honey-sweet morning air, birdsong echoing from the blooming orchards and bees buzzing thick in the rose garden lining the walls.

The manse was recovering from being submerged in the marshes with astonishing speed, seeming to evolve overnight. Nic had explained that the magic Gabriel had wrought to restore the house tended to follow its own path, that Gabriel's connection to their Phel wizard ancestors meant the manse would essentially remember how had been in its heyday and become that again. It sounded improbable to Selly, but seeing rose borders spring up without gardeners planting them seemed to confirm the truth of it. There was an awful lot about magic Selly didn't know.

Nic sat beside her, gazing out the windows also, sunlight gleaming on her dark, short-cropped curls. "Let's say you do go after him immediately," Nic mused, then flicked her an emerald-green glance. "We'll need to convince Gabriel, first, and you'll need to assemble proper provisions, so he won't worry. *And*," she continued implacably when Selly started to argue, "let's say that you, with your admirable tracking skills, find Jadren in short order. Then what?"

Selly opened her mouth to answer, and found she had no thoughts to form words. Closing her mouth again, she tried to imagine it—and to ignore Nic's knowing look. Her canny sister-in-law had a point. Once Selly caught up to Jadren, as she undoubtedly would, what would she do? Throw herself naked at him? Because she'd done that and he'd drugged her senseless to escape.

She couldn't really tie him up and drag him back to House Phel. Or attempt to reason with him, because they'd just end up arguing and he'd probably win since he could always talk circles around her, tying her up in spurious logic that she just *knew* wasn't right but couldn't seem to think her way around. When she'd first read that note—clearly meant to cow her into meekly letting him go—she'd vowed revenge when she caught up to him. That he'd be the one shedding girlish tears. But did she want that?

No, she wanted *him*. And she wanted him to want her, to love her, the same way she felt about him. The way she was sure he truly did feel, if he hadn't somehow dredged up a noble impulse from the depths of his scarred soul and convinced himself that she was better off without him. *Better off.* Why did everyone else think they had the key to her being better off? She was beginning to loathe that phrase.

What she had to do was convince Jadren that she was safe with him, that they belonged together, that together they were stronger. Together they could address whatever scared him so badly about having a familiar. Being apart would fix nothing.

Nic waited her out, sipping her tea with patience, as if she weren't Lady Phel with a million items on her many lists. Negotiating with other High Houses and so forth. More things Selly didn't know much about.

"I don't know," Selly finally said, keenly aware of how much that applied to. "I hadn't thought beyond going after him. He's mine, whether we're bonded or not. That might not make any sense to you, since Jadren and I have known each other for such a short time, but what we went through together... I just know he's mine. The only one for me."

To her surprise, Nic smiled warmly, nodding. "You're very like your brother, you know. Gabriel decided I was his from looking at a miniature portrait of me. And from a single night together during my Betrothal Trials. When I fled from him and the Convocation, Gabriel was instructed in no uncertain terms to go back to House Phel and await the outcome. But no, he came after me." Her smile turned intimate and soft. "Like you, he also had zero plan for what he'd do once he found me, which—against all probability—he did."

Selly considered that with bemusement. She'd known the bare bones of how Nic and Gabriel had come to be together, but not all of those details. "So, you're saying that Gabriel and I share romantic impulsiveness, an enthusiasm for grand gestures and embarking on harebrained quests, but lack the ability to plan for a successful conclusion?"

Nic actually laughed, eyes sparkling with affection that wasn't just for Gabriel. "I wouldn't have phrased it exactly that way. Still, you're not far off the mark." She sobered. "If I didn't make it clear before, I absolutely believe in your feelings for Jadren. Whether the product of your harrowing adventures together, the wizard–familiar bond, or your obvious compatibility—likely all three—there is a connection between you and Jadren. Even were you to agree to sever the bond, I don't know that it would change anything for either of you."

"Do you think I should agree to the severing?"

"I think it's not up to *me*," Nic answered with some acerbity. "That's a very personal choice." With a sigh, she raked a hand through her curls. "And I'm fully aware of the irony of me saying that, having participated in the decision to sever Maman's bond with Papa without her knowledge or consent, and Laryn's with Asa, which she consented to under duress." Her expression hardened. "Though arguably Laryn deserved far worse."

"You could've demanded to have Laryn executed, after what she did to you," Selly pointed out. Selly bore considerable hatred for Laryn, but she still shuddered at how that must feel, being cut off from her wizard. But, who knew? Maybe Laryn was relieved. She'd never seemed all that happy with Asa.

Nic shook her head. "Gabriel could never have stomached executing Laryn—either while she was pregnant with an innocent child or after the babe was born, as it would cast her as little more than a brood mare."

"Compromise?" Selly asked.

"The secret of all lasting relationships," Nic agreed. "The good news is, I can use that as leverage on Gabriel to prevent him from strong-arming you into having your bond severed."

"Thank you," Selly said quietly, but with intense relief. She might not be able to logically explain her reasoning to Gabriel, but she hated the idea of the severing. "Gabriel probably won't understand," she added, "and I hate for him to think badly of me for it, but..." She trailed off, not quite able to say the rest of it out loud.

Nic wrinkled her nose sympathetically. "I can offer this much: I also refused to have our bond severed."

It took Selly a moment. When she caught up, she gasped, quickly covering her mouth with her hand. "You and Gabriel... discussed having *your* bond severed?"

Nic rolled her gorgeous eyes. "Yes, of course. We didn't exactly *discuss* it so much as your foolishly noble brother suggested, then tried to insist, and even called into question whether I'm capable of making a logical decision on the topic."

Selly whistled low and slow in wonder. "And he's still alive."

Laughing, Nic put a hand on Selly's arm, squeezing in affection. "You understand me, sister. Yes, I managed not to kill him, but you should know this is an ongoing argument between us and is a disagreement that lies at the root of his concern for you. Gabriel still can't quite reconcile himself to not knowing if I truly love him or if the bond forces me to."

"Severing the bond would prove it to both of you, wouldn't it?"

"First of all, we don't know if a bond, once-severed can be reestablished. That's a risk I'm not willing to take. Also, I don't need my feelings proved to myself," Nic continued with steely resolve. "And Gabriel can learn to believe what I tell him without some kind of outside proof."

Selly sat back, considering that. Jadren also believed that she didn't know her own mind and heart. "Is it a wizard-thing or a man-thing, them thinking they know us better than we know ourselves?"

"Both?" Nic laughed wryly, shaking her head. "And it hardly matters. We'll just have to stick to our lines in the sand. So, what will you do?"

Selly really liked that Nic asked her. It seemed like, ever since she'd regained her sanity—well, and including for years before that, however dimly she recalled them—people had been telling her what she should do and why. The bitter irony was, now that someone was actually asking her, Selly only wanted to know what Nic thought she should do. This was part of being an adult, though, making her own choices. Good information helped, however. "Where do you think Jadren will go?"

Nic considered that. "That's an interesting thought problem. You know him better than anyone. Where do *you* think he will go?"

"Not back to House El-Adrel." Selly knew that much.

"No, I imagine not."

"But he doesn't have much of anywhere he *can* go, does he?" Selly asked. "He'll need a place to live, an income. You know the Convocation better than I do—can he get hired at another house without his mother's permission?"

"Theoretically, yes, but in practice no—not without an MP scorecard. Not unless he convinces someone to take him on under the table. I don't see that happening, though. Not with Katica El-Adrel retaining some kind of hold on Jadren." Nic eyed her keenly. "You haven't gone into detail about what happened at House El-Adrel—not beyond the bare bones—but Lady El-Adrel... She *does* have something on Jadren, doesn't she? Something deeper and more powerful than a Convocation high-house head or parent typically holds on one of their scions."

Selly met Nic's penetrating green gaze evenly. "I don't know what is typical. Jadren explained some—that high-house heads tend to be very controlling, that they rule with precision and total power, expecting everyone in their houses to follow exacting standards that basically result in a house of possibly thousands of people having the same characteristics and values."

Nic actually looked amused. "Did he say that? He's not entirely wrong, though he's coloring with a bit of a broad brush. Not every Convocation High House operates that way, certainly not the lower tier houses."

"Does House Elal?" Selly asked before she could lose her

nerve. At Nic's coolly raised brows, the impassively regal expression her sister-in-law could assume like a mask at a moment's notice, she hastened to explain. "Jadren used Lord Elal as an example of that behavior—he wasn't complimentary—and it just now occurs to me that I haven't asked about what you're going through, the estrangement from your father, what kind of ... pressure he might be exerting on you."

Nic's aloof expression thawed and she sagged back against the window frame, her eyes holding a curious softness. "You really are very much like Gabriel, both of you so empathetic and thinking about how other people might be feeling."

"Not really," Selly said, guilt pricking her. "It didn't occur to me until this conversation to ask you. I've been mired in my own problems."

"You have plenty to work through," Nic assured her in a dry tone. "No one expects you to just spring into action and—."

"*I* expect it," Selly interrupted. "I feel like I have to keep saying this. I'm not an invalid or a crazy girl who needs to be coddled."

Nic nearly laughed, but abruptly sobered. "Who's calling you crazy? That's unfair and dead wrong."

Jadren had called her that, but—oddly enough—she hadn't minded. At least he hadn't minced words. And he understood what that kind of magically induced uprooting from the real world felt like. "I'm aware that I'm recovering from a bad place," she answered instead, "but part of that recovery is becoming a functioning member of this house, being a friend to people. Being supportive rather than a burden." She cast about, feeling as if she needed to convince Nic of something. "Do you remember the story you told me when I was in the thick of madness? A kind of parable for my situation."

Nic nodded slowly, thoughtfully. "I wasn't sure how much of that time you remembered."

"I remember *that*." Vividly. Climbing to the balcony in the rain, creeping inside the unlocked glass doors, wanting to see this new woman Gabriel had brought home, feeling dazzled by Nic's beauty and the palpable wine-red, rose-scented magic that lushly billowed around her. The only other magical person Selly had been around until then was her brother, who had the same sort of magic she did, so meeting Nic had nearly overwhelmed her senses with her very differentness, along with the heated redolence of her magic. Nic had seemed like a glowing, living blossom—and when she'd been kind to Selly, it had warmed and settled something in her.

"You offered me a way to understand myself. By giving me the tale of the princess cursed to be misunderstood, you helped me see that what was wrong with me might not be my fault."

"Oh," Nic murmured, reaching out to take Selly's hand. "It was never your fault, honey."

"I know that. Now," she added wryly, holding onto Nic's hand. "Then…it was all so confusing. I didn't know what was real, what wasn't, even who I was." She shuddered a little internally, not liking to recall the turbulence of those mists that had held her at their mercy. No wonder Jadren had such a violently visceral reaction when reminded of his own suffering. "My point is that I've been mired in my own problems. First through no fault of my own, but since then, out of self-absorption. I haven't been a person who could be a friend to you, but I'd like to start now."

Nic smiled, a slow curve of her full lips, generous with warm affection. "You already have been, Seliah. You came to rescue me."

Selly shook her head. "I didn't do much."

"You came when you didn't have to. When, in fact, you were strenuously dissuaded from it. Then, you stayed behind to play rear guard so we could get away. You saved us." Nic waved a hand in front of her face and blinked at the tears filling her eyes before she rolled them. "I weep so easily these days. I blame the pregnancy."

"I don't know much about pregnancy, but I've heard tales that the emotions can be volatile," Selly replied, casting a dubious eye at Nic's barely rounded belly.

"Yes, well." Nic wiped away the tears, regaining her usual dry tone along with her poise. "It's a handy excuse, anyway. You asked about Papa." She sighed heavily, allowing a deep unhappiness to show.

"You don't have to—"

"Ah ah ah." Nic wagged a finger at her. "You don't get to back out now." She relented and smiled. "Really it's fine. I mean, it's *not* fine, but you asked and you should know. Papa is... Well, Jadren is more correct than he isn't on that one. As Lord Elal, Papa rules his house, his family, and his many minions, with fierce and absolute power. That includes my mother as his familiar, and me as his daughter. Or it did include me, until I ran away, a rebellion for which he hasn't forgiven me, and for which he is punishing me by denying me my dowry and even my personal possessions."

"What?" Selly couldn't imagine it.

"Yes, I know we hadn't filled you in on the details. I'm telling you now. This is one of the reasons House Phel is in difficult financial straits. It's a considerable amount of money, a large part of which is intended to redeem the cost of Gabriel applying for me in the Betrothal Trials, plus I'm owed important tangibles like grapevines from Elal stock." She rolled her head on her neck, deliberately relaxing herself, and continued. "As for my relationship with Papa, in retrospect, I can see now that, in some ways, he'd already disowned me in his heart when I manifested as a familiar instead of as a wizard, when it became clear I could never be the heir to House Elal as he'd trained me to be."

"But that wasn't something you could control," Selly burst out, appalled. While Jadren's mother was clearly a monster—he, himself, had said she was incapable of love—it seemed Nic's father was not much better.

Nic raised a single brow. "Are we admitting then that it's possible to feel bad about letting people down even though something wasn't our fault?"

Oh. "Yes," Selly agreed on a breath of a sigh.

Patting her hand, Nic continued. "Just making a point. Anyway, there's bad blood between me and Papa, trouble that goes back longer than my ill-advised escape attempt, as I'm beginning to understand. Has anyone explained alternate form to you yet?"

The apparently abrupt change of subject took Selly by surprise. "Yes, actually. Jadren explained it. I thought—when I saw Gabriel turn you into the silver phoenix—that wizards could do that sort of thing to anyone. You know." She wiggled her fingers in demonstration. "Turn people into toads."

"Ah, no. That unlikely creature is simply my alternate form, which lies hidden away inside every familiar until their wizard releases it. It's one of the reasons to be bonded, by the way, as it's only via that bond that you can take your alternate form."

"How can I know what mine would be?" Selly asked, fascinated despite herself. Jadren liked to call her a half-feral swamp creature and, in truth, she'd always loved the idea of becoming an animal.

"You don't know until you take it," Nic answered ruefully. "Imagine my surprise at mine."

A small laugh burst out of Selly. "Not what you expected?"

"Not even close," Nic acknowledged drolly, then let out a sigh. "See, Maman is a cat in her alternate form and, while these things don't necessarily run in families, I figured mine would be something like that, too, or perhaps a nice, neat peregrine falcon or some such. Nothing goes as one imagines when Gabriel Phel is involved."

"Does the wizard have an influence then?"

"Nobody knows. There are theorists in Convocation Center who collect the data and research that sort of thing, so there are some who think the wizard's magic has an effect but..." She shrugged.

"I can't help noticing your alternate form is silver." Like Gabriel's moon magic.

"Exactly." She waved that off. "Anyway, what I've been

working around to is that a wizard can force their familiar into alternate form and keep them there as long they please."

"They can keep them in animal form—as in, forever?"

"Yes, though most wizards don't put their familiars in alternate form much at all, because they can't access the familiar's magic while they're animals, and accessing the magic is the whole point of having a familiar to begin with. Still, my papa, may he be clawing out his remaining eye in misery, kept Maman in feline form since my escape. As a punishment."

"Oh." Selly could see not being able to control your own body as a punishment. She worried about Jadren's father, Fyrdo, who'd been kind to her and who'd helped them escape. What punishment had he suffered at the wrathful hands of his wizard, Jadren's awful mother? Being an animal didn't seem all that bad, compared to the things Katica El-Adrel came up with. "Did she not like being a cat?" she ventured.

Nic smiled grimly, but with a hint of wistfulness Selly suspected was for her naivete. "We don't know of a precedent for a familiar being kept in animal form that long," Nic answered, "but no, it's not good for the human intellect to be forced into the shape of an animal brain for more than a few hours or days, let alone this long. In fact, Maman has yet to recover, which is why she's in seclusion. Also why we made the decision to sever the bond without her consent."

"In the hopes that it would help her."

"And hurt *him*. I'm not sure which I wanted more," Nic replied in a hard voice Selly hadn't heard from her before. In that moment she glimpsed something of who Nic might have become, had she manifested as a wizard and become her father's heir. It was that same ruthlessness the high-house heads Selly had met all seemed to share. Lord Sammael and Lady El-Adrel both had that fiercely regal determination. "You hate him now," Selly realized.

"With the fire of a thousand suns," Nic agreed calmly, still with that murderous glint in her eyes. "I told Gabriel not to kill him—though he could have, and probably should have—which is why we instead sent my father back to House Elal missing an eye and a familiar." She sighed, staring past Selly at something only she could see. "I'm regretting that decision now."

"Because now he knows the bond-severing is possible."

Nic took her attention off whatever middle-distance preoccupied her and gave Selly a quick nod. "Exactly. I wasn't thinking clearly. Also, though he was an enemy before, we humiliated him. I know him well enough to predict he won't stay down for long—and when he rises, he'll want revenge. I haven't decided yet what to do about House Elal, but rest assured, if House Phel doesn't take care of this problem, Elal will come for us. You should know that, too."

Selly nodded, not sure she quite grasped all the implications, but determined to get there.

A reluctant smile broke through Nic's militant mien. "I didn't mean to frighten you."

"You didn't." And she hadn't. Selly wasn't afraid. She was... excited. "Whatever we need to do, I want to help."

"Good girl. A great deal happened while you were away." Nic gestured at the documents piled on the twin desks, the Ratsiel couriers collecting on the beams above like ghost versions of all sorts of strange creatures, waiting to deliver their missives and take away the replies. "Things are heating up."

"Jadren thinks Elal and El-Adrel conspired with Sammael in your abduction," Selly said in a rush, uncertain if she was betraying his trust and at the same time kicking herself for not saying so before.

Nic didn't seem at all surprised. "Certainly my father was working with Sergio Sammael, but does Jadren suspect Lord Igino Sammael, too? And what has he said of his mother?"

Selly hesitated, feeling the reluctance to spill tea that she should not, information Jadren trusted her to keep to herself. Of course, that was the same Jadren who'd walked out on her and ditched her with all the cruelty he could muster. This was how it felt to have divided loyalties. Well, if she was going to make her own choices, that was something for her to navigate. She would keep the one secret he'd beseeched her not to tell: that his ability to magically self-heal made him practically, if not in fact, immortal. The others had guessed some of it, but Selly had promised never to tell and she wouldn't.

This information, however, could affect the precarious position of House Phel. "Igino met with Jadren at House Sammael, when Jadren rescued me. They talked for some time before I was... er, 'summoned' to meet with them."

Nic wrinkled her nose in sympathy, so Selly knew her euphemism hadn't been lost on the other woman. "When Igino sent us in the elemental carriage to House El-Adrel, there was an Elal sentry spirit there to spy on us."

Sitting up alertly, Nic's eyes widened. "Can you describe

it?"

"Not really," Selly admitted. "I didn't know it was there at first—Jadren pointed it out to me—but the more I tried to pay attention to it, the more I could kind of... see."

"You'll get better with training and practice."

"That's what Jadren said."

"Well, he's not always an asshole who's wrong about everything."

Nic said the words with such earnest sincerity that it took Selly a moment to realize her sister-in-law was joking—and to bite back her instant, vigorous defense of her absent wizard. Nic nodded knowingly, sympathy in her eyes and smile. "Yeah, you've got it bad."

"Whatever 'it' is."

"Exactly. Gabriel is the one who needs to define things, to have the rules and boundaries clearly outlined." Nic shrugged, tipping her head to the side. "Not me so much. Maybe not you."

"Gabriel has always been that way," Selly said, thinking of her older brother when she was young and he wasn't yet a wizard. "He had his whole life planned out."

"Until I twisted it sideways." Nic spoke with dry humor, but Selly caught a glimpse of wistful regret in Nic's gaze, a hint of worry.

Impulsively, she reached for Nic's hand, squeezing it. "You're the best thing to happen to Gabriel," she said in all honesty and willing Nic to believe. "He needs to be twisted up a bit."

Nic's smile widened in gratitude. "And you—do you intend

to twist up Jadren?"

"Absolutely. He's not getting away with thinking he's sacrificing himself to protect me."

"There's something I know that you don't," Nic said slowly, then hesitated, chewing her lip. "It's not mine to tell and I don't know if I should tell you or not."

What would be the adult response to that? "Would it help me to know?"

"Maybe." Nic sounded unconvinced. "I think you deserve to know, either way." She nodded to herself. "Jadren told Gabriel he's in love with you."

Relief and delight washed through Selly like a spring rain thawing an ice storm. "He did?" The grin widening her face felt like it might crack her cheeks.

Nic groaned, pressing her hands to her face. "Don't be so happy. This is one reason I didn't tell you."

"All right. Why's that?"

"Because he used it as an argument for why he should leave. Because he doesn't want to love you, because he regards it as a vulnerability. He told Gabriel, 'true love makes fools of us all in the end.'"

Oh. "I see."

"Do you?" Nic searched her face. "I think in some ways this will make things even harder for you. If he didn't realize his feelings and all you had to do was be your charming self and convince him, that would be one thing. But he's taking drastic steps to separate himself from you and, if nothing else, Jadren has a strong will."

That he did. Nic had no idea. Selly had to suppress an irreverent laugh, as Nic wouldn't understand her sudden spurt of dark humor. Jadren had the strongest will of anyone she'd ever met, but they were alike under the skin. She wouldn't give up, especially now. Jadren needed her as much as she needed him.

"Will you help me convince Gabriel to let me go after Jadren?"

"Do you need his permission?" Nic asked with a raised brow.

This was a test. No, she didn't need her brother's permission to do anything. But he was also the lord of her house. "I'd like to have his blessing and support."

Nic smiled. "There you go. You need something else, especially if you're to convince Jadren he needs you as much as he wants you and is afraid to have you."

"What's that?" Whatever it took, she would do it.

"Training," Nic told her decisively. "Take a few days to learn what you need to know."

She should've guessed. "Will you teach me?"

"Absolutely. Let's start now."

"Now?"

"The sooner you master a familiar's skills, the sooner you can go after Jadren."

"Then let's start now," Selly said immediately, making Nic laugh.

~ 3 ~

A S A FIRST step, Nic took Seliah to 'meet' Maman. If asked why, she might not have been able to explain her exact reasoning. Particularly if Gabriel had posed the question, she'd have had a hard time justifying her actions. He wouldn't approve, she felt sure, just as he'd likely be annoyed that Nic had told Selly about Jadren's confession. But Gabriel had a tendency to try to protect Seliah from the harsher realities of the Convocation and life as a familiar. If Nic had to put a name to the impulse for this visit, she'd have to call it a kind of tough love.

Seliah needed to know how badly the wizard–familiar bond could wreck a person. Upon reflection, maybe Gabriel *would* approve—as he very clearly would prefer that Alise sever Seliah's bond to Jadren. Still, it wasn't his choice and he didn't truly know what he'd be asking of his sister.

For that matter, Seliah didn't know either. She didn't really know what she needed to in order to function as a wizard's familiar. Jadren clearly hadn't accessed the bond between them much. From the little Nic had gleaned, Jadren had barely tapped Seliah's magic at all. Which was curious, and raised a number of interesting questions, but the most immediate concern was teaching Seliah what she needed to know.

Had Seliah attended Convocation Academy, she'd have witnessed—and, more pointedly, experienced—how badly wizards could abuse familiars, and not necessarily out of cruelty. Sometimes, especially with young, student wizards, it was clumsiness or ineptitude or sheer bad luck. As much as Nic had loathed some of those lessons, particularly the advanced training practicums for wizards and familiars, she could recognize now how the often painful and exhausting lessons had toughened her against the brutal ways of many Convocation wizards. Nic was just fortunate that she'd wound up with someone as relentlessly gentle—sometimes frustratingly so— as Gabriel.

A wizard like Jadren ... Well, "gentle" wasn't a word she'd ever use for the jaded, sharp-tongued scoundrel. Even if he was motivated by the best of intentions where Seliah was concerned, he was still a wizard and still an El-Adrel. His mother obviously retained considerable influence over him—and Nic hadn't missed how Seliah had avoided answering that question—which meant he might lack the ability to truly protect Seliah. He could damage her through sheer carelessness. Or ignorance, as he also lacked a Convocation Academy education. Besides all of that, there was some reason Jadren hadn't wanted a familiar, and why he believed he was doing the best thing for Seliah by separating from her.

While Nic was sincere in wanting to help Seliah, part of her couldn't help wondering if severing the bond wouldn't be the best thing. Jadren was trouble. No doubt of that. But House Phel needed all the might it could muster and Jadren brought considerable power and political leverage to the table. Gabriel hadn't considered that aspect—and he hadn't asked Nic's opinion when he gave Jadren leave to go. Well, Nic *did* consider these things and that ability was one reason Gabriel had wanted her for a wife. And, in her considered opinion, they needed Jadren. If his feelings for, and bond to, Seliah ensured his loyalty to House Phel, then all the better.

As she and Seliah walked through the shaded arcade to the north wing where Maman was housed, Nic took in the lovely landscape out either side of the open arches and pondered her next steps. She was uncomfortably close to keeping secrets from Gabriel, something she'd never explicitly promised not to do, but that she knew would hurt him to discover. On the other hand, he had delegated affairs of familiars to her, so she could plausibly feign ignorance, or play on his previous directions that she didn't need to ask him for permission for every little thing, much as the familiar in her—and her Convocation training—prompted her to do.

Besides, done was done. Regardless of all else, Seliah needed training and Nic would see to it that her sister-in-law at least got a grounding in the basics.

As Nic had hoped, Alise was sitting with Maman. But then Alise spent every spare moment checking on or sitting with their mother, so her location was pretty predictable. What Nic hadn't predicted was that Alise would be asleep, her dark curls stark against their mother's white bedgown as she lay with her head on the verge of the mattress, holding their mother's hand, warm sunlight and birdsong streaming in the open window.

Nic halted so quickly that Seliah stepped on her heel, exclaiming in apology. Nic tried to shush her, but it was too late. Either that or the sound of their entry had awakened Alise, who sat up abruptly as if caught out, shoving back the curls compressed on one side of her head with fingers made clumsy from exhausted sleep. Alise peered blearily at them, her wizard-black eyes dull and fogged. "What time is it?" she asked, which seemed like an odd first question.

"Midmorning," Nic answered. "When was the last time you slept?"

Alise wrinkled her nose and gestured at the bed. "Obviously, just now."

"That's not what I meant and you know it," Nic replied with considerable impatience. "Look at you. You have shadows under your eyes I could hide a horse in. Your magic is thin and brittle enough to—"

"You're not my mother, Nic," Alise snapped, getting to her feet and almost managing to hide a wince at her stiffness. "And you don't know about my magic or—"

"No, I'm your sister. Our mother is right there and she is also totally beyond us." Nic stabbed a finger at the woman lying unconscious on the bed, her aristocratically handsome face sunken, skin dull. Her eyes, frozen in an uncanny feline shape, stared sightlessly at the ceiling. Nic almost couldn't bear to look. She wanted her mother back, to give advice, or just a hug. Maman always knew what to do. And it was all Nic's fault that she was like this. "You can't bring her back by working yourself to death," Nic continued, reminding herself, too. "And I *do* know about your magic because I'm a highly trained familiar, not an idiot, and I can feel perfectly well how drained you are."

"Fine, fine." Alise sagged, glancing at Maman. "I haven't slept much. I keep thinking there's something more I can do for her, but there's no change. Asa is keeping her alive, but he thinks that, without his healing magic, she'd just... fade away. She's basically catatonic, forgive the horrible pun."

"Do you think it's the extended entrapment in feline form that did it, or that you severed her bond with Papa?" Nic asked, nodding when Alise's startled gaze went to Seliah, understanding dawning in her wizard-black eyes.

"You told Seliah," Alise said with a sigh. "That's why you two are here. Are you considering having your bond to Wizard Jadren severed, Seliah?"

Seliah's eyes flew to Nic, who shrugged. "Everyone here knows you were bonded against your will in House El-Adrel, and yes, I know." She held up a hand to stop Seliah, who'd opened her mouth to argue. "You just heard me tell Gabriel that familiars in the Convocation don't actually consent to being bonded. While that's true, your situation is more extreme than most. As the lord of your house, Gabriel should have been consulted, with proper agreements and protections set in place, and with your consent given at least as a formality. What El-Adrel did was a major trespass against us. Just because we haven't yet demanded immediate reparations from Katica El-Adrel doesn't mean that everyone—at least everyone with knowledge of the Convocation—in House Phel isn't aware that you were illegally used. And now that Jadren has left you..."

Alise made a choking sound. "Jadren *left*? Without his familiar."

"Sometime last night," Nic answered to spare Seliah having to do so. "With Gabriel's permission," she added, thinking it best to have that information squarely out there, to put any rumors of Jadren being a pariah to rest.

"Wow." Alise seemed unable to come up with another response. Then, to Nic's surprise, Alise went to Seliah and hugged her. "I'm so sorry, honey. He's a shit. Do you want help killing him or just to hide the body?"

Seliah laughed, sounding a little watery, and held onto Alise a moment longer. "He left a note. Seems to think he's doing the noble thing. Protecting me."

Alise nodded, but looked confused. Nic didn't blame her as none of it really made sense to her either.

"I'm going after him," Seliah added. "But whether I'll have to murder him remains to be seen." She seemed about to say something more, but closed her mouth over it.

"Well," Alise said briskly, dusting her hands together. "To answer your question, Nic, as I understand now how it's especially pertinent—I don't know if Maman's condition is due more to the severing or from being trapped in a cat body. The eyes indicate lingering effects of the feline form." She gestured uselessly at their mother. "Wizard Asa says the eyes are resistant to healing, stemming from her own magic and not something he can alter. As for the severing, well, that may be a factor. Laryn is still listless and seeming very low."

Nic sighed for that. Asa's former familiar was an enduring problem, complicated by the fact that Nic hadn't liked the woman *before* she betrayed them all. "Asa did examine her, which I'm sorry he had to do, and says that she seems to be fine physically. It could be that she's depressed."

"When one's evil and treacherous plans are foiled and one is facing a possible death sentence, I doubt it makes for a happy attitude," Alise noted. "She's alive. She doesn't need to be happy."

Nic smiled at that. She and Alise understood one another. "No doubt. At any rate, Asa says that he isn't feeling any negative effects from the severing himself—aside from not having access to Laryn's magic—so if Seliah decides that she's better off letting Jadren go, there shouldn't be a concern about his health."

"*If* we even care about his wellbeing," Alise said, glancing at Seliah, "as he's the one who violated one of the Convocation's most sacred and solemn responsibilities by carelessly abandoning his familiar."

Seliah's mouth set in a mulish line. No, she didn't like having any aspersions cast on her wizard. That, more than anything else, had convinced Nic of Seliah's feelings for Jadren. Gabriel could storm and protest all he liked, but a familiar's attachment to their wizard went beyond enchantment, deeper than the softer emotions of love and affection, and drilled its way into their very soul.

Out of sympathy for Seliah's struggle, Nic went on. "The severing option is on the table—depending on what Seliah decides, but that's not the only reason why we're here. I wanted her to see the results of the severing and what Papa did to Maman, yes, but we also came to fetch you. Seliah needs to practice with a wizard." Nic frowned, not liking the idea of asking Alise to do any magic work in her exhausted condition. "But maybe I should ask someone—."

Alise interrupted with some impatience. "I can do it. I'm fine, really. What do you have in mind?"

"Let's go somewhere else," Nic suggested, not really liking being in the room with Maman and treating her like a piece of furniture.

Glancing at their unmoving mother, Alise nodded. "We can go to my rooms." She led them to the suite next door. Though Alise hadn't yet graduated from Convocation Academy and thus wasn't a full wizard, she'd been granted official status in House Phel as their resident Elal wizard. They needed Elal magic badly and Gabriel had drawn a firm, bright line against bargaining with House Elal for anything at all. And that was before they'd sent the lord of the house home missing an eye and a familiar—and nursing an enormous grudge.

In alignment with Alise's status at House Phel, she'd been given several large, interconnected rooms on the top floor, the windows open to the honeyed, midday sun, the lush lawn below rolling down to the lazily flowing Dubglass River. Through the doorway to Alise's bedchamber, Nic noted that her sister's bed was neatly made in such crisp lines that she doubted it had been slept in for days, if ever at all.

Two birds with one stone it would be then. "Let's begin with passive sensing of magic," Nic announced. "I can absolutely sense that Alise's magic is worn thin to the breaking point." When Alise opened her mouth to protest, Nic held up a hand to stop her. "I'm sure Seliah can, too, can't you?"

Seliah looked briefly startled, her amber eyes going so wide they dominated her solemn, fine-boned face. "I... think I should be left out of this argument between sisters."

"But Seliah," Alise said sweetly, while glaring at Nic, "you're our sister by marriage now. All in the family."

"Speak freely," Nic prompted Seliah. "This isn't about me being Alise's sister as much as me being Lady Phel."

"As a wizard, I outrank you, Familiar Veronica," Alise sniped.

"You're not a grown wizard yet and don't make me sic Gabriel on you," Nic retorted, planting her fists on her hips. She jerked her chin at Seliah, giving her a hard look. "Tell me what you sense. This is part of what you need to learn."

Though Seliah looked a bit like a deer facing an onrushing elemental-powered carriage, she gamely faced Alise, a line between her dark brows as she scrunched her face in concentration.

"Don't force it," Nic coached her. "Remember that being a familiar means your magic is, by definition, passive. You can't reach out to Alise, but you *can* sense her, take in the field of magic emanating from her—or that should be, if she weren't neglecting her health. Were you able to feel Jadren's magic, perhaps gauge his mood, even a sense of his thoughts?"

Seliah's face cleared in surprise. "Yes. I wasn't sure if that was normal or if..." She trailed off uncertainly, an unhappy twist to her mouth.

"You couldn't trust your magic for a long time," Nic told her gently. She didn't know what it had felt like to Seliah, to be trapped in that stagnant magic that had built up inside her for far too long and distorted her perception of reality, but Nic had tasted some of it, via Gabriel and Jadren as they worked to purge Seliah of the accumulated poisons. The magic had bent and twisted back on itself, like something that had grown out of Seliah but became a thing that wasn't her at all. "It's not surprising that you don't have a precise sense of what strong, functioning magic feels like. How did Jadren's magic feel to you?"

"Like well-oiled clockwork ticking against the inside of my skin," Seliah answered. "Is that right?"

"There is no right or wrong," Nic replied promptly, though she'd never heard anyone describe magic that way. That wasn't how Jadren felt to *her*, but these things could be very subjective. "What matters is what your senses tell you. Describe what you sense from Alise."

Seliah moved closer to Alise, who sighed in resignation— or, more likely, utter exhaustion—and sat in an armchair. "Her magic feels like yours," Seliah said, "like roses in the hot summer sun."

Nic nodded. That was how Gabriel described her magic, too, so it made sense that another member of the Phel family would perceive it the same way. "What else?"

Seliah hesitated, but Alise waved her to continue, sitting back and closing her eyes. Her lids showed blue veins, her dusky skin was that translucent. "I understand why you say brittle," Seliah continued, casting a glance at Nic. "Alise's magic feels like... a transparent sheet. As if I could put my hand through it in places."

Nic shot a significant glare at her sister, which was utterly lost as Alise hadn't opened her eyes. "That makes no sense,"

Alise said wearily.

"You are absolutely wrong, baby sister," Nic fired back. "And that is excellent sensing, Seliah. You have a gift for this."

"She can't put a hand through my magic because a familiar can't affect me magically," Alise argued, opening her eyes, but not sitting up.

"No, but a wizard could."

"I don't plan to engage in any magical battles."

"Nobody *plans* to do that," Nic replied with exasperation. "In your current state, even a minor wizard could punch metaphorical holes in you. Didn't you do that exercise at Convocation Academy?"

"I might have procrastinated on that particular practicum," Alise admitted.

Wonderful. "Training all around then," Nic declared and turned to Seliah. "Here's your first lesson in the Care and Feeding of Wizards 101."

"Do they really call it that at Convocation Academy?" Seliah asked, brows raised in wonder.

"No," Alise muttered from her chair, eyes once again closed.

"Yes," Nic said over her, then reconsidered. "Well, it's what the familiars call it. Officially it's called Wizard–Familiar Dynamics and there are a number of levels, labs, and practicums. But the course overall is primarily focused on wizards, since familiars are of secondary importance, so..." She waved a hand in the air.

"That seems so wrong," Seliah observed.

"Yes, well, you and your brother can complain about the

unfairness to each other. It's one of his favorite rants. He'd love to have a fresh audience, I'm sure." Nic said it wryly, though the truth was that Gabriel's insistence on reciprocating with the care and feeding of familiars never ceased to warm her heart. "So, when a wizard's magic feels this brittle—"

"I'm starting to hate that word," Alise said.

"Hush. When a wizard's magic feels this brittle, the best things you can offer—short of magical healing—are sex, food, and rest."

"Hey," Alise protested, cracking open one eye, "leave sex out of it."

"If the wizard in question is not sexually active, for whatever reason, then you can leave sex out. But sex is terrific for replenishing magic, for familiars, too. In particular, a lot of teasing and build-up without orgasm is one of the best shortcuts to refill the magic well. If Alise can't find anyone to play with her, she can always employ a bit of self-love."

"I can't believe I'm having this conversation," Alise commented in a wondering tone. "It's so good to be with family."

"Grow up," Nic advised. "So," she asked Seliah, "what will you do to take care of Alise?"

"Order up some food," Seliah said promptly, "so she'll eat here in her rooms and be more likely to rest afterward. Maybe a hot bath, too, to coax her to sleep."

"Good," Nic replied with a smile. "Hearty food. Also wine, to make her drowsy."

"Elal wine would be nice," Alise said hopefully.

"Yes, we all wish for that," Nic noted acerbically. "No such luck."

The ban on Elal trade included wine, as Gabriel didn't want any Phel coin going to Elal coffers. Missing out on the excellent Elal vintages was nearly as bad as relying entirely on Alise to equip the house with elemental conveniences. Moving to the newly installed Ratsiel communicator, Nic sent a message to the kitchens with an order for a heavy, fat-laden meal for the three of them. Seliah could stand to eat more, too, and it seemed Nic was always hungry these days. While Alise wasn't paying attention, Nic put in an additional request. She wouldn't call for Asa to heal Alise, not yet—though she would have words with him about not reporting Alise's exhaustion— as she had a point to prove first.

While they waited, she expounded on some of the finer points for Seliah, especially on sexuality, as she wasn't sure what all had or hadn't happened between Seliah and Jadren— judging by Jadren's note, very little—and since it was an opportunity to give Alise sideways advice. Her sister was too tense, the lines of her body to sharp with stress, for her to be sleeping. Let her overhear then.

"Not all wizard–familiar relationships are sexual," Nic said, "but if you have that aspect, it gives you an edge, and not only because of the quick magic regeneration on the fly as it were. Sexual communion intensifies the relationship, giving you another channel to communicate and interact. To reach one another when words aren't working." Though she tried to keep her mind on the abstract, Nic couldn't help remembering a couple of salient episodes when she'd managed to steer Gabriel out of his wizardly rages by diverting his attention to her, with such stirring results that her face heated at the memory.

"I think Jadren used that some with me," Seliah offered somewhat shyly.

Alise opened her eyes. "Ooh, do tell."

"Well…" Seliah fiddled with a stylus on Alise's neat desk, glancing about the room.

"You can trust us to keep your secrets." Nic sat on a chaise, deliberately nonchalant, trailing a hand over the lovely upholstery worked in a design of silver moons dancing on water alongside gold Elal spirit symbols, showing Alise's intertwined house affiliations. The Ophiel fabric wizard, Dahlia, had a knack for that sort of thing.

"Despite what you might think of him," Seliah said, "Jadren truly is sensitive and compassionate." She waited for either of them to argue, eyeing them both owlishly, but Nic nodded encouragingly and Alise listened with a gentle and attentive expression. And a fair amount of curiosity.

Though Alise would be eighteen soon, she didn't seem to have had much sexual experience yet. Not that the two of them were close enough for Nic to know. Still, though fraternization wasn't against the rules at Convocation Academy, relationships were strongly discouraged. They had a tendency to interfere with the arranged wizard–familiar pairings, as amply demonstrated by Han and Iliana's impetuous escape so they could be together. Nic wasn't at all clear why Alise had aided them. Surely her little sister—also a product of House Elal—didn't believe in true love.

"Please don't tell anyone else," Seliah said with a released breath, restlessly pacing to the window, "but I still have occasional... issues. From the madness." She turned and faced them with a brave tilt to her chin, though she was clearly braced for censure.

"It would be surprising if you didn't," Nic replied with equanimity.

"No one expects you to just get over what you went through, Seliah," Alise added, nodding.

"I expect it," Seliah replied, sounding defiant. Not surprising, as Seliah's repetition of the assertion that she expected more of herself had made it too clear to Nic just how often people told Seliah they didn't expect this or that of her. Seliah then sagged a little. "I just don't want to be treated like I'm fragile. I know I have things to overcome, but I can do it."

"Of course you can," Nic agreed, and Alise nodded, shrugging as if that were a foregone conclusion. "And Jadren understands that about you," Nic added, prompting Seliah to continue.

"Yes, well, closed in spaces, feeling trapped..." Seliah rolled her eyes and scrubbed her hands over her face. "I tend to 'lose my shit' as Jadren so succinctly puts it. But he is able to distract me."

"Distract you how?" Alise asked, bright interest in her dark gaze. "As many details as you'd like to include."

Seliah chuckled, lightly blushing. "Kissing. Caressing. Arousing." Her voice had gone throaty at the memory. "He's really good at it."

Nic didn't doubt that. Jadren might be an ass, but he was also singularly focused in his approach to everything. What was surprising was that he apparently possessed some level of empathy for Seliah, not at all typical for a Convocation wizard. Had he really left in order to protect her and not for some other nefarious or selfish reason? If so, why did he believe he was such a danger to Seliah? Though Seliah hadn't commented on that aspect, it seemed that she had some idea there.

"He has soft hands," Seliah was telling Alise, in answer to her question. "Not like the farmers around here, but gentle and sensitive. The way he touched me...it was like he could sense how I felt through his fingertips. And his kisses!" Seliah touched wondering fingers to her lips. "It was like being swept up in a dream, overwhelming, sweet and hot. I forgot everything but him when he kissed me."

Alise sighed dreamily. A knock on the door had Nic getting up and going to the antechamber to answer, which allowed the two women to keep talking. Though Seliah was substantially older than Alise, Nic couldn't help thinking of the pair of them as similar in age. Seliah younger than her physical body and Alise older than hers.

Nic opened the door to Sage and Quinn. As she'd asked, the bonded pair from House Byssan had brought up the requested food and wine, cheerfully greeting her over the laden trays, curiosity piquing their smiles. The lady of the house didn't typically ask wizards or familiars to do fetching and carrying. Of course, House Phel wasn't typical in many ways.

Nic quickly and quietly conveyed to Sage what she needed. The glass wizard, not battle trained by any stretch, expressed doubts, which Nic quickly dispensed with, confident she could rely on the wizard's solid craftsmanship to carry it off, however unorthodox the task. Then Nic kissed her old friend and sister-familiar, Quinn, on the cheek, relieving her of a couple of carafes of wine.

The kitchens had sent large servings, plus extra, which was hopefully because the lady of the house had placed the order and not a habit of profligacy. The people of Meresin tended toward generosity, a reflection of their easy, warm natures. An admirable trait, but House Phel couldn't afford to be generous, not with their finances in such bad shape. One more issue for Nic to address.

The blonde Byssan sisters, so alike they could be twins—except for Sage's wizard-black eyes—bustled into the sitting room, saying hello and setting down their trays. With an offhand glance and admirably little warning, Sage hurled a burst of fulminous magic at Alise. Caught off-guard, Alise slammed into the back of the armchair, emitting a small squeak before passing out entirely.

Feeling grimly vindicated, Nic sent for Asa while the other women exclaimed over Alise, tending to her. As Nic turned back from the summons, an angry Seliah confronted her. "Why did you tell Sage to do that? Alise is hurt!"

"I barely hit her at all," Sage said apologetically, her pretty face contorted in concern. "My magic isn't all that strong."

"That's entirely the point," Nic replied crisply, refusing to feel guilty, though Alise's skin had taken on an even more translucent hue, her face slack in unconsciousness. Wedging her way in, Nic patted Alise's cheeks briskly. Tough love was still love. Alise's eyelids fluttered, awareness returning. Good. "A wizard of Alise's MP scores, however much training she has yet to complete, should never have been taken unawares by a light punch from a glass wizard, no offense intended, Sage."

"None taken," Sage replied, clearly relieved that Alise had already come to. "Quinn, let's dish out the food for these noble ladies."

Alise glared up at Nic. "That was a rotten trick, even for an Elal."

"Brittle enough to punch holes through," Nic said softly. "I trust I've made my point?"

"Bitch."

Nic patted her baby sister's cheek one last time, gently with affection. "I love you, too."

~ 4 ~

SELLY FINALLY RETURNED to her room late that evening, after eating formal dinner with all of House Phel. She was weary to the bone. Though Alise had gone to bed—after food, Asa's healing treatment, and a hot bath, in that order—and slept the remainder of the day, that hadn't spared Selly from Nic's relentless tutelage.

No, Lady Phel had simply conscripted Sage instead, relocating them to Sage and Quinn's shared rooms, which weren't quite as spacious as Alise's, but occupied a corner and sported fabulous windows, naturally. With the tenacity and remorselessness of a military general, Nic had walked Selly through the steps of giving up magic to Sage and then refusing to allow it.

Nic had also instructed Sage to drain Selly's magic over and over, so Selly could get a feel for when she was dangerously low. That experience had been deeply unsettling. Selly had to admit, however, that she'd learned from it. Though Jadren had taught her a great deal about yielding up her magic and working with him, he'd never taken all that much magic from her at one time.

None of them had been sure how fast Selly's reserves would rebound if she were completely drained. Nic observed that Selly still generated a bounty of magic, more rapidly than most familiars, and perhaps that would settle down over time as her magic equilibrated, now that it was able to flow freely instead of being blockaded. For the time being, however, Selly seemed to replenish her magic nearly as fast as Sage could tap it.

When Sage, quite out of breath and flushed, complained that she had more magic than she knew what to do with, Nic set her to making flasks and carafes of varying sizes, commenting that they could be used for the new product line of ever-replenishing water flasks and purifying water carafes.

Sage eventually wore herself out—and Nic used that as a teaching moment, too, explaining that a wizard's endurance for performing magic depended as much on their physical stamina as on the magic available. Then Nic had dashed Selly's fragile hope of a reprieve, summoning other crafts wizards from around the house. Dahlia arrived in all her stylish glory, making new Ophiel gowns for Nic, Selly, and Quinn, who'd elected to stay and learn from observation while her sister rested.

Selly nearly didn't ask for anything for herself, but finally summoned her nerve to request some clothing appropriate for her quest to find Jadren. To her surprise, Nic not only agreed, but approved, helping Dahlia design simple, close-fitting clothing for Selly that could be layered for various climates and also accessorized to pass for more formal appearances.

"It always pays to look fashionable and wealthy in the Convocation," Nic advised, "and to be prepared for wherever your travels might take you," she added cryptically, making

Selly wonder where Nic thought she'd eventually find Jadren—
or follow him to, if she couldn't convince him to come home.
Before she could ask, Nic had set her to another round of
working, this time with the Ratisbon wizard, Wolfgang. With
the surfeit of Selly's magic, he made extra furniture for the
many empty rooms awaiting more Phel minions, to increased
grumbling from the people called in to cart the pieces off,
while his familiar, Costa, taught Quinn a risqué card game that
had them both giggling in the corner.

When Selly, feeling grumpy and put upon, suggested they
take a break—she really wanted to know what had Quinn and
Costa laughing so hard—Nic briskly told her that, unless she
was crying uncle, to suck it up and keep working. All the
while, Nic had been working on correspondence, in between
coming up with new ways to try Selly's patience and endurance, sending and receiving various messages both in-house
and out via Ratsiel courier. The woman was indefatigable, and
Selly found herself unwilling to raise the white flag of surren-
der before Nic did.

Selly sagged in physical relief, however, when Nic finally
called it a day, saying they needed to dress for dinner. When
Selly tried to beg off, Nic airily informed her that she had new
gowns to show off and that she could use practice with the
grooming imps anyway. And that, besides, as a lady of House
Phel, Selly had social obligations that she'd been allowed to
shirk for far too long. She'd have to learn, Nic added, that a
familiar's duties didn't come to a screeching halt just because
one was tired. Sitting through dinner wasn't much to ask, after
all.

Nic had swept out before Selly could form a retort to that, and Quinn caught her arm with a sympathetic squeeze. "That's exactly how Nic's maman trained her," Quinn explained, blue eyes soft with compassion. "You just received a crash course in Convocation Academy training and House Elal etiquette today. It was a *lot*—I learned quite a few things I hadn't known before—but Nic is doing this for your own good."

"Lady Phel clearly believes you'll be going after your wizard sooner rather than later," Costa agreed, managing to make the words sound suggestive. "What does it feel like, being separated from your bonded wizard?" Both familiars regarded her with intent interest. Wolfgang had also departed, leaving the three of them alone. By design, Selly wondered?

"It feels wrong," she admitted. The pulling of the attenuating bond, like part of her being extruded from her very core, had added to the grinding work of the day. Everything in her wanted to go after Jadren immediately. If she didn't trust Nic implicitly, she'd already be gone. "Like a part of me is strained, being drawn out and tugging at me. Like a fish on the line—only I'm not fighting the reel and the hook doesn't hurt. I want to go, but it's as if the other end is getting farther away and I can't leave my pond."

Costa considered that, his narrow, handsome face thoughtful. "That's probably an apt analogy. Poor little fishy with no feet," he added, not unsympathetically as he patted her arm, then gave her a sharp look. "Why did Wizard Jadren leave anyway? Everyone is *dying* to know."

Because Nic had lectured her extensively on the importance of discretion on this topic, Selly tried to look woeful.

"Who am I to understand the ways of wizards?"

That didn't satisfy Costa in the least. "Still, you must have some—"

"Will you really go after him?" Quinn asked, clearly intrigued, but also cutting off Costa's persistent curiosity with a reproving glance.

"I must go after him, mustn't I?" Selly asked in return, weariness tempting her to be melodramatic. Instead she just sounded tired. "A familiar belongs with their wizard."

Quinn and Costa nodded in agreement, though neither echoed the sentiment aloud. It made Selly wonder if the rumor about severing bonds had made the rounds also. Fortunately, she had been able to escape further interrogation by racing off to dress for dinner. She'd even taken pains to groom herself to high-house standards, if only to prove to Nic that she knew how.

It gave her an almost physical ache, however, that Jadren wouldn't see her. He'd bestowed few compliments on her, but the ones he had—especially when he'd told her she looked gorgeous cleaned up—stuck in her mind. Those *would* stick out, since they were one of the few occasions that he'd said something nice about her when he wasn't out of his head.

That probably meant their relationship was bizarre and backwards, but she craved more of that, more of his ardent attention. She deeply feared she'd never have it again. The sense of crippling loss, on top of the magical exhaustion, had almost sent her crawling under the covers. Only knowing Nic would likely come drag her out had Selly marching herself to dinner with a false smile plastered over her lips.

Gabriel had given her a somewhat surprised and definitely assessing look as she sat at his right hand—apparently her rightful and lofty place as his sister—but thankfully he didn't question her. They'd talked of light subjects over the meal, aware of the attention focused on the head of the table, Nic playing the scintillatingly entertaining hostess to the hilt. She kept everyone engaged, giving the appearance of having no greater care in the world than whether her guests were satisfied with the meal. Selly figured this was yet another lesson in comporting herself as a familiar and paid close attention, though she doubted she'd ever be able to emulate that sort of bright social chatter.

At last she was now back in her room, where she'd longed to be for hours. Perversely, she regretted being alone almost immediately. She stood in the center of the room, realizing that it still held all the detritus of the disastrous seduction attempt from the night before. When she'd come in to dress earlier, she'd been focused on the task. Now, with the leisure of aloneness, she could see only the foolish, girlish hope she'd practically oozed with the night before. The evidence of her innocent happiness now struck her as ridiculous.

Turning in a circle, she took it all in—the room that had never really been hers, even post-redecorating. Yes, she'd ruthlessly eliminated the remnants of her lost girlhood, the dolls and pastel colors gone, and had replaced them with a more adult theme, but she'd conceived the new scheme with Jadren in mind, thinking about what would please him, foolishly fantasizing about how they'd share these rooms together as lovers.

Even worse was the bedraggled evidence of her childish vision of romance—the wilted flowers, the discarded wine, the candles that had melted down and guttered out while she slept.

No, not *slept*, she reminded herself ruthlessly. While she was unconscious, drugged by whatever potion Jadren had given her. He'd held out the glass of wine and smiled at her with that wicked mouth, those wizard-black eyes staring into hers with sensual challenge. She'd offered herself naked to him and he'd kissed her with all the longing she could wish for, caressing her and arousing her... That had been a kiss like no other between them, though they'd admittedly had so few. It had been dreamily romantic, intimate, and full of all that Jadren hadn't put into words.

It had been a goodbye.

With the too-acute vision of hindsight, with her initial anger dulled into grief, she could now see how evasive Jadren had been, all the clues he'd dropped about his intentions to walk away from her, to save her from himself—or, perhaps more to the point, to liberate himself from her, the familiar he'd never wanted.

When she'd stood there naked before him, he'd said as much. *Thank you for this gift of yourself. I want you to know that, as much as I'm capable of it, I appreciate this. All of this.* And he'd watched her drink the wine he'd drugged, kissed her until she was so woozy she couldn't stand, and walked away.

As much as I'm capable of it.

I'm gone. Don't bother looking as I won't be found.

The memory simultaneously depressed and energized her magically. Apparently even the memory of sexual interaction could recharge her magic, which was good to know. At least now, thanks to Nic, she understood what was happening.

This enervating sadness though…

What if Jadren truly wanted to be free of her? It was so difficult to know with him, scathing and distant one moment, so intensely focused on her the next. Which was the real Jadren? It could be that both were equally real, that he battled himself as much as anything. She absolutely believed *that* was true.

And maybe it didn't matter because the plain truth of it was that Jadren had drugged her so he could escape her. He wasn't playing a game; he wanted to be free of her and had taken extreme steps to achieve that. Alise was right that Jadren had violated the sacred precept of the Convocation, the responsibility to care for his familiar. He'd also betrayed their friendship. Because she knew she wasn't crazy. Not about that. She hadn't imagined the connection between them. Besides, Jadren had admitted to Gabriel that he loved her. But he hadn't told Selly that very important bit of information.

The question was: what to do about it?

She couldn't just run on impulse anymore. If she wanted to be mature and responsible, she had to think these things through. Going after Jadren wasn't a foregone conclusion. So, she began cleaning up the detritus of her former foolishness and thought through her options.

The first, most obvious and most rational was that she could have Alise sever the bond. Give Jadren the freedom he so desperately sought, let him have joy of it, though she highly doubted he would be happy, but that would be his problem.

That solution would give her a new start. She could stay at House Phel, her home, where she belonged, and resume rebuilding her life as she'd begun to do before Jadren had wrenched it out of recognizability. She wanted to contribute to her house and family's strength and success. Traipsing after Jadren wouldn't do that. Learning her magic, helping establish House Phel, preparing for what might come next—all of that fit her goals. All of that made sense.

And yet...

Nothing had changed in her heart since her conversation with Nic that morning. All she wanted was to find Jadren, to close this aching distance between them. It made no rational sense, as Jadren would no doubt be the first to tell her. He didn't want her. He wouldn't welcome her arrival.

And yet...

She was going. That was all there was to it. Rational or not.

Resolved, she nearly got dressed in her new clothing right then and there. She could climb out her balcony windows and shimmy down the fretwork to the ground. She'd escaped her rooms that way any number of times over the years.

But that was the old her. The half-feral creature Jadren had named her. Nic had more to teach her, so Selly would take at least another day or two or three to learn all she could. Gabriel might not give her his blessing, but she wanted him to know she was going, and she should take advantage of any supplies he offered—or wanted to foist on her—just in case it took a while to find Jadren. And to bring him back to House Phel.

So, she put herself to bed like a responsible adult, telling herself to sleep so she'd be rested to endure Nic's fierce demands the next day.

Then she'd find Jadren and she'd show him how much better they were together. They'd figure out the rest from there.

Who knew? Maybe Jadren would be glad to see her. Maybe he'd have come to see that House Phel was where he belonged.

Turned out Selly still had plenty of foolish fantasies.

JADREN HAD NEVER been so happy to put a place behind him as House Phel.

Except that he'd certainly been desperate to escape House El-Adrel on multiple occasions, including and especially his most recent incarceration there. Getting clear of the house of his birth felt like being able to draw clean air into his lungs again after drowning.

Well, and he'd also been thrilled to get out of House Sammael with Seliah intact—more or less—and without incurring lasting damage to diplomatic relations between Sammael and El-Adrel. Even knowing he and Seliah were trapped on a surely doom-ridden chariot ride to House El-Adrel, he'd been relieved to get away from the gothic monstrosity of House Sammael.

Still, all those instances considered, he was practically giddy to be riding through the Meresin swamplands and away from the citadel of foolish optimism that was House Phel. Mad, all of them. And Gabriel Phel was their king in insanity. Offering Jadren a place in House Phel even as Jadren broke his contract as a minion, abrogating all agreements in the worst way, including and especially abandoning his familiar. *Everyone deserves a place of refuge, somewhere they can be safe,* Gabriel had said in his earnest, painfully honest way. Seriously, for a wizard, Phel had zero political game. *Seems to me you don't have one in your birth house, so I'm offering House Phel, should you ever want it.*

Jadren snorted aloud at the memory of those utterly ridiculous words. No high-house lord ever made an offer like that. The wizard was completely off his rocker and Jadren was fortunate to escape that particular bog. House Phel was going down. It was simply a question of when. Even the how didn't take much guesswork: the Convocation would stomp out their tiny grassfire of a rebellion—and that was if they didn't collapse under the weight of their debt first. Their supposed allies would be circling like vultures ready to devour the freshly dead meat soon. Nic was clever, but even an Elal at their wiliest couldn't salvage House Phel from their crazed optimism.

At least Seliah had had an excuse for her craziness. She couldn't help herself, with those ignorant country louts allowing her to go untapped all those years, not having the wit or education to recognize that she was a familiar—and a wildly powerful one. Deliciously so. Thinking of how she was very nearly destroyed by that ignorance lit a fire of burning rage in him that he had to force aside, counting his horse's steps to regain a measure of mental calm.

Of course, once he started thinking about Seliah at all, he was doomed to the thought-spiral of longing and loathing—the former for her and the latter for himself. He was experienced at self-loathing. Really, he'd refined the practice to an art, honing it to a lethal edge over these many years. That was nothing new.

Longing, however...

Oh, that was new. And unwelcome. Even as he determinedly left House Phel in the distance, the bond to Seliah tugged at him, pulling him back to her. When he had put her long, lithe, deliciously naked body in bed and left her there without touching all that soft, silky skin, without burying himself in her sensual heat and passionate intensity... Well, it had been the hardest thing he'd ever done. He'd taken extra care with the note he left her, making it excruciatingly spiteful to remind himself of what a shit he was.

Yes, Seliah would be hurt by his words, and by the intimately treacherous act of actually drugging her wine. Dark arts! He'd handed her the glass and she'd smiled with pleasure. He'd had to clench his hands around his own wine to stop himself from dashing the dread glass out of her hands. It had been necessary to do it, he reminded himself, in order to evade her artless and ridiculously effective seduction attempts. If he'd indulged in sex with her, he might not have been able to make himself leave. Hurting her was the best way to make sure she wouldn't want to come after him. Seliah was better off without him.

And he needed to be rid of her, lest he become more of a monster than he was already on his way to becoming.

I'll handle the disappearing part. You handle keeping her from thinking she needs to look for me, he'd told Gabriel. Dark arts see to it that Phel held up his end of the bargain. Seliah was a stubborn chit and the last thing he needed was her using her sleuthing and feral swamp-creature skills to track him down to… wherever he was going.

He should probably make a plan for where he was going. "As far away from Seliah and House Phel as possible," likely didn't count as an actual destination. Out of sheer instinct he'd turned in the opposite direction from House El-Adrel, too. That was just self-preservation. When his monstrous maman discovered that her least-favorite child had screwed up the one thing he'd ever done right—according to her—and divested himself of the Phel familiar she'd gifted him with, well… Everything she'd ever done to torture him in the past would fade compared to her righteous punishment. And that wasn't figuring in the fact that she'd be in a seething rage because he'd escaped her.

The only reason to go back would be for his father. Fyrdo had taken a grave risk to free Seliah and Jadren from the experimental laboratory. How he'd pulled it off, Jadren still didn't know, but he could only hope his father had successfully hidden his role in the escape.

Besides, even if Jadren went back to House El-Adrel, he had no power to help his father. As Katica El-Adrel's familiar, Fyrdo was utterly subject to her rule. And Jadren could never defeat his darling maman. No, he definitely needed to get far,

far away from his mother. Somewhere her long claws couldn't reach. Did finding a hidey-hole count as a destination? Probably not.

Ideally, he should go off on some sort of heroic quest. Show everyone his true mettle by doing... something. He had no idea what. To be honest, contemplating doing something heroic just made him feel tired. Even with wizard Asa's assistance on top of his native magical healing that made him virtually immortal—perhaps *actually* immortal, as dark arts knew his mother had tested those boundaries without ever managing to make death stick—he still needed time to recover from Phel running him through the heart.

He was also unaccountably depressed. Hating himself and his life was nothing new, but this low-level angst was decidedly *un*like him. Jaunty and acerbic self-loathing, absolutely. Directionless maundering, no. He already missed Seliah a stupid amount. Without thinking about it, he wrapped his hand around the brass widget he'd sarcastically told her to string on a chain and wear around her neck. The gadget that his body had extruded following his mother's attempt to implant it somewhere in his chest. Seliah, the sentimental monkey, had done exactly that.

Though... who was the greater fool? She'd made a necklace of it and he'd taken it from her as he left, like some sort of keepsake. Touching the brass tube, knowing she'd worn it against her skin, made him miss her even more. He forced himself let go of the thing, tucking it back inside his shirt.

Maybe he was feeling the effects of the bond attenuating. That would make sense. After all, what did he know about what it was like to have—and to break—a wizard–familiar bond? It could be that this will-sapping desire to turn around and run back to her was the prompting of the enchantment. *That* had certainly been an interesting revelation, when he'd been taught the spell to bond Seliah at House El-Adrel, a spell which naturally came with a geas to prevent him from speaking of it. Turned out that most wizards got initiated into that little trick when they graduated from Convocation Academy. Since he'd been essentially homeschooled—and ha to that milksop euphemism for what his dear maman had done to him instead of sending him to the academy like every other wizard and familiar in the benighted Convocation—it seemed he'd missed out on more than lectures on history and house seals. The revelation of a secret bonding spell made him wonder what other tasty tidbits the wizards horded like dragons atop treasure.

He needed to know more. And there was one place the dragons kept that ultimate bastion of knowledge: Convocation Center.

That was somewhere he could go. If he wanted to discover what his tyrannical mother and the many wizards firmly under her thumb had kept from him, then he should go to the source of learning.

The problem there was that no one at Convocation Center would have any incentive to help him out. Especially since he didn't exactly exist as a proper citizen of the Convocation. At least, not as a magical one, and going about as a non-magical commoner didn't sit well with him. He'd had plenty of being powerless. Now that he was, more or less, free to do as he wished, doing so as a pauper held zero appeal. Besides which, no one would teach a commoner the arcane wisdom of wizards.

To be acknowledged as a wizard, however, presented two major obstacles. First, he lacked the essential magical potential scorecard that was every wizard and familiar's official method of identification. Jadren had never been formally tested—only subjected to his mother's various experiments—and so he lacked that particular document. In order to get that all-important piece of paper, he'd need to be tested by an officially designated Hanneil wizard and the non-decaying bit of nasty human flesh in a portable cupboard that were their pet oracle heads.

Not exactly appealing, and the logistics might be daunting, but theoretically he could find a way to get it done. The aftermath might cause some trouble, as the real sticking point was what that MP scorecard would reveal. Jadren really had no idea how his peculiar brand of magic would show up on the official Convocation tests. As healing magic, sure, but his didn't work the way the House Refoel healers wielded theirs. Jadren couldn't heal anyone else to save his life—or theirs. In truth, saving his own life wasn't a concern since his healing magic worked passively to keep him alive, no matter the damage to his body.

Maman had certainly tested the limits of *that*, with excruciating (for him) and frustratingly inconclusive (for her) results. She'd been limited (thank the dark arts) by an unwillingness to lose her favorite test subject. That and the alluring potential of what she could make him into had prevented her from testing scorched earth possibilities for killing him. Therefore, he didn't know if immolation could destroy him completely or, say, full dismemberment. The parts of him that had been amputated, dissected, or burnt, simply grew back. No, the removed pieces didn't bud new hims, to his mother's disappointment and his own relief.

Gabriel Phel had ably demonstrated that destroying Jadren's heart—literally, not metaphorically—only temporarily killed him. It was Jadren's good luck that Phel had used a sword extruded from moonlight in the moment and not one of the weapons he'd enchanted with the intention of destroying any enemy. Just possibly one of those weapons, one like Jadren's trusty Mr. Machete, would melt Jadren into a pile of goo as it did to the hunters. Jadren laughed aloud at the thought, amused to categorize himself with those unhappy creations of misguided magical might.

He supposed that, if he got desperate and self-destructive enough, he could test the edge of Mr. Machete on himself and see what it did to him. Good to have options.

But not yet. The Refoel wizard at House Phel, Asa, had nearly drained himself dry saving Jadren's miserable life. While Jadren appreciated the effort, he could've told Asa to save his magical energy. Jadren would have recovered eventually. Probably. Only those soft-headed saps at House Phel would have gone to the effort to save the spy planted like a venomous snake in their midst.

At any rate, apparently destroying a vital organ only slowed him down. And, while he could drown or suffocate, he also eventually revived once given air again. Being effectively dead during those episodes, Jadren was uncertain how long his maman had tested that. She never was inclined to share data with her subjects. She always claimed that, as a scientist, she had a responsibility to control variables and having the experimental subject aware of the parameters being tested could taint the results.

Besides that, she was an insane megalomaniac who did exactly as she pleased.

Probably he needed to stop thinking about his mother, as he was beginning to feel ill, and the last thing he needed was to lose his shit in the midst of the Meresin swamps. Seliah had already seen his humiliating reaction to those dark memories; he didn't care to repeat the experience. He could just picture it. Seliah coming after him and discovering him only a few leagues from House Phel, curled up in a quivering ball of cowardice.

There, that bracing image served to straighten his spine. Jadren didn't care for the good opinion of many people—and he certainly shouldn't care what a house-poor, uneducated, half-feral familiar thought—but... Well, he did care what Seliah thought of him. The sweet ache of longing for her tugged at him sharply and he very nearly turned the horse around. Instead, he urged the creature into a faster pace.

He definitely needed to get more information on the wiz-ard–familiar bond. From the tales, only the familiar went mad from the separation, and then only because of the magic accumulation that slowly poisoned the person's mind. Phel would see to it that Seliah's magic was regularly vented, ensuring that she wouldn't go crazy again. Gabriel Phel might be a soft-brained idealist, but he loved his baby sister and would take care of her. Seliah should be in no danger from the bond attenuation.

On the wizard's end... Hard to say how that went. Without academic knowledge, Jadren had to rely on stories. The most salient tale of wizard–familiar separation was the tragic epic of Sylus and Lyndella. Sylus clearly lost his shit in a dramatic way when Lyndella was abducted, laying waste to the countryside to destroy his enemies. Had Sylus been insane or just seriously pissed off, though? Maybe it had hurt him, too. But, if Jadren had no other skills, he sure knew how to withstand pain.

But it would be better all around if the bond broke. Seemed like it should, eventually. If wizards could create the enchantment to bond a familiar, surely they could undo the spell. Convocation wizards weren't ones to leave themselves without a back door. They were too obsessed with power and control to bind themselves to a spell that could backfire on them.

No, whoever created the enchantment to begin with had to know a way to dissolve it. Because the spell was psychic in nature, he'd bet it was of Hanneil make. It had been an in-house Hanneil wizard minion of House El-Adrel who gave Jadren the bonding spell, and laid the geas on him. Coincidentally enough, Hanneil was also the house who could perhaps assist him with an MP scorecard that would pass muster as not being generated embarrassingly late in his life.

That decided it. He should go to House Hanneil, not Convocation Center. He could strike a bargain with Lady Hanneil.

What he'd offer her, he had no idea, but he'd always been reasonably glib in the moment. Half of manipulating people was discovering what they wanted. The other half was figuring out how to make them want what you could actually deliver.

Another consideration was the apparently brewing war amongst the High Houses of the Convocation, with perhaps some of the lower tier houses jockeying for position, hoping for the rare opportunity to rise in rank. The love/hate scheming between House Sammael and the house of his birth had been going on for decades, if not centuries, though the recent reappearance of House Phel seemed to have catalyzed things to a new level. Nic's house of birth, House Elal, was in the mix, too—with Lord Elal colluding at least with Sammael. Probably El-Adrel, too, given recent evidence.

House Hanneil, along with House Refoel and a smattering of others, tended to stay aloof from conspiracies. They claimed integrity as the reason, what with being healers and psychics, but Jadren was naturally suspicious of anyone who claimed ethics as a motivation. Sure, it sounded nice, but where did ethics get a person?

That's right: in the same position as the lunatics at House Phel, stripped of magic and their house status, exiled to the swamps of Meresin—though, to be fair, the Phel family had always lived there, it was just that with their fall, everybody *else* had stopped going there—and relegated to becoming a cautionary tale.

Sure, hanging with the misfits and idealists of House Phel had been educational. Likely his unexpected sentiment over his short-lived tenure there, and the people he'd come to know, stemmed from his basic exhilaration at escaping the oppressive house of his birth for the first time. He'd been like a middle-aged virgin discovering sex existed—and had been pitifully grateful for the least crumbs of pleasure. But he was realist enough to know that Phel was doomed. The Convocation would crush them all. Unfortunate, even sad, but there it was.

If he was going to look out for himself, he needed all the distance from Phel he could get. That was pure self-preservation, even without the rest. Yes, he'd strike a deal with Hanneil. Shore up his credentials. Possibly rid himself of the bond to Seliah and set her fully free of him. Create a new life for himself.

Somewhere. Somehow. Something…

No matter what, it certainly wouldn't be at House Phel. Or with Seliah.

~ 5 ~

A FEW DAYS later, Jadren approached House Hanneil and surveyed it from above. It sat in an unprepossessing valley and didn't inspire as much awe as other High Houses did, at least, not at first sight. Certainly nothing like House Sammael or El-Adrel did. Not that the Hanneil ancestral line lacked the necessary hubris and overweening sense of melodrama that characterized the other High Houses. They simply went about it a different way, probably because they were devoted to psychic magic, and spent much of their attention turned inward.

The structure of the house certainly reflected that idea, at any rate. Built of simple gray stone, the structure blended into the landscape, almost disappearing into the surrounding wind-eroded hills. It lay coiled like a snake amid the sparse pinon pines and other evergreens, apparently a single story of rounded walls and roof, hinting at a labyrinthine interior.

It gave him pause, it really did. At least, the sight put up the hairs on the back of his neck, if he didn't actually hesitate. He who hesitates is lost, after all! Besides, his horse showed no concern and kept clip-clopping along. And, much as Jadren was accustomed to being a lost soul, he had far better reasons for it than a creepy-looking house full of psychics who could plumb his mind as easily as breathing.

He'd found it odd that the Hanneil lands were so unguarded as to make the border indistinguishable. The distinct disappearance of any other traffic had been the main clue that he'd crossed into Hanneil. Most houses guarded their borders in some way—with the salient exception of the cheerfully sitting ducks at House Phel—though they all conducted the enterprise according to the vagaries of the magic they practiced. Some guarded every fingertip of their borders, like the paranoid and megalomaniacal House Elal, and others set traps and triggers on the approaches to the house itself, like House El-Adrel.

House Hanneil didn't sit on extensive lands, as their primary product lines didn't depend on acreage and because they'd forfeited most of it to the neighboring High Houses as part of that agreement struck after the wars. Maybe these people could simply hear everyone coming, so they didn't bother with going out to meet them. Probably they already knew everything about him.

Come to think of it, maybe this *was* a really bad idea. A guy with a head full of secrets shouldn't dive into a pool of mindreaders. What had he been thinking?

Not clearly, that much was certain. Seliah, fucking up his brain as usual and as seemed to be her unique gift.

Well, he was thinking now and he was seriously *rethinking* this plan. Guiding his horse away from the treacherous path ahead, he turned around, kicking himself for stupidity.

He kicked himself mentally even harder when the about-face had him confronting a group of gray-cloaked wizards in individual elemental-powered chariots, emblazoned with the House Hanneil crest of a stylized human head radiating rays in red and black. The swords, knives, spears, and bows they carried showed exactly what their job was. A border guard, after all. How charming.

Jadren supposed he should be glad that Convocation law prevented Hanneil wizards from using their psychic abilities as an offensive weapon. Even he knew that much. The Convocation had learned a few things from the wars a millennia ago and one of those things was an enemy who could burn your brains out from the inside or simply convince you that you loved them and didn't want to kill them had a distinct advantage in battle. House Hanneil had faced agreeing to those restrictions or being erased from existence by the combined might of the other High Houses, including El-Adrel. He'd be proud of his ancestors if he wasn't certain in that moment that they'd be ashamed of their scion and his stupidity in walking into what was clearly a trap.

The guards regarded him with classic Hanneil impassivity and Jadren tried very hard to look innocuous, and think about nothing. Just because the guard-wizards—and they were all wizards, with black eyes boring holes in their inscrutable faces—were prohibited from using offensive psychic magic didn't mean they couldn't and wouldn't use devastating psychic tricks of the *defensive* variety, if they could later prove self-defense to the Convocation.

And *that* would be if anyone cared to investigate his tragic disappearance. Unlikely, considering that no one knew where he was. It was only them out there. It wouldn't even be his word against theirs. If they reduced him to a gibbering mess of slobbering mental jelly, he wouldn't exactly be arguing his case before the Convocation Council.

Jadren had been lulled into a false complacency, skirting the protections set up by Hanneil's neighbors and failing to consider what he might encounter close to the house itself. Certainly he hadn't imagined he'd be so easily outflanked, though he should have, given the nature of Hanneil magic. Nothing to it but to brazen through.

"Hi," he said jauntily. "Is this the road to Convocation Center? I may have accidentally turned left at Refoel."

"Who are you, Wizard?" the point guard asked softly. "What is your affiliation? You wear no house insignia."

That's right, very deliberately so, he nearly said aloud. He really hated circular conversations. If he wanted them to know his affiliation, he'd be wearing that house's crest, wouldn't he? "I'm traveling undercover," he confided. "I'd tell you, but I'd have to kill you." He tapped the hilt of Mr. Machete at his hip.

None of the guard wizards looked even remotely impressed. They probably weren't high-caliber wizards, not ones assigned to low-level patrol duty like this, when the real gravy for the house was in thought-seeking, geas-imposing, riding herd on the oracle heads, and dark arts knew what else. He could probably take them with El-Adrel magic and the snicker-snack of Mr. Machete. But where would that leave him? A fugitive from the righteous anger of House Hanneil, that's where. He already had the house of his birth chasing him; he didn't need to add to his pursuers.

The lead wizard smiled with razor-thin lack of humor. "I doubt we have much to fear from a landless rogue wizard." They jerked their head at a subordinate. "Drop him off the cliff, but keep the horse." Wizard-black eyes landed on Mr. Machete, no doubt glowing with Gabriel's moon magic to their wizard senses. "And the weapon. Probably stolen anyway."

Better and better. Jadren danced the horse away. "Ah, let's not be hasty. I have a message for Lady Hanneil."

"Then why were you turning away from House Hanneil?"

An excellent question. "I suddenly recalled that I should have bathed at that little stream a ways back. Ditch the horsy stink. Make a good impression and all."

The wizard looked sourly unconvinced. As well they should. Jadren was normally much better at lying than this. Were they putting some kind of truth-telling pressure on him? "What about your story of looking for Convocation Center and getting lost?" the wizard inquired silkily.

"I'm going to let you in on a secret," Jadren said with a sly wink. "Anytime someone mentions turning left at Refoel, it's a joke. Maybe you mind-wizards don't get humor." Judging by the group of grayly emotionless faces regarding him, that seemed a safe bet. "*Anyway,*" Jadren added with an expansive gesture, "I claim guest-rights on Hanneil lands. I seek an audience with Lady Hanneil and await her judgment on the particulars of my case." He thought very hard on the truth of that, hoping they'd read it in him.

Several of the rearmost wizards shifted uneasily, the lead wizard looking flintily annoyed. Though no one had spoken, the lead glanced sharply at the wizard behind their shoulder. Mind-talking no doubt. Why had Jadren thought coming to Hanneil was a good idea? Oh, right—because the fair Seliah had scrambled his brains more effectively than any thought-seeker could.

"You can't claim guest rights without a house affiliation," the lead wizard pointed out in a tone that would've been smug if they'd added just a titch more energy. Instead they sounded pedantic, flicking their fingers at the lower-tier wizards. "Without a house, houseless wizard, you're nothing more than trash to be taken out. You know that, which is why you attempted to evade us."

Well, there was a conundrum. Trash, indeed. Jadren nearly informed them that he was a scion of House El-Adrel—however despised by the house of his birth—and they'd better not dare the wrath of that High House or his darling maman. Everyone feared Katica El-Adrel.

Seliah's smirking face floated before him, complete with disparaging eyeroll. *You're really going to threaten to sic your mommy on them?* she inquired sweetly. *Might as well run home to her with your tail between your legs and turn belly-up, panting for the tortures she'll inflict on you.*

"It's not like that," he ground out, thoroughly annoyed with her.

"No?" the lead wizard asked coolly. Jadren realized they'd encircled him during his imaginary conversation with Seliah. He was more muddled in the head than he'd realized. Could it be the attenuation of the bond? If so, it might be affecting her even more. The stab of concern for her at least cleared his head somewhat. *About time you pulled your head out of your ass*, she commented drily. "Then what *is* it like, wizardling?" the guard asked.

Jadren opened his mouth to explain, then gaped at the knife protruding through his chest. It seemed to have appeared from nowhere—though vaguely he supposed it had been thrust through his back from behind. Then it was gone again, replaced by fountaining blood, which looked kind of pretty. At least it wasn't gray. His horse shied and one of the guards looked at the mare, halting her with a mental command. Jadren hadn't known the Hanneil wizards could psychically control animals like Ariel wizards could, though probably that came down to proprietary magic use rather than ability. And why was he thinking about that as the wizards pulled him off his horse, dumped him on the ground, and efficiently stripped him of his stuff?

"He's carrying supplies with the House Phel sigil," one of the wizard guards noted.

"House what?" another asked.

"You know—that upstart house. Used to be a High House, lost their magic. Trying to make a go of reestablishing."

"Yeah, I heard the new lord kidnapped the Elal girl, the familiar they were so proud of."

"A houseful of losers and miscreants is what I heard."

"No wonder this one is such a poor excuse for a wizard, if he comes from that shoddy, quasi-Convocation lot. I heard the new lord never even went to Convocation Academy."

"Probably taught this one all he knows." They all laughed, relaxed now, and enjoying themselves.

"Probably kicked this one out as not even good enough for the losers."

"You have no idea," Jadren said, but no one heard him.

Mr. Machete winked at him as someone lifted it away. *You didn't even draw me from the sheath,* Mr. Machete observed. Before this, it had always spoken in Gabriel Phel's voice. Now it used Seliah's. Tricksy weapon. *I think that makes you zero for two in the self-defense department. Twice now that you've been killed without drawing a blade.*

"Wrong."

Oh right—it was three times, wasn't it? Gabriel killed you empty-handed, too.

"Not fair," he gasped. He hadn't wanted to raise a weapon against Phel.

Dead is dead, though.

"I can't die," he retorted in a rasp.

"Oh, I think you'll find otherwise," one of the gray guards replied cheerfully. "But first, you get to fly! Byeeeee."

Jadren wasn't sure if that was his own scream or the wizard's taunt that echoed as he fell. He *was* sure of hitting ground, the sickening thud reverberating through every bone in his body as they all shattered into crumbs.

His third-to-last thought was that his mother would be terribly disappointed not to be able to gather the data on whether he could heal from this level of physical destruction. It gave him grim satisfaction to deprive her of at least that much.

His second-to-last thought was: not again.

His final thought was only her name. *Seliah.*

SELLY CLUTCHED HER head and screamed bloody murder. Dimly aware of the concerned shouts around her, she fell to her knees in the midst of another of Nic's grueling training sessions, feeling as if she needed to keep a tight grip on her skull to keep the pieces from flying apart, sending her brains to splatter the walls. When someone tried to pry her fingers away, she sobbed for them to stop.

Jadren.

She must have lost a little time, because the next she knew, strong arms were lifting her, carrying her with solid familiarity, a warm voice telling her all would be well. And it would be, now that Jadren had returned to her. Jadren still loved her, holding her close, promising to help her. "Jadren," she murmured in relief and gratitude.

"Don't you worry about him," Gabriel replied in a tone that threatened violence. "He'll pay for doing this to you. I should've insisted you have that bond severed."

Feeling better every moment, Selly became aware that Gabriel was carrying her through the manse with ground-eating strides, Nic jogging beside him to keep up on her shorter legs, her keen green gaze fixed on Selly's face with concern and discernment. "This isn't about the bond attenuation," she told Gabriel.

"No, it isn't," Selly agreed. "Put me down, Gabriel."

"Not until you're in the infirmary under Asa's care. You

have blood pouring out of your nose," he added, giving her a baleful black glare as if she'd done it deliberately to upset him. "You have no ground to give orders at the moment."

With considerable exasperation, Selly wiped her nose on her sleeve and frowned at the quantity of bright blood on it. What was happening? She groped for the bond with Jadren, not finding him there at all. The last time this had happened was when Gabriel had run him through and Jadren had... She began squirming, Gabriel's arms tightening more to contain her. "Put me down!" she demanded, desperation making tears well up. "I need to get to Jadren."

"Not a chance," Gabriel growled, his magic condensing silver in the air.

"Gabriel, please, I—"

"*If* this is about something that's happened to that reprobate and *if* there's anything you can do about it and *if* you convince me you're rational and healthy enough, *then* we can discuss you hurling yourself into danger to save a man who abandoned you without a backward glance and subjected you to *this* kind of damage."

Selly started to protest, but caught Nic's warning look and raised brows. Be rational, right. She needed to be calm and focused. Not a half-feral crazy girl. Instead, blowing out the breath she'd taken, she tried to calm herself, using the meditative techniques Nic had been teaching her. Control of magic depended on a clear mind and precise control. Even though familiars couldn't wield magic externally, they could regulate the flow of it internally. Part of keeping her internal environment healthy was knowing when her magic needed to be tapped or replenished. Right now, it needed to be released, which would help her handle this situation with the sane and logical arguments that would sway her difficult brother.

And if that didn't work, well, she could always escape. "All right," she said, pleased with how smooth her voice sounded. She relaxed into Gabriel's hold. "How did you come to be carrying me?"

Gabriel gave her easy capitulation a suspicious glance, but Nic nodded approvingly from over his shoulder. "Nic called me." He glanced at her and she smoothed her expression into one of attentive concern. "Which was the right thing to do. Asa!" he called, as he turned into the healer's offices. "Something happened to Selly. Seliah," he corrected himself. He carried her directly into the infirmary and laid her on a bed with tender care—and Selly reminded herself that Gabriel loved her and that overrode all other considerations for him.

The dark-skinned Refoel wizard hastened over, calling out for a wash basin and cloths. "Is all this blood yours?" he asked, his magic twining just ahead of him, tingling bright green, brushing over her senses. She must indeed be getting better at using her magic because she'd never felt the workings of Asa's wizardry on her like this before. It seemed she could almost track the changes he wrought on her physiology, the probing of her flesh as palpable as if he ran his hands over her, checking for injury. That reminded her of how Jadren had done the same, frantically searching for wounds, the action speaking more loudly of his feelings for her than any words could—and making her ache anew in fear and longing for him.

Surely he couldn't be dead. If he'd promised her nothing

else, it was that he couldn't die. She'd depended on that foundational truth more than she'd realized. In a life of shifting sands of insanity and uncertainty, she'd already begun to rely on the surety that Jadren would somehow always survive.

"Seliah?" Asa asked, arching a fine dark brow, elegant in his concern. "Can you understand what I'm asking?"

"Yes, the blood is all mine," she answered belatedly, aware of Gabriel's scowl of concern and Asa's mental probing. It seemed people would forever be first assuming she was slipping back into crazyland, as Jadren so flippantly phrased it. "Something has happened to Jadren," she explained, wrapping her fingers around Asa's wrist as he gently mopped the blood from her face. "I think it affected me through the bond."

Asa nodded consideringly, not shaking her off, but continuing to clean the blood away, her hand on his wrist like a trailing guide, his other hand casually resting on her bare skin at the join of her shoulder and neck. Through that contact, his magic still twined into her, assessing and testing, a deft and meticulous use of wizardry she only now appreciated. No wonder Convocation-trained wizards and familiars looked down on rogues like Jadren, Gabriel, and her. They were bumbling amateurs by comparison.

"The solution is clearly to sever the bond," Gabriel announced, surprising Selly that he'd said it aloud, but then she realized he'd warded the space around their cluster, preventing anyone else from overhearing.

"Is it, Lord Phel." Asa returned mildly, not exactly posing that as a question. There was the required respect in his tone, but also a firmness that conveyed he wouldn't be swayed by the orders of the high-house lord if his healer's responsibilities dictated otherwise.

"Look how it's damaging her," Gabriel pointed out tersely, gesturing at Selly with an impatient hand. "This can't be normal." Even as he confidently uttered that declaration, he glanced at Nic for confirmation.

She pursed her lips and shrugged. "Asa can say better than I can. I don't have direct experience with any wizard–familiar bonds but our own." Slipping her hand around Gabriel's tensely bulging upper arm, she squeezed, drawing his attention and smiling warmly. "Let Asa do his job, my only love. You know he'll tell you true."

"Whether Lord Phel wants to hear it or not," Asa muttered under his breath, giving Selly a hint of a smile.

She smiled back, tremulously. "I think Jadren died," she confided to Asa.

"He has a bad habit of doing that," Asa agreed on a sigh. "I suppose it was too much to hope that he might honor all the work I put into healing him and keep his sorry flesh intact for longer than a week."

Laughing despite herself, Selly agreed ruefully. "He does seem to be unduly careless about it." Jadren was an unhappy combination of sharply cynical, jaded beyond the experience of most human beings, and scarily naïve. He waltzed through the world as if it couldn't hurt him. But just because death didn't stick to him—hopefully that was still true—that didn't save him from suffering. And, someday, something would damage Jadren so much that he wouldn't be able to recover from it.

She shivered with a sense of foreboding at that thought and

firmly set it aside. That day had not yet come. She'd make it never would.

"I can't feel the bond," she whispered, through Gabriel frowned reprovingly, apparently thinking she was trying to hide the information from him. In truth, she hated to say it aloud.

"From what I understand of the nature of the enchantment governing wizard–familiar bonds, your bond with Jadren should have dissolved upon his previous untimely death at Lord Phel's hands."

"I've apologized for that," Gabriel said tightly, proving he was listening with close attention to their murmured conversation. It was his right as lord of the house, Selly supposed, but she wasn't above glaring at him for intruding.

"So," Asa continued placidly, "either the wizard–familiar bond *doesn't* dissolve with death, as is commonly assumed, and we've simply lacked resurrected participants to provide evidence—"

"Now there is a daunting thought," Nic noted.

"—or Wizard Jadren's physical deaths, which I've yet to determine are full deaths rather than near-death experiences, as I haven't been present when he ostensibly died, are not enough to dissolve the bond. That is, whatever magic allows him to survive massive physical destruction and rebuild his body against all probability, may also keep him alive on some level. Enough to sustain his end of the spell."

"Except this time," Selly said with thin despair, her voice lifting in question at the end.

"That remains to be seen," he answered gently, his magic

still probing her. "Have you experienced this kind of sympathetic damage as a result of injuries to your wizard before?
Because that *is* what happened, Lord Phel. Seliah's physical
reaction is essentially self-induced by her own magic, apparently as a sympathetic response to her wizard's magic."

"I thought a familiar's magic can't be wielded by them,"
Gabriel said sharply.

"Not outside themselves," Nic countered, "but our magic
clearly affects our own bodies, or magic build-up wouldn't be a
problem. And we wouldn't have the ability to control
extraction of magic from us, or use magic as a passive field to
sense the magic of others."

"Then what prevents you from using it outside your bodies?" Gabriel demanded, as if Nic were deliberately being
difficult.

She gave him an owlish look and thumped the center of
her forehead. "Something in here."

"Nobody knows," Asa supplied without looking at them.
"Great minds—familiar and wizard alike—have assailed the
problem. Something in the brains of wizards undergoes a final
maturation that enables the wielding. Comparisons of
dissected brains reveals the anatomical difference, but no one
knows why *that* region of the brain is important, nor why it
takes on the wizard-configuration in some and not others."
He'd been speaking absently, clearly lecturing on a familiar
topic, all while delicately probing Selly with his magic. His
wizard-black gaze focused on her face. "Experiments on living
subjects didn't yield any further information, perhaps because
the participants, all unwilling, as you might imagine, didn't live

long enough."

She shuddered at that—as if the brain-dissection bit hadn't been bad enough—and sincerely hoped Jadren's mother didn't take it into her diabolically cruel mind to investigate that particular research question. Jadren would be an ideal test subject. "I have felt Jadren's pain," she answered Asa's question. "And at times maybe experienced some of what he did? Though not nearly on the same level of what he experienced. I'd get maybe a headache—and I thought that was because of the magic drain. I'm not well-trained enough to know the difference," she added apologetically.

"You *weren't*," Nic put in, "but you're getting there. She's a very quick study."

Asa nodded, expression remote. "Difficult to say then, why this episode affected you so dramatically, but you're fine now. You may sit up." Though she didn't need it, Asa helped her into a sitting position, his long, elegant hands both caring and impersonal. "She's in perfect health," he told Gabriel. "In truth, she'd already begun to recover before I performed any healing. I suspect that she would have fully recovered on her own in short order, without assistance."

"Healing herself?" Gabriel asked with a frown, Nic's face the reverse, eyes widening and expression brightening with intrigued excitement.

"Yes." Asa patted Selly on the shoulder. "The bond is still there. It's attenuated, and whatever Jadren did to himself this time, it appears to have taken him well out of the realm of the living, if not exactly into full death, but I suspect our unlikely immortal will return. I can sense him clawing back along the thread between you. Soon you will, too."

Selly nodded, swallowing back tears, the relief at hearing that news overcoming her flinch at hearing Asa refer to Jadren as immortal. It really hadn't been a very well-kept secret, at least, not within this group.

"Interestingly, you appear to be using Jadren's magic to heal yourself unconsciously," Asa offered in a thoughtful tone, projected for Gabriel to overhear.

"Should she be able to do that?" Gabriel asked sharply.

"Especially at this distance," Nic noted with interest.

"Wizard Jadren's inherent ability to heal is unprecedented, so far as I know. It's almost like a familiar's passive field in that he doesn't seem to consciously control it."

They all looked at Selly, but she had nothing to offer. She certainly wouldn't say more about what Jadren had specifically made her promise not to tell.

Gabriel read it in her and sighed. "Are you determined to keep this bond and go after Jadren?"

Flushed with relief and desperate hope that Gabriel was even asking, Selly nodded, trying to look calm and rational. "I believe I must."

"She's in good health, you promise?" Gabriel asked Asa, and Selly heard the unspoken question that included mental and emotional health.

"As previously stated," Asa returned mildly.

"You could still have Alise sever the bond and have done with him," Gabriel said to Selly, searching her face, sounding almost beseeching.

"I don't want that," Selly replied softly, but firmly, holding

Gabriel's gaze, letting him see how she felt. "It might not make sense to you, but this is important to me. I can't turn my back on him."

Gabriel sighed, glanced at Nic, and shook his head. "Too much alike, you and I, Seliah," he said. "Neither of us able to just let go as we should."

"Hey," Nic protested. "Chasing me down made good economic sense. Or," she amended, "it will eventually." She grimaced, softening when Gabriel put an arm around her and snugged her close against him.

"That was entirely why I did it, my practical wife," he murmured in a tone that said anything but.

"I know." She laid a hand against his cheek. "I love you, too."

Selly's reunion with Jadren wouldn't be anything so heartwarming. No doubt it would involve him hurling insults at her in further attempts to drive her away. Oddly enough, the prospect filled her with anticipation.

~ 6 ~

"ALL RIGHT, SELIAH," Han said, laying out an array of weapons on the rough table outside the stables. The handsome blond familiar with a dancer's body and startling teal eyes gave her a very serious look. "You don't have to take all of these, but they're all potentially useful, all refined from moon magic, so lethal to any hunters you may encounter."

Selly nodded, surveying what Han had brought her. He was more than a pretty face. Another late bloomer, Han had only recently manifested as a familiar. While biding his time at Convocation Academy, hoping to become the newest of the mighty house of Hanneil wizards, Han—having completed all the coursework available to an uncategorized student—had devoted himself to weapons training. He'd become so proficient that Gabriel had appointed him trainer in weapons work for all the House Phel denizens. Magic-workers tended to rely on their magic for self-defense, but Gabriel, also a late-bloomer, had grown up using the manual chop-chop method as Nic sardonically called it. He'd decreed everyone should learn to use physical weapons as well as magical ones.

Selly had not been exempted and had spent the time in the last few days when Nic hadn't been draining and training her, practicing with Han. Anything to reassure Gabriel that he could let her go with a clear conscience. Though they still weren't telling their parents.

"You're obviously already good with the bow," Han continued, "so I've rounded up as many silver-tipped arrows as I could." He gestured to several quivers of arrows, then selected one and handed it to her. "These bolts are shorter and lighter than what you've been using, with the idea in mind that you won't need accuracy over distance. These aren't for hunting, but for killing magically animated creatures like the hunters, and for fighting off people. It's a trade-off, but smaller means you can carry more."

"I already have too much *stuff*," Selly agreed on a sigh and an irritated glance at the stable. As with everything at the resurrected manse, the stables had become bigger and more complicated. She couldn't simply grab a horse and scavenge tack. No, a horse had to be "readied" for her. Which apparently took forever. She'd like to get a better sense of which horse she'd be taking so she could make decisions about what to take or leave.

Gabriel had been adding more and more supplies that she'd absolutely need, according to him, as if he hadn't ridden across Convocation territory—and beyond, into mundane lands—with far less. Selly didn't weigh much, but one horse could only carry so much stuff besides her and she'd put her foot down on bringing an additional pack horse along. She might need to move fast. In fact, she'd rather have gone on foot, to be even more flexible, staying off the roads, moving through the wilds of the marshes as she'd learned to do while trying to run away from her madness, but that idea had been firmly vetoed by not only Gabriel, but Nic as well. They felt she'd be too slow and vulnerable on foot and she'd finally conceded the point, if only because she wanted to get to Jadren as fast as possible. She shifted impatiently from foot to foot.

"Important *stuff*." Han smiled with good humor, then pointed to a series of blades. "You've proven good with the smaller daggers, but you need a longer blade, too. With your long arms and legs, you've got good reach for close-in, hand-to-hand fighting, but no sense getting closer than you need to, especially if you encounter someone with an even greater reach. Also, it's good to have a few back-up blades. I suggest these five, plus your favorite that you're already wearing."

"Five?" she repeated, hesitating.

"They weigh less than the food supplies," Han pointed out.

"I did manage to survive on my own for years without hauling food and water around," she grumbled. She'd scavenged and hunted and yes, maybe she was too skinny from years of going lean, but she'd survived.

"Having to hunt would slow you down," Nic reminded her, arriving with Gabriel and a host of others apparently coming to see her off. Selly had hoped that the early departure would discourage an assembly, but apparently she was wrong. At least her parents were nowhere in sight. Ducking their worries and remonstrations had been highest priority. Her mother would have enough of a fit when she found out Selly had left, yet again.

"At least you don't actually need to haul water," Gabriel said gruffly. He'd stopped arguing about her going, but had retreated into what Nic called grumpy-wizard mode. "This is for you," he said, extending a silver object.

Selly took it with curiosity and no small amount of wonder. It radiated moon and water magic, mostly Gabriel's, and as like to her own as a hand in glove—but Jadren's clockwork infused it also, clean-oiled magic ticked against her skin. The sensation gave her a rush of longing for him and she imagined for a moment that she sensed him along the bond, stirring in shattered agony. There was so much pain that she didn't know whether to hope that it was real, confirming that he lived, or to hope it was simple wishful thinking. Except that she'd never wish for him to be in pain.

Unless she caused it herself during the course of justifiable revenge, of course.

"It's a self-replenishing water flask," Gabriel said.

"One of the new product line Jadren helped design," Nic put in.

"He left before he finished all his proposed tweaks," Gabriel clarified, "so it's not perfect, but it's better by far than my first one. I personalized it for you."

Selly traced her fingers over the design, the sigil of House Phel: a full moon shining over still waters. Etched into the silver in scrolling letters, her full name encircled it. Seliah Phel, not El-Adrel, as Lady El-Adrel had pronounced her following her bonding to Jadren. Selly wasn't sure how she felt about that. Phel was her house, not El-Adrel, yet the cleaving of Jadren's house of birth from her name seemed like an unfortunate sundering, an omen of ill things to come. And of Gabriel's opinion about them. Selly didn't care for the sensation of being tugged between Lady El-Adrel and Lord Phel in some political dispute.

To give herself a moment to recover her poise, she traced the design with a wondering fingertip, marveling at how it almost seemed to be part of the silver rather than scratched into the surface, all smooth edges that glowed like moonlight as she turned it in her hands. "Did you do this?" she asked Gabriel. "I mean," she fumbled, knowing that he had and realizing she'd been unclear, "did you... draw this?"

"I used moon magic, yes," Gabriel answered, then cleared his throat, glancing away. He frowned at the array of weapons. "Han, that sword has got to be too heavy for her. Surely there's another?" He turned away as Han argued the point.

"He stayed up most of the night working on it," Nic confided, looping her arm through Selly's. "He tweaked the water spell, too, so it only fills when you open it. Otherwise it stays empty once drained, so long as you affix the lid while it's upside-down. That way it's lighter. He worried about you throwing it away in order to move faster."

"I would never," Selly breathed, awed and immensely touched, despite her overall aggravation with her bossy big brother.

"Yes, well, he made sure of that," Nic replied drily. "There's something else and I'm asking you not to argue about it. He wants to do this. *Needs* to," she amended.

"Do what?" Selly asked with renewed suspicion, alerted by Nic's tone. Nic simply shook her head and pointed Selly at the horse emerging from the stables led by a groom. "Vale?" she gasped in shock.

The big black gelding—Gabriel's horse that he'd raised from a foal, trained himself, and treated like another sibling—tossed his head and whickered as he danced sideways, looking terribly pleased about going on an adventure.

Selly whipped her head around to Gabriel. "You can't send Vale with me!"

Nic squeezed her arm warningly before stepping away. Gabriel glared at Selly, appearing more angry than anything. "I can and will," he retorted, stabbing a finger at Vale. "Vale is the best-trained horse we have. He's fought hunters before. He can aid you in a pitched fight. He's strong, has speed, stamina, and heart. If you're going out on this fool's mission, then you're taking the best House Phel has to offer. You're not some beggar at the doorstep, Seliah. You're a lady of House Phel, a citizen of the Convocation whether they like it or not, and you will have the best. We might be poor and less fancy than those other houses, but we have *some* resources."

Selly blinked at her brother's speech, somewhat taken aback. "But he's yours," she said faintly, pretending she didn't see Nic sending her significant looks.

"Ours," Gabriel corrected softly, taking the water bottle—with its magically etched declaration of exactly which house Selly belonged to—and setting it aside. Gabriel folded her hands between his. "What's mine is yours, too. Please take Vale. I know you don't want me to worry about you and I want you to know I believe in you and your ability to complete this ill-advised quest. I would feel better if you had Vale to assist. Besides…" Gabriel's lips quirked at a perfectly timed and excited whinny from the gelding. "He's been bored,"

Gabriel added in a confiding tone. "Cooling his hooves around here while I'm buried under paperwork and correspondence isn't good for him. If you won't do this for me, do it for him."

"All right," Selly conceded. It was truly a gift beyond price. She didn't know what she'd do if something happened to Vale though. "I'll bring him and Jadren home safely," she promised.

"You and Vale would be enough for me," Gabriel commented sourly.

Laughing, she put her arms around Gabriel's waist and hugged him. "I know you like Jadren better than you're pretending."

"I only like him as far as he's good to you," Gabriel corrected. "Feel free to run him through on my behalf if he's anything but."

"Yes sir, Lord Phel," she replied with a saucy grin and a salute.

He tweaked her nose, mock scowling. "Just come home," he said. "Anything else we can handle together."

IT WASN'T EXACTLY a relief to head out, but it seemed as if a weight fell from her shoulders as Selly rode away from House Phel, the gentle white gables of the gracious manor quickly disappearing amongst the wildly blossoming orchards. Vale seemed equally delighted to be on the move, giving no sign he minded having her astride instead of his best friend in all the world. He pranced with vigor, eagerly following the direction she set, unbothered by the weight of the full saddlebags.

She'd had no trouble deciding which direction to go, even with the bond so tenuous. A brief scouting foray during a rare bit of downtime in the last days had revealed Jadren's path. As wily as he might be in any number of arenas—notably ones where she was hopelessly inadequate, which boded well for them as a team—he was shit at concealing his trail. If he'd even tried. He might've been so confident that his scathing note would keep her meekly at home that he hadn't anticipated her tracking him. All the better for her, then.

"Keep underestimating me, wizard," she muttered under her breath, and Vale tossed his head in emphatic equine agreement.

Regardless, Jadren had left a trail as clear as if he'd been riding a herd of elephants, so obvious even several days later that Selly could practically hear him swearing and stomping around in his perpetually foul mood. His presence was so vivid that it felt like he traveled along with them as a remanent of himself, almost visible at times. Here he'd stopped to pee against a tree. There he'd eaten lunch, leaving a few scraps of fruit peels on the ground, spoiled scion that he was, so accustomed to being picked up after. Because there was no one to witness but Vale—and Vale didn't judge—she plucked up one of the rinds, picturing Jadren's clever fingers removing it, imagining that she sensed his lingering presence in the moldering peel. She wasn't so sentimental that she kept it, but she was crazy emotional enough to consider the thought before discarding it. *Just trash,* she told herself.

Jadren's trail got more difficult to follow the deeper he penetrated into the marshes. The ground grew less forgiving— or more, depending on how you looked at it—with water filling in and absorbing the signs of passage. Even Vale's deep hoofprints vanished behind them, the mossy turf springing into place as she looked back, the trailing gray mosses hanging from the blackly glossy trees muffling sound so that Selly began to feel like a remanent herself, a shade of someone not quite alive. If not for Vale's vitally alive presence, she might have begun to doubt her own existence.

She hadn't expected this sense of disassociation, but she should have. These marshes had been her refuge and her nightmare. Being alone in the depths of the wetlands of Meresin felt like returning home—and like falling backward. This had been the landscape of her madness. No wonder she'd thought of the magic-induced insanity as shades of shifting mist. As daylight fell away, victim to the deeper shadows of the twisted canopy and the lowering sun somewhere beyond, and as fog swirled in over the softly clicking, croaking waters, she imagined the boundaries of her mind similarly darkening and dissolving. In the marshes, there are few clear lines. Water becomes ground becomes bog becomes twisted roots. That silvery shape might be mist or moss. The next step could be shifting sands, solid ground, or a black and bottomless pond. There's simply no solidity, no reliable, definable reality.

More than ever, she missed Jadren's caustic wit and barbed demands. He'd teased her so relentlessly about being a crazy girl that she'd risen to the challenge, determined not to lose her shit. She was still determined, but... she found it difficult to hold onto the boundaries of her self in the trackless lands.

When Vale suddenly balked, she came to her senses, only just then realizing how far she'd drifted from the present. Night loomed in the shadows of the trees, a chill in the air. She shivered, from the gloom and at the temperature. The heat of the spring day had yielded entirely to the dank of nights not yet entirely free of winter's grip. Irresponsible of her not to have been paying better attention. She should have made camp on dry ground by now, with a warming fire. She peered around at the surrounding glimmers of open water and water-logged ground. This wasn't a place they could stop.

Patting Vale's neck, hot and damp with sweat, she dismounted, wincing at the stiffness of being so long in the saddle, and at the sucking squelch of her boots in the muck. Vale was hock deep in it, poor guy, and must have been working hard to forge ahead. Once away from the warhorse's body heat, she shivered harder. This wasn't good at all.

How crushing the humiliation would be if her big talk and grand quest ended less than a day's ride from House Phel.

Time to dig herself out of memories and focus on the present. With a hand on Vale's bridle, mostly so she could grab on in case she foolishly put a foot down on unstable ground, she took a step forward. Vale nickered a protest, jerking his head back. Her fingers, numb with cold, slipped off the bridle and she went down.

And down.

Suffocating sludge closed over her head.

JADREN WAS HEARTILY tired of waking up dead.

Or mostly dead. He supposed that someday his death would actually take instead of being temporary and he wouldn't wake up at all. Or maybe he'd wake up in some paradisial land free from pain and suffering like some people insisted lay on the other side of the veil.

If he woke up dead and *not* in agony for once, then he'd know.

Of course, many people would say that the likes him deserved to end up in a place of eternal suffering and punishment for his many faults and transgressions, which meant he'd wake up in torment and... how would that be any different from the usual waking up to agony?

Dark arts, don't let me find out, he thought to himself, aware that he couldn't move his jaw to speak the words aloud. In fact, he couldn't seem to move anything at all, not even his eyelids to see where he was. That couldn't be good. Especially since he couldn't seem to feel his eyelids at all. Pain, yes. He could sure feel that. As usual for the standard return-from-the-dead scenario, agony ruled, shimmering over him in waves like heat magic. He'd never understand why, if he had to be cursed with this self-healing thing, it couldn't have come with a pleasurable sensation. Why couldn't healing feel like an orgasm? Or, failing that, something sweet and soft, like the caress of Seliah's fingertips over his skin, her pliant body sleeping with languid warmth beside him.

But no—healing had to hurt as badly as receiving the initial wounds. Even worse, really, as incurring injuries usually came as a surprise, swift shock fading into a blessed escape from consciousness. Healing, not so much. It took too long for his body to repair itself for shock and surprise to buffer anything, and his body flinging itself out of unconsciousness seemed to be part of that process.

Though, maybe that wasn't true in this case. It occurred to him, in a bemused, fragmented way, that he was swimming back and forth through murky tunnels between consciousness and unconsciousness—and that his brains weren't working at all properly.

Good and smashed them this time, didn't you? Seliah asked. She was standing over him, fists on her hips as she raked him with a scathing look of disappointment, lip curled in disgust.

He tried to say something flippant, a bit of pointed sarcasm, and failed utterly. Instead, he wanted to beg her to hold him, to help him. Not something he could recall ever wanting, much less asking for. A bad sign. *I think I might be fucked this time*, he confided to her.

You think? She shook her head sadly. *And you believe you're qualified to protect me.*

From myself, yes. He knew that much, though he couldn't recall why it was true.

She didn't seem to hear, pointing to something above. *You really believed you could survive falling off of a fucking cliff, Jadren?*

Oh right. He remembered the cliff. Kind of. Enough to be pretty sure it wasn't his fault. *I didn't fall*, he retorted indignantly. *I was thrown!*

She didn't reply. Because she was gone. With the whole lack of working ears and eyes, it occurred to him that he couldn't have seen and talked with her anyway. She hadn't been there at all. And why would she be? He'd ditched her. Abandoned his familiar, the one person who could help him heal from this. If he really was nothing more than a pile of messed-up flesh at the bottom of a cliff, would his shattered pieces be able to come together? It was possible that he'd simply remain conscious in this pulped state. Ooh, unless wild animals ate him. Would he finally die if he were digested into little bits?

Regardless, it seemed he'd awakened in a place of eternal torment, no matter what the reality. Exactly what he deserved, and it appeared he'd done it to himself. He'd wanted death to take and this time it might just happen. Except that it was taking an excruciatingly long time.

A very, very bad sign.

~ 7 ~

S ELLY PLUMMETED IN slow motion, retaining enough of her wits and wiles to close her eyes and keep her mouth firmly shut. The marshes were full of such sinkholes and this wasn't her first. Though she should have known better. Vale whinnied in alarm from a distance, which reassured her that the horse hadn't fallen into the slimy pit with her. Good thing, as she didn't know if she could've gotten Vale out again.

She'd been stupid to have kept going so late, to take a step in the dark on unfamiliar land. *What were you thinking, crazy girl?* Jadren's ghost-voice asked bitingly. *Oh, wait—let me guess—you* weren't *thinking.*

"Shut up, I've got this." She couldn't fail. Before when she'd wandered the marshes, out of her mind, she hadn't cared what happened to her, and that unconcern had seemed to protect her. Now, she cared. Cared so ferociously it cut through her like a knife, spearing her heart as surely as Gabriel's sword had impaled Jadren. *Jadren.* He needed her and she had to get to him.

Her feet touched bottom, the rock she'd hoped for catching her feet. The trick was not to react too soon. And not to yield to the urge to take a breath. Allowing her weight to settle, her body to compress, she thought about her muscles, the texture of the mud, Val whinnying for her—anything but air and the lack thereof. She didn't dare hope she'd have enough in her to allow a second slow sinking, another desperate push upward.

She'd have once chance at this.

Bending her knees, tensing her calves, her thighs, her entire lower body, she waited one agonizing beat longer, then *pushed.*

Going up was faster than going down—something true only in the sinkholes of the marshes. Mud going down; water going up. Her upturned face broke through the surface sooner than anticipated, and she sucked in a great, gasping breath, trying not to choke on the clumps of mud and plants that came with the blessed air. Wasting no time, she struck out sideways. It didn't matter which direction, the sinkholes were never that big and all she needed was one slim handhold of solid ground. Without that, she'd go under again.

Her flailing hand sank down, along with her spirits. *Giving up already?* Jadren asked, shaking his head. *Some brilliant metaphor of yours this is.*

The metaphor works, she thought fiercely at him. *You'll see, you nervous Nelly!*

In her mind, he guffawed. Heartily. Not dead or wounded at all. *Nervous Nelly?* he echoed in astonishment. *Are you mentally twelve years old after all?*

Ignoring him, she made herself move slowly. Swimming, not flailing. She reached, trying to see through the darkness.

Not there, Jadren said with impatience. *There. An arm's length to your right. Next time, Nelly, consider using your magic.*

Not daring to hope, to trust that any of this was real, she figured following the advice was only practical. It wasn't as if she had a better plan. Moving carefully to maintain her fragile buoyancy, she moved an arm's length to the right.

And put her hand on not only solid ground, but a muddied hoof and horsehair above it. Vale lowered his head and snuffled her hair. Sobbing her gratitude and relief, Selly extracted her other arm from the muck and wrapped both hands around Vale's leg, beneath the matted fall of his once-luxurious fetlock. The gelding's training held true—another reason to thank Gabriel—and Vale began backing up slowly, not shaking her off, but dragging her along.

Selly collapsed on the soggy, but decidedly solid ground and caught her breath. She needed to get up, get them both clean and warm, but no sense in charging off into trouble again. Waiting for Jadren's sardonic agreement, she heard nothing. He seemed to have abandoned her again. If he'd been anything more than a figment of wishful thinking to begin with.

Vale whickered, nudging her shoulder with his muzzle. Yes, she needed to get up and handle this, which she should be able to do. She'd made her way safely through this landscape when she'd been out of her mind; she could do it with her wits about her. Or perhaps a combination of both.

Next time, Nelly, consider using your magic. She wasn't sure if she'd heard that—then or now—but it was good advice, especially since she knew a great deal more about her magic than ever before. Of course, anything would be an improvement over "nothing at all," but still…

Getting to her feet, she leaned against Vale's solid bulk and wiped the mud from her eyes. She was surrounded by water, and Nic had said that Selly almost certainly generated her magic from water and moonlight, as the theory went that familiars grew their internal magic from the world around them, able to drink in and feed on magic in ways that wizards couldn't. By contrast, wizards generated their own magic to some extent, but nothing like familiars did, especially powerful ones like Selly, Nic had explained.

When Selly had asked if the mysterious brain-thing that made them unable to wield magic might be less of a dysfunction and more of a talent in a different direction—generating magic as opposed to venting it—Nic had looked briefly bemused. Then she'd pronounced Selly as bad of an optimist as her brother and resumed the lecture.

Keeping in mind Nic's lessons about passive fields of magic, and trusting her instincts honed over those years of surviving on her own, Selly felt her way through the shadows. Letting her magic draw on the surrounding water, she mentally tasted its nature. *Show me where solid ground is,* she willed it, and a path opened up before her as if highlighted in moonlight. Beyond pleased with herself—and deeply relieved that she wouldn't be sinking Vale and herself in another bog of doom anytime soon—Selly picked her way along the path, gaining confidence as she went.

Soon she wasn't fighting to lift her boots from the sucking muck with every step, though they were filled with the goop, disgustingly squishy. Vale's labored breathing eased as he followed her with more alacrity, his hooves actually making reassuring soft thuds on ground that didn't give with every step. Letting the water show her high ground, Selly led them to a place of grassy peace under the spreading limbs of a tree with palm-sized leaves casting silhouettes against the silvery sky. Good thing, too, as the air felt dense and heavy with the onset of rain. Sure enough, as she unburdened Vale of the packs and his tack, a low rumble presaged the opening of the clouds, and rain thrummed on the thick canopy above.

She gave Vale a cursory rub-down, but figured the rain would remove the majority of the mud and she'd finish the job in the morning light. He seemed happy grazing on the lush grass, keeping her company as she stripped down and stood in a clearing to rinse herself and her gear. Nothing but a real bath would get all the grit out of her hair, but she felt better afterward.

No building a fire tonight. A memory tugged at her with a sweet ache, reminding her of that night she and Jadren had argued whether or not to have a fire. She'd won the argument, but then hadn't been able to bring herself to get in the box Jadren had made to ward them against the dangers of the night. Then hunters had attacked, the event that had launched them on the tangential adventure that brought her to this moment.

Alise had assured Selly that her spirit spies hadn't detected any hunters on Meresin lands, and Gabriel had sent out descriptions of the vile creatures, too, asking that any sightings be reported to the house. So, she and Vale should be safe for the night. Still, she felt oddly alone. And lonely. Stupid to feel that way, since she'd lived for years alone and had enjoyed Jadren's company for only a few days.

But she missed him. Dreadfully. Wrapped in an oiled cloth—and grudgingly sending mental thanks to Gabriel for bullying her into taking it along—she ate a cold meal and listened to the rain fall in the darkness, the splashes and night-songs of life around her making the island that much more isolated. Vale cropped grass quietly nearby, and her long blade and bow and quiver sat on either side of her, easily reached. Afraid to be disappointed yet again, but unable to resist, Selly reached along the fine thread that her bond to Jadren had become. As of late, it felt as if it spun off into nothingness, tethered nowhere, simply vanishing into an attenuated point in the far distance.

The bond hadn't disintegrated completely, however, so there was hope. As long as it remained, even connected to apparently nothing, that had to mean Jadren was out there somewhere. She couldn't imagine what condition he must be in, that he hadn't regenerated more than this yet. It had been more than a full day since she felt him die. Jadren should have healed somewhat by now and the fact that he hadn't...

Worry consumed her and she considered the possibilities of where Jadren might have ended up. She didn't kid herself that he'd be found at the end of this trail she followed, waiting for her to show up. If his mother had captured him again—a strong possibility, as she'd have been seriously unhappy about his escape and would no doubt send people after him—he'd be back in one of those glass-walled cages she maintained for her experimental animals. That might or might not explain his failure to heal.

Or if he was at the bottom of a lake or in some other situation that kept destroying his body as rapidly as it healed. She felt vaguely ill contemplating those possibilities, and what Jadren might be suffering, so she set the thoughts firmly aside.

She simply must follow this tenuous thread of connection until the end. Hopefully whatever she found there would give her direction for her next steps.

Dark arts make it so.

SELLY AWOKE, FULLY alert, to thickening birdsong and thinning mists as dawn brightened the marshes. It took a bit longer for her to shake the cloying dregs of the dream. Jadren, his body broken beyond belief over a scatter of sharp boulders. He barely looked like a human being at all—more like a smear of blood and bone at the bottom of a steep cliff. Nobody, not even her semi-immortal wizard, could survive damage like that, so it must have been a nightmare, born of her wild imaginings before sleep.

Setting aside the sick dread and worry, she made herself replace those dream images with others of Jadren from her memories. His black eyes full of wicked mischief as he teased her. The taste and feel of his lips on hers, the glide of his hands over her skin. With that shimmer of remembered erotic connection, she fancied she felt a sense of him, as if he were actually present. Could it be?

Yes, the bond felt stronger. And, at the end of it, instead of billowing nothingness, there was... something. Not quite Jadren as he'd felt before, but a definite presence. A wafting scent of him, as if she'd just walked into a room he'd recently left. He was alive. No matter what horrible condition she might find him in—*please don't let it be the cliff*—he would live. Repeating that to herself, she rose and briskly prepared to get moving.

Vale whickered a good morning greeting, barely pausing in his gleeful grazing, though he stomped one hoof pointedly. Erg—right. She'd have to clean out his hooves lest the frogs of his feet suffer from all the rot-inducing moisture. Jadren might have a point about the elemental-powered carriages of the Convocation being easier than dealing with horses, but could they pull you out of a sinkhole? Vale cocked his head at her and shook it, black mane rippling. That's right—no, they could not.

Fortunately there was lots of water and they might as well both get a decent bath before moving on, so she coaxed Vale into the shallow verge of the pond, picking the sandiest spot. With a towel from the bags, she scrubbed them both clean of last night's mud. Then, with Vale back on the grass, she used the pick Gabriel had sent, along with every other tool imaginable, to clean the mud packed in around the frogs of Vale's feet.

It took a while, but afterward she felt less like an irresponsible horse-owner, promising herself that Vale's speed would make up for the delay. If that nightmare vision of Jadren had been true and not just a figment of her worst fears, then she needed to get to him as soon as possible.

She kept her head together better that day, focusing on finding the best route through the marshes, relying now on the insistent tug of direction that whispered of Jadren's presence, rather than following his trail. That would save her some blundering like the near-disastrous one of the night before. Following in the footsteps of someone as ignorant of nature as Jadren would only lead to more calamities.

It helped her confidence, too, to know that she and Vale were definitely headed to Jadren's current location. If that dream proved true, Jadren wouldn't be moving anytime soon.

IT TOOK SELLY two more days to get close enough to Jadren to recognize the landscape from her dreams. She had only a vague idea of where she might be. School had never really been one of her strong points, then the whole losing-her-mind thing had cut her education rudely short. Besides which, the teachers in Meresin didn't emphasize the geography of the rest of the Convocation much.

It wasn't as if she could ask where she was, either, as she'd been assiduously avoiding people, easier in some places than others. She'd gotten good at discerning when they were approaching population centers. Keeping to the natural camouflage of the roadless, trackless wild places allowed her to spot the cleared avenues for roads before they came upon them. Those big throughways were like rivers cutting through the forests and hills, creating low points in the landscape where elemental carriages streamed along in a frothing current of color. People went on foot, too, and occasionally on horseback, but the carriages dominated. She and Vale both eyed them warily, mutually agreed that they wouldn't get too close.

Selly couldn't articulate to herself her exact reasons for making sure she wasn't seen. Some of it was habit. She'd spent so many years avoiding people that it was in her blood and bones. *Stay hidden. Move fast. Don't let them catch you,* her old, feral self whispered in the back of her mind. Yes, that was her crazy-girl self, but that side also possessed certain skills. Besides that, she didn't know who might be an enemy, and one didn't have to be taken captive more than once to exert effort to ensure it didn't happen again. The last thing she needed was to be captured by hunters, recaptured by El-Adrel, or snagged by some rogue wizard thinking she was an unbonded familiar ripe for stealing, and carted off somewhere where she couldn't get to Jadren.

So, she avoided the inns with their enticing smells of gravy wafting in the evening air over the meadows. She slept on the ground, keeping company with Vale, and dreaming of Jadren—battered and broken beyond repair—every night.

From how he looked in the dreams, he didn't seem to be improving at all and he hadn't "spoken" to her again. That is, if the dreams represented any kind of reality. She'd begun to nurse a sick dread and anxious worry that they *were* real. The landscape in the dreams didn't change and, though he wasn't improving, Jadren continued to strengthen at the end of the tether between them, the sense of him increasing with every dream moment, every league she closed between them. The bond had begun to feel as it had before he left, with none of the fraying attenuation.

That was the good news. The bad news was her magic seemed to react to the strengthening bond by billowing up. Oh, it had been building all this while, which she'd anticipated and had been warned about umpteen times by everyone at House Phel, as if she didn't know from extreme personal experience what having untapped magic would do to her.

She hadn't expected this effect, however, like Jadren was the moon pulling on the tides of her magic. His need raked her, tugging at some visceral core with an almost painful hunger. She found herself urging Vale to go faster and harder, until the gelding galloped through the scrublands, the dirt turning redder and spraying in a cloud behind them. As usual, she had no idea which High House ruled the lands she crossed. It wasn't as if the Convocation put up signs. She only hoped it wasn't anyone too awful, because she didn't think she could bring herself to slow or halt their headlong travel.

Even when Vale skidded on some loose shale, the shock momentarily clearing the haze of urgency from her mind, she only managed to slow him somewhat. The horse was breathing hard, sweating in the intensifying mid-afternoon sun so that his black coat gleamed wet, and yet he didn't seem to want to stop either. As if Vale also sensed Jadren's need.

So it was with vast relief that Selly recognized the cliff she'd dreamed about far too many times. Dusty red like the rest of this landscape, starkly dramatic, it stood out against a searing blue sky free of clouds. Even without the bond pulling at her like a rope inexorably wound round a winch, she'd have been able to go right to the spot, as if she knew it well.

Vale skidded to a halt at the immense spread of rocks tumbled at the base of the cliff and Selly launched herself from the saddle, half-running, half-climbing to scramble over the scree. White shards stood out among the rocks, like bleached wood stranded on the riverbanks after a flooding rain. As one snapped with a splintering crunch beneath her foot, she realized with horror that they weren't made of wood at all. They were bones.

Countless bones littered the sharp rocks, filling the interstices and sticking out in thorny bunches. Her throat tight, she resisted looking up at the cliff's edge high above, not wanting to picture how many people had met their deaths falling from it. *I didn't fall,* Jadren's voice echoed in her mind. *I was thrown!*

She looked around wildly for Jadren, but his voice had been only in her mind, maybe only in memory. Still, Jadren had to be here, somewhere in this graveyard of scattered bones. She could feel him at the other end of the bond, but he was still absurdly weak even this close, and she couldn't quite triangulate on him. What would she do if he was unconscious or too injured to pull magic from her in order to heal? *Whatever it takes,* she told herself grimly. She wouldn't flinch from whatever it took to bring him back. She hadn't come this far to give up on them.

A whimper of despair escaped her when she finally found him, despite her resolve to be strong. The birds pointed the way, the crows concentrated black against the sere expanse of dusty red rocks and white bones. At her approach, they lifted in a cloud, croaking reproachfully, revealing a bright crimson smear, gleaming wetly amongst the rocks. Jadren.

He was nearly unrecognizable, a heap of crumpled body draped over and between the rocks, bone shards sticking up through him. No wonder he hadn't been able to heal.

The wonder was that he still lived. Which he did, as evidenced by his continued fresh bleeding, the blood oozing in some places, flowing in sluggish fountains in others, otherwise, she might not have been able to tell. She couldn't bear to look at his face for more than a quick glance, his skull grossly misshapen, features so mashed as to be unrecognizable. That wasn't like the dreams at all—though mostly what she remembered of Jadren's face in those were the sense of his presence and his intense wizard-black eyes. They were closed now, at least so far as she could discern in the puffy mess of his face, sunken deep into bruises that were a disconcerting mix of old and fresh.

In a haze of utter despair, Selly considered that it might be better to put him out of his misery rather than attempt to save him. Surely no human mind could survive days of this kind of agony intact. If she had known of anything that would actually put him out of his misery for good, she might have done it in that moment. As it was, however, she was afraid any attempt to truly kill him would only prolong his suffering. Dark arts knew that others before her had tried to murder him with no luck.

"Jadren," she said, patting his cheek over his beard, a spot relatively unscathed for no discernible reason, keeping her palm against his skin. "Take my magic." She hoped against hope that he would draw on her reflexively, his wizard senses knowing unconsciously what to do. But no. Nic had said wizards needed to consciously draw magic from others, and that was holding true. Jadren's skin felt both papery thin and weirdly clammy under her hand, especially odd given the hot sun. He didn't feel alive to the touch, only in the fluttering of his presence along the bond.

Well, first things first—he couldn't heal with so many intrusions reinjuring him. So, she did the only thing she could. Working bit by bit, she freed his limbs from their twisted positions, methodically extracting the bits of rock and bone that had impaled him. She started with his feet, figuring she could begin to inure herself to touching his broken body, steeling her stomach against the gore and her heart against the debilitating fear of somehow hurting him more, as little sense as that made. Even so, just touching the boots he wore, seeing that they were the same ones he'd complained so bitterly about walking in, moved her ridiculously—and she became aware that tears ran down her face in a continuous, silent stream as she worked.

With her hands covered in his blood—she'd seriously had more than enough of Jadren's blood getting all over her, though if they remained a bonded pair, she might have to get used to it, assuming that past experience could be extrapolated to the future—she focused on working her way up his body, straightening the long, lean legs, aligning his narrow hips, meticulously rearticulating the fingers of one mangled hand.

Maybe she should remove his boots and do the same for his toes, but considering that task felt like more than she could bear.

As it was, his clothing was mangled in with his flesh. Taking off his boots might take the toes, perhaps the whole foot with them. He could likely regenerate anything that came off, but whether her sensibilities would recover from that experience was something else entirely.

She'd just cross that bridge when she came to it. Getting Jadren ambulatory was a goal for the future. Top priority at the moment was prying him free of the impaling bones trapping him among the rocks. The biggest challenge facing her was a splintered femur—not his—thrusting up through Jadren's chest. It impaled him imperfectly, wedged perhaps on a shoulder blade, so that his body bowed up in a rictus of ongoing agony.

Feeling around beneath his back, hoping that maybe she could roll him over, and pull it out the way it went in, she discovered the sharp-ended bone was wedged solidly in a crevice. Just Jadren's bad luck that he'd landed on something so fixed, and hit it so precisely, that it had gone through him rather than splintering.

You have no idea, she imagined him agreeing in his dry, sardonic voice, glad that it was only her imagination as he needed to be blessedly unconscious for this. With a nearly audible click, his eyes opened, snagging her immediate attention. Wizard-black, starry with pain, they focused on her. There he was, fully himself beyond that horribly battered face.

"What in the dark arts are you doing here?" he demanded,

his voice barely there with no breath behind it, his words slurred and sloppy from broken teeth.

"Saving your life," she snapped, happy for the opportunity to snark back at him, beyond relieved that he had enough mind and spirit to bite at her. "Speaking of which," she added, laying a hand against his cheek again, "take my magic."

"Unhand me, foul beast," he muttered, but unable to jerk away.

"Do it, wizard," she ordered.

"Just let me die." His eyes drifted closed again. "In peace."

"You tried that. It's not working."

"You're telling me."

"You need help, Jadren. Let me—"

"No. I left you for a reason."

"Yes, well, we can talk about that later, when you're not food for crows. Take my magic."

"Can't make me."

She sighed. Stubborn fool. "Fine. Go back to sleep. You'll want to miss this part."

"Wasn't sleeping, crazy girl."

"Unconscious then."

"Resting my eyes," he corrected, a scary rattle crawling up his throat. "That sun is brutal," he added on a dry whisper, eyes opening again to stare up at the relentless sky with a hopelessness she'd only seen in him once before, when they'd been consigned to his mother's experimental torture chamber.

"Here." She withdrew the flask Gabriel had given her and unstopped it, inverting it so that it would fill. "Do you want some water?"

"No," he answered, not looking at her. "My master plan is to lie here under this punishing sun, bleeding out, until I'm a desiccated husk of rawhide and bleached bones like my friends here. At last I've found my tribe. And you're not in it."

"You belong with the living, Jadren." It was easy to hold his head so that he couldn't turn it. Pouring water into his mouth in short intervals, she hoped it would do him some good. It couldn't hurt.

"I have living friends. My crow buddies visit all the time."

"People. Not scavengers. You have a family and a home waiting for you."

"Lies." He struggled feebly against her grip, accomplishing exactly nothing. "You're all just crows to me now. Get away from me, you feral swamp creature."

All right, she hadn't expected a joyful reunion, nor gratitude, but no way was she going to fight him every step of the way. She drank the rest of the flask's contents herself—the sun was indeed intense—and hooked it on her belt again, surveying the femur staking him. With luck, he'd pass out once she began to lift him. She only hoped she possessed the strength to do it. The best method would be to break it off, since it couldn't be pulled from the back. But the bone looked too solid. It would take forever to saw through. And something told her she didn't have forever. A sense of foreboding crawled over her and she kept glancing warily at that cliff's edge. Whoever had bested Jadren and tossed him over to his doom clearly frequented this spot. She didn't want to be the next candidate for an impromptu flying lesson. "Who did this to you?" she asked.

"Gray birds," he answered, fluttering the fingers of his less mangled hand. "Not like my crow friends. *They* love me."

Delaying wouldn't solve any of her problems, so she began gathering smaller rocks, wedging them under his shoulders and hips to straighten his body from the agonizingly bowed arch, aligning his shattered spine as she did. He cursed her, but vaguely now, his mind blurring and wandering with the pain and the mess it was in. Truly it was a wonder he was capable of speech, much less thought. He mostly talked about the crows, calling them by various names he'd apparently assigned to them. Several had returned, perching on nearby rocks and watching her with white eyes stark against their glossy black feathers.

She pitched a handful of gravel at them. "Go on," she snarled, taking out her exhausted and helpless ire on them. "Free lunch is over."

"Wasn't free," Jadren whispered. "I made them pay good coin for every mouthful. Beakful? Made a tidy sum. Maman would be pleased."

Selly couldn't decide if she loved or loathed Jadren's dark and twisted sense of humor in that moment. Finally deciding she had Jadren as level as she could get him, she stood and straddled him. A good half a forearm's length to lift him. She could do this, especially if she used her leg strength. It would be ideal if she could tie a rope around him and loop it over a branch, so she could use Vale to lift Jadren up, but there were no helpful overhead branches. Only that merciless sky.

Squatting, she wrapped her arms around Jadren's lean torso, securing her grip, her cheek next to the impaling bone.

Fortunately, Jadren was built skinny—and was all that much lighter with so much flesh and blood lost. She couldn't dwell on that. He batted feebly at her head and shoulders, muttering unintelligibly. Ignoring him, she instructed herself to do this in one pull, with all her strength. Just like escaping that sinkhole.

One. Two. Three.

With a grunt, she pushed up with her legs, Jadren flying up with her—far more easily than she'd expected, he weighed so little, barely more than skin over bone—and they tumbled backward with the force of her pull. She landed painfully amidst the rocks, Jadren on top of her, both of them groaning at the impact. The crows croaked in excitement, circling overhead, no doubt anticipating a double meal.

Jadren gasped out a laugh, sounding not unlike that crow family. "Oh honey, I know you're hot for me, but not tonight. I have a headache."

And he promptly passed out.

~ 8 ~

SELLY DIDN'T KNOW exactly how long it took her to transport Jadren off the immense field of rock and bone, and over to where Vale waited. No way was she risking Vale getting a hoof stuck in those treacherous rocks, possibly breaking a leg. It took hours, at least, as the sun was definitely declining by the time she half-dragged, half-carried Jadren off the rocks. She was spattered with his blood, shaking with exhaustion, and drenched with sweat and despair.

Jadren hadn't regained any kind of lucidity again, instead mumbling about not leaving the crows behind and calling out for Mr. Machete. Selly had noted that he'd been stripped of weapons and all of his belongings, before being flung off the cliff to dispose of what they'd obviously assumed was his dead body. They'd kept the horse Gabriel had given Jadren, too, so it could have been a robbery, a random attack, and not one targeted against the scion of El-Adrel or the wizard minion of House Phel.

It seemed they wouldn't have so carelessly discarded Jadren had they known who he was. Jadren, of course, was unable to tell her anything. It made her nervous, the not knowing. Especially the part of the not-knowing when whoever it was might return.

Bless the stalwart Vale, he didn't shy at having the bloody, gore-covered and occasionally thrashing and shouting Jadren draped over the saddle. Selly didn't much like hanging Jadren there like so much broken-spined baggage—and it couldn't possibly be comfortable for him to be lying on his wounds, head down like that—but she also didn't have much choice. There was no part of him that *wasn't* damaged and she wanted away from that ominous cliff and whoever had done this to him. Jadren would eventually heal, but not if his attackers decided on a more thorough approach to destroying him.

So, she led Vale away at the most direct angle she could manage, with no real destination in mind beyond "as far away as possible," walking beside the gelding with a hand on Jadren's shoulder in case he should start sliding off, which meant they weren't going fast at all. Somewhere in the back of her weary brain she considered that she should figure out a destination. But what would it be? All along, bringing Jadren back to House Phel had been her plan, but she could hardly walk him there at this painful pace on Vale's back.

Though… why not? It wasn't as if Jadren was a normal person who needed healing as soon as possible or he'd die. If that death trap of rock and bone hadn't killed him, not to mention dehydration and being (partially) eaten by crows, then possibly nothing could, especially if he continued to stubbornly refuse her magic. The major drawback was that several days of slow travel in his condition would be agonizing. Even though she knew he'd already suffered excessive torment, she couldn't bring herself to inflict still more on him.

If Jadren continued to refuse to take her magic, the only other option would be finding a magical healer. A Refoel wizard wouldn't need Jadren's assistance or even consciousness to heal him. And it seemed to her that House Refoel should be in the area somewhere. Once again, she kicked herself for not knowing the Convocation territories. The next chance she got, she planned to memorize the map. If she knew the marshes well enough to navigate them in the dark and gloom, then she could learn the lines on a Convocation map.

Combing through her memory, she recalled that Asa had come from House Refoel to Meresin and that it hadn't been far. He and Laryn had given a ride to Sage and Quinn Byssan—and someone had said that was because House Byssan was on Refoel lands. She was fairly sure the others had referred to House Refoel as being an exception from the usual rule of Convocation politics and brutal high-house ways. The healers held themselves to a different ethical standard.

Selly was pretty sure they would help Jadren—and her by extension—no matter who they were.

Short of going all the way to House Phel, she couldn't think of another place that would offer a similar kind of sanctuary. Or, if not actual sanctuary, at least not a headlong plunge from the cooking pot into the woodfire. Maybe Refoel would even send a Ratsiel courier to House Phel. There would perhaps be some sort of bargaining required, an exchange of payment for services rendered. Nic naturally handled that sort of negotiating for the house—and Selly should probably learn how to do that, too—but she had no idea what all was involved or how anyone knew what counted as fair. If she did it wrong, she could end up costing the house a fortune, which they already couldn't afford.

Maybe going to House Refoel wasn't such a great idea and she should just commit to dragging an unconscious Jadren all the way back to Meresin. Now she was just dithering, which would get them nowhere. It occurred to her that maybe she was too tired to think clearly.

Vale had no particular advice when she asked him for his opinion, bobbing his head agreeably to both options. Well, and they wouldn't get there that night, even if she could figure out in exactly what direction Refoel lay. She needed to make camp and tend to Jadren, get his bones aligned as best she could. Maybe deal with his boots and feet, though nausea welled in her at that prospect.

She just needed a decent spot. Running water—it would be really good to wash some of the gore off of them—some shelter to hide behind, maybe a campfire, if only for the spiritual comfort, since the nights had been warm in this region.

Spotting a goat track leading up a wooded hill a short time later, she turned Vale onto it, hoping for a bit of high ground with some decent screening. The slope made her excruciatingly aware of the ache in her leg muscles, which seemed to radiate out into her entire bruised body. *Nothing compared to what Jadren is suffering,* she reminded herself.

"Trouble," Jadren whispered.

She almost didn't hear him, thinking the hoarse sound was a scuttle of gravel or the rustle of wind through the scrub pines—except that the bond tweaked at her in the same moment, a twinge of alarm that wasn't her own. She froze, Vale instantly taking the cue from her.

Someone was following them. Several someones, by the feel of the magic that now brushed across her senses with a ping of an unfamiliar flavor. Another aspect of her vast ignorance, that she recognized so few kinds of magic. Nic had gone through the Convocation Magic Potential scorecard with her, meticulously reviewing the columns that showed the various major categories of magic and then the rows that reflected the subcategories within that group, along with the numbers at their intersection that showed the degree of potential. But that hadn't given Selly any idea how most of those magics *felt*. She'd probably recognize the magic types of the wizards she'd worked with during those few days of training with Nic, but that was only a few varieties. Most of the wizards beholden to House Phel had been too busy with their legitimate tasks.

This magic felt... odd. It sort of reminded her of the flavor of Han, though this had more of an uncomfortable edge. That could be because Han was a friend and one of the gentlest people she'd ever met, in contrast to his sharp warrior skills with weapons. Or it could be because Han was a familiar and these were—

"Wizards," Jadren hissed, not so much struggling under her hand as twitching spastically. Still, even him being able to move that much was a good sign. "Hide, you idiot," he growled.

Oh, yes—he was definitely feeling better.

"Where?" she asked quietly near his ear.

He grunted in disgust. "I can't see anything but horse. You're the wild swamp creature, expert at fleeing and hiding. Figure it out. Fast," he added. "Or we're fucked."

These must be the wizards that had tried to kill Jadren then. Or some other enemy known to him. She touched his skin, annoyed that he flinched away from her. "If you use my magic, can you fight them off?"

He huffed a sardonic laugh. "If I open to your sweet, sweet magic, my sweet..." He trailed off. "No. Not opening that door. You wanted to be the rescuing hero. Step up to the challenge."

Considering he was the one who had gotten himself practically dismembered, she nearly snarled a retort—but she decided to take the high road. Besides, she could explain the many and varied flaws in his thinking later, after they'd escaped.

JADREN FOUND IT nearly impossible to think, which was a serious drawback in a scenario where some cleverness would come in exceptionally handy. Unfortunately, every time he managed to pull two thoughts together, pain would explode them apart again. Even with Vale's extraordinarily smooth gait—Jadren had assembled enough brain power to recognize Gabriel's steed and recall his name, though not sufficient to figure out why Seliah had him—the least jostling made him hurt all over.

And crave Seliah's magic.

It took far too much of his self-control not to suck down every bit of that deliciously thirst-quenching, moon-bright magic practically oozing out of her. *If I open to your sweet, sweet magic, my sweet...* Had he really said that? He grunted in disgust at himself and no small amount of bone-separating pain as Seliah got Vale moving again, finally. Not like her to be paralyzed by indecision—except when she was losing her shit. Could be the stress was too much for her. She had to be exhausted, after all those countless hours of extracting him. Another reason not to take her magic, besides the fact that he'd probably kill her doing it, given his wretched condition. Just as he'd always feared. So wrong that he'd gone through all of this just to be right back at the monstrous outcome he'd fled to begin with.

Those Hanneil wizard-guards were getting closer. It was the same lot, so far as he could tell through his fractured senses. How and why that crew had tracked them, he had no idea. They weren't moving fast enough, that was certain, the Hanneil psychic magic thickening as the wizards closed on them. Curse it, that magic was actively questing, ferreting out the trail of their thoughts. Figures.

"Mount," he gasped to Seliah.

She didn't reply, but picked up her pace.

"Get on the horse, Seliah," he ground out.

"No," she hissed. "I'll hurt you."

"Do as I say, Familiar!"

She coughed out a laugh under her breath, at least breaking into a jog and urging Vale into a faster clip. "You can't both abandon me and lay claim to me at the same time, Wizard. Screw you and your orders."

If Jadren's teeth hadn't been a jagged mess of splinters, he'd have clenched them. "Think of it as revenge."

"Tempting," she spat. "But I won't hurt you more than I have to. Yet."

"If you don't mount and get us out of here, you won't get to punish me." He sensed her hesitation, perhaps finally believing him.

"Fine." To his intense relief, she halted Vale and reached for the saddle. Then she stopped, the vivid sense of her burgeoning magic suddenly muffled. *Uh oh.*

At the same moment, a fist clamped over his already weakened brain, his feebly moving thoughts losing all momentum. They slowed, then skidded to a stop. Vale and Seliah went similarly motionless.

Shit shit shit. Desperately, Jadren reached for any wizardry in him. Something, anything to shake the hold of these Hanneil wizards. But he came up empty. Worse than empty, because apparently being on the edge of death for days, and then his body attempting to make up for the healing it had been unable to accomplish all that time, had dug into his reserves so far that he'd begun cannibalizing himself. The only positive here was that Seliah hadn't frozen in a posture touching his skin, or he likely would lose even that slim thread of control that kept him from seizing her magic.

The need inside him—that coiling magic that never felt wholly born of himself, but often like some kind of rapacious parasite devouring him along with anything it could feed from—would fasten itself upon Seliah and take everything from her to its satisfaction. It had taken everything in him to refuse her offers of help so far. *Why and how in the dark arts had she come after him to begin with?* And now all that self-restraint could be so quickly and easily foiled by a slip of the hand.

Worse, he couldn't help wondering if, had he accepted her help back at the bone field, maybe they wouldn't be in this fix now. Maybe he could've controlled himself. Maybe.

"Well, look what we've found," a familiar voice observed, though Jadren could still only see—through blearily unfocused, semi-healing eyes—an expanse of black horse hide and a glimpse of hooves below. Ignominious didn't begin to describe his current ass-up, humiliatingly helpless position. "Imagine our surprise when we detected the presence of a powerful familiar in our territory," the Hanneil lead guard-wizard said. "One with *such* an unusual flavor."

Seliah didn't make a sound, but her thrum of distress echoed down the bond to Jadren. He thrashed against the inside of his skin with the desperate need to get to her, to protect her. Later he'd make her sorry she'd put herself in danger coming after his pathetic self. Sorrier, that was, since she should be greatly regretting the misguided effort by now.

"And now we find that familiar is bursting with magic—though what taste *is* that, precious one?—loosely bonded to a dead rogue wizard we dispatched days ago. Except he's not so dead. Wasn't this intruder thrown over the cliff, as instructed?"

"He was," another too-familiar voice protested. "I watched for his body to hit bottom, even though he was dead when he went over."

"Not quite so dead, apparently," the Hanneil wizard observed with bland interest, coming over to Jadren and lifting his head by the hair, then making a sound of disgust when the clump came loose from his barely healed scalp, Jadren's chin thumping back down against Vale's flank.

It was a measure of his overall level of pain that none of it hurt noticeably. Though he did wonder how truly awful he must look. Poor Seliah, saddled with him with his monstrous nature showing fully on the outside for once. Good cautionary experience for her though. Maybe now she'd listen. *If* they got out of this.

The Hanneil wizard shook their hand free of the stuff, wiping a hand against their gray robe. "Lady Hanneil will want to know about this. Bring them along."

To Jadren's intense dismay, Vale obediently turned, carrying him like so much baggage in the direction of House Hanneil. Considering that had been his initial plan, it was galling to confront how very much he did *not* want to face Lady Hanneil with Seliah present. This could only go badly.

Even worse was Seliah at the other end of the bond, her anxiety at being unable to speak or move her own body as she was loaded into one of the Hanneil guard's chariots almost more than *he* could bear. If small, enclosed spaces reminded her of the powerlessness and vulnerability of being restrained, how much worse would this be for her?

Viciously, he wished he possessed Gabriel's trick for turning his familiar into alternate form without touching her. It didn't escape him, trapped as he was with too much leisure time with his thoughts, that it wouldn't do him any good to have that trick as he was 1) so far into magic debt he was as bad off as House Phel, and 2) by refusing to embrace Seliah as his familiar, he wouldn't be able to change her into alternate form regardless.

That's what he got for attempting to be noble and do the right thing—he just fucked things up even worse. And didn't that just figure?

SELLY USED HER newly acquired breathing and meditative techniques to fight off the mind-fragmenting panic of being unable to move. *Now is not the time to lose your shit,* she told herself fiercely, wishing it was Jadren's disembodied voice drawling the sardonic order instead. It was so much more effective, but he apparently only talked in her head when they weren't in each other's company. It also bothered her intensely that she couldn't turn her head to check on him, but at least she had the bond to reassure her that he hadn't fallen off Vale and been left behind.

Not that Vale would ever let that happen, but he wasn't his own horse right now and couldn't control himself any more than she could and—

This is not meditating, she told herself. *This is spiraling into crazyland and it helps no one.* Since clearing her mind and thinking of a bright light, as Nic had taught her, wasn't coming even close to working, Selly concentrated instead on the bond between her and Jadren. Why had that loathsome wizard called her loosely bonded? Maybe because of the attenuation. She had to focus past all the muddying pain to get a sense of him within it. So far as she could tell, he was all right. Immobilized like she was, but there and conscious. And afraid, definitely worried for her.

Whatever Lady Hanneil wanted from them, it couldn't be good. Especially since this group of wizards who must be from House Hanneil—and apparently she was on Hanneil lands?— had tried to kill Jadren. They would have succeeded, had he been killable. From what little Selly knew of Convocation politics, for House Hanneil to murder the scion of House El-Adrel would be a big problem. So, they couldn't have known who he was. And they didn't recognize her magic. Somehow this should work to her advantage. She could use their ignorance against them.

"Or," said the impassive wizard who seemed to be the leader, moving into her line of sight, "your ignorance can work in our favor, little familiar. How is it that you don't know Hanneil wizards can read thoughts as you're longing to do with your broken wizard? The scion of House El-Adrel, eh? That makes things interesting."

"That makes things downright difficult for us," another put in.

"We should've killed him when we had the chance," a different one growled in disgust.

"We tried, didn't we?" The lead wizard sounded almost cheerful. "You've seen him. There's no way he should be

ROGUE FAMILIAR

alive—unless magic is afoot. Perhaps something like the sort
Ariel and Tadkiel are using to create those unkillable hunters.
Yes, Lady Hanneil will be very pleased with us."

"Enough to get taken off guard rotation," one of the group
muttered. "I tell you—hey! What's that?"

At that moment, four things happened: Selly suddenly had
control of her body again. Jadren shouted something incoherent. Vale took off at a gallop.

And the oily feel of hunters smeared across her senses.

The group of wizards that had been surrounding them
now scattered like rain before a gust of wind. Hunters seemed
to be everywhere, darker shadows whisking out from the
shadows under the surrounding trees, leaping with their
unnatural weasel like lope combined with canine slinking. One
of the creatures appeared suddenly before them. A swipe of
taloned paws and the wizard that had wedged Selly into the
chariot with her was knocked away, leaving her alone.

Vale had disappeared from sight. A relief there, that the
warhorse had carried Jadren out of the melee. The Hanneil
wizards added their screams to the din, yelling to each other
that their weapons weren't working, that they couldn't seem
to get a mental grip on their attackers.

Selly smiled grimly to herself, not at all sorry to see their
smug superiority so thoroughly shattered. They'd been so
confident of their hold on her that they hadn't relieved her of
weapons. Not exactly in control of her situation, but closer.

Taking a moment to assess her situation as Han had taught
her, she also drew an extra dagger to clench between her
teeth—remembering to place it dull side inward—just in case

137

she ended up in hand-to-hand. The hunters savaged the Hanneil wizards, though a couple kept a keen eye on her. Odds on they had tracked her here. Apparently just being a familiar lit up the magical landscape like a beacon, just as Nic had warned her. The upside of the hunters wanting to capture her was that they'd avoid damaging her too much, which gave her a tactical advantage.

The downside, naturally, was that she needed to do everything in her power to avoid capture. Never mind how badly she didn't want to become the prisoner or possession of whoever had tasked these particular hunters. Jadren needed her. She wouldn't go so far as to say he wouldn't survive without her help, but he certainly wouldn't thrive. Especially when he had people after him, too.

She'd already picked her tree. Choosing her moment, she dashed for it, using all the wily speed and agility Jadren regularly accused her of having. Though the hunters howled at her move, two dashing after to stand guard at the base of the tree, none of them managed to stop her—or even appeared to try. They were perfectly happy to have her treed, no doubt, planning to dispense with the Hanneil competition for her capture first, and then retrieve her at their leisure.

A miscalculation on their part. Glad she'd had the presence of mind—well, and Han's insistent training—to keep her primary weapons on her body instead of on Vale, Selly settled on a sturdy branch and unclipped her bow from the strap holding it. She strung it, using the familiar motions to center and calm herself. Jadren was safe for the moment, carried away from the fighting by the clever Vale. The hunters were preoccupied with increasingly bloody scrimmage below. The Hanneil wizards had realized their predicament and had resorted to using their hand-weapons, quickly discovering that they couldn't kill the hunters, or even slow them much.

Not without the specially enchanted moon-magic silver. Feeling cool as moonlight, herself, still as deep water, Selly began firing the short, moonsilver-tipped arrows at the hunters. It took her a few tries to adapt the trajectory for the shorter bolts, but soon she hit each target as she selected it. And she picked them off carefully, remote and ruthless from her aerie. She waited for a hunter to dispatch one of the Hanneil guards, leaving the unfortunate wizard twitching in a bloodied mess. She felt no remorse for these people who'd done their level best to kill Jadren. Once a wizard was down for good, she sent an arrow into the hunter, melting it over its erstwhile victim.

It took a surprisingly long time for the hunters to catch on to what was happening. Though, to be fair, they hadn't been created to be clever. Persistence and obedience to their mission had been layered into the enchantment that made them, not the ability to think on their feet. With the possible exception of the lead hunter, who finally noticed its minions falling to Selly's arrows, hissing at the hunters guarding her to put a stop to it.

The two at the base of the tree immediately leapt onto the trunk, bark flying as the talons on all four paws dug in. They leapt toward her with alarming speed, closing the short distance with unnatural alacrity, as she hadn't climbed all that high. Her heart hammered like a trapped bird, but she would not yield to the panic. She would be cool, bright, precise.

She fired an arrow into the open maw of the hunter coming up the face beneath her, gratified when its shriek faded to ghostly echoes as it dissolved into chunks of rotten meat, leaving the four sets of talons incongruously attached to the tree. The other hunter came up behind her and she had to twist in place, something digging sharply into her spine.

It swiped at her, cutting through the leather of her pants and opening four grooves into her thigh as it fastened on her. They burned like fire but she was water; she was ice; she was moonlight congealed into hardest silver. Pulling the dagger from her teeth, she plunged it into the creature's unsettlingly slanted yellow eye, having the presence of mind to hold onto the hilt as the thing shuddered, then melted away.

"How did you do that?" the Hanneil wizard who'd seemed to be in charge shouted up at her. The wizard was embattled, no longer in their personal chariot, barely fending off three hunters with desperate swings of a long sword. Even to Selly's amateur eye, the wizard barely knew how to get by with it. "How?" the wizard screamed. "Who *are* you?"

"*You* will never know," she answered, using the dagger point to dig the talons out of her thigh, flicking them away. It would hurt later, but at the moment she was encased in cold moonlight, feeling nothing. Some distant part of her wondered if she'd entered a new phase of madness, pushed past panicked immobility and frozen into some other level.

"Help me," the wizard begged, though it sounded an awful lot like a command. "Save me—you know you can—and I will see you're rewarded."

Selly *thunked* the dagger into the tree trunk near her hip for safekeeping. No way was she putting that thing in her mouth again. Nocking an arrow, she picked off one of the wizard's tormentors, mostly to toy with her enemy, show how easily she could help, if she chose to. She would not. Gabriel likely would, but she wasn't her brother. She'd become something harder, crueler. "Rewarded how?" she asked idly, curious.

The wizard yelped as one hunter broke through, raking one shoulder with its claws. The wizard managed to lop off the hunter's arm, but that did nothing to stop the creature, naturally. Or unnaturally, as the case might be. Another hunter circled behind the wizard's unprotected back and the third stood back, the leader, eyeing Selly with interest. Selly kept her eye on that one in return.

"Anything you want!" the wizard howled. "Anything!"

"I want my wizard back, healthy and whole," she said quietly, and watched as the two hunters leapt on the Hanneil guard, tearing him limb from limb.

The lead hunter's jaw fell open, revealing double rows of sharp teeth. "Lady Ssseliah Phel," it hissed, slinking toward her, "you will come peasssefully with me."

"I don't think so." Satisfied that the hunters had dispatched all the Hanneil wizards, Selly fired an arrow into the lead hunter.

It didn't melt.

Instead, it dipped its muzzle thoughtfully at the bolt embedded in its lean hairy chest, then gave her a canine grin full of slobber and self-satisfaction. "You will not find me ssso easssy to dissspatch, I think," it said, and advanced on her.

~ 9 ~

GABRIEL GLARED AT the missive dropped by a fleeting Ratsiel courier directly onto his desk. He'd been absorbed in reading a demand for payment—one of several that had arrived overnight—when the thick packet of envelopes smacked onto the polished wood with an impressively heavy thump. The crest of House Elal shimmered balefully from the center of the excellent paper of the top one, stuff that Gabriel now knew to recognize, thanks to Nic's careful tutelage, as the most expensive House Salis had to offer.

Gazing with trepidation at the oval of entwined golden spirit glyphs gliding in the infinite circle that formed the Elal sigil, Gabriel steeled himself for the inevitable bad news within. At least Nic had gone to consult on wedding plans, though grudgingly. She still viewed a lavish ceremony as being a waste of money, time, and energy. Of course, Nic also darkly predicted there might not *be* a House Phel at which to hold a wedding at midsummer, so it was hard to blame her for not being enthusiastic. Though Gabriel could wish that she cared a bit more about marrying him, she'd say that was his soft heart talking, his incurable romanticism, and she'd likely be correct. For Nic, their relationship was a foregone conclusion. She

ROGUE FAMILIAR

didn't need a public demonstration or vows to cement what for her was already true.

It perplexed and annoyed his wife that Gabriel still needed more than that. In truth, it wore on him that he needed it, too. What would be enough for him to believe Nic truly loved him and wanted to be with him, rather than being compelled by magic or the considerable social pressure of the Convocation? He didn't know.

And this self-excoriating philosophizing, as Nic would call it, only postponed the inevitable. With a sigh for their uncertain future, Gabriel used a touch of wizardry to unlock the seal on the missive. A nice bit of elitism there, ensuring that only he could open the envelope. Lord Elal had pointedly written to Gabriel and not his daughter, wizard-to-wizard or lord-to-lord, Elal wanted Nic excluded from this communication. Yet another way of showing his daughter how inconsequential he considered her.

At least Nic would be spared the initial reading. If only Gabriel could figure a way to spare her the information entirely... But he doubted that would be possible. Even if he managed it, Nic would cheerfully eviscerate him for both keeping secrets from her and not allowing her to help him. Besides which, Gabriel wouldn't make her father's mistake of treating Nic as a pawn in the struggle between their houses. This was Nic's battle more than anyone's—and had been since she manifested as a familiar rather than a wizard. Perhaps since her birth.

Gabriel unfolded the multiple pages, skimming the flowery formal greetings that embodied everything Convocation he hated most: all lies and double-talk, a polite pretense of conviviality that did little to cloak the lethal dagger grasped in the velvet-gloved fist.

And there was the edge of the blade: Lord Elal demanded the return of his wife and familiar, Lady Elal. He made no mention of the severing of their bond, which was interesting. He also demanded the return of his daughter as unlawfully abducted from House Elal. Gabriel snorted aloud at that. He might not know all the intricacies of Convocation law, but he'd followed the Betrothal Trial rules scrupulously—well, with one glaring exception, but no one knew about that but Nic and him, and there was no reason to believe anyone *would* find out—and he was absolutely in his legal rights to refuse to yield his familiar to the house of her birth.

The rest of the missive contained a variety of threats and promises of escalating enforcement, a lot of it couched in bureaucratic language Gabriel only partially understood. He'd need help parsing the exact implications, and appropriate measures to take, but perhaps he could get that aid from Wizards Wolfgang and Asa, as well as Familiar Quinn, who'd apparently all been champions in mock trial tournaments at Convocation Academy. Nic could accuse him of circumventing her, but he could plausibly argue that she herself had recommended those three as experts.

The other envelopes in the packet contained letters that were even more inscrutable, except that they were clearly marked with the sigils of Houses Sammael, Tadkiel, and El-Adrel, along with a few others he didn't recognize and couldn't easily decipher. Various complaints and demands for monetary compensation, he could follow that much. What he wasn't sure of was how seriously to take the floridly phrased offenses. In a few cases, he couldn't quite discern what they referred to. It made his farmer's brain swim, trying to decipher all the legal obfuscation, and he considered just burning the cursed packet and going for a ride to see how the fields were coming along.

Except that Seliah had Vale—and that thought set him to worrying about his sister. They'd heard nothing from her. Not that they'd truly expected to, but the foolishly optimistic part of himself had rather hoped she'd be back at House Phel by now. With or without Jadren, he didn't care. He certainly didn't miss the acerbic and very likely duplicitous wizard.

The library doors opened and Nic burst in. He jumped guiltily, but it was just her normal high-energy entry to a room, he decided, not a result of anger, urgency, or emergency. Nic never did anything by halves, including simply moving from place to place. Gabriel had come to know his wife well enough to assess her mood and not be alarmed by her sudden entrances.

"Gabriel, my only love," she sang out, "we have *got* to talk to the kitchen staff about portion size." And that confirmed she was only on one of her standard rampages and nothing was wrong. Nothing more than usual, anyway.

She turned to close the doors behind her and he took advantage of her momentary inattention to slide the packet of letters under a pile of documents. Unfortunately, that left the original demand for payment front and center, but Nic probably already had that problem at the top of one of her lists.

She strode toward him, skirts swishing with her swaying

hips, a warm smile on her generous mouth. The buttery yellow of her gown wasn't a color he'd have picked for her, but it deepened the bronze of her skin, making her dark hair and brilliant green eyes stand out. Those eyes lost a bit of sparkle as they hardened and narrowed, going unerringly to the pile he'd just hidden the packet under. "What's going on?"

He slid the payment demand toward her. "Another house wanting payment."

She took the paper, barely glanced at it, and tossed it onto a pile of similar bills on her desk. "I'm aware. They don't have nearly the leverage they think they do to be hounding us this way. We might not be a High House yet, but neither are they. I'll handle them."

Relaxing now that his diversion seemed to be working, Gabriel raised a curious brow. "What's your plan for handling them?"

"I'll answer that question with a question—where are you on training those water-wizard apprentices on cleaning wells and the ones sent from House Ishim for the ice production?"

Grimacing, he scooted back his chair, and came around the desk to be closer to her. Some of that wanting to be near her came from her magic, the scent of fire-warmed roses as alluring as Nic's vivid and sensual beauty. He also couldn't resist taking the opportunity to touch her, to breathe in the feel of her skin as he traced the shoulder bared by the low swoop of the gown's neckline. Though Nic gave him a look that warned she wouldn't forget the question, as soon as he touched her, she trembled under the caress, her lush black lashes lowering to screen her gaze, her breath shuddering audibly now as the

ROGUE FAMILIAR

sensual heat flared instantly to life between them.

They'd always had that spark. He'd sensed it just from the miniature of Nic that had been enclosed in the Betrothal Trials packet, the mutinous set of her lips and arrogant tilt of her chin so compelling to him. When he'd first glimpsed her in person, all that restless energy of hers contained in that tower room, he'd known instantly that she felt it, too. Their magics knew one another. And when they'd touched, the sensual connection between them had billowed into burning flame.

Would it always be this way between them? Difficult to know, but Gabriel thought so. As Nic lifted her heated gaze to his, the sexual tension thrumming palpably between them. "Gabriel?" she murmured.

He brushed a kiss over her cheek, sliding a hand down her narrow waist to the generous flare of her hip. "Yes, my heart?"

"The apprentices learning to purify wells and water for ice... you're not ducking the question, are you?"

"Maybe I just want to enjoy time with my wife." He kissed along her jaw, savoring how she yielded, tipping up her chin and shivering at the caress of his lips along her sensitive, swanlike throat.

"Maybe you just want to divert me from the problem at hand."

He paused, lifted his head, made himself think about something besides triggering the fastenings on that lovely Ophiel gown and getting her naked. Apprentices. Right. That had indeed not been going all that well. When he'd had time for it. "I'm not a good teacher."

She stepped back, gave him a hard look. "Gabriel."

"What? I'm not." He threw up his hands in exasperation. "You, better than anyone, know how little I understand about my own wizardry, let alone trying to teach what I do to someone else. I feel like there are more important things I could be working on."

Her stern mien didn't change one iota. "First of all," she replied, holding up a single finger, "this *is* a high priority. It's just as important, if not more so, as getting those flasks tested and out to market. We need functioning water wizards to clean wells because we promised that service as collateral for exchange of services like this one." She pointed the finger at the pile of bills. "We need to teach the House Ishim wizards to purify water for ice so we can get that income source going."

Unexpected guilt assailed him. "I know, I just—"

"Two," she continued over him, "it's well known that we learn best by teaching. These wizards have all received excellent academy training on wielding magic in general, so they have the necessary framework to learn, they lack only the expertise of the lone water wizard worth his salt in all the Convocation. Teaching them will not only give them the insight only you can provide, it will force you to interrogate your own methods. That's a good thing, by the way."

It didn't *sound* like a good thing. For all that Nic loved to tease him about his introspective tendencies, Gabriel didn't like thinking about his magic much. From the owlish look Nic was giving him, she followed that thought easily. "Not thinking about it doesn't make it go away," she said in a softer tone. "Third," she added more loudly, preventing him from replying, though he didn't really have a good response to that, "you're attempting to divert me from whatever you hid under that pile of documents." She smiled thinly at his wince.

"Do you have eyes in the back of your head?" he grumbled.

"I know my wizard." She held out a preemptory hand, snapping her fingers, then opening her palm. When he didn't immediately comply with the implicit command, she shook her head slightly, eyes full of surprising compassion rather than the anger he'd expected. "I know you want to protect me from the world, but even you, my mighty one, cannot keep the world from reaching out to us. Stronger together, remember? This is why you wanted me for your familiar."

"I wanted you because I fell in love with your portrait," he retorted, annoyed enough to tell the truth, even as he reached for the packet of letters. He'd known all along that there wasn't any point to keeping them from her.

"Nobody falls in love with a portrait," she huffed, though the high color on her graceful cheekbones gave away that she was pleased. That and her magic coiling warmly around him, like rose-infused wine, redolent as the roses blooming outside the open library windows.

"It was that stubborn tilt to your chin that did it. And the mulish set to your lovely lips." He set the packet on her still open palm, lifted that chin, and gave her a lingering kiss on those tempting lips. She even tasted like roses and wine. "This won't be easy to read."

She didn't pull away, instead smiling ruefully up at him. "I know, but have you ever known me to look for the easy way out?"

"No." He had to agree there. Much as he'd like to protect her, he wouldn't change that about her either. Her courage and determination delighted him as much as they alarmed him.

"And I'm not stubborn," she added, pulling away and going to her own desk to lay out the letters, stacking them with crisp ease into an order she grasped with a single glance at each.

"She said, stubbornly," he retorted. Unwilling—perhaps unable—to sit, he folded his hands behind his back and paced to the windows as she read. Paced back again. Made another circuit. Nic said nothing. He walked to the windows again. This was unbearable. "Well?"

"Shh. I'm reading."

"I know you don't read that slowly."

"Reading *and* thinking, then. Give me a moment."

Her voice sounded steady, even absentmindedly irritated about his interruptions, no hint of the tears he'd more than half anticipated. When her father had sent her previous messages expressing his anger and disdain, Nic had been hard hit. Not this time. In truth, she'd had a far more fierce, even militant air about her lately. She'd always been determined on her courses of action, but something about the abduction had changed her. At least, Gabriel assumed it was that, as she'd been different since. The change worried him on some level—though Nic would no doubt tell him he worried too much. Which was in no small part why he'd said nothing to her about it.

Finally she sat back, glancing up thoughtfully as he came around to edge a hip onto her desk. "What do you think?" he prompted.

"Other than that we're fucked?" she answered drily.

He couldn't say his hopes sank, as they hadn't actually been high to begin with. Still. "I considered that some of it might be Convocation hyperbole."

She raised one elegant black brow in question, glittering nails tapping a light rhythm on the documents.

He gestured vaguely. "You know—making it all sound worse than it is in order to intimidate us."

She pursed her lips, then blew a stream of air between them, nearly soundless, but enough to make the longer curls draping over her forehead flutter. "It would be difficult to make it sound worse than it is."

He decided on a preemptive strike. "I'm not handing you over. No matter what."

Biting out a sigh, she raked a hand through her hair, the curls going wilder in the humidity of late morning. "We don't need to have that argument again, though I might point out that these are official documents very clearly directing that you don't have a choice."

"Even the Elal ones?"

"House Elal filed an official complaint with the Convocation." She pinned one document with a fingertip and spun it to face him. "That's what this one means, that you stole me." She did the same with five others. "Same with this one, accusing you of stealing a second familiar from House Elal, Maman. This one from House Iblis, documenting the theft of their familiar, Narlis."

"We settled the question on Narlis."

"No," she corrected calmly, "we paid them off. The action was still against the law. Besides which, these two from Houses Ariel and House Phanuel, accuse you of same with Iliana and Han, respectively. As does this one from House El-Adrel, regarding Seliah. They describe this as a pattern of behavior and they're not wrong."

"I didn't steal *you*," he argued. "That one was perfectly legal."

She actually laughed. "You realize that's not a compelling argument."

He supposed it did sound bad, put that way. "Seliah was illegally bonded to Jadren. El-Adrel didn't have a contract with us. They owe us compensation, because—if we're going to pretend that human beings can be owned—Seliah belongs to House Phel. You said that much."

"We can argue that point, but our case is weakened by the weight of the rest of this. Besides, there's more."

He sighed. "Of course there is. Might as well hit me with all of it at once." He grimaced at the pile of documents. "They certainly did."

"Standard Convocation tactics," she replied with an arch look. "Hit the enemy with all the heavy weaponry at once for maximum impact. In the ancient wars, they did it with magic massed from all the minions of the houses. Apparently that was really something to see. At least now they only barrage you with paperwork." She reached for the other pile. "To summarize the rest, they're all from Convocation Center, regarding misplaced—their term—Convocation citizens."

She brandished the top sheet. "This one demands that you

deliver me for retraining, as previously conveyed via their proctor, with substantial fines for failing to comply to the initial request and more fines, plus censures against you for threatening said proctor."

When he opened his mouth, she gave him an hard stare. "Let me finish, so I can save a single, emphatic 'I told you so' for the end." Tossing that document aside, she held up the next. "I bet you can guess on this one: deliver Seliah for assessment and training, as previously conveyed, etc., etc., plus fines and censures. Then there's these two from Convocation Academy, demanding the return of their student wizards, Alise and Sabrina." She raised a brow. "Apparently House Sammael hasn't bothered to mention to anyone that we sent Sabrina home."

Gabriel waited. "Nothing about returning their other students to the Academy?"

Nic snorted. "Familiars? No, and be glad for it. It's one less charge to deal with."

"All right. I'll let that go as this is indeed more than enough."

Cocking her head, Nic studied him. "Is this when I mention that I warned you?"

"Not necessary." He sighed. "Out with it. What is your plan?"

"I'm curious," she said, instead of answering. "Had you succeeded in keeping this from me—including, not incidentally, the summons for you to appear at a hearing before the Convocation judicial council—what was *your* plan?"

"Get Wolfgang, Asa, and Quinn to advise me on the legalities."

"That's not a bad approach," she conceded, which made him feel slightly better. "We'll do that, although I suspect the best they'll come up with are stalling tactics. I assume this was sent sealed to you specifically, so you had to open it with your magic?"

He nodded, wincing internally. "Shouldn't I have?"

"I could wish you'd asked me that before you opened it, but you're your own wizard. By doing that, you confirmed receipt, so that started the clock ticking on our reply to the allegations."

"How long do we have?"

"A month."

He brightened. "That's not terrible. It gives us time."

"Time might not make a difference." She gazed past him, deep in thought. "The wheels of the Convocation turn slowly, but they move with relentless might, grinding all resistance beneath the weight of centuries," she added darkly.

"That's quite poetic, if awfully defeatist."

She blinked at him, deep green eyes focusing again on him. "It's a quote. By the lawmaker and wizard-philosopher Lord Redlin almost three-hundred years ago. He thought that then; imagine how much greater the solidification of time-honored institutions now."

"Is philosophy a category of magic potential?"

"If it were, your scores would be off the charts," she retorted, but she smiled ever so slightly in amusement and he was pleased to have lifted at least some of her dark mood. Then she sobered, tapping another sheet to the side of the others. "Do you understand that this document requires that you remand Seliah into the custody of either Convocation Center or House El-Adrel immediately?"

He'd gathered that much. "At least we're unable to comply on that one, so long as Seliah stays away."

"A very slight comfort." Propping her elbows on the desk, Nic dropped her face in her hands, showing rare dejection.

Concerned, Gabriel moved behind her and set his hands on her shoulders, the tendons in the exposed nape of her neck visibly corded. So tense. He dug in his thumbs, massaging the tight knots, gratified by her moan of pleasure of an entirely different sort than before. "I'm sorry," he told her, willing her to believe it. "I've done everything wrong from the beginning. I should have listened to you. I'm the stubborn one and now I've put us all in jeopardy."

She grunted, though whether in agreement or in response to him finding a particularly sensitive spot, he wasn't sure. Then she lifted her head and turned, eyeing him. "I'd love to be able to enjoy this moment of vindication more, but I can't." Reaching up, she slipped a hand behind his neck, drawing him down and tipping her mouth up for a kiss.

Never able to resist her, he eased into the kiss, brushing his lips softly over hers in a kind of apology and benediction. Not that Nic ever held anything against him. At least, not for long. He might agonize within the quiet of his thoughts over whether Nic loved him willingly, but there was no denying that she loved him unconditionally. Even if he made mistake after mistake, stubbornly forging down the wrong path, she'd stay doggedly by his side, he knew, giving up everything—

including her life—to support him.

Could he offer her anything less?

Her whole body relaxing, Nic tipped her head back against the high seat, murmuring into his mouth as he deepened the kiss and stroked light fingers down her throat, teasing the upper curves of her lush bosom. "What did you say?" he asked, withdrawing from the kiss just enough to whisper the question against her lips.

"Better than a massage," she answered, lips curving under his, a smile in her throaty voice. "But you don't have to apologize."

"I don't?"

"Not at all." Moving languidly, she eased out from under his hands, standing and gathering up the documents in exacting order. "I'll call a meeting of our informal, in-house legal team and we'll plan our defense." She gave him a questioning look. "What?"

"I didn't think you'd agree to that plan."

One raven-brow flew up. "You thought I'd insist on caving to these demands?"

"I considered the possibility," he admitted.

"No, Gabriel. To answer your question: no, you don't have to apologize because none of your decisions were made out of willfulness, stupidity, or maliciousness. Every single one—even and perhaps especially the ones I disagreed with—was made because you follow your own code of ethics. And you now have a House full of people who are following you in turn, because of those ideals."

"I thought it was because you recruited them."

"Not all of them, and the ones I did specifically recruit, I attracted on the basis of the House shaped by *you*. Remember how I told Seliah that Jadren was right when he said that the heads of the High Houses govern their people with such singlemindedness that the houses *do* develop an identifiable character? Wait, or maybe you weren't there for that conversation."

"You spent quite a lot of time instructing Seliah without telling me much," he pointed out. It hadn't been easy for him to keep his nose out of it, but he'd managed.

"Do you mind?" she asked, an usual hesitation in her manner, nothing about her hard now.

"I've told you over and over that you don't have to report to me or ask permission."

She narrowed those penetrating green eyes. "Which does not answer the question."

No, it didn't. "I don't like to think of us keeping secrets from each other."

"You mean, as you just now attempted to do?" She tapped her glittering nails on the documents she held.

"That was to protect you."

"Exactly."

It took him a moment to catch her meaning. "You don't have to protect me, my heart."

"Do I need to say 'exactly' again?" she inquired archly, but her lips curved with warm affection.

Going to her, he caressed her cheek. "I can't help wanting to protect you, but I also want us to be honest with each other."

"I know, and likewise." Her gaze flicked up to his consideringly. "I was, in part, protecting Seliah from you."

Ah. That stung. But he could also see her point. Heaving out a long breath, he nodded, mostly to himself. "I'm not entirely rational about the people I love."

"I know. It's not a bad quality. Just bear in mind that holding onto people too tightly makes them squirm to escape the grip." Nic smiled at him, laying one hand over his heart, her magic flowing into him and infusing his body with the essence of her via his bloodstream. "As for one of your other capacities as Lord Phel, shaping the direction of House Phel and the people who belong to it is absolutely as it should be. It's even more meaningful that you are creating something new, something noble and meaningful. This didn't come about due to capriciousness or selfishness. It's happening because you chose not to accept the way things are, no matter how I told you that you should. That you *had* to."

"Those documents you're holding say otherwise."

She shook her head slowly. "No. These just draw the lines of the battleground. Now we know where we're going to fight."

"Fight?" he echoed uneasily. Though they'd discussed it before, had indeed fought skirmishes, this sounded like more.

"Yes. This is war. And we're going to win or go down fighting, but we're not capitulating." That militant gleam was back in her eyes. "They're going to be sorry they dragged me back to the Convocation. And my father will be the sorriest of all."

"In point of fact, *I* dragged you back."

Laughing softly, she patted his cheek. "A figure of speech, my only love." Expression hardening, she bared her teeth in a grin that had nothing to do with happiness. "They could have been rid of me, but no. Now I'm going to help you turn the Convocation upside down. They say you ran afoul of the law? Then we change the law."

"All right then," he said, though she obviously didn't need his agreement.

Nodding crisply, she strode back toward the library doors. Paused. Turned back. "Gabriel?"

"Yes, my heart?" he asked bemused.

"Deal with getting those water wizards trained and out the door, would you?"

Though she phrased it as a question, it wasn't one. "As my love commands."

She simpered, fluttering her lashes, then blowing him a kiss. "Back at you, Wizard."

~ IO ~

I F RIDING BELLY-DOWN over Vale's back, every bone in his
body broken, jabbing into organs he never knew he had,
injured worse than he'd ever been in his entire, wound-riddled
lifetime and going at a painstakingly slow walk had been
agonizing, then there were no words for the mind-melting
experience of doing same at a full gallop.

And that was on top of the knowledge that their headlong
flight through the crappy little forest was leaving Seliah behind
to be captured by hunters. Or remain a captive of the Hanneil
border guard. Which was worse—the cooking pot or the
campfire?

Answer: both sucked for the one trapped in either.

Jadren tried to fling himself off Vale's back, in order to 1)
stop the jouncing agony at all costs, 2) get back to Seliah and
help, somehow, some way, and 3) get himself back in control
of his stupid life. Not necessarily in that order.

This, however, was where riding a highly trained warhorse
worked against one's best interests. Vale cagily managed to
balance Jadren in place, even as the gelding ran at top speed
through whipping branches and thornily clinging underbrush.
Of course, it didn't help that Jadren's efforts to dislodge himself

resembled those of a gutted fish left to uselessly flap its gills in fingernail-deep water. Apparently losing most of your body mass left one unable to do stuff an infant could do, like lift their own head.

Finally, Vale came to a halt. By dint of much wriggling and flopping, Jadren managed to slither off Vale—fortunately feet-first—and slumped into a briary thicket of some sort. Vale's good manners came in handy in that the horse didn't step on him, which took a bit of fancy footwork, and returned immediately to nuzzle Jadren's face in equine concern.

At which point Jadren fully processed his foolishness. He couldn't extract his own sorry self from said briary thicket, let alone go back and help Seliah. However... he could send her more able assistance than his. "Go get Seliah," he told the horse, which came out sounding like "hunh hent shshlah," given the fact that a prickly set of leaves had thrust itself into his mouth and couldn't be dislodged.

And then he passed out.

SELIAH FACED THE lead hunter warily. Why hadn't the enchanted arrow melted the creature like it had with the others? Was the hunter immune to only the arrows tipped with Gabriel's special formulation of moonsilver or all the enchanted silver weapons? One thing was certain: she would not climb down from her safe perch to find out.

She only hoped that Vale had gotten Jadren clear. No sense contemplating other possibilities. The Hanneil wizards were all dead and so were all but one hunter and her. If she could dispatch this remaining hunter, even if it killed her in the process, that would be better than leaving it capable of tracking Jadren.

There was also the option of complying with its demand to go quietly. That might work equally well to lure it away from Jadren. Then she could be the one nobly sacrificing herself for him and let's see how much *he* liked it. It occurred to her that exacting revenge on Jadren by destroying her own life might be self-defeating, but hey—a win was a win, right?

She was starting to sound like Jadren.

"Lady Ssseliah Phel," the hunter hissed again, "you will come peasssefully with me."

"To go where?" she called down, readying another arrow. Maybe that one arrow was a dud.

"My employersss identity doesss not consssern you, Familiar. You will come peasssefully with me."

"I don't think so." She let the bolt fly, embedding it in the thing's eye as it looked up at her. Shadows had deepened with encroaching night, but she still hit the mark.

It didn't even flinch. Instead it actually tutted at her. "I sssaid you would not find me ssso easssy to disssspatch." It advanced toward the tree, patient as a stalking feline, apparently unbothered by the arrows sticking out of it. "You will come peasssefully with me."

"Not a brilliant conversationalist, are you?" Seliah scanned the tree above her, quelling the urge to flee higher as the thing advanced. Her previous sangfroid during the battle had melted and now dribbled away, leaving panic behind. Above her perch, the branches rapidly thinned, the trees in this region not very tall and less robust than the ones she knew back home. No likely candidates to leap to laterally, either. She was as treed as a wild cat from the western marshes.

Making herself think past the panic, she clipped the bow back into place on her shoulder harness, stowing the couple of arrows in her hand back in their quiver. She still had a good supply of them and they'd no doubt come in handy in the future, hunter-melting qualities or not.

"My wordsss ssserve my purpossse," the hunter replied, pausing at the base of the tree and gazing up along the trunk. "Come down peasssefully."

"Or what?" she taunted. "Seems to me that we're at an impasse. You're too scrawny to carry me out of this tree and I am *not* coming down, peacefully or otherwise."

It appeared to consider, though hunters weren't known to have much ability to think. This one was different in any number of ways. How could it be immune to the enchanted silver? She tried to recall Nic's lessons. There had been a lot of information crammed into very few days. She knew enough to understand that working magic involved a lot of methodical problem-solving. Thus wizards had their arcaniums for working up new magic and perfecting old spells. The wizard minions of House Phel had the big workshop to practice in. She'd been in there a couple of times, seen the set up where Jadren and Gabriel had collaborated to enchant the weapons condensed of moon magic, to make them able to defeat any enemy.

Hmm.

"I can sssimply wait you out," the hunter said. "Without food or water, you will die."

"That will take days," she pointed out. She was used to going without food, though water had always been plentiful. How long could she go without? She'd left the water flask in the bags on Vale, unfortunately.

"Posssibly, but you are mortal and mussst sssleep. I am not mortal. I have time. I can wait."

"My people will come to rescue me." It sounded good, anyway.

The hunter grinned, tongue rolling out between rows of fangs. "I will sssoon have reinforsssementsss."

Well, shit. It could be bluffing, but Selly definitely was. She highly doubted Jadren would heal in time to heroically rescue her, especially not without the help of her magic. It was burgeoning inside her, too, which didn't help, her mind beginning to swim with the potency of the stuff trapped inside with nowhere to go. She should've prevailed on Jadren's guilt and made him tap her magic to save her, since the obdurate wizard wouldn't do it to save himself. In the meanwhile, the overstuffed sensation only combined with the incredible frustration of not being able to use all that power to do anything to help herself.

Well, there was always Gabriel's manual chop-chop method, a classic for a reason. Melting the hunters was fast, efficient, and permanent—but cutting them into pieces too small to do damage also worked. Gathering her legs beneath her, she extracted the big dagger she'd wedged into the tree, adjusting her grip on it. She didn't bother to disguise her actions, as she doubted the hunter cared whether she was armed or not, in its immortal confidence.

"All right," she announced, "I'll come down."

It nodded, still grinning in its canine, weasel like way. It didn't seem to question her easy capitulation, pleased that she was cooperating as it expected familiars to do. She gauged the distance. Farther than she liked to jump, especially given the difficulty of assessing the exact drop in the deepening shadows, but she'd scaled greater heights. The hunter remained obligingly right beneath her.

Deciding not to give it any time to question her motives— or for her to lose her courage—Selly gathered all her considerable, moon-bright, dammed-up-water frustration, and dropped onto the hunter, blade angled down.

She didn't catch it entirely by surprise. That would've been too much to hope for. As she fell it opened its arms in a parody of an embrace, talons flaring wide, a cage to imprison her.

No more cages, the feral creature within her snarled.

Then she didn't have to think anymore. Couldn't have, even if she'd wanted to. She whipped the blade across the hunter's eyes, blinding it in one stroke. Its fangs and talons ripped at her, but she felt nothing, only the burning fury to dismember, dismantle, destroy. Crimson rage filled her vision and she drew a second blade—another of Gabriel's enchanted ones—with her left hand and attacked the hunter as if the knives were her own claws. Wild cat from the western marshes.

The bespelled weapons didn't melt the hunter any more than the arrows had, and it fought back with desperate ferocity. Gradually, however, it fell to her determined onslaught, soon no more than a pile of severed limbs, still twitching with unnatural life. She was almost sorry, as she had plenty of the killing rage left and no target for it. So, she redirected the urge to destroy, applying it with meticulous thoroughness and cutting the pieces ever smaller, hurling the bits into the underbrush, scattering them as far as possible. From what Gabriel had told her about the hunter he'd chopped up and locked in a trunk, those pieces might grow into new, individual hunters—possibly also resistant to the enchanted weapons, unfortunately, if they retained the properties of their parent—but what mattered most in this moment was to get Jadren and herself clear of the things.

Finally, with nothing left on which to vent her fury, she realized she'd better find Jadren and Vale. That meant walking and trying to track Vale's passage in the dark. Plus side, it would be a big trail. Downside, it was really dark. Where was the moon when she needed it? She briefly considered lying down to sleep and finding the trail in the morning light. She wanted nothing more than to sit down and rest her increasingly weary bones. But more hunters might arrive and Jadren definitely needed her.

Screwing up her determination, she made herself search the bodies of the Hanneil wizards. They'd taken Jadren's supplies and she might not have another opportunity to reclaim them. It was a gruesome, depressing task. Though it had been easy to harden herself against her captors' fate when they were alive, the dead bodies saddened her, their slack faces those of regular people, their lives unnaturally cut short, and in savage ways.

Sure enough, however, she found Jadren's treasured machete. She also found the bag she herself had scrounged from House Phel supplies, the one she'd left in Jadren's rooms there, containing all the bits and pieces his mother had attempted to install in him and that had been extruded during his healing process. She hadn't thought to check to see if he'd taken that, but he clearly had. For what purpose?

It didn't matter. If they both lived, she could ask him. She also scavenged her arrows from the piles of goo that were the former hunters, and anything else that seemed useful. Jadren had convinced her of the usefulness of supplies, though she began to regret the decision as she started walking. It was a lot to carry and she was ridiculously weak. Her legs felt both impossibly heavy and flimsy as overcooked vegetables. She really hated overcooked vegetables.

As she stumbled through the dark, boots catching roots and rocks as if they leapt out to trip her, it occurred to her that she probably wasn't in her right mind. A different kind of not-in-her-right-mind than usual. Though the magic overload pulsed within her, this wasn't the crazyland of shifting mists. This was something else and she had a very strong feeling that she should figure it out before it was too late.

Too late for what though?

Suddenly, a black shape loomed before her, huge and heaving hot breath. She screamed a little, a frightened yip and fumbled for a weapon. Somehow she ended up on her back in the prickly leaf litter, head swimming and not remembering how she fell. Something whuffed over her face, scented with grass. Vale?

"Jadren," she gasped. Managing to roll over—why did everything hurt so much?—she used her arms to push into a more or less seated position, then reached up to cradle Vale's head. Peering up, she could see Vale still wore all of his gear, but lacked the most important baggage. Jadren was gone.

Despite the crushing disappointment, she held onto Vale's lowered head with relieved gratitude. He'd found her and maybe he could take her to Jadren, clever horse that he was. Vale whickered, which she took to mean he would, and backed up a careful step. Ah yes, just like when he pulled her out of the sinkhole. Only this time he was lifting her out of her own weakness.

It took a stupid amount of effort to get her clumsy feet under her, but after several tries and failures—and really only because of Vale's determination—Selly managed to get upright. It was a precarious state, full of wobbling and an enervating dizziness that threatened to drop her to the ground again. Turning his great head, Vale nudged her hip, clearly intending her to mount. The saddle might as well be the moon, as far above her as it seemed to be. She considered the monumental effort of lifting a boot to the stirrup and discarded it as impossible.

"Sorry, Vale," she mumbled against his sleek, warm hide. "I don't think I can."

He nudged her again, then rumbled what sounded very like a long-suffering sigh. Under her clinging weight, he shifted, lowered, and was soon kneeling beside her.

"I didn't know you could do that," she breathed, overcome and close to tears for no good reason. Except that she was so very tired. She collapsed onto Vale's back more than climbed on, barely managing to swing a leg over to straddle him. As if he understood her difficulty, Vale waited for her to settle, then got to his feet with only a bit of lurching. She stayed on, anyway, though her thighs seemed to be too numb to grip as they should.

Vale, best of all possible horses, carried her so smoothly that she didn't have to worry about falling off. And she could stop thinking about which direction to go, because Vale knew the way to Jadren. Good thing, too, as her thinking continued to degrade. She rode through the dark night, her mind similarly obscured, everything drifting in an ungentle haze. Pain and dizziness tangled together, so that she imagined them as dance partners, sweeping around in the ballroom of her head, bobbing and spinning, egging each other to go faster and faster. Queasiness chased after them, bound to catch up eventually. That would turn the party into a real mess.

Gradually, she became aware that Vale had stopped, and that some of the swaying motion she'd attributed to the wild dance was him lowering himself down so she could dismount. Poor horse. She did her best to scramble off, which resulted in a mouthful of dirt as she faceplanted at the final moment. The ground, hard and prickly as it was, felt really good. She melted into it, lassitude filling her, darkness washing over and through her, taking her down like the sweet, slow fall of the sinkhole.

Like the sinkhole. Which meant death.

That still-alert, quite-alarmed-though-much-quieted voice in the back of her consciousness started shouting that yes yes yes, *this* was the problem. Though she didn't understand why it would be. Jadren was the wounded one. But, according to the prodding of her internal panic, she couldn't just lie there and sleep. Besides, where was Jadren? Surely Vale would have taken her to him.

Worrying about Jadren galvanized her when worrying about herself hadn't. Making herself *move*, she looked around.

Sure enough, there he was: sprawled bonelessly over a spindly bush and looking pretty much like a ragged set of black leathers left to dry. His pale skin showed through the rents, the rest of him in shadow. The bush didn't look very comfortable and she wondered why he'd picked it, until her groggy brain figured out that he'd fallen from Vale's back and landed there.

And it was up to her to get him off and into a more comfortable position. Selly was pretty sure that dislodging your wizard from various hazards upon which they'd impaled themselves was not covered in Nic's Care and Feeding of Wizards lessons. Of course, she doubted that even the much-vaunted Convocation Academy taught how to handle scenarios where both wizard and familiar were so injured they couldn't help each other. She certainly was in no shape to help Jadren and vice versa.

But he was capable of healing and she wasn't. Therefore she needed to do whatever it took to put Jadren on track to accomplish one of his healing miracles, so he could save her in return. How she was going to do that with him spackled to a thornbush, she didn't know. Vale nudged her shoulder, snorting softly and she reached up to stroke his velvety muzzle in appreciation for the comfort. He nudged her harder, this time on the side of her head. "Hey," she protested, though without much force, her eyes widening as she took in the unexpected sight of a small cabin tucked back in the trees.

"You are the best, smartest horse in the entire Convocation," she breathed, "and beyond!" She didn't know if Vale had chosen this spot to dump Jadren on purpose—though she suspected he had—but she'd take advantage of this opportunity. Occupied or not, the cabin presented the best opportunity for safe haven. Deciding she only had it in her to traverse the short distance once, she hauled herself to her feet a final time, using the ever-patient Vale as a scaffold. Her whole body hurt, stinging and aching with countless wounds from that hunter that she must have failed to register in the heat of the fight, awash with whatever insane rage had overcome her.

Finding the oilcloth in Vale's packs, she spread it on the ground, then tied a pair of ropes to one bunched-up end of it, tying the other ends to either side of the chest strap of Vale's saddle. Leading Vale to the bush—and leaning on him, too— she got the cloth positioned beside it. At that point, she simply needed to lever Jadren off the bush and onto the cloth, where he collapsed in a boneless heap with a pained groan.

"Sorry," she said, meaning it, but also knowing this was the best she could do. Jadren grunted again, though she couldn't tell if he accepted the apology, rejected it, or simply reacted to the ungentle landing. "All right, Vale, let's go." She clung to the saddle as Vale moved forward at a slow walk, telling herself she needed to make sure Jadren's weight didn't shift the

JEFFE KENNEDY

girth, but really because she couldn't walk without the horse's support. She must have lost a lot of blood.

Feeling a bit foolish, she knocked on the cabin door. What would she say if someone opened it to find her, no doubt looking like a victim of the scavengers that plagued the outskirts of Meresin, hanging onto a massive warhorse, dragging an apparent corpse? *Hi, mind if we stay the night?* Though it might've been prudent to have a weapon at hand, just in case the potential occupants were hostile, she decided against it, as no one would react well to this scenario, let alone with a big dagger on display.

Fortunately, no one answered the door. Until the relief hit her, Selly hadn't realized how much she'd dreaded having to talk to someone, even a friendly face. Trying the handle, she found it fortuitously unlocked. Well, they deserved some good fortune after this long run of bad luck. Vale ducked his head and wedged through the doorway, barely fitting, but making it. Selly peered around in the darkened interior, then happily spotted the low glow of a sleeping fire elemental in a lantern. It was the sort that Alise had been installing in House Phel, with a switch anyone could trigger, and the small spirit inside leapt into bright light at her touch.

The place was small and plain. It could have been a farm cottage in Meresin, which made her feel right at home. A small kitchen area appeared to be scrupulously clean and well-stocked, looking very like her parents' kitchen, giving her a kick of nostalgia and comfort. She'd love to have her mother there right then, to kiss and pet her, to take care of Selly in exactly the way she'd been rejecting this last little while, wanting to prove she could handle things on her own.

Guess this was her opportunity to prove it, so she'd best handle them.

Deciding the dark room through an open doorway was the bedchamber—and that no way was she getting Jadren onto a bed—she untied the ropes from Vale and dragged her wizard over to the fur rug in front of the cold fireplace. That hearth came with a fire elemental, too, so she triggered it, comforted by the cheerful flames it made as it leapt joyfully over the fuel the cabin's owners had efficiently placed there. She kept Jadren on the oil cloth, so neither of them would soil the rug. The cursed thing was coming in handy.

While Vale stood there—and really hoping the gelding's hooves weren't scarring the wood floors—Selly relieved him of the packs and his tack, letting it all fall to the floor. She couldn't do more and hoped the horse would forgive the neglect, especially unfair to him given all he'd done to rescue them. Liberated, Vale went out the still-open front door, head high, and Selly trusted that he'd be fine overnight. Wishing she'd thought to hold onto the horse before he left, she gave up on any pride and crawled to the door to close it and put the bar in place. People who locked doors to guard people inside, but not their possessions when they were gone, were people she understood.

She crawled back to Jadren, thinking vaguely that she should get some food into them, but only capable of digging the ever-replenishing flask out of the packs and setting it by his side after she drank as much as she could hold. Only a bit longer to last, she told herself. As best she could—feeling slightly stronger for having drunk the water—she began arranging him into an at least well-aligned, if not comfortable position on his back. It could be her imagination, but he looked somewhat less terrible than he had, his face more recognizable, regaining its shape. She stripped him as she went, which was easy, given the sorry state of his clothing.

Once Selly got the scraps of Jadren's shirt off, she spotted the chain around his neck, the brass tube threaded through it. She'd worn it around her neck for a while. At some point Jadren had reclaimed it. Moved, brushing her fingertips over it, she wondered at the significance of him wearing it.

Going to his boots, this time she didn't hesitate, probably numbed by exhaustion and all the violence, pulling them off and throwing them aside. His feet were long and pale, oddly vulnerable looking, but miraculously not mangled—or at least not that Selly could discern. All of him was sunken, blue-white as a dead thing, and she could only hope that his wizard's instincts would take over and seize her magic when he wasn't in any state to fight it.

Nic had said that wizards naturally craved magic, particularly from their bonded familiars, and that they had to control themselves to not take it. Not many wizards really wanted to restrain themselves from draining their familiars dry, she'd said; they only hesitated for fear of draining their familiars to the point of death or beyond.

If she did this right, Jadren would be in no condition to restrain himself. She'd seen him come out of injury-induced unconsciousness before and he wasn't in his right mind in that state. Jadren had understood that about her from the beginning, how the madness affected her, what she needed to come out of it and recover when it overtook her. She could turn that around, use that shared understanding against him. Or, rather, to save him. His instincts would do what he would stop himself from doing, given the time and opportunity to think. She'd make sure he didn't have the chance to do something stupidly noble.

With him laid out to her satisfaction, so he'd heal as cleanly as possible, she removed her own clothing, grateful for the ease of the release of the Ophiel fastenings. Her clothes were torn in places, but not to rags like Jadren's. Still, the burn and tear of wounds reopening as she pulled the leathers away made her aware of the injuries she'd only guessed at till then. That hunter had hurt her far worse than she'd realized, the deep bites from its fangs and the scores from its talons bled anew, some of them frighteningly deep. She didn't look too closely, however. Her strength had run out and she had nothing left in her to attempt to staunch any of the bleeding.

Laying herself down next to Jadren felt like the easiest and most natural act in the world. She laid her head in the fold of his shoulder, draping her upper arm over his chest and her thigh over his groin, sighing at the deliciousness of the skin-to-skin contact. Even if she never had more with him than this, even if she never tasted the passion he'd promised and taunted her with, she had this moment, this deeply satisfying if fleeting present. Losing herself to the drag of sleep, to the bliss of finally letting go, she felt safe as she never had.

She was with Jadren, and that was all that mattered.

~ II ~

JADREN WALKED THROUGH a nighttime marsh flooded with the light of the full moon. Tree limbs hung heavy with waxy ivory blossoms over still water, the reflection of the flowers twining with the white moonlight. Night creatures sang unfamiliar songs, the chorus oddly charming—quirky and yet beautiful, reminding him of Seliah.

"Quirky, but beautiful makes you think of me?"

Jadren turned, catching his breath at the sight of Seliah, clad only in her long dark hair. Distantly, he wondered at that flowing hair, thinking that perhaps he should realize something about it. But the thought fled, dispelled by the sheer seductiveness of her. Her skin glowed in the moonlight, the sensual curves of her long, delicately boned body shadowed here, revealed there. Her full lips curved and she lifted one hand to a branch above her, tilting her head and swaying there like one of the water reeds, like another blossom of the marshes.

"Where are we?" he asked, unable to take his eyes off of her.

"You don't recognize it? I suppose you haven't ever been here. Still, I thought that you might recognize this place, having been inside my magic."

"This is your magic?"

She shrugged a little, her breasts rising and falling with the movement, her hard, dark nipples peeking briefly through the screen of her hair as she gazed over the landscape. He wanted her with consuming passion, his hands aching to touch her, so he moved closer. Glancing back at him, Seliah smiled invitingly. "The landscape of my magic... Perhaps so, yes. A familiar's arcanium, as it were." She held out a hand to him. "You're welcome in this place, wizard of mine."

Delighted by the invitation—though a puzzling part of him shouted that he could not, should not touch her—Jadren took that final step and clasped Seliah's hand, interlacing his fingers with her long, slight ones that felt so fragile between his, yet also shimmering with magic that flowed into him like water coming to the desert. He was parched and she nourished him.

She smiled as he drew her close and gathered her naked body against his, running his hands over her, his breath quickening at her shiver of heated response. He'd wanted to touch her like this from the first moment he saw her—wild, strange, more than a little insane. The perfect woman for him.

When she drew him down to the cushioned bed of moss, waxy white petals showered around them, and he luxuriated in the sense of her. Kissing her, he drank her in, pure water and radiant moonlight filling every empty, aching part of him, banishing the pain and giving him what he so desperately needed.

JADREN AWOKE, DEEPLY confused, sizzling with magic and well-being. Also hugely aroused. The naked woman who was draped over him explained the last bit, though he couldn't imagine who she was, how she'd ended up in his embrace, or where in the Convocation they were. Though this was far from the first time he'd awakened magically sated with a naked woman, usually he was sexually sated, too. And this didn't look like House El-Adrel, by any stretch.

Nor did he understand why he felt like he'd been drenched in pure water from the inside-out, leaving him brimming with bright white magic that reminded him of moonlight and—

"Fuck me!" he yelped, thrusting Seliah away from him. Far too late. She rolled away with boneless lassitude, limp as a wilted flower, not even making a whimper of sound. At the other end of the bond between them gaped a vast nothingness, a void complete and depthless.

She was dead.

He'd done it after all, the one thing he most feared, what he'd always suspected lay within him and what even his mother didn't realize he was capable of doing. He'd felt it before, all those times of waking up with the various women his mother had bred him to, the infinite hunger within him that would drain anyone dry of their magic to feed itself.

To devour and become… What?

He still didn't know, and didn't want to. Though he'd find

out now that he'd finally become the monster. And Seliah had paid the price. Of all the people who could've been sacrificed to the voracious beast within him, it just had to be the one person who'd ever mattered.

"No no no no no," he chanted under his breath, coming onto his knees and rearranging her lax limbs on the... tarp? Yes, some kind of primitive treated cloth—of Meresin farmer-make, no doubt—laid over something cushiony.

Seliah wore only underwear, some incongruously lacy stuff, and he ran his hands over her chilled skin. Cold as death, despite the warmth of whatever the fuck kind of shack she'd somehow stowed them in. Her normally dusky skin was gray and bloodless, covered in fresh bruises, the many wounds savaging her long, lean body giving evidence to a fight that had to have been hunters, given the tooth and claw marks. Indeed, the foul, oily feel of the hunters' magic clung to her, like the scent of rot and cruelty. How she'd survived and escaped, he didn't know.

He knew that the hunters hadn't killed her, however.

He had.

All that magic surging within him was hers. He'd healed so completely that he felt better than he remembered ever feeling, as if he'd lost years and gained a new level of youthful vitality. He'd taken so much of Seliah's magic that he'd not only fully healed, but filled himself to bursting. With a despairing laugh, he lowered his forehead to Seliah's cold breast, thinking of all he could do with that magic, all of it either selfish or useless. He could heal himself—of anything, apparently—or make an unending supply of widgets and gadgets. But no gadget would bring Seliah back to life and he had no ability to heal anyone else.

So ironic that he experienced the pinnacle of personal power at the moment that he fully realized how worthless that power was to him, holding the empty corpse of the woman he loved. The only person he'd ever loved.

As he lay there, contemplating new levels of self-loathing, bits and fragments of what had happened came back to him: their capture by the Hanneil wizards, the hunter attack, Vale carrying him off at breakneck speed. He could kill that horse, wherever the creature had escaped to now. From where Jadren lay, Vale's tack and packs sat clearly visible not far away. Seliah had to have been the one to relieve the horse of his burdens. Before she deliberately set herself up to be drained by him as soon as he recovered just enough for his instincts to kick in, for the insatiably greedy and ruthless monster at his core to awaken and take all she offered and more, and before his better self—if he even possessed such a thing in the rotten core of his soul—realized in time to call a halt.

Alone with Seliah's cold corpse, Jadren found himself weeping as he hadn't since he was a boy. He couldn't claim that he grieved for her death, as he'd never been so unselfish and was unlikely to develop that ability now. No, he wept for himself, for all that he'd lost. And he wept from impotent rage at his inability to do anything right, ever.

He'd tried to get away from her, hadn't he? He'd tried to spare her this fate, but no. No, she'd just *had* to come after him, had to find him and drag him away from what should have been his grave in the boneyard at the bottom of the cliff.

Tears flowed onto Seliah's clammy skin, and absurdly he thought of a gruesome childhood poem, of a young woman crying over her slain lover and how flowers had grown from his decomposing body, blossoming with white petals and drooping heads.

That dream... It hadn't been a dream at all, no more than the others of her had been, when he'd been repeatedly dying from that fall. Seliah had known how to manipulate him into taking her magic and she'd done so with the finesse of an experienced familiar. She'd clearly learned a few tricks. And he knew just which tricky Elal familiar to blame for it.

Oh, he'd make Nic pay for this all right. Once he was done watering his dead lover. Only he'd never gotten to have that with Seliah, another bitter regret. If this were a romantic tale, he'd die here in this stranger's hut with Seliah, the two of them entangled in death as they'd never managed in life. The tragic romance of it appealed to him, even as he observed the additional irony that, not only couldn't he die, but he was bouncing with health.

As he lay there—all right, as he wallowed in self-pity—he became aware of a slow sound, a deep, soft thud, followed by a long pause. Then the thud came again. Not from outside, but from beneath his ear.

Seliah's heart. Beating.

Slowly, oh so slowly, but there.

Some part of her yet lived.

Hope, a very strange, painful, stabbing emotion he didn't quite recognize, shattered through him like the lightning bolts of his family crest. It galvanized him, and he leapt to his feet,

Seliah's wilted body in his arms. He could still save her! A healer. He needed to find a Refoel healer for her. He glanced wildly about the decrepit little cabin, as if a Refoel wizard might emerge from a crack in the woodwork.

No such luck, of course. Wizards: they popped up and captured you when you wanted to be left alone, but couldn't be found when you needed one.

That meant he had to get Seliah to a healer, and dark arts only knew where they were now. Somewhere not far from Hanneil lands, most likely—and also not far enough. If that border patrol had made it back to tell the tale, House Hanneil would be coming after them. Realizing he was standing naked in the center of the room, holding Seliah as if he meant to dash out the door, he figured he'd better get ahold of himself and make an actual plan. Seliah seemed as dead as ever, her swanlike throat exposed with her head draped back over his arm, her hair short from the bonding ceremony. It had been long in that dream that wasn't a dream.

With each passing moment, one of those slow, labored heartbeats could be her last. He had to find a way to save her. And standing there naked, in a panic—and apparently still weeping like that girl from the childhood poem—wasn't going to do a thing. He started to set Seliah down again, observed the gory state of the tarp they'd been sleeping on, and decided against it.

There must be a bed in this place. Spotting the doorway to a dark room, he carried Seliah in there and laid her gently on the bed, then took stock of his surroundings. Someone's tiny cottage, nothing fancy. Barely the basic conveniences. It was night, but no telling *which* night or how long it had taken him to regenerate. By the looks of it, the residents had only left temporarily, which meant they could be back soon. That little confrontation could go either way.

He covered Seliah with a blanket. Reluctant to leave her, he feathered fingers over her face and kissed her softly, showing her far more gentle affection than he'd ever dared while she was awake, so ready to misinterpret the least gesture from him.

And look where it had gotten her.

Deliberately turning his back, he strode out to rummage through the packs. To his surprise, he found his own supplies, including Mr. Machete. Somehow Seliah had retrieved the stuff the Hanneil wizards had taken from him—which didn't bode well for that group—including, very interestingly, the bag of relics once implanted in his body. He'd saved them, carried them with him, largely because his dear maman had invested time and energy in them. She might be a megalomaniacal sadist who kidded herself that her love of torture came from a sincere interest in experimentation, but she was also insanely intelligent and didn't waste time on random efforts. When she'd cut him loose to be a spy in House Phel, she'd spent that time preparing for when she'd have her favorite experimental subject back in her greedy paws.

And when she could again attempt to implant these widgets for whatever nefarious goal she had in mind. Emptying out the bag onto the primitive wooden table, he spread them out with trembling fingers. None of the metal, mechanical things made any more sense to him than they ever had. His mother believed in the purity of scientific effort, which meant that her test subject shouldn't know the purpose of the experiment, lest that skew the results. Never mind the additional barrier of his lack of education. Very likely any junior wizard in House El-Adrel would know the purpose of these gadgets—or could use their mechanical magic senses to discover it.

Jadren could use his inherent El-Adrel wizardry to make minor gadgets. He could do basic warding and a few other standard wizard's tricks, but no one—least of all his dear maman—had ever expected or wanted him to become a full El-Adrel wizard. Not like his siblings. No, his mother had seized on him in his youth to mold him into something else. She'd recognized his great potential, not to ever head House El-Adrel after her, but to accomplish what she never had: employ their shared resistance to death to some purpose other than saving their own skins.

One of these inscrutable mechanisms—maybe all of them—were designed to allow him to use that unconscious healing magic deliberately. He'd never before been so replete with magic, thanks to Seliah's foolish martyring of herself, so the least he could do was attempt to use one of these to save her.

But which one? All? And how? He couldn't very well implant them in himself as his mother tried to do. Besides, that had never worked, his body always extruding them again, no matter how deeply and firmly his maman tried to affix them.

Still, she'd never had his true cooperation. No matter what kind of extortion she'd used, regardless of what techniques she'd employed to attempt to bend him to her will, she'd never quite broken him. Even when he'd promised cooperation in order to spare Seliah a terrible fate in House El-Adrel, he'd retained a shred of stubborn will. Oh, he'd stilled his struggles and hadn't overtly resisted, obeying his maman's every instruction, but he'd never truly submitted to her.

And he knew that must matter because she kept trying so very hard to get him to do it.

And none of this was saving Seliah's life. Gathering up the array of widgets, he carried them into the bedroom and dumped them on the quilt covering Seliah. It was a colorful thing, made of many small pieces of cloth stitched together in circles of rings. Some kind of marriage deal, he guessed, the room speaking of a couple who shared the bed, each with various belongings on the little tables on either side. Stacks of novels and a pair of reading glasses on one, a collection of manuals and packets of herbs on the other. Not a life he or Seliah had ever had, or would have, even if he managed to save her.

But he'd figure out their future later, once he was sure they'd have one.

Since he had no knowledge of the gadgets to go on, no basis to logically choose, he nearly despaired. There was no time to try each one, even if he had the vaguest clue of what he was trying to do.

He'd overheard Nic harping on Gabriel about using his "wizard's intuition" enough times, and there was no denying Phel was an impressively powerful wizard who performed feats no one should be able to pull off. Jadren had always thought that talk of intuition and instinct was a fancy way of saying someone was simply guessing, but what else did he have?

It wasn't as if magic made logical sense at the best of times anyway. Closing his eyes, trying to screen out the worry that he hadn't heard Seliah's heart beat in far too long—*you wouldn't be able to hear it from here anyway, idiot*—he let his fingers drift over the gadgets. Waiting for one to speak to him. As if a metal doohickey could speak.

You're wasting time, his inner voice observed. *Wasting what little life Seliah has left.*

I'm not. She wouldn't survive a trip to find a healer. She might not survive the next few minutes.

At least finding a healer has a chance of working.

An infinitesimally small chance.

Still a non-zero chance, whereas this… What are you even thinking? You might as well dance around the bed beseeching the spirits of our ancestors to intervene.

He paused. *Is that something people do?*

You're asking me? I am you. I don't know anything more than you do.

I'm not asking you. I'm wanting you to shut up.

Then shut up.

You shut up! Cursing in frustration, Jadren took his own advice and attempted to quiet his mind. If this had any chance of working—*It doesn't. Shh.*—then he needed to give it his all. Quiet mind. Trust his wizard's intuition. Seliah deserved his best effort.

Something snagged his memory. He closed his hand over the brass widget still hanging from the chain around his neck.

It had a feel of Seliah's magic, from lying against her skin. It also had a bit of buzz, that zing of his mother's magic, deeply embedded in the device. Turning it over in his fingers, eyes still closed, he found he had a clear image of the thing in his mind. It had rattled around in his lungs for some time as he and Seliah crawled through that tunnel to the catacombs below House El-Adrel. He'd told her to keep that one, since it scintillated with his mother's magic. At the time he'd thought he had an idea of what it was or did. He clearly recalled having that thought, but not the understanding behind it. Why had he thought he knew? *What* had he thought he knew? Surely not some blasted wizard's intuition thing.

Was it?

Opening his eyes, he studied it. A kind of brass, mini-telescope, inset with crystal lenses. His maman's magic coiled through every bit of it, inlaid in every pore of metal and crystal. It had come out through his ribs, after a painful journey through his lungs, but where had it started? That intensely long and agonizing session with her trying various devices, forcing him to use Seliah's magic in an effort to heal and seal those things into a permanent position in his body came back like a fever dream. He couldn't remember much detail of that blur of blood, pain, and despair. But that memory had to be in his head somewhere.

Jadren wasn't big on remembering those sessions with his dear maman, but that was mere selfishness. And this was for Seliah, who'd knowingly sacrificed her life for him. Staring fiercely at her lovely profile, he set aside his squeamishness and forced himself to delve through those memories. This device in his mother's hands. The glitter of anticipation in her wizard-black eyes. The slice of the scalpel over his chest as he attempted to hold still, the bite between his ribs, the excruciating widening as she inserted the device... next to his heart.

How romantic, his snide inner voice observed.

He ignored it and placed the brass device over his heart—and over his skin, thank you very much. If he had to resort to self-surgery he would do it, but not yet. He needed all of his magic for Seliah. It didn't feel right, but it felt like... something. It tickled his mechanically attuned magic, not exactly speaking to him, but still communicating in some way.

His inner critic rolled his eyes, muttering about woo woo nonsense.

Jadren didn't care. He'd been a fool for Seliah's sake many times over. At least this time was *for* her. Focusing on Seliah, he laid a hand over her barely living but (hopefully) still beating heart, holding the device over his own heart, slowing turning it until *click.*

He couldn't quite define the sense of rightness, except that it felt like when an enchanted device worked correctly, when he'd found the exact way to make it function smoothly. A sense of being well-oiled and perfectly fitted. A harmonizing of gears and wheels. He gave his magic to it as he would to any device he created, enchanting it to do its job, to carry his healing ability to Seliah and into her, infusing her body with his own self-healing.

Her heart thudded under his palm, a drumbeat of response. The wizard–familiar bond snapped into vivid life and Jadren had to sternly leash himself so as not to take from her, but to give instead. The bond resisted momentarily, then seemed to accept his will and reversed the flow, creating another venue to pour healing into Seliah's blood-starved, exhausted body.

It was odd, viewing the process from this side. Not so much accelerated healing as a kind of rejuvenation. As his unusual magic permeated her cells, they began to renew themselves, repairing damage of all kinds, resetting to their previous state with astonishing rapidity, like waves of lightning ricocheting through her body. Was this what his maman saw in him? It could be, and—though he couldn't quite grasp the significance of it—he began to understand why she'd been so focused on harnessing this particular magic.

And on keeping the Convocation from knowing about it.

He set that aside to puzzle over later. At least he'd begun to believe there would be a later, for Seliah, and perhaps for him. Color returned to her complexion as her poor, strained heart regained its rhythm, her body producing blood to flow through collapsed vessels. She twitched, muscles and nerves reawakening. And her magic followed, gaining strength like a rising, waxing moon, water flowing into dry creek beds, bringing life to cracked soil.

She took a deep breath, undulating, becoming alive again before his eyes. In a bizarre and unexpected development, her hair visibly grew, spiraling, then stretching until it reached its previous glorious length. Finally, she sighed into a real sleep. How he knew that, Jadren wasn't sure, but his internal sense— all right, probably his stupid wizard's intuition—told him it was done. Carefully withdrawing his touch, just in case Seliah relapsed without it, he remained there a while longer, assuring himself that she indeed lived. In truth, she looked healthier than he'd ever seen her. She'd lost the gaunt hollows of her madness-induced, feral life and now looked... absolutely radiant.

Thoughtfully, Jadren turned the small device over in his hands, still not entirely sure why it had worked. Wasn't it enough that it had? Maybe, maybe not. Certainly he never wanted to be caught without it. He'd even be willing to have it surgically implanted, if someone like Asa could find a way to do it and have it stick. Although, with Jadren's terrible luck, he'd likely end up shredded again and lose the thing. He'd have to figure out how to make a new one, should this one be lost. He certainly didn't want to be in the position of going back to his mother begging for another.

Finally able to believe Seliah would sleep this off and be all right if he left her alone for a bit, he took himself off to wash and find clothing. They needed food, too, and he'd better see where Vale had gotten to. Seliah might've mustered the strength—Jadren didn't know how she'd done it—to bring the horse's tack inside, but he doubted she'd been able to groom him. Hopefully he hadn't run off.

Come to think of it, how had Seliah come to be riding Gabriel's horse? And how had she found Jadren? Surely Phel hadn't sanctioned this ill-advised pursuit. In fact, he'd promised Jadren he'd handle keeping Seliah at House Phel. Jadren snorted. *Fine job there, Lord Phel.*

It was, no doubt, a crazy, ill-conceived, and infuriating tale. Oddly, he found he couldn't wait to hear Seliah tell it to him. With one last, lingering look at her, he went out to assess their situation.

Maybe they weren't completely fucked, but he doubted it.

~ 12 ~

S ELIAH WOKE ALONE, in an unfamiliar bed drenched in late-morning light, wearing only her Ophiel lingerie.

The last thing she remembered, she'd been wandering her dream-marsh, enjoying the peaceful beauty of the place without the enervating mists of insanity to foul it. Jadren had been there, whole and well, and his dream self had…

She sat bolt upright. The lovingly handmade wedding-ring quilt fell away. How had she ended up in the bed? She distinctly recalled laying herself beside Jadren's broken body on the oilcloth so as not to mess up the linens of these unknown people. If she'd gotten blood all over the white linens, she'd never get it out again. Household magic had never been one of her fortes. Probably because she was a familiar, she realized for the first time. Nic had told her that many of the folk of Meresin were minor wizards, able to use water magic to dry out their homes and fields in the saturated landscape, and probably wash linens so they looked like new.

But she hadn't bled on the sheets—though plenty of dried blood had flaked off on them. Those disturbingly deep injuries from her battle with the hunter had all closed up as if they'd never been. The bruises from her falls in the rock-strewn boneyard were gone, too. She felt... quite good. And her hair. It spilled around her, reaching again to her waist as if it had never been cut in the bonding ceremony.

Jadren. He had to have done this. Her plan had worked!

Tossing aside the quilt, she leapt out of bed, finding some-one—hopefully Jadren—had left her a pitcher of water and soap to wash with, bless them. She efficiently stripped off the sheets, too. Finding a clean set in a chest against the wall, she made up the bed again. Later she'd wash the soiled ones.

Hearing the sound of footsteps, she ran into the main room of the cottage—just as Jadren walked in.

He stopped, hand on the handle with an arrested expression, emotions stark on his face for once, fleeting in such quick succession she couldn't identify them all. Her heart thundered, feeling as if it echoed his somehow, recognition simmering in the space between them. He looked good, to her immense relief. Perfect, even, with his auburn hair bright and beard neatly trimmed, wizard-black eyes intent on hers, magic sharp-edged in the air, clicking like well-oiled gears. He wore a commoner's plain, working clothes, but looked anything but mundane.

His gaze dropped, leisurely scanning her from head to toes and up again, before he met her gaze with a sardonic lift of his brows and a twist of his fine lips. "Still trying to seduce me, poppet?"

Once, she might've been bothered by the scathing tone, but she knew better now. Erotic tension fulminated along the bond, echoing hers, repeating and intensifying. "Why," she answered in the same tone, "planning to drug me insensible again?"

"I should, as clearly the message didn't take the first time." He shut the door behind him and prowled toward her, her skin prickling with awareness. And longing. "What in the dark arts were you thinking, coming after me? I seem to recall that I *specifically* ordered you not to!"

"I was thinking I was saving your miserable life!" she retorted. Jadren could bring up her ire like no one else—and yet she felt almost giddy to be fighting with him again. "You're welcome, by the way."

"I don't need to thank you because I saved yours in return," he snarled, "which I wouldn't have had to do if you'd *stayed put* as you were told."

"If I'd stayed put, like a child or a pet who can be ordered about—which I might mention, I am not—*you* would still be at the bottom of that cliff, dying and healing over and over again, being eaten alive by scavengers." She poked him in the chest with her index finger to emphasize the point. At the physical contact, the bond sizzled to a higher level, nearly stealing her breath. "How would you have liked *that*?"

"I liked it fine." He seemed to catch himself on that, a haunted look crossing his face before he firmed his jaw. "At least I knew you were safe. Turns out I was sorely deluded on that point, but apparently all bets are off when it comes to feral swamp-creatures."

"I could say the same of you." She skewered her finger in harder, furious, relieved, and aroused. All emotions swirled together when it came to him. "How can you be so hapless?" she demanded. "How did you get yourself attacked by a crew of dimwitted wizards, robbed of all your things, and thrown off a cliff?"

He bared his teeth, seizing her skewering finger in a hard grip. "It wasn't like I planned it that way."

"What *did* you plan then? Where were you going?" *How could you leave me?* she nearly added, but swallowed back at the last moment. She knew the answer to that. The real question was, how did she keep him from leaving her again?

"I was going as far away from you as possible," he fired back. "And now look at us." He wrapped his hand around hers, gripping it tightly. "We're right back where we started, only this time I very nearly killed you. What in the dark arts were *you* thinking?"

"That you needed my magic to heal. You wouldn't take it before, so I did what was necessary to make sure you'd get the magic you needed."

"Yeah, well, I took so much that you were a desiccated husk. Exactly what I knew would happen."

"And then you saved me, just as *I* knew would happen."

"How could you know that?" he demanded, bewildered and outraged, shaking her hand clasped in his as if he could wring the truth out of her. "*I* didn't know I could use my warped healing ability on someone else. How could you possibly have guessed it? I shouldn't have been able to do it! That's an enormous risk you took, Seliah. A foolish one, and you are not a stupid woman."

So that's how he'd done it. This would change things. For the moment, however, she decided not to mention that she'd envisioned him fetching a Refoel healer for her. "It wasn't a risk, Jadren," she replied, willing him to understand that she meant it. "I trust you. I believe in you."

"You shouldn't." He sounded more like he was pleading with her, emotion stark in his black eyes before he dropped them to their clasped hands. With great care, he unfolded her fingers, then pressed her palm against his chest, lifting his gaze to meet hers. "Your heart was barely beating," he whispered, like it was a confession. "How do you think I felt, waking up beside you, thinking you dead and knowing it was all my fault, Seliah?"

"I didn't think it would bother you that much," she answered, realizing in the pained depths of that heart that it was true. She didn't have high expectations of Jadren. After all, he'd told her not to, and she understood, better than perhaps anyone, how damaged he was. Sure he'd told Gabriel he loved her, but it was salient that he'd never told *her*. And he might've healed perfectly on the physical level, but Jadren carried emotional and psychological wounds that were so twisted over with scar tissue that he might never be whole. Jadren had even described his mother as a monster incapable of love, and had called himself a monster, too. People that messed up didn't become loving life partners. He'd never be like whoever occupied the other side of that bed inside, sharing the handmade quilt, and quiet days in the cozy cottage.

Right now, he was looking at her as if she'd thrust a blade into him. "How could you think I wouldn't care if you died?" he asked in steady, but ghostly tone. "After all I've done to protect you, to save you from several and assorted terrible fates. Repeatedly."

"But you left me," she protested, feeling perilously close to tears. She hadn't thought she'd say that to him, but the words dragged out of her of their own accord, demanding to be heard. "You drugged me and you left me, leaving that awful note behind."

His jaw flexed, black eyes darker than ever. "I left you *because* I cared, Seliah. I care too much about you."

She swallowed back the tears, taken aback that he sounded so angry and yet also so relieved to hear the words directly from him. "I did what I had to in order to save you, too, Jadren. I couldn't do anything less. I love you." There, she'd said it out loud, and she held her breath, waiting for his cruel set-down.

He stared at her, looking positively aghast. "No, you don't."

Of course that was his reply. "Don't tell me what I feel."

"I will tell you when you're being an utter fool," he retorted. "You don't love me. You can't love the likes of me. That's the wizard–familiar bond making you think that."

Now she understood Nic's loudly voiced frustrations over Gabriel's doubts regarding her feelings for him. She started to tug free of Jadren's grip, but he held onto her, black eyes hard. "Running away?" he taunted. "You can't flee every time you're uncomfortable, Seliah."

"That's rich, coming from the guy who ran away because he couldn't deal with our relationship."

He barked out a dry laugh, releasing her hand and stepping back. "Our *relationship*? You're just like the rest of those House Phel *Phools*," he sneered. Very funny. "What do you imagine—

the pair of us all happily wedded like the commoner denizens of this shack, living some kind of cozy, domestic life? They only have this because they're obviously mundane citizens, buying whatever basic magical conveniences they can afford and muddling along. They aren't us. We belong to the world of wizards and familiars and the politics of the Convocation, whether we like it or not."

"Being those things doesn't mean we can't care about each other," she insisted, well aware and vaguely ashamed of her girlish fantasies of marrying him in the gardens at House Phel, carrying a bouquet her father picked and arranged just for her, perhaps Gabriel presiding over the ceremony. "I might be bonded to you, but that doesn't stop me from loving you."

"You're wrong." He shook his head repeatedly. "You don't love me. You and I don't have any kind of relationship beyond wizard and familiar—and I tried to release you from that particular obligation. I was being fucking noble!"

"Noble," she scoffed. "You don't have a noble bone in your body, Jadren. You were being a coward."

At last, she'd struck him mute. He gaped at her, clearly stricken, and at a loss for words.

"You were afraid *because* you care about me," she continued remorselessly. "You admitted it. 'Too much,' you said."

He recovered, face pinching in sardonic disdain. "So, in your estimation, I'm a frightened coward. I must say, Seliah, your wooing technique leaves something to be desired."

She eased closer to him, and laid a hand on his cheek, stroking the silky beard. "Only sometimes. You're only a coward when it comes to your emotions. The rest of the time you're so terrifyingly brave it defies rationality."

"Are we talking about me or you now?"

"I'm not brave."

"You are." His voice softened and he leaned into her touch, setting a hand on the round of her shoulder and smoothing down, lightly caressing her skin. "Terrifyingly brave. I'm not afraid of death—sometimes I wish I *could* die—but you put real fear in me, because I can't bear the thought of you being gone from the world."

"Truly?" she breathed. That he'd say this to her was so much more than she'd dared hope for.

"Why couldn't you just stay put, Seliah?" he asked, sounding wistful this time. "I wanted you safe from me, safe from what nearly happened. From what *did* happen. I can't control this thing in me and you're the last person in all the world I want to hurt."

Her heart thrilled to the words. It wasn't exactly a declaration of love, but coming from Jadren, it might as well be. "Because you care about me," she insisted.

"Too much," he agreed on a whisper. His mouth drifted closer to hers as he slipped his hand under her hair to caress the back of her neck. "This is your last chance, Seliah. Be smart for once and walk away from me. You could have a life with someone better than me. You don't have to do this, but if you do, I don't think I'll be able to let you go again."

How do you know it's real, how you feel? Selly had asked Nic.

Does it matter? Nic had asked in turn. *Feeling how you feel, even if you didn't have a name or reason for it, would you go after Jadren anyway?*

"I can't do anything else." She'd said that then and said it again, aloud and without meaning to.

Jadren frowned at her, though he didn't let her go, his fingers flexing on the back of her neck. "You can, Seliah," he said with quiet intensity. "I'm giving you that option. Don't worry about the bond. It will attenuate again, if you let it. I felt it go when I was at the base of that cliff. The next time I almost die, it will—"

"Don't say that!" she interrupted fiercely. "Just because you can't actually die doesn't mean you can be so careless with your life."

"The point," he said, enunciating the word, "is that you can be free of me, of this. Don't let the wizard–familiar bond decide your fate. You can have your magic tapped by those friendly Phel wizards. You'll be fine without me. Better, because we're bonded, no other wizard can bond you. You can be free in a way that no other familiar can be."

With a flutter of shock, she remembered Jadren didn't know Alise could sever the bond. And she decided in that fraught moment between them that she wasn't going to tell him. He'd find out the truth eventually—especially if they went back to House Phel—but she had this reprieve to convince him they were better together and she'd ruthlessly exploit that.

"You don't need to pay the price of putting up with the likes of me," Jadren continued, more earnest than she'd ever seen him. "I am not an easy person to be with."

"Neither am I."

His lips twisted ruefully. "Oh, Seliah, that is so not true.

And you deserve so much better than being tied to a heartless monster like me. No, I'm not noble. You're right about that, but I *am* an expert on pain and that is all I'm capable of giving you."

She slid her hands up his shoulders, winding them behind his neck. "I seem to recall you bragging about being an expert on pleasure, too. You said you could make it very, very good for me."

He winced, fingertips softly stroking the nape of her neck, giving her delightful shivers. "I was not in control of myself at the time. You know that. You should know that it could happen again."

"You're in control now."

"Yes, which is why should stop me. I'll let you go, Seliah, if you tell me *no*."

"I don't want to," she breathed, and closed that last distance between them. Their lips touched, and she moaned at the sweet shock of the kiss, almost as if it were their first. Bright and new, full of promise.

His warm lips barely moved at first, tense and withholding, as if he tried to resist her. Then he groaned, a sound echoing her own, his hand firming on the back of her neck and keeping her there as he deepened the kiss, devouring, sending delightful sparks all through her. He stroked his other hand down her naked spine, shivers of heat following the wake of the caress. Such soft hands. Wizard's hands, sensitive and sensitizing. No one had ever touched her like he did, like she was something precious to savor. No matter his words, his attempts to put her off, the way he touched and held her couldn't perpetuate the lie.

Jadren wanted her as much as she wanted him. The bond shimmered between and around them, less like a ribbon or tie than like a blanket that wrapped around them both. She leaned into him, trembling with need, doing her best to savor the moment in case he changed his mind yet again. If nothing else, she'd have this memory, this moment, forever.

"Seliah," he said, his voice hoarse, hand going to her bottom and pressing her against his groin. "I really think you should tell me *no*."

Back in that cage in House El-Adrel, she'd told him *no*, had held off against his determined seduction. His behavior had been a product of his deranged mind in that moment, and they'd had witnesses, wizard-scientists observing them through the glass. But now they were alone and she would not refuse him again. She wanted, needed this, him. "Yes," she replied. "Yes, Jadren. Yes, yes, yes. More than yes. *Please*."

He made a sound of frustration, kissing her almost punishingly. She reveled in it, writhing against him, lifting her hands to slide them through his thick, fire-bright and silky hair. Breaking the kiss, he stared at her for a long, wild moment. Then swept her into the balcony of his arms, and carried her toward the bedroom.

"We should bar the door," she protested weakly, not really wanting to take the time, but an interruption would be even worse. "Whoever lives here could—"

"Could be consumed by the fires of House Hagith for all I care." He laid her on the bed with gentleness at odds with his words, lavishing her with kisses. "I warded the whole fucking shack. No one is getting in."

"It's a lovely cottage," she argued, gasping as he flipped her over, undoing the fastening on the Ophiel lingerie that covered her breasts. He yanked it out from beneath her and it landed somewhere with a clatter as it knocked something over. Sweeping her hair to one side, he pressed her flat to the bed, hand stroking down her body and hot lips pressing to the hollow at the nape of her neck. She moaned, adjusting her face in the pillow so she could breathe, but otherwise yielding to his desires. Whatever way he wanted to have her was just fine.

Jadren kissed his way down her spine, melting her more with every touch, each lick of his tongue. He reached the small of her back, lingering there, then shifted to kneel beside her, tugging on the panties. "Lift," he ordered gruffly, and she complied, raising her hips, though she felt a bit self-conscious letting him strip her of them, displaying her bottom with the movement.

She wasn't a virgin, but she felt as shy as one. And, back when she'd lost her virginity, she hadn't been quite right in the head, though not as far gone as she'd ended up. She'd been sixteen and considered silly with it, and already a bit wild, gravitating to the lonesome quiet of the marshlands. The boy had been the same age as her, a farmer, awkward and sweet. They'd gone swimming and fishing as much as they'd fooled around, and it had all been equally fun for her, the sex no more exciting than the rest. Mostly it had been a release from the brain-fogs that plagued her, the pleasure there and gone again.

Being with Jadren was nothing like that. He consumed her, set fire to her every nerve, his skill in touching her every bit as expert as he'd once promised. Sliding the panties down her thighs with excruciating slowness, he kissed the path of skin behind. She sighed, melting down, and he tutted in disapproval, slipping a hand underneath her hips to lift them again.

"Like this," he murmured. "I like how this looks."

She squirmed, complying, pressing her thighs firmly together, and he whispered a laugh. Resuming his meticulous removal of her panties, he worked them from under one knee, then the other. She didn't miss that he set her knees down again slightly wider apart. "Jadren," she muttered into the pillow, sounding plaintive, her face hot.

He stroked a hand down her thigh, then traced the back of her knee which shouldn't have been so unbearably erotic. Bending her knee so it inched forward, he pulled the panties over her ankle, repeating the process with her other leg, her bottom now high in the air and her thighs far enough apart that he must be able to see everything. She tried to wriggle them together but he stopped her by dint of putting himself between her spread ankles, caressing the upraised globes of her bottom.

"Why do you have to be so fucking gorgeous?" he asked in a philosophical tone. "I mean, look at this adorable ass. Tiny, tight, perfect. And then this treasure." He trailed light fingers down one side of her sex, not quite touching the most sensitive part, teasing her.

Mortified, feeling her face hot against the pillow, she writhed, knowing her sex must be swollen and dripping wet. All on display.

"So responsive, too," Jadren whispered, continuing to tease

her, still not touching her where she wanted, needed it most. "But shy. I thought you insisted you're not a virgin." His fingers tangled in the soft hair at the apex of her mound, petting her, tracing the exterior of her sex. "Are you embarrassed?"

She groaned, glad he couldn't see her face.

"Answer me, Seliah," he commanded softly, settling a soft fingertip at the exact spot where her nether lips converged, where the hair gave way to tender flesh, stroking very gently, not nearly enough to send her over. "You're very wet, so I believe you're aroused and enjoying this, but is it too much? You can tell me if it is."

And then he'd stop. She understood his game now, why he was pushing her comfort levels like this. He'd never believed that she wasn't a virgin and this was his way of testing her. Well, she'd known this about him. Jadren couldn't help playing his little games, taunting, testing, and challenging her. Probably he hoped she'd lose her nerve and let him off the hook.

She pushed up on her elbows and looked over her shoulder at him. He met her gaze, seeming a bit startled, his wizard-black eyes intense in his handsome face, rigid lines of controlled passion in the set of his jaw. "I'm not a virgin," she told him, "but I've also never done anything like this. Still, there's nothing I won't give you, Jadren. Nothing you can't see or have." Very deliberately, she spread her thighs wider, offering herself to him.

He stared her down, a humming growl coming from him. Slowly, holding her gaze, fingers digging into her hips to keep her still, he bent and licked one globe of her bottom, then gently sank his teeth into a bite.

It was exquisite. She shuddered, whimpering, feeling her sex weeping, her limbs weakening with sapping desire. Jadren murmured something incoherent in reply, hands skimming up her body to cup her breasts and tease her nipples. Collapsing, unable to hold herself up any longer, she pressed into his hands, into his marauding mouth.

And he still hadn't fully touched her sex. She whimpered, pleading wordlessly, but continued to yield to however he wanted to see and touch her. She could give him this, her utter trust, her complete compliance. Whatever he wanted or needed from her, he could have. He'd promised he'd give her utmost pleasure and she believed him.

When he flipped her over, she went with the movement, lying back in the disarrayed tangle of her hair. He knelt between her splayed thighs, still fully dressed, his black gaze hooded as he looked at her, almost idly feathering light fingers over her belly, the sensitive hollows of her hips and groin. Rolling her hips, she held up her arms to him, but he smiled, thin and sly as a fox, and shook his head.

Setting his hands on her knees, he pressed them wider, tickling the backs of them so she shuddered wildly. "Such interesting places to torment you with," he murmured thoughtfully. "I look forward to discovering every one, but for now, I'm going to indulge myself and you'll patiently allow it, yes?"

She nodded, mouth dry, not quite certain what he meant, but on board for whatever it might be. Pushing her knees back,

Jadren slid down and settled himself, blowing lightly on her quivering tissues. Threading her hands through that thick hair, she made sounds of encouragement. His tongue touched her, right at that spot where he'd set his finger, and she convulsed at the sheer extremity of the sensation. Jadren laughed, darkly amused, and shifted his grip to hold her still.

Kissing her in that exact spot again, he wiggled his tongue, wet to wet, the deft and delicate caress of his lips joining to press another, fuller kiss to her sex, so intimate, so drenched with sensual affection that she sighed into it, offering and accepting more.

And there was more. He explored her with his mouth, making her aware of the fine petals of flesh so they felt almost foreign to her. She'd touched herself before, of course, with her fingers, and knew how to make herself come, but this felt entirely different in a way she couldn't have anticipated. He seemed to know what felt good before she did, finding which spots and rhythms drove her wild. She lost all sense of self-consciousness, of self at all, a creature of sensation, an instrument played by the mastery of his expert kisses and caresses.

She sobbed at the exquisite sensations, begging him, and he brought her to climax, not pausing in his ministrations as she convulsed, driving her still higher, increasing the tension before she had a moment to release, to catch her breath. Until finally she was screaming, thrashing wildly in the firm command of his hands and the determined assault of his mouth.

At last he let her drop, slowing the caress of lips and

tongue, releasing her hips now that they no longer leapt. He set a firm hand on her belly, the still strength comforting and grounding, calming her. She cracked her lids to find him smiling at her, smugly pleased. She breathed a laugh. "That was amazing."

"Yes," he replied, almost reverently. "Yes, it was."

Crossing his arms, he took hold of the hem of the rough-spun shirt he wore and pulled it up, over his head, treating her to a view of his excellent chest, the brass tube hanging on its chain around his neck. He pulled that off, too, at set it aside, lean muscles flexing with chiseled lines under his pale skin, which sported a dusting of auburn hair, like flames licking over snow. Selly sat up, suddenly reenergized, and splayed her hands over those muscles, tracing him with her fingers. He stilled under her touch and she glanced up to find him watching her almost warily. "Is this all right?" she asked, and he nodded, a bit uncertain.

Bending her head to his chest, she tongued one nipple, then the other, delighting in their copper color and velvety softness—and in how Jadren caught his breath, a thrum of response shivering through him. Giving him this was a delight of its own and she intensified her efforts, gratified by how he melted under her ministrations. He combed his fingers into her hair, stroking the heavy fall of it away from her face and moving it to stream down her back, otherwise holding still for her exploration, giving little sounds of appreciative pleasure.

Making her way down his flat belly, she tasted and tested, enjoying discovering what made him quiver under her caresses. She reached the tied waist of the trousers, glancing up in inquiry, finding him watching her with stark intensity, dark eyes fixed on her. With him holding her hair back like that, she realized, he could watch her as she pleasured him. His lips quirked at her knowing. "Quite a stirring sight," he acknowledged wryly. "I'm not often on the receiving end."

Often… or *ever*? She hadn't really contemplated Jadren's sexual history, beyond knowing that he'd essentially serviced any number of women—wizards and familiars, both—under the supervision of his mother and tormentor. Coming out of the magical healing put him in a crazed and aroused state where he had little control of himself. He'd learned to pleasure those nameless women, but who had they been and how had they treated him? In his somber gaze she caught a hint of that answer, a well of sorrow in him, and a glint of anticipation.

"May I?" she asked, hearing the sensual throatiness of her own voice. At his nod, which seemed slightly uncertain, though not in giving permission, but perhaps in him wondering how he'd handle this, she slowly loosened the ties, sliding the pants down so his erect cock sprang free, framed in its nest of fiery hair.

Following his example, she knelt up and, placing her palms on his chest, gently pushed him back on the bed, then worked the loose trousers off his legs, having to pull off first one boot, then the other. When she had him naked, she worked her way back up his long legs, kissing and nipping, letting her nipples graze him and her hair stream over his skin. He watched her still, almost warily, anticipation thrumming through their bond, through his quivering responses. She spread his legs as she advanced, settling herself between them and kissing around his scrotum drawn tight up under the hard cock lying on his belly, inhaling the scent of him, of sex and man.

"Seliah," he said roughly, his breathing uneven with anticipation, "you don't have to do this for me."

She looked up his long body and smiled. "I want to." Knowing he wanted to watch, she moved her hair out of the way.

He gathered it up. "I'll be responsible for your hair," he said on a hoarse laugh, then groaned as she licked her way from the looser skin of his balls up his hard shaft. Because she hadn't done this before, she experimented, judging by the way Jadren moved under her, by the sounds he made, what worked best. Gripping the base of his shaft firmly in one hand, she swirled her tongue around the velvety tip, now licking, now sucking harder, until his movements became increasingly urgent. Finally he dropped her hair and seized her shoulders, stopping her and pulling her up, his fingers sliding into her sex. She gasped at the sheer pleasure of it and he groaned at her wetness, turning her onto her back and settling between her spread thighs.

He looked serious, even grave, his expression set into intense lines and those black, black eyes staring into hers. Positioning himself at her entrance, he pressed slowly in, pausing at the resistance, assessing her expression, a question in his eyes.

"It's been a very long time," she explained, aware of how very tight she must feel. "Don't stop."

He breathed a ragged laugh. "Good, because stopping right now might kill me. Oh, Seliah…" Flexing his hips, he pushed in deeper, filling her, both of them sighing at the intimate connection of skin.

Their bodies joined to the hilt, Jadren began moving inside her, slowly at first, then increasing the pace as they found the right rhythm for them, a song shared by only the two of them. He leaned to the side, half turning her, so her right leg came over his hip and his face lay close beside hers on the pillow, dark eyes half closed in utter sensuality. She clutched at his shoulders, buffeted by the waves of intimate, erotic connection, needing to hold onto him. He wrapped an arm around her waist, anchoring her as the impending climax tossed her on tumultuous waves. Convulsing, she cried out throwing her head back. Jadren's face contorted and he increased pace, breathing hard, then crying out also, his body pounding into hers with devastating results, prolonging her climax and unraveling her so she felt her edges blur and the world dissolve.

There was only him, inside and around her, his face softening, black eyes deep as luminous pools. She lay there, gazing at him, catching her breath as he did the same. He looked softer, sweeter, more vulnerable than she'd ever seen him, and he smiled slightly, a bare twitch of his lips, a hint of wistfulness, of some other emotion she couldn't quite identify and thought likely he couldn't either. "That was intense," he said softly, stroking light fingers down her arm.

"Yes," she answered quietly. Intense, yes, and intensely moving. The sheer bliss of being with him was one thing, but the devoted focus he gave to her, of seeing to her pleasure before his own, of how he stayed present, immersed in their bodies and how they moved together—it all rocked her, physically and beyond. She never wanted to lose him and, in that moment, if she could have wrapped him up and kept him from ever knowing that their bond could be severed, she would have.

It would be unfair to him, selfish and wrong, to keep the knowledge from him, but Jadren would seize on the severing to separate himself from her, and she couldn't let him do that to either of them. They were alike in so many ways, connecting on a level she didn't quite understand. Yes, the bond was there, her magic flowing into him in a slow trickle that felt like her love for him, her desire to nurture him, to care for him, to make him happy. Was this her familiar's inclination toward the care and feeding of her wizard?

Or was it love? It felt like love, and she nearly said the words to him again. They crowded against her lips, wanting to fly to him, but she was too afraid of ruining the moment.

He pulled her close, snuggling her against him, their legs tangling together as he placed a soft kiss on her forehead. She sighed in utter bliss, wanting this, only this, to be with him, intimately entwined. The truth resonated in the depths of her being. Apart, they suffered. Together, they had this.

And she wanted exactly this, always.

~ 13 ~

JADREN WAS RATTLED.

Of course, the interior of his head wasn't the most stable of places to begin with, and the recent sequence of events hadn't done anything to *improve* his relative sanity. Nothing like having your brains literally scrambled to destroy any hope of rationality.

That unfortunate scrambling had to explain how he'd ended up in bed with Seliah. Well, that and walking in the door of that rustic shack and seeing her alive and well, standing there in all her glory, wearing only that devastatingly sexy lingerie, illuminated by the morning light through the windows so her dusky skin seemed to glow golden against the dramatic cloak of her newly restored long and flowing hair.

As if that hadn't been enough to rivet him in place, the delighted shine in her amber eyes, the glad cry that escaped her, and that radiant smile—all for him, when no one in his entire life had ever been happy to see him—had nearly put him through the floor.

He'd tried to resist her allure, he really had. The way he'd planned it in his admittedly fragmented head, he would have convinced her to walk away, to seize a chance for happiness that being stuck with him would never provide. But no. Not Seliah. Somehow she'd not only sucked him back into her magnetic field, but she'd seduced him into bed with her.

Yes, fine, he'd carried her there, and had done most of the actual, physical seducing, but those were details. He'd done it entirely because she had manipulated him into it. And because she needed only exist to be seductive. And *then* she'd taken over, with her sensitive, sensual mouth, and unraveled him entirely. Being inside her, the bond shifting and shimmering between them... Well, he'd once sneered at the people who insisted on calling sex "making love," but now he understood on a visceral level. There was a distinction and he wouldn't be the same again.

Seliah lay cuddled in his arms, a drowsy weight, all sweet curves and silken heated skin, impossibly long and lovely legs tangled with his, and he felt like he was bleeding inside. Not like an injury, but a kind of slow-seeping that tenderized the parts of him he'd thought forever toughened with scar tissue, callused over and jade-hard from knowing far too much about the world. He'd realized a while back that he was in love with Seliah—stupidly, head over heels, against all kinds of good sense and good judgment in love—and also that love had made him a fool in the end, an irony that hadn't escaped him.

He seemed doomed to be smart enough to recognize the worst mistakes he could make—and foolish enough to fling himself into making them anyway.

He had become a fool as great as any in House Phel. And now, these feelings for Seliah, for his bonded familiar of all people, threatened to make him weak as a babe. He actually wanted to *stay* in that bed with her, to spend his days and nights exactly like this, safe and cocooned, feeling... loved? Was that what this odd feeling was? No wonder he didn't recognize the enervating sensation.

You should run, his internal voice advised. *Run now and run fast.*

Oh right. I'm sure Seliah won't follow this *time.*

He still couldn't believe she'd come after him, that she'd managed to rescue him from that cursed boneyard of impaling death. And again later, from the ensuing entanglements. "How did you get away from the hunters and the Hanneil wizards?" he asked as the thought hit him, realizing the abrupt question probably wasn't appropriate for the mood. Oh well, she should know better than to expect romance from him. If she didn't, she'd do better to learn fast.

She tipped back her head to look at him, and he couldn't resist brushing the long locks of tenebrous hair from her face. "It was easier than you'd think," she answered, speaking the completely absurd words in a very serious tone as only she could. "The wizards—House Hanneil is psychic magic, right? Things make more sense now, knowing that—tried to control the hunters with their mind magic and went into disarray when it didn't work. I think they also hadn't battled hunters before because, by the time they started fighting with physical weapons, they were at a major disadvantage. The hunters killed them all." She chewed her lower lip a moment, clearly remembering something more, but didn't give it voice.

Too tempted to resist and not really wanting to, Jadren sucked that full lower lip between his, moving it into a kiss as she stirred against him, the sexual connection between them heating rapidly, as if they hadn't just sated themselves. "And how did you deal with the hunters?" he prompted, though he also traced the enticing curve of her perfect bottom, tempted to smack it a little, just to hear her squeal. Time enough to discover the edges of those boundaries with her. Probably. He hoped so, he suddenly realized. He wanted years to explore every way of having her and being had by her, from the heady lovemaking to the sharp-spiced games of pleasure and pain.

"I would've gotten them all cleanly," she was saying, and he realized—upon speedy mental review—that she'd been telling him about shooting the hunters from a tree with enchanted moon-magic-tipped arrows. "Well, if you can call melting them into that disgusting stew 'clean,' except the arrows didn't work on the leader."

Jadren came alert, all thoughts of alluring sex-games with Seliah fleeing from his mind. "You definitely pierced the leader's flesh with the silver? Correctly enchanted moon-silver? You're sure?"

Huffing in exasperation, she rolled her eyes. "Of course I'm sure. You think I didn't try multiple weapons? Once I decided I couldn't stay in the tree and committed to the hand-to-hand fight, I used a blade that had worked fine to melt other hunters. I tell you, this hunter was different. And it wasn't surprised that it was different. It knew."

This development didn't bode well at all. It implied that whichever wizard—or house of wizards—created that lead hunter had both known about Phel's enchantment and its effect on the hunters and had come up with a counter-spell. It worried Jadren greatly that his own darling maman just happened to be one of the few outside of House Phel who knew about the enchanted artifacts. She'd had that first blade of Gabriel's in her possession long enough to use her wizardry to analyze its properties. He figured she already knew all there was to know about how it worked, so he'd gone ahead and fed her the information confirming it, by way of assuring her he was being a good little spy. "Who sent the hunters?" he asked.

"I don't know."

"You should have asked."

"Jadren." She said his name with an edge of impatience, though she also caressed his back with sensual affection that made him want to sink into her and never stop. "Give me some credit. I *did* ask. The hunter refused to say. I'm pretty sure they were after me and not you, though. They didn't even blink at Vale running off with you, and they only fought the Hanneil wizards because those guards wouldn't give up." She shrugged against him and Jadren imagined it had been far worse than she wanted him to know.

She was likely correct about the hunters being after her, which set his teeth on edge. In general, the hunters seemed to be tasked to recover familiars, as a guiding principle. The fact that the one had been made immune to House Phel weapons only further indicated that Seliah was their target. It could be Convocation Center that wanted her, as they had sent that proctor to fetch Seliah for training. Though El-Adrel should have filed the paperwork confirming the legal bonding, which should be the primary claim. Of course, that claim would be complicated by the fact that Jadren didn't officially exist. The fact remained that any number of houses would be interested in acquiring or recovering Seliah—with the house of his birth at the top of the list.

"You *could* have stayed up in that tree," he pointed out. She'd been relatively safe there, but could she stay put? No, not Seliah. "That lone hunter couldn't have gotten you down on its own."

"It said reinforcements were coming," she argued. "Even if it was lying about that, I couldn't stay in that tree indefinitely. Especially with you needing me and—"

"I did not *need* you," he interrupted, immediately annoyed—and chagrined.

She didn't respond in kind, simply raising her brows and sliding a slim thigh along his hip in a most distracting caress, the heated slickness of her sex grazing his skin enticingly. He didn't shine at arguing under the current circumstances. "So, you were reclining in that thorn bush because it was so comfortable?" she inquired sweetly.

"I would have healed eventually. It's what I do." The words came out with a bitter tinge he hadn't realized was there.

"Not without my magic, you wouldn't have," she countered implacably. "You were down to the dregs from being unable to heal at the base of the cliff. What magic you generated on your own got immediately used up for partial healing, and you were back in the same place."

"Suddenly you know a lot about my magic."

"Not sudden, but yes. I've made a study of how your magic works, how the healing progresses, and Nic gave me a crash course in wizard–familiar dynamics. It's important for me, as your bonded familiar, to know how to support and care for you. Without an infusion of my magic, I think you would've eventually gone past the point of being able to recover."

Interesting. Perhaps that method would be a way for him to die then. Her theory was plausible. Deliberately, he turned onto his back, extracting himself somewhat from her embrace.

They should really be thinking about leaving this place.

He should really figure out where they could go.

Undaunted, Seliah leaned up on one elbow, fitting herself against him, sliding her thigh over his rapidly rousing groin. She laid a hand on his cheek, drawing his attention to her earnest gaze, the lovely amber of her lustrous eyes dark with concern. "I understand why you have a death wish, Jadren," she said softly, "but you do have things to live for."

"You?" he retorted scathingly, only it came out in a sensual murmur, apparently too affected by the sinuous twining of her lithe body against his. He wanted her again, rather desperately, which made no sense given how they'd exhausted each other only a short time before.

"Me," she answered with a slight smile. "I'd like to be that to you, but also for you to be able to actually live your life. You've never really gotten to."

"I'm pretty sure I have been living my life, all these years," he replied drily, though that funny, sensitive place inside him began its subtle twitching again. Something about the way Seliah looked at him made him feel oddly raw—as if she saw into him, perhaps saw the person he could have been, if he hadn't been distorted and twisted into this false construct.

She shook her head slowly, solemnly, then bent to give him a soft, quick kiss, her dark hair falling around his face. Reaching up, he tucked the hair back behind her ear and she smiled, coming in again for a longer, more lingering kiss. "I mean *live* your life, Jadren, for you. Not as a puppet of your mother's. Not as a minion of House Phel, if you don't want to be. Not even as my wizard if you'd truly rather be rid of me."

"Oh, *now* you'll be all compliant and not come recklessly chasing after me?" He added a snort, a bit of jaded sarcasm to counter the pang her offer gave him. He'd become accustomed to the idea of her determined pursuit and the thought that she might not actually care enough to persevere pained him more than he liked to admit. So much for her declarations of love. That must be a thin devotion indeed, for her to relinquish it so readily. But then, consider the focus of that supposed affection. He knew himself to be a monster. Seliah was no fool. At some point, she'd have to recognize that loving him would be pouring herself into an empty pit.

Seliah considered his question somberly, toying with hairs of his chest, her eyes downcast. "If me letting you go means you getting to be your own person, then yes," she said quietly. "That's what it means to love someone, Jadren. Your happiness is more important than my own. I believe we're stronger together, but I don't want to fight you on that point for the rest of our lives. I want you to *want* to be with me, to want this." She swept a hand down his body, the caress stirring, despite the serious, even depressing conversation. "But I want you to choose this even more. You got stuck with me. I'm very aware of how that played out. You made me your bonded familiar because you really *are* that fucking noble."

She flicked up her gaze at his huff of a laugh, ardent emotion in her quiet amber eyes. "We both know you did it to save me from a worse fate," she insisted, "that you didn't want a familiar at all, least of all a half-feral swamp creature. I can be noble, too. I mean it: if you truly want to be free of me, I'll go home and never come after you again."

Why couldn't she have come to this decision *before*, when he'd mustered the strength to leave her? Before he'd known the sweet succor of her body, before he'd discovered what it felt like for her to touch him with such reverent affection, to look at him with love in her eyes that he didn't, couldn't deserve.

"It wasn't noble," he told her, figuring he'd kick himself for it later, but unable to stop himself. "When I said I only bonded you in order to save you, that was an excuse."

She gazed at him in mute question, a tentative hope in her expression. Lifting her hand, he interlaced his fingers with hers, marveling anew at the delicate feel of her slender bones. Drawing her down again, he kissed her, her hair cascading in a dark veil, screening them from the world. It would come for them soon enough, but for the moment, they were the only two beings in existence, intertwined. Whole, in a way he'd never thought he could be made whole.

"I was horribly selfish," he confessed in that shrouding place of comfort. She needed to know the truth about him. Maybe then she'd finally wake up and see him for what he was. "I wanted you so badly, Seliah, that I took the opportunity to have and keep you when I could." He waited for her condemnation.

She said nothing.

"You shouldn't forgive me for that," he told her. "You should hate me for it."

"There's nothing to forgive, nothing to hate," she insisted, showering kisses over his face. "All I've wanted is for you to want me. Knowing this means that's true."

A tendril of dread curled in his gut. This couldn't possibly work out well. "I do want you," he said, fully aware that he didn't sound like it. The words came out more like growl of pain, a howl in the wilderness of the beast that has no companionship because it devours anyone who comes too close. "And that is a problem, Seliah. I want you to the point of consuming you entirely. You might not survive how much I want you. You almost already didn't."

Even still, his magic drank from her on a subtle level beyond his conscious control, as so much of that ability of his seemed to work. He should be replete, but the hunger in him had no limits. He'd always sensed that, suspected that the monster within could and would consume anyone.

A flicker of memory came back to him, of a woman being carried away, her body limp, skin gray with lifelessness. He'd been lying on the floor of his cage, barely aware—indeed his keepers thought him asleep, but he'd been in that twilight state of emerging from deep injury, his body healing at an accelerated rate that left his awareness behind—but he'd watched through cracked lids as they carried her away. A naked woman whose scent still clung to him, a familiar whose magic ran through him like a cool winter wind. A woman he'd killed.

And she hadn't been the first, or the last.

With a harsh cry of revulsion, Jadren thrust Seliah away, scrambling out of the bed as if she'd set fire to it.

"What?" Seliah asked, not angry, but concerned for him. For *him*. More the fool she. She sat up in the bed, the blankets falling away from her naked body, her long black hair framing her exquisitely sensual figure with loving contrast. Her amber eyes were fixed on him with compassion, with that love he'd sensed from her.

And it was wrong. So very wrong. He scrubbed his hands over his face, digging his fingertips into his eyes as if he could erase Seliah from his mind. Maybe if he could somehow not *see* her, he could manage to walk away. As if he could manage to again forget what he now remembered with horrifying clarity: all those familiars he'd drained to death over the years. So many dead at his hands, faceless, nameless, their magic forever a part of him now. They lived in him, part of the makeup of his fleshly form, incorporated into his blood and the smallest tissues.

As was Seliah. She was in there, too, devoured to make him whole.

That wasn't love; it was predation. A gruesome form of parasitism.

Then she stood before him, prying his hands from his eyes, and he became aware of moisture streaming down his cheeks. Tears? No—blood. His vision was smeared with it, his eyes unfocused from the damage he'd done to them. He'd nearly clawed out his own eyes.

Seliah's voice told the truth of it, crisp annoyance and fear.

"Stop it, Jadren," she commanded, her grip on his wrists firm. "Just because you can heal from any injury doesn't justify this self-destructiveness. You have to stop this."

He tugged away, but she held on with fierce tenacity. She always had been a surprisingly strong little thing. "Funny," he drawled, layering on extra sarcasm, tasting blood on his lips, "I always thought the one upside of my monstrous condition was that I could inflict on myself at least some of the same punishment I dole out to others."

"Who have you punished?" she asked with far more compassion than he deserved. "Not me. Not anyone I know of, not of your own accord. You aren't responsible for what happens when—"

"Then who *is* responsible?" he snapped, breaking her grip on his wrists—if only it could be so easy with the non-physical hold she exerted over him—and striding away. His eyes were already healing, the plain little room coming into focus with its homey things of simple lives and loving comfort. A sudden rage possessed him to tear it all to shreds.

He turned his back on it, gazing out the little window to the unpretty garden beyond. He had no idea what was growing in it, but it seemed to be a mess of vegetables as well as flowers, which made no sense. Who planted those together? The inferior quality glass made it all look warped, so maybe that was the issue. Still, he hated the people living here even more for their stupid garden and bad windows.

"Sometimes things just *are*," Seliah said. "You told me that about the magic, and so have others—it does its own thing. I didn't want to be driven mad by mine, but it happened, and it wasn't anyone's fault."

She was sorely mistaken there; it was absolutely the fault of those countrified idiots at her fallen house who'd had no idea what she was. He didn't say so, however, as that argument would go nowhere. Besides, her point about magic applied, just not in his case. "You don't understand what I've done," he said, hearing the hopelessness in his voice and hating himself for it.

Maybe that terrible fall had broken him in more than body. He'd always been able to summon insouciance in the face of despair. He had no idea what was wrong with him. His body was whole again, but he was still falling to pieces.

"Then explain it to me," Seliah said. Rustling sounds made it clear she was getting dressed. No doubt he'd blown any chance of another round of sex. Just as well. "Actually," she continued, sounding absurdly cheerful, "I'm kind of disappointed that you didn't trot out your usual old saw, 'you have no idea.'" She lowered her voice as she said it, making the imitation of him sound extra gloomy.

He turned to scowl at her, meeting her impishly pleased smile. "It's not funny, Seliah."

Her smile faded and she faced him somberly. "All right. Then let's talk about this. What are you responsible for that's so terrible?"

"Murder," he answered bleakly. "So many deaths. Believe me, you don't want to know what I..." He trailed off unable to say more. With his back to the wall, he slid down until he was sitting, legs drawn up and face pressed to his knees. Might as well fully commit to a full losing of shit. Fetal position just made sense at this point.

The gentle tapping of her footfalls faded as she went into the other room. Maybe she was finally wising up and leaving him alone. Unable to motivate himself to… do anything at all, he sat there. Numb.

Soon enough, however, Seliah returned, seating herself beside him on the wooden floor. "Here." She took his hand and wrapped it around a warm mug. "Drink it. You'll feel better."

He held the thing dully. It smelled weird. And it was a discomfiting yellow color, like old urine. "What is it?"

"Herbal tea. It's good for you."

Lifting his gaze from the dubious mixture, he scrutinized her apparently innocent and helpful expression. "Is this revenge?" he asked drily. "Drugging me as a bit of gotcha-back?"

"I considered it," she answered seriously, drawing up her own knees and wrapping her arms around them. Tipping her head back until it met the wall, she gazed thoughtfully at the ceiling. "I entertained all kinds of fantasies of how I'd exact my revenge. How I'd puni—that is, make you pay for jilting me like that."

She'd stopped herself from using the word "punish," he realized, dancing around him so whatever she thought had set him off wouldn't happen again. How demoralizing.

"But no, this is only herbal tea," she continued, rolling her head to look at him, her scrutiny palpable on the side of his face. "A blend of soothing herbs."

"I don't need to be soothed like a fussy infant," he said,

tempted to fling the mug across the room, which would unfortunately only prove her point about his state of mind. "Besides, what do you know about herbs?" He'd tried for a sneer, but the question came out plaintive.

"Some. You know, before Asa arrived, we didn't have magical healing in Meresin. We didn't even know it was real and not something made up for stories. We just had regular healers, and home remedies that used herbs. Everyone had a kitchen garden like the one here, with standard herbs for cooking and addressing the usual ailments. I figured the people here had a stock of dried herbs, and they do. Nice little hot water elemental, too. The herbs were all well-labeled," she added, before he thought of that potential problem. "Besides, I recognize them from back when I learned how to harvest and use them. I promise the tea will make you feel better."

"That's presuming you know what's wrong with me. I doubt Nic's crash-course in the care and feeding of wizards covered this."

"No, but I recognize shit-losing when I see it," she replied without judgment. "Having been there. Whatever you remembered can wait until you're calmer, then you can tell me about it. I feel I should point out that I'm very much alive, so whatever it is you think you do to familiars isn't true."

If only. Deciding he'd get no peace until he drank her probably vile concoction, he sipped, finding the stuff tasted pretty much like dried flowers—big surprise there—but otherwise more pleasant than it smelled. Or looked. Drinking a bit more, he found the twisted knots of his innards relaxing, and the sky no longer seemed to loom so low. The day had flown by, sinking toward mid-afternoon somehow. They should have gotten on their way long before this. Though that begged the question of where they'd go. Besides away from this little house with its accusatory happiness.

"I wasn't exaggerating when I said I drained you to death," he found himself saying, lulled by the easy companionship and the slanting golden light. "It's part of what my magic does. Just as I heal myself unconsciously, I can drain a familiar without being aware of it. I have no control."

She nodded in his peripheral vision, unperturbed. "You've taken magic from me before in small doses. Very small doses. And from Nic and the others. Clearly you have control."

"I *thought* I had it under control. I worked hard at it and Maman—well, it was the one of the few useful skills she managed to teach me. But you… You easily figured out how to circumvent that control. You *guessed* and were able to do it."

She was quiet a moment. "To be fair," she finally said, "it didn't take a lot of guesswork. I could feel your magic reaching for mine through the bond, and I knew we needed skin to skin contact—that's a given—and I have experience with how you behave when you're coming out of that healing state. I don't know if you recall, but you'd been refusing to take any magic from me after I found you at the cliff."

"Oh, I recall." He'd at least had enough presence of mind then to refuse her, knowing that once whatever lived in him latched onto her, he wouldn't be able to stop. "Because I knew what would happen, even though I didn't consciously remember until now. It's happened before, over and over. I murdered countless familiars back in those labs. I remember their faces now. I can see their corpses being carried away." He tossed the empty mug aside with a clatter and pressed his fingertips to his eyes again. "How could I forget?"

Seliah slid slender fingers around his wrist. "Don't," she commanded softly.

"It could've been you," he continued. "It *was* you. If I hadn't figured out a way to heal you…"

"How did you do that anyway?" she asked. "Heal me. I kind of had it in my head that once you recovered fully, you'd either take me to a Refoel healer or go find one and bring them back. I told you I had a plan," she added into his stunned silence.

Her belief that he'd save her staggered him. "That was an extraordinarily stupid plan," he ground out.

"I feel compelled to point out that it worked."

Jadren didn't know which was worse: the idea of her martyring herself for him—sacrificing her own life to save his—or her blithely trusting that he'd somehow wave his magic wand and fix everything.

She nudged his arm with her shoulder. "So, spill," she said in a light, teasing tone. "How did you do it? I'm guessing it's some kind of breakthrough, right? Because you've always said you couldn't heal anyone but yourself."

"I used one of Maman's dread devices," he admitted, pointing at the table beside the bed where he'd set it when undressing. He hadn't wanted to take it off, but he also hadn't wanted the thing clunking between them. Having it at hand had seemed to be a good compromise.

Seliah uncoiled gracefully, rising and going to fetch the

thing, and returning to sit cross-legged in front of him, turning the tube over in her slender fingers, the chain dangling in snakelike brass links. "This is the one you told me to keep as a souvenir. That I could string it on a chain as a memento of you."

"Which you clearly did." He took it from her and looped the chain over his head. "It's good you did keep it. Turns out I could use it to focus my healing magic into you."

Seliah cocked her head thoughtfully, considering him. "So, she did have some method behind her mad experiments."

"She's sadistic and insane, not stupid," he replied drily. Though he had to admit it surprised even him that one of those devices had actually worked, his mother had tried and failed for so long.

"And it worked outside your body," Seliah mused.

"It would be a distinct advantage to have it implanted in me." He plucked at the thing, letting it dangle from the chain. "Then I wouldn't risk losing it or having it taken."

"Did any of them stay?" Seliah asked. "The devices she tried to implant in you—are there any still in you?"

He shook his head. So strange to be having this conversation with another human being. The only other person in the world who'd known about what his maman had tried to do to him was his father, her familiar and necessary assistant to her magical workings. And now Seliah, his own familiar and... necessary? He hoped not. "Not so far as I know. My body forces them all out."

"*Would* you know?" Seliah persisted. "I mean, if one or more had taken and stayed implanted, it doesn't seem like she would've told you about them."

"True. But she was always so frustrated that I doubt it. Also, if she'd found a way to get some of them to take, wouldn't she have replicated that success?"

"Logical," Seliah agreed. "So what are you going to do now?"

He scrubbed his hands through his hair. "No fucking clue." He met her thoughtful gaze. "I suppose you want us to go back to House Phel."

"Not necessarily. Gabriel sent plenty of supplies with me. We can continue with whatever purpose you had in mind."

"I did wonder what in the dark arts Phel was thinking, letting you tear off after me. Especially when he promised—" Jadren broke off, too late, realizing how incriminating that particular confession would be.

But Seliah's eyes sparkled cannily. "That he promised to keep me there? That my brother gave you permission to leave and desert me? I know everything, Jadren."

"Figures Phel would cave and spill it all."

She wasn't in the least offended. "Nic took my side. And they both knew I'd couldn't do anything but come after you, so Gabriel finally agreed it was better I go *with* his blessing and support."

With a sigh, he extended a hand to her, and she took it with a soft smile. "I wish you hadn't been compelled," he said, wanting to tell her so much more than that.

"I wasn't compelled by anything more than my own desires," she replied without hesitation. "I am now exactly where I want to be. Wherever you want to go, I'll go with you."

"I'm not sure where that is."

"Where *were* you going when you were diverted by a near-lethal fall from a cliff?"

"I didn't fall, I was thrown," he protested, laughing a little along with her. How he could be laughing at this juncture, he didn't know, but it felt good. "I was going to House Hanneil," he admitted. "I just didn't expect the border patrol to do away with me as a landless, rogue wizard."

"Didn't you tell them who you were?"

"Explaining who I am is a bit difficult. I did tell them that Lady Hanneil would want to see me, because I'm just that important. Shockingly enough, they declined to believe me."

Seliah snorted in appreciation. "Why Hanneil?"

He considered lying. But what was the point? "I thought they could assess my magic and get me an MP scorecard, so I could perhaps get a job in the Convocation. And I thought I could ask them about whether our bond could be severed."

Seliah regarded him steadily. Too steadily, and with a flush of color rising on her dusky cheekbones. She was covering something up there. "Do you think they can sever the bond? I've been told it's impossible."

"I figured that since they—" The geas kicked in, stopping his tongue. Figures. He shook his head. "I figured if anyone knew, they would. Turns out getting an audience with Lady Hanneil isn't so easy as riding up and asking for it."

"It won't be easier now, with us having killed their wizards—so far as they know."

He patted her cheek with his free hand. "Aw, look at how well you've come to understand the Convocation. Does my heart proud."

She rolled her eyes at him, then turned her face, holding his gaze, and pressed a kiss into his palm, her talented tongue flicking out in a most stimulating caress. Lightning arousal jagged through him and he forgot everything but wanting her again. More and more.

Sliding his hand behind her neck, he pulled her into a kiss, sinking into her avid, delicious mouth. She came eagerly, meeting him with equal desire, trailing a hand down his naked chest to clasp his hardening cock in a deft and arousing grip. "Let's get back into bed," she murmured against his lips, and his member leapt her in hand in full agreement.

"We should get on the road," he countered, though without much conviction. At least his brain had kicked in. Somewhat. "At least figure out where we should go."

"Not House Hanneil," she said, stroking him so he groaned and fisted his hand in her hair.

"Definitely not," he gasped. "But where?"

"I have an idea." She bent and took him in her mouth, so he didn't find out her plan for quite some time.

~ 14 ~

NIC PURELY SIMMERED with fury, only some of it directed at herself. She wasn't much of one to revisit past mistakes. Of course, other than the unavoidable error of failing to manifest as a wizard, Nic hadn't been much of one to *make* mistakes in the first place. She worked hard, to the utmost of her ability, never giving only a mediocre effort. As best as she could, she'd always made sure that she did everything very well. If she didn't hit the mark, then she recalibrated, practiced, and refined until she was satisfied with her performance.

After all, her beloved papa had expected nothing less of her, his pride and joy, his heir. He'd been an exacting taskmaster and she'd been the brilliant pupil that rose to even the highest expectations. Until she'd failed the final test.

But that wasn't worth thinking about. She'd spent too much time dwelling on what she'd lost by being a familiar, unable to take over as Lady Elal and head the house of her birth as she and her papa had always believed she would. Her life had changed for the better as a direct result of that apparent failure. A more philosophical person than she might produce a pithy saying worthy of the wizard-philosopher Lord Redlin: Something something about what seems like a failure at the time leading to better things.

She'd found those better things: friendships she'd never expected, Gabriel's love, the true partnership they enjoyed, the opportunity to rebuild House Phel and make it into something truly extraordinary. Had she become Lady Elal, she wouldn't have any of these things. The path to heading House Elal had been very clear—basically becoming her father—and also tremendously circumscribed. With this life she'd fallen into, arguably as the result of a single, wildly impulsive and unwise decision, she'd given up all predictability, along with convention, all on an improbable dream. One she'd actually begun to believe in.

Now, she fumed, she'd already jeopardized the venture before they got it off the ground, because she hadn't been paying enough *attention*. How many times had she warned Gabriel that the hammer was poised to fall? Countless. She'd known this was coming and yet she'd allowed herself to drift through the days on a haze of love and sex and spring flowers, actually talking about *wedding planning* like she was living in a romance novel instead of an epic tragedy.

How disgusted her papa would be. Or perhaps he felt smugly vindicated. Clearly she'd never been the right material to head a High House. *Where is your spine, daughter?* Her father's voice echoed in her head. *Perhaps that familiar's brain has sapped away your will and intelligence. Pity.*

Clutching the sheaf of intimidating documents, she strode through the arcade, deliberately ignoring its graceful airy lines, the gorgeous spring sunshine glittering off the lake, and the scent of blossoms on the gentle breeze. Those things were illusions, distractions. Out here in the peaceful beauty of remote Meresin, it was easy to drift from day to day and forget the giant wheels of the Convocation endlessly turning. Growing up in House Elal, attending Convocation Academy, she'd been constantly immersed in politics. In that milieu, she'd have heard the rumor about this summons being drafted long before the Ratsiel courier was summoned.

She'd been unforgivably careless, disgustingly soft—and that was going to change. Gabriel had applied for her in part because she knew the Convocation. She'd been trained to be a warrior for House Elal and she'd use that to fight for House Phel.

At the end of the arcade, the doors stood open to the vast ballroom. As with the rest of the manse, it had been cleaned and largely repaired through human efforts, but the magic had taken over from there, embellishing and polishing with loving detail. The dance floor seemed to glow, attractively beckoning, the strains of absent music almost audible in the warm air. Tempting as it was to linger, she had no time to admire the changes—she never did—so she turned the corner to take the hallway to the larger feast hall that they'd converted into a dining and study hall for the minions, students, and apprentices. If they ever did host a ball, like everyone kept imagining they'd do for Nic and Gabriel's wedding—fat chance of that—they'd have the feast in there.

Dreams and illusions. There would be no wedding, no balls, no dancing and feasting by elemental light. What killed her was that she'd come to believe it would happen.

She nearly collided with Alise, coming the other direction.

Alise grasped Nic's arms, steadying them both—ironic as Nic's little sister was both smaller and slighter than she. Nic was supposed to be the rock.

"What lit your ass on fire?" Alise snapped, then reeled back her attitude as she studied Nic's face. "The baby—is everything all right?"

Nic blew out a breath and some of her wild fury with it. She hadn't given her pregnancy a thought in the last little while, though everyone else seemed to have it at the tops of their minds. The baby had begun to feel less theoretical to her, and yet their future seemed so uncertain that it was difficult to imagine this unknown life inside her ever entering the world. It actually made her sick to contemplate the child's fate, should House Phel lose everything.

"Maybe you should sit," Alise said gently, urging Nic toward a window seat overlooking the back lawn. "You look pale and flushed."

Nic resisted, tugging out of Alise's hands. The last thing she needed right now was compassion, as she'd likely burst into tears, which wouldn't be helpful to anyone. "How can I possibly look both pale *and* flushed?" she asked tartly.

"You're practically white except for the flags of red on your cheeks," Alise replied evenly. "Your eyes are glittering like a snake's and your magic is blazing hot, too. What made you so angry?" Her gaze fell to the sheaf of documents. "Papa?"

"Among others," Nic answered grimly. "Nothing for you to be concerned with. How is Maman?"

"No change," Alise answered shortly. "Do I have to point out that, as a wizard of House Phel and as a daughter of House

Elal, this absolutely *does* concern me?"

"No, because you're a minor still and not a full-fledged wizard."

"Nic." Alise caught her arm. "Let me help, please."

About to shake her sister off again, Nic met Alise's earnest black gaze, then peeled off one of the documents and handed it to her. "Among other things, you are ordered to report to Convocation Academy and to House Elal. On pain of expulsion from the academy—with no recourse to continue your education—for the former and on pain of disinheritance for the latter."

Alise read the document, quickly and with a wrinkled nose, as well-trained by their father in understanding legal language as Nic had been. Say what you would about Lord Elal—and Nic had plenty to say—but he'd never shirked training his progeny in critical skills for surviving Convocation society. Alise handed the document back to Nic, expression impassive. "It goes without saying that I'll do neither."

"Does it?" Nic asked with considerable impatience. "This is your opportunity to wipe the slate clean. You can go back and be forgiven, finish your education, be reinstated as our father's heir."

Alise made a rude noise. "I don't care about any of those things."

"You should," Nic insisted. "This is your future we're talking about."

"*Our* future," Alise corrected crisply, their mother's regal poise in her bearing, the insistence on partnership all learned from Gabriel. "House Phel is my house now. Your family is my family." She reached out a hand, then hesitated, wizard-black eyes flashing up to Nic's for permission. With a sigh of resignation, for more than just the gesture, Nic moved the documents aside for Alise to lay a hand on her gently rounding belly. "I'll be an aunt to this new person," Alise breathed. "My family, too, right here."

"There's nothing to feel yet."

"Not true," Alise said, stepping back and rubbing her hands together. "There's everything to feel. Don't ask me not to feel it, Nic." She clearly meant far more than Nic's pregnant belly, something that Nic supposed she understood.

"Then use your head and not your heart," Nic advised, reminding herself of that advice at the same time. "If you don't graduate from the academy, your professional options outside of House Phel will be severely limited. If you don't go back to House Elal, our father will name Nander heir."

Alise blew out a pfft of disgust that fluttered her bangs. "Our little brother couldn't head House Elal with our father's hand up his ass working his mouth for him like a puppet."

"Younger siblings grow up," Nic observed, though she had to laugh at Alise's colorful metaphor. At least this conversation had bled off some of her edgier anger. "Nander could be a formidable enemy of House Phel someday. I'd far rather have you as Lady Elal, and our ally."

"And how many years in the future might that be?" Alise countered. "Papa could live decades more and what if House Phel is destroyed before then, while I stood by and did nothing but ensure—what?—a prosperous career for myself? I'd much rather focus on the present and near future, thank you very much. And," she added archly, "need I remind you that you personally already gave me permission to stay. Even if you regret it, you can't renege on your word."

"I know." If only she *could* regret it. Things would only get uglier from here. Selfishly, however, Nic was profoundly glad of her sister's company. With their mother perhaps permanently comatose, and her father and brother probably permanently estranged, Alise was the only Elal family she had left. "I don't regret it."

"Good," Alise added impishly, "because no way am I missing the wedding."

Nic groaned. "There is no way we are spending time, energy, and coin on planning a completely unnecessary wedding."

"Completely *necessary* wedding," Quinn corrected, joining them with a cheerful smile and a bounce in her step. "Everyone is looking forward to it. Once Seliah drags her reluctant wizard back here, we'll set the date in stone and send out invitations." Her happy blue gaze fell to the sheaf of legal documents, dimming with canny understanding. "Ah, now I know why you summoned me. At last the other legal shoe has dropped."

"An entire wardrobe of them," Nic agreed wryly. "I thought we could—"

"Lady Phel." Asa strode up and bowed, barely contained exasperation in his voice and movements. "I do have patients and while I am obviously obligated to answer to you and Lord Phel, it's most distracting to be pulled away by an unexplained summons like this."

Nic waved the documents at the healer. "Not interested in some amateur legal wrangling?"

Asa's expression blanked, then sharpened. "My patients can wait."

Unable to stop herself, and despite everything, Nic laughed again. Yes, this was better than being so incandescently furious. "I'm told Wolfgang is in the study hall." She glanced at Alise. "You might as well come along."

Feeling a bit like she was leading a parade, Nic continued into the study hall. As she walked, she concentrated on breathing deeply from her belly, running a fast meditation exercise to calm her over-excitement and subdue her magic. The various wizard minions of House Phel would never step out of line and violate Gabriel's trust by messing with their lord's familiar, but waving an abundance of magic around wizards was akin to throwing a bloody steak in front of a hungry dog. Even the most obedient and well-trained canine would struggle with itself and its baser instincts. One should always be wary of a wizard's essentially predatory nature. They craved magic and no veneer of civilization would ever completely tame that voracious need.

As she'd been informed, Wolfgang, the Ratisbon wizard, and his familiar, Costa, lingered at a table in the study hall. They sat near the terrace doors, which stood open to the lovely spring morning, the remnants of breakfast between them, and both nursed cups of coffee as they pursued separate interests—Costa reading a novel while Wolfgang appeared to be sketching him. The morning light fell nicely over Costa's hair, gilding it and his aquiline features, making the handsome young man look like a creature out of a tale, so Nic could hardly blame Wolfgang for appreciating the view and wanting to commemorate it.

A few other folk were scattered around the common area, some browsing the shelves, others seated at work tables or on deep-seated couches, books and documents scattered around them as they studied. In the area of the hall designated for conversation, several lively groups debated points of magic and politics. It did Nic's heart good to see her vision coming to life. This was worth fighting for.

The hall lay adjacent to a secondary kitchen, which they'd begun staffing to provide morning and midday meals for the various minions—and evening meals for those who didn't rank highly enough to join the lord and lady of the house in the formal dining room. As Nic had originally envisioned, the large hall had become a convivial gathering area, the shelves filling the walls from floor to ceiling not exactly bursting with books, but not as gapingly empty as they had been, either. It helped that those who'd brought materials with them had been—for the most part—persuaded to store them in the study for common use. House Phel would need far more than this if they were to be a proper house, but new acquisitions would have to wait until they were no longer in arrears on their accounts with House Calliope.

Though perhaps they could ask for duplicate materials from other houses, even Convocation Academy. Nic made a mental note to look into it, wryly amused at herself that she could apparently continue to look that much toward the future. Still, she did give herself a moment—the meditative breathing was helping—to appreciate how much the place had begun to look like her initial vision of it.

As Nic moved through the hall, wending her way around desks and conversational groupings of chairs, the occupants all looked up and acknowledged her with unfailing courtesy. Gabriel had made that very clear: Nic might be a familiar and thus of lower rank to many of the House Phel denizens, but she was Lady Phel first and foremost in his mind, and woe to any who failed to treat her with the courtesy he demanded. She loved Gabriel for it, more than she ever wanted to tell him. Her vain heart that had been groomed to be an arrogant high-house wizard thrived on the deference. As much as she'd tried to reconcile herself to a familiar's lowly status, it had always stung her pride to be looked down upon.

As an Elal, she possessed more than her fair share of pride—likely too much—but that was an emotion that could be useful, if wielded properly. Righteous anger could be channeled into a rage to bring down the Convocation. Weddings could be postponed or canceled entirely, but her child *would* have a future. She would see to it.

Wolfgang and Costa glanced up as she approached, then both rose and bowed to her. Casting an interested eye at Nic's entourage, the Ratisbon wizard lifted a brow. "Good morning, Lady Phel. I see you've brought the House Phel quasi-legal team."

"The best we can muster," she agreed, setting the pile of documents on the table.

Costa hastily rescued his coffee cup and novel. "Since I'm useless at law, I'll take myself off."

Wolfgang caught his familiar's hand. "You don't have to go. Stay. I value your insights."

Costa smiled radiantly and gave his wizard a kiss. Had Wolfgang always valued Costa as a person rather than solely as a magical appendage and lover—or was that only since arriving at House Phel, with their laxer rules on the status of familiars? Most likely, this unusual pair had been drawn to House Phel, like so many of the other round pegs who didn't fit precisely into the unrelentingly square holes the Convocation offered its magical citizens.

"You can tell me all about it later, darling," Costa told Wolfgang, batting his lashes flirtatiously, "and I'll offer my *insights* then. Iliana wanted help in working with Nethys, so I might as well do that while my wizard doesn't have need of me."

Wolfgang's expression went dense with a desire Nic recognized well from her own wizard. Alise cleared her throat and looked away, while Asa's green healing magic took on such a tinge of bitter longing that Nic inadvertently lifted a hand to soothe him, withdrawing at his black, warning look.

For her part, Quinn exchanged air kisses with Costa, then sighed after him as he left. "What a thing to be in love with your wizard," she said wistfully. Quinn was bonded to her sister, so they shared a strong magical connection that, while affectionate, was obviously not sexual.

"It's overrated," Asa said shortly, going to the chair Costa had vacated and holding it for Nic to sit. Alise dragged over chairs for herself and Quinn, while Wolfgang began perusing Nic's stack of documents. To her satisfaction, he quickly discerned her organization and piled them accordingly.

"Not that you're bitter," Alise said to Asa.

"Didn't you have affection in your relationship with Laryn?" Wolfgang asked Asa. "You seemed to have a loving marriage on top of the wizard–familiar bond, her eventual betrayal notwithstanding."

"I thought we did," Asa bit out, "but apparently I was deluded." He snatched up one of the documents, glaring at it fiercely.

"You were not the only one she fooled. She betrayed everyone in House Phel," Alise told him gently, with a wisdom beyond her years. "Some more than others," she added cutting a glance at Nic and away again.

Asa visibly set his jaw. "Some cuts go deeper than others, too. Can we focus on the matter at hand? I *do* have patients to tend to."

"Yes," Nic said briskly. "Would one of you wizards set a ward so we can't be overheard? Then let's read and discuss."

IT TOOK SOME time for all of them to read, passing the documents around the circle, Wolfgang and Quinn both making notes as they went. Nic took the opportunity—why not?—to read each again as they were passed to her.

The threats, no matter how floridly couched, hadn't gotten any more pleasant in the interim.

Finally, Wolfgang sat back with a sigh, tossing the final document onto its appropriate pile. He raised a brow at Asa. "Do you want to take the lead or shall I? Your debate team won the Convocation Academy championship also."

"You captained," Asa conceded with a nod. "Quinn, you won the mock trial championship?"

"In trademark law," she replied, blushing faintly at the attention. "A lot of this stuff is beyond me."

"I bet that's not true," Wolfgang told her warmly.

"I'm regretting I didn't join the debate or mock trial teams," Alise said ruefully, then cocked her head at Nic. "You didn't either, did you?"

Nic snorted. *"Extracurriculars?* Of course not, for the same reason you didn't. Lord Elal wouldn't stomach *his* heirs wasting their time on clubs. Those are for people with nothing better to think about!" She deepened her voice and waved her arms in red-faced bluster in what she knew was a devastatingly accurate mimicry of her father, even before she'd reduced Alise to tears of laughter. "Apologies," Nic said to the rest of the group, abruptly aware that she wasn't behaving as befit a lady of a High House. "Kind of an inside, family joke, I guess."

"There are few in the Convocation who haven't encountered Lord Elal in some capacity or other," Asa remarked drily. "The imitation was uncannily accurate."

"My championship ability, apparently. Who needs extracurriculars?" Nic quipped, making everyone laugh. Again this feeling of camaraderie, of family—in a way she'd never felt with her actual family. Alise caught her eye with a half smile. Not the only one to observe this feeling then.

"Well, that and being the most powerful familiar in the Convocation," Quinn put in, rolling her eyes, "plus being bonded to possibly the most powerful wizard in the Convocation. You are an undefeatable pairing."

"Unless we're defeated before we barely begin," Nic said, gesturing to the documents. "Is it as bad as I think?"

"Probably," Wolfgang acknowledged. "You are no fool Lady Phel and, lack of extracurriculars notwithstanding, Elals have a reputation for canniness in these arenas. What we have here is—" He broke off at the same moment that Nic sensed Gabriel enter the study hall in a swirl of silver moonlight and deep, still waters.

Good. He'd calmed down somewhat. Nic had hoped that making him concentrate on training the water-wizards would focus his attention on what he could control. She studied him as he crossed the room, devastatingly handsome with his white hair blazing, elegant black coat flaring back to frame his broad shoulders and lean waist, delineated by the fitted Ophiel suit, also in black, and worked with silver embroidery. His dark eyes fixed on hers with an intent smolder, even as he courteously acknowledged the greetings of the people he passed, accepting their bows and curtseys with all the inherent grace and arrogance of any of the natural-born nobility.

Gabriel might still see himself as a humble farmer, but the magic had changed him. So had taking his rightful place as Lord Phel. Just as the house seemed to be restoring itself according to a pattern set by the Phel ancestors, Gabriel himself seemed to be maturing, fleshing out into the fully powerful wizard and leader where before there had been only the promise of it. Nic shivered inside, feeling the leap of answering passion elicited by her wizard's clearly prurient thoughts. Perhaps tonight would be an arcanium night.

As if he'd divined her thoughts, Gabriel gave her a slow, wicked smile, the sounds of conversation and birdsong resuming as Wolfgang dropped the wards. They all stood to acknowledge the lord's arrival, Nic smiling to herself at Gabriel's discomfort. Not all the way to noblesse oblige then.

"Let me get you a chair, Lord Phel," Quinn said, but Gabriel stopped her with a hand, which he then extended to Nic, drawing her to her feet as he took her chair, then settled her comfortably in his lap.

"No need," Gabriel replied smoothly as his hand followed the narrow of her waist and round of her hip, snugging her a bit closer against his groin and chest. His magic sipped at hers, a refined touch that spoke of his practicing. It was more of a chaste kiss of affection, a taste of her magic, than any replenishing. "I can listen and avail myself of my familiar at the same time."

Nic's ardent reaction to that remark, particularly him referring to her as his familiar—something normally confined to sexual intimacy—was probably less discreet. Certainly Gabriel sensed it through their bond, and the press of their bodies, a ripple of heated amusement coming from him. "I thought you were working with the water wizards," she murmured in his ear, taking the opportunity to press a kiss to the hollow beneath the lobe, which always affected him.

He squeezed her hip lightly, thumb brushing very high on her thigh. "I gave them exercises that will take a considerable

amount of time to solve. And I wanted to hear this. Continue,
Wizard Ratisbon."

With a flick of his fingers, mostly for their benefit as the
physical gesture was unnecessary, Wolfgang restored the ward,
outside noise abruptly ceasing. "As I began to say before Lord
Phel joined us, what we have here is a multi-pronged attack.
There are three main thrusts—complaints from other houses,
censure from Convocation Center, and summons from
Convocation Academy. All coordinated to arrive at once."

"Nic said this is standard Convocation tactics, to create an
avalanche of legal problems to overwhelm us."

"Indeed," Asa said, tapping lean fingers on the table.
"That's why I suggest we employ the strategy of refusing to
allow the avalanche and instead deal with this stone by stone."

"Exactly." Wolfgang nodded. "They're trying to handle
everything in the single hearing, attempting to use this pattern
of behavior they're trying to establish as the foundation for
everything else."

"Because any one of these offenses taken singly wouldn't
be enough to indict," Quinn said. "That's how they go after
trademark infringements, too. It's rarely worth the expense for
the Convocation judicial council to chase every infringement
complaint. They bide their time and compile evidence of
infractions, until the problem becomes significant enough to
create an impact beyond the houses involved, or if it will create
precedent. Otherwise, they leave it to the individual houses to
handle it through business negotiations. Fortunately, House
Phel has no trademark infringement issues, so that's not a
consideration."

Gabriel's strong thighs tensed beneath her bottom and Nic wriggled a little to distract him. No one but the two of them knew about Gabriel's infringement on House El-Adrel's trademark—well, besides Lady El-Adrel, Jadren, and probably Seliah, at this point—and that was because Lady El-Adrel chose extortion as a resolution. Still, given Quinn's summation, the single enchanted dagger shouldn't be enough to draw the Convocation's attention. Beyond whatever scheming led her to ensure Jadren's placement at House Phel as her spy and agent, it could be that Katica El-Adrel had elected that path because she knew one violation—particularly from a brand-new house—wouldn't get her much leverage.

"So, we file countersuits and legal arguments in a staggered pattern," Asa mused, tipping his head back to gaze at the ceiling as he thought, "forcing Convocation Center to splinter their responses and deal with each separately."

Wolfgang grinned broadly. "Yes. They tried to avalanche. We will nibble them to death."

"With any luck we can get the hearing delayed multiple times." Asa returned the smile, not as broad, but quietly anticipatory.

"And Convocation Academy?" Alise asked.

Asa leveled a look on Alise, stern, but not without sympathy. "I'm going to say what Lord and Lady Phel will not. The best solution is for you to return to Convocation Academy and complete your education as quickly as you can. Once you graduate, you will no doubt be welcomed back at House Phel."

"Without doubt," Gabriel agreed solemnly. "You have my

word on that."

Surprised that he hadn't argued about Alise going back to school, Nic waited, not quite avoiding Alise's stricken and pleading eyes.

"But you need me here," Alise argued, sounding young and uncertain.

Nic opened her mouth, but Gabriel squeezed her hip. Fine then.

"You've done incredible work for House Phel," Gabriel agreed, "and this will always be your home. You are welcome here any time, Alise, but I've given this thought. You know I'm no lover of Convocation customs, but even I can recognize that a Convocation Academy education—and degree—is critical for a magical citizen of this world. Hear me out," he said firmly when Alise opened her mouth. "I realize I'm an exception to that rule, as are Jadren and Seliah. But there's an old saw that the exception proves the rule—and all three of us have experienced difficulties because we lack that training and degree."

"Nic taught Seliah," Alise replied with a stubborn tilt to her chin that Nic absolutely recognized from the mirror. "I can learn what I need to know from the other wizards of House Phel."

"Not in your expertise," Gabriel corrected before Nic could. "The more that Nic tutors me based on her general understanding of wizardry, and all that Asa graciously shows me given his more advanced understanding in a tangential field, and every time I attempt to train others in water and moon magic, the more I realize how great my disadvantage is."

Alise snorted. "I was there at House Sammael when you ripped off the roof from across the valley, Lord Phel. You have power to spare and your lack of Convocation brainwashing is an advantage, not a—"

"It's both," Gabriel interrupted. "And the ways that my lack of education are a disadvantage are ones I bitterly regret. It's too late for me to change that. It's possibly too late for Jadren and Seliah to change that, if we're to keep them safe from the Convocation, but three of us in one house is more than enough. If you want to do your best by yourself, this family, and this house, then you'll go back to the academy—not incidentally taking one legal challenge off our plates—and you'll get that degree."

"Is this because I tired myself out?" Alise demanded, glaring at Nic. "I can't believe you told him about that."

"I didn't," Nic answered, and Alise flushed at her misstep. Gabriel said nothing, but the slide of his fingers down Nic's spine promised this conversation would be continued later. "Still," Nic added, "that incident only further supports the point that you would benefit from finishing your education."

Alise firmed her lips, giving Nic one last beseeching glance. "Maman is here. You are here. All of my friends are here. I don't want to go back to the academy."

Nic sympathized, she truly did. To her surprise, Quinn jumped in. "Buck up," she advised Alise briskly. "Every person here, with the exception of Lord Phel, survived Convocation Academy. If you don't have friends there, make some. Think of it as a service to House Phel if you have to, because the more friends you make now, the more allies we'll have in the future. If you don't want to go to back House Elal, you can come here for school holidays and other breaks."

"I've been disinherited," Alise pointed out, brightening and finding the relevant document. "My father won't pay my tuition so I *can't* go back!"

"House Phel will pay your tuition," Nic said, before Gabriel could. Dark arts knew where she'd find the money, but that was the least they could do for Alise. "And, when you see Nander at the academy—because I'm asking you to seek him out, make him give you the time of day, give him my love and good wishes whether he wants to hear it or not—and tell him that we'll cover his education, too, should he wish to separate himself from Papa."

"Diabolical," Gabriel whispered in her ear, his admiration as erotic as the caress of hot breath.

"You'd just better come through on those water-wizards," she whispered back.

"Have I ever failed you?"

"Fine," Alise said, sounding more angry than glum. "I'll go back to school. But I'm upping my course load and getting done as fast as possible. It'll be more expensive."

"In the short term," Nic agreed, "but we'll save long-term on your room and board."

"All right," Gabriel said, "that handles the Convocation Academy complaint."

"Not the question of Sabrina Sammael," Nic countered.

"The Sabrina Sammael summons is fishing," Asa put in decisively. "She trespassed on House Phel grounds without invitation and we have dozens of witnesses to the effect that Sabrina aided her brother in a hostile attack on the house. They're only guessing that we kept her captive, or killed her. Whatever reasons House Sammael has for keeping her home instead of sending her back to school, they have nothing to do with us. I suggest sending a reply to that effect."

"I wish I knew that Sabrina is all right, though," Nic commented unhappily. She didn't like feeling as if she'd sent Sabrina home to be abused in some way. Yes, the little bitch was awful, but she was also young and had been molded to be yet another terrible Sammael.

"You can't save everyone," Gabriel commented.

"Surely that's my line." It helped that he patted her with affection.

"All right, I believe we have a strategy for dealing with Convocation Center," Wolfgang said, reviewing his notes. "I'll come up with some specifics and Asa and Quinn can review. That leaves the question of the complaints from the various houses. I suggest we handle House El-Adrel by counter-suing over them illegally bonding Seliah. And that we ask for considerable compensation."

Nic easily sensed how much Gabriel didn't like that, but he swallowed back his reflexive argument and nodded. "I can draft that," she offered. "If nothing else, I know a great deal about the relative worth of a familiar like Seliah and how those negotiations ought to be handled."

"Good," Asa acknowledged. "I'll prepare the paperwork to file for Seliah's contract to Jadren, and review Jadren's contract as a minion to House Phel. Those transactions are so commonplace we can have them notarized and accepted into the Convocation Center records before El-Adrel realizes we went around them. If we play that correctly, by the time Jadren and Seliah resurface, there will be no question that they both belong contractually to House Phel."

"There are two complicating factors," Gabriel said. "The first is more straightforward. Jadren has no MP scorecard and, naturally, neither does Seliah. Neither officially exists to the Convocation."

Asa frowned. "You do have the Hanneil wizard, Ziv, on staff now. They weren't asked to test Jadren and Seliah?"

Gabriel shook his head. "It frankly didn't occur to me."

"And Wizard Ziv has no oracle head," Nic put in. "Isn't that needed?"

"I'm not fully certain," Asa answered thoughtfully. "I'll discuss with Ziv. And, as neither Jadren nor Seliah are in residence, it's something of a moot point at the moment. I'll mull what we can do about the problem of their citizenship."

"That won't stop us from responding to House El-Adrel, however," Wolfgang said, with a canny smile. "Katica El-Adrel might be more amenable to dropping charges on both sides if she's invested in keeping Jadren off the record."

Nic said nothing and neither did Gabriel. The problem of Jadren and whether to protect him from the house of his birth could wait.

"And the other complication, Lord Phel?" Asa inquired.

Gabriel gave Nic a questioning look. She nodded, encouraging him to share. If not now, when? "We have reason to believe that El-Adrel, Sammael, and Elal are conspiring together against Phel," he said.

Quinn sighed philosophically. Wolfgang and Asa exchanged considering looks. Wolfgang kicked back in his chair, extending long legs and folding elegant hands over his lean belly. "I did wonder. It explains a great deal."

"Besides, this is the Convocation," Asa agreed wearily. "It would barely count as having a new house rise up if at least some of the other High Houses *weren't* conspiring to bring them down."

"Let alone a 'new' house that's the resurrection of a previous High House brought down under questionable circumstances," Nic said darkly, drawing everyone's attention. Gabriel tightened his grip on her waist, but it felt more like a gesture of support than warning.

"Questionable in what way?" Alise asked, frowning. "All I know is that houses lose their Convocation status if the family doesn't produce at least one wizard in a generation. Now that I think of it, all the High Houses have so many branches of family that it sounds almost impossible for a High House not to produce at least one wizard. How did it happen in the Phel family?" she asked Gabriel.

He shrugged, his magic fogging a bit. "How does the old joke go? Gradually and then all at once."

Nobody laughed. "The very slowly part," Quinn said thoughtfully, "has been seen throughout Convocation history. One of my study concentrations at the academy," she added as an aside.

"True," Asa said. "But the typical descent of a High House is the mirror of its ascent—a High House is demoted to second tier, then gracefully declines to third, as others rise to take their places. Why have we never questioned why House Phel simply vanished?"

"Because we're still right here," Gabriel answered drily.

Asa waved an apologetic hand. "From the Convocation rolls, I mean."

"And arguably from collective awareness," Nic put in. "When we received your application for the Betrothal Trials, Maman had to research the house and family. Even the Elal spies didn't have a lot to go on."

"Which is saying something," Asa remarked with a wry wince for Elal's famed ability to find out anything about anyone they wished to.

"All we knew offhand was that the house had sunk into the swamplands of Meresin," Nic said very seriously. "I expected to live in a ramshackle houseboat, or a hut on stilts." Gabriel growled softly, giving her hip a little pinch, and she giggled, pleased to have teased him about it.

"All families tell tales," Quinn said, looking to Gabriel. "What does yours say about the loss of your high-house status, Lord Phel?"

"Very little, in truth. I grew up believing myself to be a simple farmer. The manse indeed was mostly underwater and we regarded it as an ancient ruin—fascinating, but belonging to another time, place, and people." He tipped his head back to gaze at the ceiling, with its beautifully finished woodwork.

This hall, this entire wing had been submerged, home to marsh creatures, until only a short time ago. Nic, who was infinitely more familiar than Gabriel with the miracles magic could perform, found the massive transformation startling to contemplate. She could only guess how unsettling it might be for him. She laid a palm over his heart and he dropped his gaze to smile at her, laying a hand over hers.

"The old family never seemed relevant to us," he continued. "We had little to do with the Convocation or much of the world beyond the borders of Meresin. The old tales of wizards and magic... well, they seemed like a colorful mythology that had nothing to do with planting crops and tending orchards. In truth, I think most of us didn't really believe in magic at all until..."

"Until you manifested as a powerful wizard, stunning everyone," Nic finished for him, full of pride and affection. She turned to the others. "I've talked to various people—including Gabriel's parents—asking what their grandparents said of the time before. They consider those stories to be tall tales, full of fancy and nonsense, but the elements point to the involvement and collusion of several High Houses in a concerted attack, namely Sammael, El-Adrel, and Elal."

Everyone looked grave, Wolfgang whistling low under his breath. "Not for the first time, I'm glad to have been born to a second-tier house."

"Agreed," Quinn said fervently.

Alise gave Nic a rueful look. "I suppose it was too much to hope that Elal's involvement in House Phel's misfortunes was a recent development."

She didn't know the half of it.

"I suggest you consider a fourth house for your list of colluding traitors," Asa said. "It hasn't been *that* many generations since the fall of House Phel. Not nearly enough time has passed for a Convocation-shattering event like the utter collapse of a High House to have disappeared from memory."

"And the textbooks," Quinn put in. "I should have read about it and I never did, I'm sure of that."

"There have to be records, at least of the official version of events," Wolfgang said, "even if they're sealed. The Convocation never gets rid of anything."

"When Gabriel applied to Convocation Center to restore Phel as a house," Nic told them, "they somehow neglected to give him access to the old House Phel records."

"They didn't tell me such things existed," Gabriel corrected.

Asa looked unsurprised. "The conspiracy runs deep. For this to have been so thoroughly covered over, we have to look to a house capable of altering memory."

That hadn't occurred to Nic and it should have. "You suspect Refoel of interfering?"

He looked briefly startled, then shook his head. "No. I could be idealizing the house of my birth, and Refoel has its faults certainly, but Refoel cleaves to its ethic of using magic only to heal and nurture, never to destroy. We do, however, share a border with a High House easily capable of such nefarious actions, an ancient enemy we keep a very close eye on."

"You're thinking of House Hanneil," Alise said.

"Hanneil with the psychic magic to alter memory," Nic said on a sigh of resignation. "Perhaps even to suppress magical ability in a family?"

Gabriel sat still beneath her, absorbing that information. "Then why was I different?"

She rolled her eyes. "Besides the fact that you are different in every way?"

"Lord Phel has a point," Asa put in. "Why Seliah and why him, after all this time? Two siblings in a single generation. Something changed. Some sort of repressed magical break-through? I need to research this." He gave Nic and Gabriel a thoughtful look. "You should consider asking House Refoel for aid."

Gabriel frowned, not understanding. "We have an alliance with House Refoel. That's why you're here."

"No." Nic shook her head at him. "We have a business contract. House Refoel never allies or gives aid to any house," she explained, looking at Asa. "They stay neutral."

"I think in this case," Asa said slowly, "if they can be per-suaded that Hanneil is moving to create a multi-high-house alliance, they might make an exception."

"But is that what is going on?" Quinn said into the ensuing silence. "This is all supposition."

"We need a lot more information," Nic said, as Gabriel seemed still stunned into silent contemplation. She leveled a look on Alise. "Will going back to school with your dutiful tail tucked between your legs sit easier if we task you to infiltrate the records and copy and send everything you can on House Phel?"

A smile gradually lit Alise's face. "It will, yes. Challenge accepted."

~ 15 ~

"I THOUGHT WE decided that trying to go to House Hanneil, again, was definitely a bad idea," Seliah said to him, far from the first time. "I think we should go to House Refoel," she added, also far from the first time.

"Why didn't you mention that idea before this?" he inquired sarcastically, rewarded by a fierce amber glare. "Besides, when I apparently agreed that House Hanneil was a bad idea, my cock was in your mouth and I can be excused for not listening to a word you were saying."

"If your cock had actually been in my mouth, I wouldn't have been able to speak," she retorted with a cheeky smile. "You're well endowed enough that a girl wouldn't be able to talk around it."

He swallowed a laugh, not wanting to encourage her. Seliah continued to be a puzzling blend of wide-eyed naivete and an earthy sensuality beyond her years and actual experience. That she could give as good as she got in the scathing insults department made it difficult to shut her up with a well-aimed remark. It also made him love her all that much more, which was equally distressing, although on an entirely different scale.

"I changed my mind," he informed her. "Besides there's no point in going to House Refoel. We're both of us healed. Even Vale is in tip-top condition, you admitted that much."

Seliah's relief at hearing he'd groomed Vale and put him in an enclosed pasture to eat his brains out on fresh grass had been almost embarrassing, she'd clearly thought so little of his abilities in that arena. She'd been less pleased when she reviewed his efforts in detail, going to pains to instruct him in the finer points of equine care. Because he considered Vale to be their heroic savior in equal weight to being a hot-headed fart-beast who'd galloped off with him at the worst possible moment, Jadren made an effort to pay attention and didn't make a single remark about this being work for hostlers and beneath a scion of House El-Adrel, tempting as it was to annoy Seliah by saying so. Besides which—clearly in this new life he led, replete with freedom even as it lacked basic conveniences like elemental-powered carriages—it was useful information to know.

Also... He was in simply too good of a mood to dredge up his normally caustic outlook on life. The spring morning was bright and sunny, delightfully mild. He was brimming with Seliah's magic and replete from sating himself in her deliciously sensuous body. They'd spent the remainder of the afternoon and the entire night in bed, alternating bouts of intense sex with sleeping entwined around each other, and taking turns fetching snacks. Never had he slept so hard or so peacefully. And, even though the sleep had been interrupted by them reaching for each other, the blaze of desire billowing them into wakefulness, he figured they'd easily spent around twenty hours in bed, so he was surprisingly well rested.

He almost caught himself humming a jaunty tune before he realized and stopped in horror. That was a bridge too far.

Glancing over at Seliah, who was performing the final checks on the packs strapped to the patient Vale, he surreptitiously admired her unusual beauty. Tall and lean in her black Ophiel fighting leathers, with legs that went on forever, she moved with the grace of a wild creature. She'd braided her dark hair at her temples, to keep the long, silky strands out of her face, but otherwise acceded to his request that she leave it loose. He'd never been in the privileged position of having a lover he could make such requests of and it gave him an odd feeling of triumph mixed with trepidation. He both treasured the intense joy of having her and obsessively worried about the pain of losing her, which would inevitably occur, no doubt sooner rather than later.

What a mess he was.

"The *point* of going to Refoel," she was saying and he hastily paid attention when she raised a brow at him, "is to discover more about your healing ability. This is something we both agree you need to know."

"House Hanneil does all the MP score testing," he replied. "They can assess exactly what kind of magic I have *and* they can give me an official scorecard."

"Why do you even care about that?" She stretched herself up to reach higher on Vale's back, the position showing off her perfectly round and delectable ass, and he couldn't resist sidling up behind her and cupping it with both hands.

"They could give you a scorecard, too," he murmured,

kissing the side of her neck as she stilled, then tilted her head to give him better access.

"Why would *I* even care about that?" she reframed the question in a dry tone, but her throaty voice softened the sarcasm.

He slid his hands over the narrow flare of her hips, savoring the neat curves of her pelvis that arrowed down to the triangle of her mound, so nicely delineated in those close-fitting leathers. Sliding his fingers into the gap between her thighs, he caressed her mound, marveling at the addictive heat radiating from it, and lifted his other hand to mold over her small breast, loving how her nipple hardened in response, leaping to his touch. She let out one of those little moan-sighs that never failed to get to him, and leaned back against his chest. "We can't mess up the bed again," she purred. "I already put clean sheets on it."

"I recall," he said on a snort. She'd insisted on doing that menial chore and others, cleaning up the little cottage and leaving coin for the occupants on top of it. A soft heart and softer head, not that he'd make the mistake of saying so. Seliah might be soft in some ways, including the most enticing ones, but never forget what a vicious and ruthless fighter she could be when provoked. Feeling reckless, he nipped her on the ear for a bit of extra provocation. "Nothing wrong with the grass right here," he suggested.

"Except that we're out in the open, anyone could come by, and *you* are avoiding the subject." She turned in his arms and slid her hands behind his neck. "Why would either of us want an MP scorecard? A useless piece of paper that only establishes rank in the hoity-toity world of Convocation princes and princesses."

Dark arts how he loved her. Nobody said things like that. "Is it useless or is it good for establishing rank?" he teased.

"Exactly." She wrinkled her nose at him. "Jadren, you don't need an MP scorecard or to impress anyone with your rank. What you *need* is to find out the nature of your magic and how that device of your mother's allowed you to focus it to use on someone else. House Refoel's expertise in healing magic exceeds anyone else's in the Convocation, right? We wouldn't go to Refoel with questions about moon magic. We shouldn't go to Hanneil with questions about healing magic."

"Suddenly you're an authority on Convocation houses and their areas of specialty."

"I know a few of them anyway. Besides which, remember when you approached House Hanneil only a few days ago and they tried to kill you?"

"Did a pretty thorough job of it, too," he pointed out.

"Don't remind me."

"It would be different this time," he argued. He'd been mulling this exact question. "That patrol apprehended me because they thought I was a houseless, rogue wizard. I couldn't tell them I'm a scion of House El-Adrel as I had no identification that way."

"Which you still don't have," she pointed out relentlessly while softly stroking the back of his neck, which felt lovely, but also seemed like petting him to be calm, so he pulled away, stalking a few strides toward the empty road that wended past the farmed clearing. He didn't need to be managed, least of all by his familiar. Care and feeding of wizards, indeed.

"Jadren," she continued, still in that sympathetic tone that rankled, "you were able to waltz up to House Sammael and knock on the door to rescue me because Lord Igino Sammael knows you, you told me that." She paused. "Is that why you want this MP scorecard so badly, to prove that you're a wizard to be reckoned with? Because you are that. You don't need a piece of paper saying so."

"Aren't you so wise?" he sneered. *Ouch.* Seliah saw into him far too well for comfort. "Stop calling it a piece of paper. You don't understand the significance of having that documentation. I can't get a job anywhere without it. I'm not even a citizen of the Convocation without it. Even commoners have citizenship papers or marks that show they have the right to be where they live. I have *nothing*, which means I am nothing. For all intents and purposes, I don't exist, Seliah. My beloved Maman saw to that."

"You *do* exist, though. You don't need anyone else to say so for that to be true."

"Tell that to the Convocation," he retorted bitterly.

Seliah regarded him with that same sapping sympathy, her amber eyes soft with compassion. "What your mother did to you is heinous, Jadren, but you're free of her now. You *are* someone and you have a job—at House Phel."

"That's just another kind of servitude," he snarled. "I'm trapped no matter which way I turn. I might as well be still confined to one of my mother's glass cages for all the real freedom I have."

At last her sympathy faded, her gaze hardening. "Trapped

by your bond to me, you mean."

Yes. No. He didn't know. "The bond confines you, too," he pointed out, with a sense that he'd stepped onto the slick, shifting sands of one of those lethal sinkholes she'd warned him about.

"This again?" She tapped her foot. "I don't feel confined by my bond to you. I feel strengthened by it. More, I know that *you* are strengthened by your bond to me. So, in your flailing about to find your identity or whatever it is you're doing, don't pretend that this is anything rational. I get that you're deeply messed up, Jadren. Guess what? So am I. But that's what makes us good together."

He stared at her, practically speechless. "You're actually arguing that adding fucked-up to fucked-up doesn't equal twice as fucked, doesn't even result in the one canceling out the other, but somehow winds up in the positive column?"

She frowned at him, punching her hands to her hips. "As we're talking about human beings, not numbers to be added and subtracted, yes!"

"We are not human beings," he informed her silkily. "We are wizard and familiar." He stabbed a thumb at his chest and then pointed at her to emphasize their roles, as if she might be unclear.

Seliah actually rolled her eyes at him. "We are human beings with magical ability. That doesn't take away from our humanity."

"So you admit adding and subtracting makes sense in this scenario," he crowed triumphantly.

She gazed at him blankly. "I've forgotten what we're arguing about."

To be fair, so had he. "For some absurd reason, I'm arguing with my familiar about what I plan to do. If you're so determined to be bound to me, to follow wherever I go, then you'd best learn to be obedient to your wizard's will," he informed her, rather enjoying as she reacted first with shock, then with annoyance. Far better than that sympathy that only weakened him. "Wizard," he declared, repeating the thumb-stabbing gesture, then pointing at her again. "Familiar. We're going to House Hanneil."

She gazed at him for a beat, then raised her brows in supercilious question. "Are you done beating your chest at me now?"

The woman could sure take the wind out of his sails in a trice.

Before he could summon an appropriately scathing answer, she continued. "How do you know you're the wizard and I'm the familiar?" she asked in a falsely sweet tone, eyes wide with mock innocence. "We have no paperwork saying so."

"I see what you're doing there," Jadren ground out. "And your ridiculous argument and baseless logic won't sway me."

"How about the argument that your desire to go to House Hanneil is entirely about your ego and possibly your ongoing self-destructive tendencies?"

"If so, that's my problem."

"Is it?" she asked with quiet intensity. "Seems like that's *our* problem. What happens if they throw me off the cliff with you? I can't survive that fall."

"They won't kill a valuable familiar." Though the image of Seliah, smashed and shattered at the bottom of that cliff made his blood run cold.

"Oh, right." Seliah rolled her eyes and cocked one hip. "They'll toss *you* off again—and this time there won't be anyone coming to drag you off those rocks—and me, they'll just capture and bond to whatever wizard they decide I'd serve best as a living asset."

"They won't be able to, since I can't die," he replied before thinking.

"If that was meant to be reassuring, it fell far short. Not even as far as you fell off that cliff."

"I didn't fall, I was thrown," he retorted before he realized he'd just taken another dive, falling for that bait. Seliah could twist him up until he couldn't see straight. "At any rate, my decision is final. I'm going to House Hanneil. You can either go home or come with me."

"Or I could go to House Refoel," she said, thoughtfully tapping a finger against her lip. "Or I could report to Convocation Center for testing and training. Really, if I'm free to do as I like, I have all sorts of options."

"You are *not* free to do as you like," he replied, setting his teeth. "I gave you *two* options, which is more than most familiars get. Pick one."

"You're not the boss of me."

"I *am* the boss of you," he fired back, part of him in the back of his mind observing that this sounded like a children's argument.

She turned her back on him, hair rippling in a dark wave

with gleaming blue highlights that reminded him of moonlight on still water, the curling tips pointing at that enticing rear end, just to taunt him and make him even more miserable. "Vale is *my* horse," she was saying, then looked over her shoulder at him with a narrowed gaze. He hastily yanked his own avid stare off her pert bottom. "If we part ways, he goes with me."

"He's your brother's horse," Jadren retorted, mostly to annoy her. And because arguing with her was like a drug he couldn't quit. Vale swung his head around and blew out an equine remark between grass-slobbered lips that Jadren couldn't interpret.

"Vale is his own horse," Seliah amended, scratching under Vale's forelock. "But he's on loan to me."

"Fine. I'll take my things and walk to House Hanneil."

She spun around, fully exasperated. "Do you seriously have a death wish?"

In truth, he probably did. Just as everyone wished for the one thing they could never have. "I have a gut feeling I should go to House Hanneil. Call it my wizard's intuition."

"Your wizard's idiocy and stubborn short-sightedness more like," she grumbled. "Do you want to walk or ride first?"

"What do you mean?" he asked, feeling a bit stupid.

"Only one horse." She pointed to Vale, as if he might've failed to notice the big gelding. "Despite what the romantic novels say, it's not all that feasible for two people to share one horse for any length of time, especially not with this much baggage. We'll have to take turns riding."

"Who are you accusing of having baggage?" he quipped, unable to resist the joke. It helped to justify the smile widening his lips, even though the real reason for it was the sheer giddy relief that she'd decided to come with him. It meant far more than it should that she chose him. Yes, it called her good judgment into question, but that just showed how alike they were.

"I fully own my baggage," she replied with an answering smile. "Even if most of the literal baggage here is mostly what Gabriel foisted upon me."

"We could make an argument that a fair amount of the metaphorical baggage is, too."

Her lips twisted ruefully and she dipped her chin to acknowledge the point. "Family can be that way. How about we start out walking? We're both rested and that will keep Vale fresher longer. Maybe we can buy another horse along the way. Who knows? Maybe we can even talk your murderers at House Hanneil into giving us your mare back. She does belong to House Phel after all. There have to be Convocation rules about that, as there are for every other cursed thing."

She was probably right, though he didn't know what they were. "Then you're coming with me?" he asked, with a sense of relieved gratitude.

"Where you go, I go, Wizard," she answered with a hint of a smile on her naturally grave face. "Besides, you need someone to keep your skin intact. I like it the way it is."

Unable to resist her, he pulled her close. "I like your skin, too."

Almost lazily, she looped her hands behind his neck, toying with the short hairs there as she liked to do, inclining her long body against his. "You certainly spent enough time examining every fingertip of it."

How well he remembered. Her tawny, satin-soft skin held endless fascination for him, especially when she purred so delightfully in response to his explorations. "You truly will come with me to House Hanneil, even though you think it's a bad idea?"

"I truly will," she answered, making it sound like a vow. In a way, he supposed it was.

He kissed her, sinking into the welcome of her full, sensual lips. Maybe they could stay in the little cottage another day. To his surprise, he found himself thinking of the place with nostalgic affection, not as a poorly ventilated hut, but as a cozy nest of peace and safety. When had he ever had that? Never. And he wanted more.

But, he reminded himself, it wasn't truly safe. That was an illusion, a delusion to believe that he was in any position to take care of Seliah. She would never be safe until he figured out how to be wizard enough to protect her. "What did I do to deserve you?"

She shook her head sadly. "Terrible things, no doubt. But it's too late to repent of your past ill deeds. You're stuck with me now."

Sliding his fingers along the glossy, intricate coils of the braid alongside her face, he let out a dramatic sigh. "I shall just have to bear my punishment with good grace. Off we go to House Hanneil, then."

"All right, but I reserve the right to—"

"I say House El-Adrel," a cool voice interrupted.

Jadren whirled at the sound of it, shocked out of his skin at the incongruity of his sister suddenly appearing there, of all places—and by the fact that she had apparently stepped out of thin air. "Ozana," he said flatly, and surreptitiously palmed a couple of tools from his vest. Good thing Seliah had thought to bring a spare set of clothing for him, along with his usual tools. She knew his propensity for disaster far too well. "What an unexpected displeasure."

Ozana smiled thinly, a close-lipped echo of their Maman's elegant charm, and ran a hand to unnecessarily smooth her sleek cap of auburn hair, her wizard-black eyes hard on him. She wore white and gold, a shimmering tribute to the El-Adrel colors, even wearing lightning-bolt earrings that dangled nearly the length of her long neck. The figure-skimming sheath dress showed off her long legs and gold heels—though the grimace she made as her stilettos sank into the turf somewhat ruined the effect.

"You've been a naughty tyke, Jaddy-boy," she said accusingly, lifting one heel to glare at the soil and tufts of grass on it, as if he'd put it there. "Leaving without permission. Making off with House El-Adrel property." She plucked off the offending turf and flicked it aside, the oil-sheened black of her eyes shimmering as they slid to Seliah. Ozana looked her over with greedy and proprietary interest. "Pretty," Ozana remarked, showing teeth in predatory delight. "Nummy magic."

"Mine," Jadren said, stepping in front of Seliah. Her magic had gone silver-sharp and ice-cold. He was familiar with that particular flavor from being around Gabriel Phel when he lost his temper and truly unleashed his powerful magic—to the point of summoning torrential storms and manifesting silver spikes from moonlight. Seliah couldn't manifest her magic, naturally, but the explosive levels of it built just the same. And similarly would need somewhere to go.

"The familiar belongs to House El-Adrel," Ozana coolly corrected, "as do you. It's convenient that you can return together. Still, I wouldn't get too full of yourself. I have no idea why Maman gave her to you instead of to me, but I've lodged a complaint and requested that the decision be reversed. I'm elder, the familiar is mine by right of birth order."

"She is already bonded to me."

"Easily dealt with if you're dead, then she's mine as she should have been to begin with."

"You know," Seliah put in, "I'm standing right here."

"I'm not so easy to kill, if you haven't noticed," Jadren said, ignoring Seliah's words, but backing closer to her.

Ozana waved that off, though a pair of unattractive lines puckered her elegantly winged brows. "You do have a cat's knack for escaping danger, but all cats die in the end, and so will you, brother dear."

"Everyone dies in the end," he corrected, sidling another step closer to Seliah. "The only question is when that end occurs."

"So philosophical when you're not yammering with insanity and don't move another step. Here, let me help."

Too late, Jadren dodged. But even had he been faster, he couldn't have outpaced the golden lasso Ozana shot at him from her sleeve. She cackled in pure delight as the enchanted metal chain wrapped itself around him at lightning speed, pinning his arms to his sides, his hands flattened against his thighs. A silver blade shot past his head and *thunked* against Ozana's hastily erected ward, his wizard-sister raising her brows in interest as the dagger fell harmlessly to the grass.

"How interesting," Ozana observed. "She bites. A fighting familiar makes this new pet even more exotic. Don't struggle, Jaddy-boy, the noose only tightens if you do. And gets sharper. I made it myself."

He'd already discovered as much, the metal loops digging in, lacerating his flesh so that blood soaked into his leathers and welled up to run down his arms. Great, and he'd had this new set on for, what? Maybe a whole hour. Behind him Seliah yelped, and he spun to see as Ozana strolled past. Though he tried not to move his arms, the enchanted lasso clearly interpreted the movement as struggling, and tightened further. Jadren gritted his teeth against the pain. At least that was something he had plenty of practice doing.

One of his mother's automatons had clasped Seliah in its arms, though it seemed to be struggling with its next steps. Instead of meekly resigning herself to her captor's superior strength, Seliah had—naturally—lost her shit and gone into feral wildcat mode, shrieking and squirming. She raked her nails across the automaton's eyes with no result, as the thing wasn't alive, kicking her booted feet against its metallic legs with a clanging sound like bells. Ozana glanced at him. "Make her stop before she hurts herself."

"Good luck making Seliah do anything," he drawled, morbidly amused by Seliah's rapid de-evolution into her wild self. The automaton, clearly inhabited by a spirit, no doubt harnessed and tasked to the job by an Elal wizard—the amazing part was that he hadn't seen it before—wasn't intelligent enough to adapt to the confusing behavior of its captive. Still, it didn't need to be. It simply had to hold on.

Ozana walked around the little scene as if taking in an art installation. Every once in a while, she looked over to Jadren, assessing his reaction as Seliah's foul-mouthed cursing rolled over them in waves. Finally, with an exasperated sigh, Ozana pointed at Seliah and a metal and leather gag clamped itself over Seliah's mouth. She'd learned that particular trick from their mother and it looked exactly the same.

"You know," Ozana said conversationally into the new silence, broken only by Seliah's muffled grunting. "I thought Maman had exaggerated, but the creature really is quite untamed, isn't she? Clearly you've made no progress at all. Don't you know how to use the bond to ensure obedience?"

Ah. Actually Jadren did not. Beyond forcing a familiar into alternate form and keeping them there until they agreed to be more biddable, he didn't know of any way the bond could be used to force submission to a wizard's will. Another area of ignorance left by his lack of Convocation Academy education. At the same time, he wasn't sorry on this one. He liked Seliah's fire.

So long as it didn't get her killed. Ozana sighed sadly at his lack of response and snapped her fingers. Two more automatons stepped out of nowhere, going to aid the first. Since Jadren had the wit to observe this time, he saw how they had actually moved through a dense patch of air, only appearing to be transported from nothingness. More Elal wizardry, using spirits to mimic the air and hide their El-Adrel allies. That

meant this group had arrived some time ago, to have surrounded him and Seliah so effectively. Dark arts only knew
what Ozana had overheard before she decided to show herself.

More critical—did the people back at House Phel realize
this possibility? Nic was savvy about Elal wizardry, but she
might not have been privy to this particular application. And
Alise was too young to have been initiated in all of the Elal
defensive—and offensive—secrets. It wouldn't take much to
distract the trusting denizens of House Phel with some kind of
feint, legal or otherwise, while spirits obscured the approach of
a physical army. They'd be sitting ducks, happily quacking and
dabbling or whatever it was ducks did. Jadren cursed himself.
He should've realized Elal wouldn't take his defeat at Gabriel
Phel's hands lightly. He'd want revenge.

Ozana positively twinkled at his catching up to what she'd
no doubt known for ages. "It's too bad, really, little brother,
that you couldn't ever figure out how to please Maman. Being
in her confidence is so much better than not. Too late now,
however, as she's most displeased with you for absconding
with your lovely present. However did you manage to
escape?"

He bared his teeth at her, which was the most defiance he
could muster under the circumstances. "You never could
figure out how to sweettalk the house," he gritted out, trying
to sound insouciant, but the words definitely coming out
pained. "She's always hated you."

The perfect oval of her pale, delicately freckled face began
to spiderweb from the edges with the maroon of old blood and
sibling rivalries. "The house!" she scoffed, a hint of a frustrated

screech in her voice. "It's not sentient, you know. That's a bunch of superstitious claptrap. It's just a building with magical elements, like any other enchanted artifact. You don't *talk* to the thing!"

And she wondered why the house didn't like her. Yes, the house—meaning the literal, physical House El-Adrel—could be a real bitch, mischievous, mercurial, and occasionally downright sadistic, but she also loved her denizens. At times, the house reminded Jadren of a cat whose loving affection included treating her people like mice to torment. You never knew when you'd get the purring, cuddling version of the house or the swat with claws extended that drew blood. But it did help if you knew how to pet cats. Or if you were at least willing to try. Ozana's insistence on treating the house like an inanimate object without feelings had not endeared her to their childhood home.

"Remember when you got trapped in the atrium and the house changed the whole thing into a globe?" The memory cheered him enough that he could speak over the pain. Come to think of it, the chain was hurting less now. He was healing rapidly, thanks to the massive sex-infusion of Seliah's magic. *Stronger together, remember? This is why you wanted me for your familiar.* Seliah's words echoed annoyingly in his mind, emphasized by her mute glare at him from the confining embrace of the automaton.

"Then the globe detached itself from the rest of the house and rolled downhill," he reminded Ozana gleefully. That had been truly fucking hysterical, his already startlingly malicious eight-year-old older sister had been tossed inside the rolling ball like a furious, red-furred rodent, beating her fists against the glass and screaming without sound. He'd been only five at the time—and sporting numerous cuts and bruises from Ozana playing scientist on him, a foreshadowing of things to come— and he'd fallen to the lush grass in fits of laughter, unable to catch his breath from the hilarity of it all. Their parents had been summoned by the panicked wizard-nanny and it had taken hours for their mother and father to charm the house into releasing Ozana.

Mostly it had been their father who'd got it done. The house resisted being leveraged by wizardry, even a wizard as powerful as their Maman, but it had a soft spot for the gentle, loving Fyrdo, which was probably how he'd managed to effect Jadren and Seliah's escape from the labyrinthine laboratory where his mother had imprisoned them. No way would Jadren even hint at his father's involvement in their escape, however. Hopefully Ozana's apparent ignorance of how they'd escaped meant their mother hadn't figured it out either. A relief to know, as a wizard could make a disobedient familiar's life very, very unpleasant. Jadren met Seliah's irate amber gaze and tried to send reassurance along their bond. "What more evidence do you need?" he taunted Ozana. "It took a special hate to do that to a kid."

The spiderwebbing of maroon humiliated rage had blossomed into a full flush encompassing Ozana's entire face. "That was *not* the house acting on its own. It was an embedded spell that I accidentally activated. The cursed place is riddled with layers upon layers of enchantments carelessly left behind by our wizard ancestors. The fact that the house is so resistant to wizardry is just proof of that."

"Yeah, keep telling yourself that, Zany." With the use of her hated childhood nickname, Ozana's face purpled further. She always had been ridiculously easy to infuriate. A special gift of his. "You know that you'll never be Lady El-Adrel if you can't manage the house."

"At least *I* have a shot at being Maman's heir," Ozana snarled, stalking closer to him. "Unlike you. She will be very pleased with me for returning her errant lab rat—and this potent familiar. You'll see when you're dead and the Phel familiar is mine. I will be a force to be reckoned with."

"You sound like a villain from one of those books our nanny read to us. Hasn't your reading material matured at all?" He didn't bother pointing out the flaw in Ozana's logic. She never had been much of a thinker, as evidenced by the fact that she'd never quite put together just how difficult Jadren was to kill. She was, however, an impulsive fireball of emotion, and he'd always known how to light her fuse.

With an incoherent screech, Ozana leapt on him, knocking him to the ground as she flailed at his face. Perfect. He whistled for Vale as he'd heard Gabriel do and, at the same time, fast-enchanted the tool he'd palmed. He stabbed the tool, a simple spike, into Ozana's leg where she straddled him, then jabbed a second spike into her back above her heart—and fired his magic into it. The electric current sent Ozana into a paroxysm. With any luck, it would stop her heart, at least temporarily. The shock of his lightning fed back into his own nerves, which hurt, but his healing magic, nicely boosted by Seliah's shimmering moon and cooling water, buffered the worst of it.

As Ozana lost consciousness, her magic vanished from the chain binding him, releasing its hold. She toppled over as he shrugged her and the chain off, his sister jerking spastically. The shock wouldn't kill her, as she'd also inherited their mother's resistance to injury—not to Jadren's immortal extent and probably not even to their mother's—though how much Ozana understood that about herself was debatable.

Jadren pushed up, a bit more rattled by that shock that he'd anticipated, though his head was clearing rapidly, and looked to Seliah. As he'd hoped, Vale had used his excellent horse-sense and charged the automaton holding Seliah. She had escaped its clutches and staggered away, the gag having fallen to the ground, and seemed to be watching in some astonishment as Vale trampled one automaton beneath his hooves while battling the other two.

The creations moved too ponderously to fight the excellently trained war horse, even with Vale laden with their bags, and they were shortly all piles of scrap metal. Seliah started when Jadren set a hand on her, her still mostly feral gaze swinging to him wildly. "It's me," he told her, stroking her back. "You're safe now."

Her eyes cleared somewhat, her stare a bit less full of animal panic. "Safe?" she squeaked. "This is what you call *safe*?"

He grinned at her, beyond relieved to see her regaining her equilibrium again so quickly. Good thing, as they needed to put a move on. "I'd say safe as houses, but... well, you've met House El-Adrel and she's the last thing from safe. Fortunately she likes me much better than Zany here. I'd introduce you but..." He waved a hand at the satisfyingly incapacitated Ozana. "She's a bit out of sorts."

~ 16 ~

SELLY LOVED JADREN'S resilience and darkly irrepressible humor—both no doubt key to his having survived everything that had been done to him with his sanity (relatively) intact—but at this particular moment, she wasn't amused.

"*That* is your sister?" she ground out, not really a question, pointing at the auburn-haired woman still twitching on the grass. Green and brown smears sullied the striking woman's once pristine white sheath dress and smoke wafted from her skin rather disconcertingly. "What did you do to her?"

"Nothing that she didn't deserve," Jadren answered, a bit defensively. "We really didn't need her carting us back to House El-Adrel."

"Oh, I'm not arguing the result," Selly said. "I'm just fascinated by this thing I didn't know you could do. Also, if you could zap her like that, why you didn't do it sooner." Like before that bitch muzzled her, or before the metal monster nearly crushed her. She'd be all over bruises and she'd *just* been enjoying feeling fully healthy and rested again. Speaking of injuries, she went to check Vale. A few lacerations marred his glossy dark hide, mostly on his lower legs, but he seemed sound overall.

When she patted him comfortingly, he rolled his eyes wildly at her, clearly displeased by the repeated attacks by unnatural creatures. "You and me, both, buddy," she said, stroking his long nose. He bumped her with it, blowing out a breath through his lips as he ducked his head, and she obligingly scratched the itchy spots between his ears and under his forelock.

"I'm sorry," Jadren said, sounding genuinely contrite and putting his arms around her from behind, sandwiching her between horse and man in a most comforting way. He'd done this before, only with much more erotic intent, and she surprised herself at how it settled something deep inside her to be held this way. "I know you were afraid, but I had to wait for her to get close enough for me to jab her." He took her hand and pressed a metal piece into her hand. "I had to make this on the fly and I wasn't sure how well it would work."

She edged back from Vale, just in case, and looked at the innocuous-seeming spike in her hand. "Will it... go off again?"

He chuckled and moved her hair aside to kiss her neck in that spot he'd discovered melted her with alarming speed. Indeed and against all practicality, given their circumstances, her blood leapt in eager response, desire shimmering through her.

"No," Jadren murmured against her skin, nipping lightly, like a lightning bolt right there, zapping her arousal to the next level. She moaned and he echoed the sound, vibrating through her from his chest against her back, his hardening groin against her bottom. "It needs wizardry to work. Probably only mine, though I could maybe make one that anyone could use."

"That would be handy," she agreed in a throaty voice. Vale bumped her peremptorily in the stomach, shattering the mood. "Vale is right—we can't dawdle."

"Right," Jadren agreed, letting her go immediately. "Stop trying to seduce me, you wild thing." Despite his teasing, when she turned to face him, he was regarding her with a concerned expression. "Do you feel all right? Can you ride?"

"Yes, or walk," she reminded him. "I'm going to be bruised up, but probably better to move so I don't stiffen up."

"Ride," he told her in that arrogant tone of command that simultaneously turned her on and irritated the fuck out of her. "Up you go." He held the stirrup for her foot and offered a hand for balance."

"I'm not that badly hurt," she protested, not moving.

"Both of us will ride. We'll need the speed to put some distance between us and Zany and any other henchmatons she might have with her. There might be more lurking, cloaked by Elal spirit magic. I'd rather not be here when she recovers her wits enough to uncloak them and have them subdue us before we can fight back."

"We have the advantage now. Use your wizardry against her."

"I can't defeat my sister—or any of my siblings—any more than I can battle my mother."

Selly cocked her head, studying him. "You don't know that."

"Yes, I do. I have a whole lifetime of evidence from growing up in that house. Believe me, I'm not being overly modest. I am well aware of my personal limitations."

"You *just* defeated your sister." Selly pointed to the prone wizard. "Maybe you need to reconsider what you do and don't know about yourself."

He offered Selly a crooked, half-smile. "I'm good at taunting Zany into a frenzy, but it won't be so easy the next time. She's not exactly a brilliant strategist, but she's much more powerful. I got the slip on her this time. That won't happen again. We need to go, now. She's already recovering."

The woman did seem to be looking healthier, no longer smoking or convulsing quite so much. Her magic, much like Jadren's in feel and flavor—quite disconcerting to Selly to feel that from the wizard when she first appeared—seemed to be rebounding somewhat. "Why not just kill her? I mean, I know she's your sister, but you don't seem to be on friendly terms."

He made a choking noise. "You have no idea. She tried to kill me often enough when we were kids. Unfortunately she is also not so easy to kill."

"Does she have your healing gift, too?"

Jadren shifted restlessly, glanced at his sister. "Can we discuss on the hoof, as it were?"

If they weren't going to just kill the wizard, Selly supposed they had better flee. She relented and took the offered assistance to launch herself into Vale's saddle, her body creaking with protest already. She'd be in a world of hurt after a few hours of hard riding. Jadren swung up behind her, snugging in close to her body. "You're a better rider, so you direct Vale," he said, moving her hair to nuzzle her neck again, most distractingly. "Consider me baggage."

"I already do," she replied tartly.

He laughed. "That's my girl."

She wanted to retort that she wasn't his girl, but she most emphatically was, in every way imaginable. No sense pretending otherwise, to herself or to him. She turned Vale's head in the direction of House Hanneil and urged him into a fast walk.

"Other way," Jadren said.

"House Hanneil was back this way, wasn't it?" She might not be an expert in Convocation geography, but she had an excellent sense of direction.

"We're going to House Refoel."

A surge of relieved pleasure that wasn't sexual, yet still wasn't without an erotic edge, swept through her. She turned Vale around and urged them into a trot as they circled around the inert wizard sprawled on the ground. "I'm really not that badly hurt."

"I'm delighted to hear it, though I must say my balls will need medical attention if you intend to jounce us all the way to Refoel like this."

Smothering a laugh, she moved Vale into a smoother canter, the overhung forest trail like a shadowy tunnel to a sun-dappled land beyond. They weren't away and safe yet, but she had a good feeling about going to House Refoel. Healers were nice people. And she and Jadren had escaped yet another attempt at capture and they were together. "Better?"

"Some." His teeth clacked, however, and he was way too stiff in the saddle.

"Lean into me," she advised. "Think about it like sex, how we had to find the rhythm that worked for us both.

"That worked very well," he agreed with a dark burr in his

voice. He snaked his arms around her waist, after a while finding the sync with the movement of her body and horse. "Good analogy. Though this is faster than we ever did it. So far."

A surprisingly giddy laugh escaped her. "We'll have to work on that."

"Deal. If my balls survive."

"You wanted to make time."

"True. The sooner we get to House Refoel, the happier I'll be."

"Why the change of heart?" she asked.

"Maybe I'm just that worried about my ability to ever get it up again."

"You chose Refoel before the jouncing began."

"It's closer," he answered. "Which we might be extraordinarily grateful for, if Zany recovers soon enough to pursue with vigor, which might as well be her middle name. I'm reasonably certain Refoel will offer us sanctuary, as it's part of their ethic and they're not fond of El-Adrel, from way back. And you might have a point about me learning about my abilities being more important than obtaining a piece of paper."

Would wonders never cease? "Did you just admit I was right and you were wrong?"

She almost felt him roll his eyes. "Not everything is a competition."

Not *everything*, but she'd definitely won that contest. "Just watch me win this race." She urged Vale into a faster gallop, the wind of their passage too fierce for further conversation.

But Jadren lay against her back, strong thighs snugged against hers, and his arms tightly embracing her. From time to time, he caressed some part of her or other, or kissed her cheek, temple, jaw, throat, his face alongside hers so her hair whipped out behind them on the other side. He wasn't one to express affection with words or romantic gestures, but the way he touched her said everything.

They might be racing for their lives to safety, but it was also one of the best moments of her life.

"YOU WERE GOING to tell me about your sister," she said several hours later, when Jadren estimated they should be near the Refoel border, or perhaps over it, if they left it unguarded and unmarked. Besides, Vale was drenched in sweat and tiring. For fear of pursuit, they kept moving, this time walking alongside Vale to let him cool. As she'd dourly predicted, Selly felt like one of those El-Adrel automatons, moving stiffly and painfully. Jadren offered to try to heal her, but she demurred, saying he should save his magic in case they were attacked, and since she could get healed soon enough anyway, once they reached Refoel. Besides, it wasn't as if she hadn't walked off aches before.

To her surprise, instead of taking up position on the other side of Vale's head, Jadren elected to walk beside her, even holding her hand, interlacing her fingers with his. For all his brusque attitude, now that he'd stopped trying to push her away, he treated her with a surprisingly sweet level of affection.

"Ozana is a psychotic, evil bitch," Jadren said. "Oh wait, that describes my entire family. Was there something more specific you wanted to know?"

"Fyrdo isn't psychotic or evil."

"True. Apparently his paternal contribution was entirely too nice and gentle to battle the psychotically evil El-Adrel side from dear Maman, because we're all like her and not him. Alas. Not incidentally, the ability to heal slash resist death seems to come from Maman's side, too. So, yes, to answer your earlier question, Ozana, like all of my siblings, seems to be more difficult to kill than the average person. I'm not sure she knows about it, though. Maman isn't exactly chatty on the topic. I mostly know it about myself because I'm the most extreme example and, after a few years of my mother doing her best to kill me, I eventually figured it out."

"I don't remember meeting any of your siblings when we had those dinners at House El-Adrel."

"No, they were all conspicuously absent. Not that I blame any of them. Far away from Maman is always wisest."

She contemplated that a moment, how it would be to regard your own mother and your siblings as the worst of enemies. It made her heart ache for him, a sentiment she knew he wouldn't welcome. "Are you all wizards—no familiars?"

"Exactly. Makes for lovely family dinners, each one clawing to be heir to the glorious El-Adrel legacy."

Selly ignored his sarcasm as being of his light, knee-jerk

variety and not the cutting version that indicated she'd come too close to something truly painful. "Except for you."

"Correct. I have no desire to be Lord El-Adrel." He mock shuddered.

"Even though the house loves you."

"The house loves only herself. I suspect she sussed out my lack of useful wizardry early on and, correctly discerning that I wasn't a contender for ruling her life, let me off easily. The others have a much harder go of it, which Maman observes closely. To head House El-Adrel, a wizard must be able to govern the house itself. Can't have your house eating everyone in it. Before you ask, no that's not the case with other houses, even High Houses, but falls in line with the El-Adrel magical concentration on enchanted artifacts. The house is our greatest and worst invention."

"In a way, Gabriel had to govern the manse for Phel. He had to raise it from the water and make it whole again."

Jadren gave her a thoughtful look. "That's true. Perhaps there is an element of the heads of houses having to deploy a certain level of wizardry to manage the physical house to rise to leadership of the non-tangible aspect." Then he waved his free hand, making Vale bob his head and snort. "At any rate, none of this is here nor there. Maman has numerous wizard-lings to choose from and Ozana is one of her favorites. And, not incidentally, why I fought to bond you as my familiar, lest you ended up in Zany's evil clutches. Or the equally evil clutches of one of the others who are as yet unbonded. You're facing enough trouble being in mine."

"You're not evil," she protested.

He slid her a dark look from glittering wizard-black eyes. "Seliah, darling, you really have no idea."

"Then tell me. What is this thing that you're so afraid of becoming?" When he hesitated, his magic developing a decided unhappy clanking, she pressed on. "Because I think the worst has already happened. Your automatic healing ability inadvertently drained all of my magic so you could save yourself and it turned out fine. You saved me in turn. You can do it again. I really don't understand what—"

"No," he snarled, dropping her hand. "You don't understand anything, Seliah! You have no idea what it's possible for me to become, especially with unlimited access to all of your magic that rebounds so bountifully."

"Then, tell me what—" She broke off at the same moment his head whipped up. That sense of magic, so like and unlike Jadren's impinged on her senses.

"Get on the horse," Jadren ordered tersely, seizing her by the waist and tossing her bodily across the saddle. *Ow.* "Ride straight for the house and claim asylum. If you encounter a border guard, tell them who you are and do the same."

She scrambled to a sitting position and held a hand out to him. "You're coming too."

He shook his head. "Go. I'll play rear guard."

"I remember what happens to the people playing rear guard," she shot back. "Either we both run or we both fight— and you told me that you can't defeat Ozana, so fighting her on your own sounds like a really bad idea."

He gave her a look of pure frustration. "I'm trying to be fucking noble here. Go!" With that he smacked Vale's rump, clearly expecting the horse to take off running. Instead, Vale obeyed his rider's implicit command to stand solid, swinging his head around to give Jadren a look of mild indignation. A whirring sound hummed in the distance, one Selly recognized as belonging to one of the elemental-powered carriages.

"Can Vale outrun one of those carriages?"

"Doubtful," Jadren answered, finally taking her hand and clambering up behind her. "Let's hope he's rested enough to get us to someone with Refoel authority."

"Hold on." Without waiting for him to settle, Selly urged Vale into a flat-out run. He wasn't a racehorse, but he possessed plenty of heart. Maybe they'd get lucky.

THEY DID NOT get lucky.

Vale did his best—beyond what most horses could do—but he'd already been tired and carrying two people, plus bags was more than even he could muster. Ozana caught up to them not long after.

Selly sensed the phalanx of Elal spirits preceding the wizard, the ones Jadren had said were clouding the air and providing camouflage for the El-Adrel automatons. She had no time, however, to congratulate herself on her growing ability to sense magic passively, as the path ahead suddenly disappeared in an apparent cloud of fog.

Undaunted, Vale didn't even slow, plunging into the

mist—then tripping, staggering, and nearly falling as something snagged his feet. Afraid the valiant steed might break a leg, Selly reined him in, soothing him with calming pats on the shoulder. He was soaked in sweat and breathing hard, so much so that Selly feared she'd foundered their staunch friend.

She opened her mouth to ask if they'd be at a disadvantage on the ground, so they could unburden Vale, but Jadren had already leapt off. Facing back the way they'd come and extracting tools from his vest, he cursed a steady blue streak under his breath. When she dismounted and joined him, he gave her a nasty glare. "I don't suppose you'll hide."

"Nope." She readied her own weapons, quiver at her back, a few arrows in hand, and daggers at the ready. Sticking one blade in her teeth, she grinned at him around it, making it clear that conversation, at least on her side, was over.

He growled in supreme frustration, wizard-black eyes glittering in suppressed ire—and also a hint of humor. "Why did I have to fall hopelessly in love with a half-insane, feral swamp creature?" he muttered, facing down the trail to the increasing hum of the as-yet invisible carriage.

"Funny," Ozana sang out from nothingness, "that's exactly what Maman would like to know." The sound stopped and spirits swirled in the air like heat shimmer over sunbaked earth, drawing aside to show a fancy open carriage of white and gold, Ozana—mud-smirched and quite scorched—perched on the seat.

Selly didn't wait for the taunting. She fired a sequence of three arrows at Ozana, aiming for each eye and the base of the throat. All three bounced harmlessly off an invisible shield, just as in their previous confrontation.

"Wards," Ozana told her with considerable disgust. "Are you truly that ignorant?" She smoked with fury, her magic palpable as she aimed some sort of device directly at Selly. "Maman is most anxious to explore the depths of your attachment to this idiot, Jadren. Get in the carriage. Both of you."

"Or what?" Jadren challenged, edging slightly in front of Selly.

A streak of fire like a horizontal lightning bolt shot out of the device and hit Selly in the shoulder. It burned with agonizing heat—and kept burning. After her first yelp of shock and pain, she clamped her teeth on further whimpering, but the burning continued to intensify, feeling as if it burrowed down to the bone. Jadren glanced at her, his face so white and strained that his eyes looked like black pits of despair.

"Or I'll kill her," Ozana said flatly, her own gaze fastened on Selly like a snake about to strike. Except she'd already struck, her wizardry a connection pumping venom into the wound, weakening Selly rapidly. Though she fought the sapping weakness, Selly fell to her knees. Jadren reached for her...

"Don't," Ozana's command snapped out, freezing him. "Make one move in any direction except toward this carriage and I'll blow her head off. You know I never bluff, Jaddy boy. You won the first skirmish, but the war will be mine."

"Seliah is too valuable to kill," Jadren said.

Ozana laughed. "Not to me. The pleasure of depriving you of the one familiar Maman would ever let you have is beyond value to me. You might be harder to kill than an alley cat, but at last I know how to hurt you." She blew a kiss at Seliah, the magic making the liquid fire blossom into her blood and spread through her body.

She couldn't help it: she screamed, the shriek scraping out of her throat and fading into a sob, the dagger she'd had uselessly clenched in her teeth falling to the ground. Jadren made a sound, too, a faint echo. Then he walked toward his sister. "Fine. Make it stop now."

"Not until you're both in the carriage."

"She can't even walk," Jadren bit out. "And you won't let me touch her, so how in the dark arts am I to get us both in the carriage?"

"All right," Ozana said after a pause that seemed to last forever. "Carry your precious darling into the carriage and then I'll make it stop. But no false moves. Even look at her wrong and I'll blow a hole through you to kill her. Don't think for a moment that I'll hesitate."

"I know you better than that," Jadren replied in a grim voice, turning slowly back to Selly, keeping his hands in plain view.

"You should." Ozana gloated. "Who'd have ever predicted that sniveling little Jaddy would fall in love with a familiar. It's so unsavory. Makes me sick to my stomach, honestly."

Jadren crouched before Selly where she sat shuddering in pain, the edges of her vision going black, setting his hands gently on her. "I'll figure a way out of this," he reassured her softly. "Put your arms around my neck and let me lift you. As soon as you're in the carriage, she'll stop the pain and you'll be all right."

She did as he instructed, putting her mouth near his ear, panting pauses after only a couple of words. "I have. Plenty of. Magic. Use it. Kill her."

"I don't dare try," he answered with barely a sound. "Besides there's nothing I can—"

"Healing tube. Round your neck. Reverse it."

"What?" He lifted her and turned, walking toward the carriage and the gleefully smiling Ozana.

"Do it," Selly hissed against his ear.

"Won't work."

"Better. To try. Die on. Own terms."

"Seliah…"

"For. Me. Kill her."

Jadren pressed a kiss to her forehead, fervent emotion in it coursing through their bond, a deep shuddering reverberating through his chest. He stepped into the carriage and sat, holding Selly on his lap. "We're here. Release her."

Ozana made a rude sound, but the enchantment released with a pop, the cessation of pain such an intense absence, such a relief that it washed through her with almost orgasmic pleasure. Selly gasped and needed a moment to focus. Then, tipping back her head, she met Jadren's intent gaze and nodded infinitesimally, slipping a hand under his leather vest and shirt to find the tube on the chain around his neck.

Doubt flickered through his black eyes and she did her best convey confidence in him and determination in equal amounts. He could do this. He had to do this, because they were *not* going back to House El-Adrel. From where she sat on

Jadren's lap, Selly faced Ozana, who regarded them with a smug sneer. Making it look as if she fearfully clung to Jadren—which didn't take much acting skill, given what had transpired—she turned the tube under Jadren's shirt to point at Ozana. Jadren gently put his hand over hers, and nudged the tube into the reverse. Oops.

"Aren't you two just the picture of—" Ozana began, breaking off into a croak that shouldn't come from a human throat. They would never find out what Ozana thought they were a picture of, because, as Jadren pulled hard on Selly's magic, Ozana's black eyes bulged, then popped like overripe grapes, followed by her head.

The explosive shattering of Ozana's eyes, skull, then body—which seemed to occur in a grotesque slow-motion cascade—showered Jadren and Selly with gore, though Jadren quickly turned a shoulder and tried to shield her from the worst of it.

They sat there a moment in shuddering silence, Selly too shocked to muster two thoughts, let alone put them together. Jadren stirred finally, lifting his head and meeting her gaze, his face stark and eyes bleak. A thin mist of red coated him. "And you wonder why I think I'm a monster," he said in a hoarse, horrified voice.

"There seems to be no question of it to us," someone said.

~ 17 ~

A N UNSETTLING FRISSON of déjà vu curdled Jadren's blood. As if having just exploded his sister into a fine mist wasn't enough to do that. Cautiously, he turned his head to assess this new threat. A trio of wizards faced them calmly— one in an elemental-powered carriage, another holding Vale's reins, and a third forward of them, hands folded, posture serene, but black eyes intently assessing what must surely be a truly gruesome scene.

"Murder is prohibited on Refoel lands," that wizard said, in that same mildly disapproving tone.

"Then we have crossed into Refoel?" Seliah asked, sitting up straighter. "We claim asylum."

The Refoel wizard regarded her with some bemusement. "It seems your wizard's victim should be the one claiming asylum from you."

"*She* attacked *us!*" Seliah protested, trying to wiggle from his grip. Jadren held her tighter, trying to convey the wordless warning. "She wanted to take us to—"

"Asylum has been requested by a guest on your lands," Jadren interrupted Seliah before she could reveal too much damming information. Refoel wizards were unlikely to interfere with internal House El-Adrel business. Their code meant House Refoel stayed clear of most Convocation political conflicts, but that therefore meant they couldn't really be counted on to help with anything either. Upside was, they didn't conspire with your enemies against you; downside was that they didn't help you against your enemies either. And enemies who were your own family? Well, you were pretty much fucked there. Covered as he was in his sister's exploded body—he doubted even *he* would be able to recover from that sort of discorporation, much less Ozana—he was fully aware of the extent of this particular fuckery.

The Refoel wizard considered. "The familiar has requested asylum and cannot be blamed for the actions of her wizard. Therefore, asylum is granted." Jadren sighed internally in relief, and tightened his hold on Seliah, who immediately bridled and opened her mouth to protest, before sinking into mutinous silence at his glare of warning. A miracle there, that she actually heeded him. "You, however, El-Adrel wizard, are a murderer and cannot be granted asylum."

How had they known he was from... *Oh.* The late Ozana's ostentatious carriage, absolutely shouting the House El-Adrel affiliation. So much for anonymity. Also... so much for Ozana. He'd yet to fully assimilate that he'd successfully murdered his awful sister. Probably he should have some kind of emotion about it, but at the moment all he felt was a queasy sense of relief.

Well and anxiety about what new mess they'd gotten themselves into.

"I'm bonded to him," Seliah burst out. Apparently the

miracle only covered one response. "You cannot separate us. Also that's *my* horse."

The Refoel wizard lifted one brow a Seliah. He had the look of Asa, which made Jadren wonder if they weren't related. Not a standard border patrol in that case, but a member of the family. "No one plans to steal your horse—or you from your wizard. You will both accompany us to House Refoel. We will give you succor—food, rest, such healing as you might require—but you must relinquish your weapons as they are not allowed on Refoel lands. And the El-Adrel wizard will be prevented from using magic."

An odd cloaking sensation settled over Jadren, a muting of the bond between him and Seliah. Though she remained in physical contact with him, he could no longer sense, or—he presumed—draw upon her magic. It felt like a sort of ward, but one fitted to his skin, which he hadn't known was possible.

The wizard who'd cast the ward watched Jadren with opaque calm, perhaps waiting for a challenge, but Jadren held up his hands, palms out, then eased Seliah off his lap, helping her to her feet as he stood. "Can you stand?"

"I'm not a fainting damsel," she bit out, but she also swayed on her feet, and he kept a steadying arm around her.

"We'll cooperate," Jadren called to the Refoel wizard, "but my familiar was injured in the duel with the wizard I killed. She needs healing." In a lowered voice, he added, "Try to avoid giving our names, or any other hints about who we are. They haven't asked, so don't volunteer."

She pressed her lips together, a stubborn lift to her chin, but she nodded acknowledgement. The fact that Seliah didn't argue about being treated immediately said a great deal about just how badly Ozana had hurt her. He jumped out of the carriage, then helped Seliah step down and walk over to the Refoel wizard.

"I am Chaim," the wizard told Seliah with gentle warmth, saying it in such a way that it was clear he wasn't offering his name to obtain hers in return. "I wish only to help you. Maya will lead your horse." He turned, leading Seliah to the Refoel carriage while the wizard inside stepped out and walked toward them. "Liat will ride with you, Wizard El-Adrel, and help bring your carriage with us."

"It's not mine," Jadren hastily assured them, wrestling an irrational urge to snatch Seliah away from the wizard. "Leave it here."

Chaim gave him a reproving look. "You would have us litter our forest with abandoned carriages, not to mention neglect the air elemental bonded to it? We are not so irresponsible in House Refoel."

"All living creatures are precious to us," Liat added sternly, making it sound as if Jadren might not be able to understand the concept. She was also dark-skinned with bone-structure similar to Asa's aquiline face. "We will not cause harm to any living creature, either by direct action or by inaction. Refoel is not so careless of our responsibilities of stewardship to the world as other houses."

Jadren barked out a laugh at that. Describing El-Adrel's malevolent activities—not to mention those of other houses like Sammael and Elal—as "careless" seemed so mild as to be a joke. "You have no idea," he said on a sigh.

Liat softened somewhat, following Jadren's gaze to Seliah, Chaim's hands all over her. He'd love to cut those hands off. "Your familiar will not be harmed."

"I know." Making himself look away, and curling his fingers into impotent fists, he climbed back into the fouled carriage. Liat, despite her prissy stance on all life being sacred, didn't seem daunted by the gory remnants of Ozana. He supposed healers must become accustomed to seeing parts of the human body normally kept *inside* the skin.

"It is difficult for wizards, especially one with such violent tendencies," Liat said, using her sleeve to clean off the elemental's cupboard in order to redirect it, "to restrain their possessiveness toward their bonded familiars."

Was that what he was feeling? Wonderful.

"Dare I ask what sort of enchantment created this... effect?" Liat queried, looking at the gore and showing distaste for the first time.

"That is something I'll have to discuss with Lady Refoel."

"Lord Refoel," she corrected without rancor. "Lady Refoel recently retired and Chaim is now Lord Refoel."

The overly solicitous Chaim was Lord Refoel? Jadren couldn't decide if he was more surprised that the lord of a High House had been out doing the job of his minions or that the mild-mannered man had managed to win the typical feeding-frenzy of high-house heirs competing for the metaphorical throne. The wizard's powerful ability to prevent Jadren from being able to extend his magic past his skin made more sense, as this was no ordinary patrol wizard. However, the fact that Chaim was tending to Seliah's healing personally instead of him delegating the task became more concerning.

"Where is Chaim's familiar?" Jadren asked, belatedly hearing the ripe suspicion in his own voice.

Liat set the carriage into motion, leaving Chaim and Seliah behind. "Chaim has not bonded a familiar."

Jadren's brows climbed his forehead as his misgivings curdled into sour jealousy, sinking his spirits further. He'd known they should have headed toward House Hanneil. "That's odd for the head of a High House."

"Quite the opposite for House Refoel," Liat replied serenely. "For a healing wizard, a familiar provides magical resources for major works such as traumatic injury or severe illness, or for serving many patients in a short time frame. Chaim has always been focused on the administrative side of House Refoel, thus hasn't felt a familiar is a high priority for him." Liat slid him a look that clearly took in Jadren's blood-smeared appearance with both pity and censure. "In House Refoel, there are no battles for primacy among siblings. The magic from our familiars is used for healing and nurturing, not murder and destruction."

"She tried to murder me first," Jadren muttered.

"You will have an opportunity to present your case before Lord Refoel."

Great. The same guy who wanted to steal his familiar would be his judge, jury, and likely executioner. "What happens if I'm found guilty of murder?"

"You are guilty of murder. Three witnesses, including Lord Refoel himself, saw you kill the other wizard in cold blood."

"I wasn't cold at all. In fact, I'd say my blood was boiling at the time."

He didn't think he imagined that Liat struggled to suppress a smile. "By that I mean that the other wizard was simply sitting there, not being aggressive in any way."

"You'd have seen plenty of aggression had you arrived a few minutes earlier." Jadren craned his neck to see if Chaim and Seliah were following after them. "Those injuries to my familiar were caused by that other wizard. She used it to make us get into the carriage."

"You will have an opportunity to present your case before Lord Refoel."

"Circular argument is circular." When Liat didn't reply, Jadren asked, "Speaking of which, why did you all come out to find us?" And why had these supposedly noble healer types simply stood by without helping Seliah and him?

"We may not guard our borders as some High Houses do, but we do observe them. We became aware of the trespass and investigated."

The very blandness of Liat's explanation pricked Jadren's suspicion further. "And Lord Refoel, Himself, investigates every border trespass? No wonder he has little time for healing. I'm shocked he has time to sleep, what with trotting out to the border every time someone wanders past."

For the first time, Liat showed emotion—though it was a bare flicker of irritation. "You talk too much, El-Adrel wizardling."

Jadren had to laugh. "You have no idea. Too late to pretend I didn't strike a nerve. Why did Chaim Refoel drag himself to the border just for me?" *Or just for Seliah,* his darkly suspicious self wondered.

"You may pose that question to Lord Refoel yourself."

"When I have my opportunity to present my case?" he inquired drily.

"Exactly." After that, she wouldn't say more.

"THERE," CHAIM SAID, giving Selly his trademark warm smile. "You should feel much better now."

She definitely did, so she returned the smile and thanked the healer, then added, "I didn't need to be separated from my wizard, however."

"Was I that transparent?" Chaim sat back, surveying her. "Given the scene we witnessed, I thought it prudent to have an opportunity to speak with you without the need for you to censor yourself. It is difficult for a familiar to speak against their wizard. What is your name, bright one?"

Mindful of Jadren's caution not to reveal names, Selly debated what excuse to use for refusing to say, what sort of attitude to feign. Unfortunately, she had almost no idea how a proper Convocation familiar behaved. Nic hadn't covered that in her crash course—the Proper Comportment of Familiars?—and she had gone on plenty about how Gabriel's insistence on having things his way at House Phel meant they were all sideways of the rest of the Convocation. All Selly knew were the obedience aspects and the care and feeding stuff... which gave her at least something to go on.

"I'm not comfortable divulging personal information without my wizard's permission," she confided, hoping to sound meek, which wasn't her strong suit.

Chaim sighed. "How about if I promise that the El-Adrel wizard will be unable to seek retribution against you?"

That didn't sound good. She blinked in what she hoped looked like innocent confusion. "I'm bonded to my wizard. We cannot be separated."

"You can be separated via his execution," Chaim replied grimly, setting the elemental to put the carriage in motion.

Finally. Her relief at going toward Jadren again—not from the bond's prompting but by her own need to be with him, if only to keep him out of trouble—was mitigated by that declaration. "Execution?" she squeaked, not needing to fake her distress. "Can you promise that?"

"As Lord Refoel, yes, I can." He gave her an apologetic smile. "I apologize that I wasn't fully transparent earlier. I've only recently taken on the leadership of House Refoel, so I can claim that introducing myself as such is not yet habit. However, the full truth is that I didn't want you to be so intimidated that you wouldn't confide in me. But you won't do that, regardless, will you?" He waited, but Selly said nothing. Chaim sighed again. "I know who you are, Seliah Phel." At her startled look, he laughed softly. "Your identity was not difficult to discern, besides the fact that your name is inscribed on the silver flask we found on your horse. We did send a wizard–familiar team to House Phel. Due diligence on the Phel family should be expected." He slanted her a look. "Though before this I rather understood you were not… fully functioning, shall we say."

She decided to dispense with the playacting. "I am much improved. Wizard Asa has been a great help to me. As have the others of my house."

"Have they? You are demonstrably in excellent health, mentally and otherwise, and you are an enviably powerful familiar, as well as a beautiful woman. I know very little about water magic and nothing about moon magic, but the feel of you is intoxicatingly pure and bright. You would be an excellent familiar for a healing wizard."

Selly kicked herself for taking so long to catch up to what was going on here. Of course, she wasn't accustomed to being noticed, much less wanted. Chaim watched her with decided interest—and she sensed no wizard–familiar bond from him. "You're shopping for a familiar," she said flatly.

He inclined his head. "I've been waiting for the right woman."

"Unfortunately I'm taken."

"As I indicated previously, that is likely temporary. You deserve better than this violent, unstable El-Adrel rogue murderer. Tell me what happened. Did he steal you?"

She narrowed her eyes. "If you know who I am, then you know who my wizard is."

Chaim chuckled, relaxing against the bench seat and draping an arm along the back, fingertips close enough to brush her shoulder if he extended them a breath more. "Ah, I expect I'm meeting the *real* Seliah now. From what I've heard of your brother, I didn't think you could be so meek as you were pretending to be. I like that you have spirit. And no, I do *not* know who your wizard is, beyond that he is clearly an El-Adrel. Besides the circumstantial evidence, his resemblance to his father, Fyrdo, cannot be mistaken. I plan to check Convocation archives, but I think this El-Adrel scion won't be found there. Which makes me wonder, and is why I ask—how did you come to be bonded to an El-Adrel wizard in such a short span of time? The last I knew, a Convocation proctor had arrived to take you for testing and training."

She shrugged. "There was a ritual. He cut my hair, I said the words. We were bonded."

Chaim narrowed his black eyes at her in disappointed irritation. "Seliah, you know perfectly well that answer, while true, is an obfuscation." He held up a hand as if to stop her from saying more, though Selly hadn't been about to volunteer anything. She wasn't quite sure where this odd interrogation was going, but she worried it was nowhere good for Jadren. "You need not say more," he continued, "or be concerned about retribution from your wizard. I suspect this bonding was not done legally, which will be easy enough to discover. My greater concern is why an unknown El-Adrel wizard is fulminating with healing magic that he's somehow learned to weaponize."

Selly opened her mouth, aghast at the wizard's words and feeling that she needed to say *something* to protect Jadren, but she closed it again, unable to think of a thing—except that it had been her idea and she seriously doubted it would help their situation to say so. Chaim watched her in grim satisfaction.

"I will know the truth soon enough," he said with resolve. "Mark my words: I will not allow this travesty of the magic Refoel holds in sacred trust to be abused in such a way. I consider you to be an innocent, not an informed accomplice. No familiar can be expected to govern their wizard, much less one as innocent of the world as you." He extended his fingers that breath of distance, stroking the bare skin of her shoulder. "I have so much to offer you. You will see."

He waited, but Selly said nothing, watching stonily ahead. That was all she could do for the moment: watch and wait. And hope to the dark arts that they could escape this bind.

SELLY CAUGHT HER breath at her first glimpse of House Refoel. She hadn't known what to expect, especially as every High House seemed to imbue the physical structure that was their core and home with their own unique aesthetic. What she hadn't imagined was that House Refoel wouldn't have any kind of central structure at all. Instead it appeared to consist of a scattering of buildings across a lovely peaceful valley.

The road brough them around a soft bend about halfway up. Low hills rose on either side, with a creek tumbling over rocks and boulders down below. Groups of cottages formed circles at various levels, with some larger buildings clustered together at several different points. Steam rose from pools of different sizes, some overhung with spring-flowering trees, others open to the sunlight. Verdant gardens wound through everything, with enticing winding pathways and sculptures in alcoves. People wandered about or soaked in the pools, or bathed in the abundant sunshine.

Above all, the whole place felt blissfully serene, as if the very air contained healing magic. Selly gazed about in wonder that she tried to disguise. Nothing she'd seen of the Convocation thus far had prepared her for this kind of beauty and peacefulness. She'd wanted to hate everything about House Refoel. She had loathed House Sammael. And House El-Adrel had been so bizarre and frightening at first. With House Refoel, though, she found herself rather adoring all she saw. But then, she supposed that the places themselves were neither good nor bad. All lay in the intent of the people dwelling there, and even that was as varied and changeable over time as the weather.

From the corner of her eye, she caught Chaim watching her knowingly. "Beautiful, isn't it?"

Reluctantly, she nodded, unwilling to give him more than that.

"I thought you would be able to appreciate this place, given your love of nature. We of Refoel share that love. Asa campaigned heavily for the position at House Phel as it would provide him with the opportunity to explore the unspoiled countryside of Meresin, a rarity in the Convocation. He wrote to us of your knowledge of the marshes, your ability to commune with the wildlife there. I think you will find yourself very much at home here."

She nearly spat out that this would never be her home, but

JEFFE KENNEDY

she didn't want to alienate the wizard who would pass judgment on Jadren. Besides, it would be a lie to say that she didn't like what she saw and felt. Much as the El-Adrel house was sentient—Selly had experienced that, no matter what that awful Ozana had said—this "house" might also hear her words and be hurt by them. "It is a lovely, harmonious place," she acknowledged.

"We go to pains to make all aspects of our home healing and healthy in every way." Chaim smiled broadly at her praise, charming and handsome as he beamed. "Very often the people who come to us are in need of recovery from more than physical hurts. Disease and injury leave scars beyond what a healer, even a wizard gifted with magical ability, can knit together. The body may be whole, but the mind, heart, and spirit can take longer to recover—if they ever fully do. Now, perhaps, you better understand why we go to lengths to protect the sanctity of our lands, and why we cannot allow someone steeped in violence to come and go as he pleases."

"Sometimes it's necessary to fight," she said quietly, thinking of the deaths she herself had caused. Even the hunters, though monstrously created and alive only through magic, had nevertheless been living creatures, whose lives, however twisted, she'd forcibly removed from them. "Look at you. You've taken vows to only help, not harm, but you're speaking freely of executing my wizard."

Chaim nodded, a line creasing his otherwise serene brow. "Sometimes it's necessary to fight," he echoed. "As head of my house, I must do what's needful in order to protect what is sacred to us. I would not, however, carry out the execution myself, nor would any of my people. Once his guilt is determined—"

"Don't you mean *if?*" she interrupted.

The look he gave her oozed sympathy and more than a little long-suffering patience. "Your loyalty does you credit—it's a fine quality in a familiar—but you must also be realistic. We all witnessed the murder. My point is that that he will be sent to the Convocation for execution. No one here will harm him. You may put your mind at ease on that count."

"That isn't remotely reassuring."

"It is what it is, no more, no less. What I mean to counter is your argument that I am somehow lacking in integrity. I am a wizard of my word. I will not break my vows by harming your wizard."

Selly regarded him with some astonishment. "Are you saying because you'd let someone else be the one to get actual blood on their hands that you would bear no guilt for the decision?"

"I would bear guilt for the decision, but not for the action."

"That is a ridiculous rationale."

"A time-honored one," he corrected, "long considered by minds wiser than yours, or mine, for that matter."

"Is this how you justify to yourself standing back and refusing to aid others?" she demanded, incensed.

"To what are you referring?" Chaim asked in return, unruffled.

"You could have helped us against the wizard attacking us."

"It was not our fight, therefore we did not choose a side."

"By declining to help us, you helped her. That's choosing."

The carriage glided to a halt in front of a low, graceful building. Glassed in windows showed an airy interior, a peaked roof reminiscent of the surrounding hills holding more glass cut in shapes to fit. "We sometimes dance a fine line," he continued, "but House Refoel will be no one's enemy."

"The El-Adrel wizard injured me. She captured us, planning us both terrible harm. Why are my wizard's actions worthy of condemnation and hers are not?"

Chaim shrugged. "I'm viewing this in terms of the outcome. He committed murder; she did not."

"That seems like a very convenient moral position to take."

With a sigh, he stepped out of the carriage. "Come inside, Seliah Phel. He is inside, awaiting us, this wizard to whom you are so fiercely loyal for reasons that surpass understanding."

"Your understanding, you mean."

"Perhaps." He held out a hand. "I think I understand more than you realize. Your loyalty speaks well of you, of your earnest heart and ability to offer unconditional affection. Come, you want to see him and you will. There's no reason to refuse my company."

Not taking his hand would only be rude, and she couldn't afford to offend him. Setting her hand lightly in his, she stepped out of the carriage. He didn't move immediately, instead enfolding her fingers in a loose, warm clasp as his wizard-black eyes gazed into hers. Unlike other wizards, his eyes didn't glitter or seem depthless. They had a soft warmth to them, like a hot summer night, his healing magic green and verdant as the marshes in full bloom. She didn't at all like that she found him attractive.

"I'm only asking you to consider what you know of him, how you came to be bonded to him," Chaim said with soft urgency. "You may have an opportunity few familiars ever enjoy, the chance to *choose* for yourself."

"At the cost of my wizard's death," she pointed out relentlessly.

"His death will be the result of his actions, nothing more, nothing less. If that sequence of events leads to you being free of him, of you receiving the great gift of the freedom to choose your own path in life, that is simply the way of things. You can receive the gift without paying the price."

"*He* will pay the price."

"Of his own misdeeds? For being an abomination. Yes, as it should be."

"An abomination," she echoed, aghast. All of Jadren's dark mutterings about being a true monster rattled around in her mind, chattering against each other. He'd said all along that having access to her magic threatened to bring out the very worst in him. Had she, by encouraging him to use their combined power, by suggesting that he reverse his healing ability in order to kill, fulfilled his insistent prophecy? "He was only acting to protect me."

Chaim gave her a look of such soft pity that she cringed. "Oh, bright one," he murmured. "You are wise in the ways of nature, but not of wizards. He used you to save himself, to viciously murder a competitor. What do you truly know of him?"

"He's damaged," she whispered. "You have no idea what he's been through."

Chaim nodded, his expression full of regret. "I sensed that in him. His mental turmoil is truly terrible. And yet, while we can regret how a monster has been birthed and shaped, that does not mean we must offer our throats to its ravages." He turned and led her inside, holding onto her hand. The interior smelled of soft spices, oiled wood, and sweet flowers. The placement of the many windows and the open grace of the large room made it seem as if the gardens outside entered the space. It was the closest thing to being outside while being indoors that she'd ever experienced. She hated how much she loved it.

Canting his head, Chaim observed her reaction. "There is nothing wrong with appreciating beauty when you find it. Nothing wrong with recognizing a place that speaks to your heart and spirit. It's not disloyal to discover what you want, to receive the answer to a question you didn't know to ask."

How did he seem to see inside her head? "Can you read my thoughts?" she asked in sudden alarm. She'd thought only Hanneil wizards could do that.

Chaim smiled, placing a gentle fingertip between her brows, smoothing away the furrow, a nourishing trail of healing magic shimmering behind, easing the headache she hadn't been aware was building until it was gone. "I have psychic magic, yes, but not so much that I can read your actual thoughts. Consider me more of an empath. I can sense how you feel, your yearnings, what causes the moonlight in you to sharpen with distress, the water magic to turn to ice." He

314

trailed the finger lightly down the bridge of her nose, dropping his hand to press it over her heart. "I sense the turmoil in your heart, Seliah. You have suffered much. I want only health and happiness for you. I see you flourishing here. That is not a bad thing to want for you."

"I—"

"Don't need to decide anything right now," he interrupted gently. "Maya will show you to your room, so you might bathe and change into clean clothes. Eat, drink—I will arrange for refreshments ideally suited to what your body needs right now. Rest, nap if you can. In a few hours, I'll send for you."

"I want to see my wizard," she said, though all of that sounded really good. Dangerously enticing, in truth.

"And you will," Chaim assured her, handing her over to Maya, who gave her a welcoming smile. "He is also bathing and refreshing himself. It is our ethic to give everyone who comes here what they need."

"Except their freedom," she retorted.

"None of us may act without consequence, Seliah," Chaim replied with a hint of sternness. "Our actions create reactions. At this moment in time, I am the vehicle for assessing the correct reaction to your wizard's action. I am sorry that you blame me for it, especially as I yearn for your goodwill, but I must shoulder that responsibility, also. Maya?"

With that he glided away, murmuring greetings to the people he passed.

"If you'll come with me, Lady Seliah?" Maya gestured with one hand, holding some of their packs from Vale, Selly belatedly realized. "Your horse has been cared for, his injuries healed and his exhaustion eased," Maya assured her. "He has a noble heart. An exceptionally fine companion."

"I can take those bags," Selly said, feeling a bit ungracious, but not caring for how much she liked Maya's recognizing Vale's extraordinary qualities. These people were the enemy; they shouldn't be likable. Maya handed over the bags without protest. They walked down a long hall, the healer wizard seeming to drift almost insubstantially. One side of the hall was entirely glass from floor to high ceiling, giving onto a garden in the near view and then falling away to a stunning perspective over the greening valley below. On the other side were doors, some closed, others standing open to reveal inviting rooms, pristinely made-up and apparently unoccupied.

"This is our guest house," Maya explained. "For visitors and other temporary guests. Those who choose to stay on with us move out to other domiciles of their preference."

"Is my wizard behind one of these closed doors?" Selly could sense Jadren only vaguely on the other end of the muffled bond. He was here somewhere, but she couldn't pinpoint his exact location.

"I couldn't say," Maya answered, firmly enough that Selly knew Maya meant she wasn't allowed to say, not that she didn't know. They reached the end of the hall and the Refoel wizard opened a pair of double doors, standing aside to gesture Selly within. "For our most important guests," Maya said, dimpling.

With a sense of guilt-inducing awe, Selly surveyed what had to be the most beautiful room she'd ever seen in her life. More windows, all floor-to-ceiling, gave a panoramic view of the valley and hills, while careful plantings screened anyone from being able to look in from below. A huge, enticing bed all in white sat near the back, while scatterings of chairs, settees, and large, colorful pillows beckoned one to sleep, sit, or recline. All so very restful. Several pairs of glass doors stood open, allowing cross-breezes, and led out onto a lovely terrace with three pools. "I'm being seduced," she murmured to herself.

"Chaim wants nothing spared to please you. Hot, warm, and cold," Maya said, pointing to each pool in turn. "They are self-cleansing, so you may bathe in any of them. Leave your soiled clothing there and they will be cleaned for you."

Selly wondered if the self-cleaning water counted as a trademark infringement on House Phel's planned product line. Nic and Gabriel would want to know about this. In fact, she should let them know where she was and what might occur. "Could I have some paper and pens, and access to a Ratsiel courier?" she asked, doing her best to make it sound deserved and normal.

Maya's forehead creased in doubt. "Chaim wished for you to rest and relax."

"I need to tell my brother, Lord Phel, where I am," Selly replied, imitating Nic's regal poise that exacted obedience. "So he's not concerned about my wellbeing. After all, I'm not a prisoner here, am I?"

"I shall inquire about providing you with materials for correspondence, Lady Phel," Maya said instead of answering directly, bowing in acknowledgment, then seeing herself out.

Belatedly, Selly realized that she should have been addressed as an El-Adrel, since they knew Jadren was an El-Adrel wizard and she his bonded familiar. The Refoel insistence on calling her by her name or the rank that came from the house of her birth now seemed vaguely ominous.

~ 18 ~

JADREN MARCHED TO, if not his immediate execution, then the penultimate step before it. Knowing that they'd find it difficult to execute said execution—ha!—gave him scant comfort. If anyone could figure out how to permanently kill him, it would be a houseful of healing wizards who wished him ill. This marked a new level in the escalating achievements in irony of his life: he'd managed to make enemies of the people everyone else in the world regarded as friends. It was like he had a special talent for fucking things up.

They'd allowed him to bathe and eat, but they'd also taken away his clothing. In exchange they'd given him one of their flowing robes that everyone here seemed to wear. He felt like an idiot in the swirling pale-green thing. What really bothered him was that, along with everything else, they'd taken the widget on the chain around his neck. Even though his magic remained muted by whatever whammy Chaim had placed on him, he would've felt much better having that weapon available. They also refused to tell him where Seliah was, though he could sense in a muffled way that she was nearby. Frustratingly, he couldn't discern much more than that.

They escorted him into a round chamber, ringed with

windows open to the sunshine and serene views that looked much too pretty and benign to be a place of judgment. Lord Refoel sat behind a white stone desk, polished to a high shine and carved elaborately with flowers pollinated by bees. Liat and the other Refoel wizard, the one who'd taken charge of Vale—Maya—sat demurely nearby. No one else was in the room.

"Where is my familiar?" Jadren asked, using preemptory challenge to cover his concern. He'd expected Seliah to be there and it worried him greatly that she wasn't. The last few hours of waiting, he'd been anticipating her arrival at the door of the room they'd stowed him in. Knowing her determined nature, she should've been demanding to see him.

Unless she didn't want to see him, which was a distinct possibility and one that shouldn't sting so much to contemplate. He wouldn't blame her for getting a good look at what Chaim was clearly offering her in this place and deciding to opt for a much better deal. Still... he'd believed her declarations of love. Would she turn her back on him that quickly? Maybe so. Seliah had so little experience in the world. He was likely the equivalent of a teenage crush for her. She *should* grow out of it. All along he'd known in his gut that Seliah needed someone better than him.

But not fucking Chaim.

"Lady Seliah Phel is resting," Chaim said, answering Jadren's question as if speaking to a querulous patient.

Jadren cursed internally that they'd discovered Seliah's identity, though he wasn't going to give Chaim the satisfaction of knowing he'd scored a point, so Jadren kept his face blank, much as the possessive crawling need inside him wanted to correct them that Seliah was an El-Adrel now, for better or worse. *Mine.*

"Seliah has suffered a great deal and must recuperate," Chaim continued, when Jadren said nothing. The reproach in his demeanor demonstrated beyond a doubt that Chaim blamed Jadren for Seliah's need to recuperate. Not that he was wrong, but it still rankled to be judged by Mr. Perfect. "Your magic has been nullified, so there is no reason for you to have your familiar present."

"Except that she's the lone witness on my behalf." And because he... Well, he didn't *need* her, but he did *want* her with him. *Stronger together.*

Chaim smiled in gentle sympathy that made Jadren want to rip the healer's perfectly white and even teeth out one by one and stuff them down his throat. "Even in Refoel where we honor all life paths, we also comply with Convocation law. Familiars may not testify in a court of law."

"I'm surprised you'd uphold Convocation law."

Chaim considered that. "I am the lord of a Convocation High House. Of course we are subject to Convocation law, just as we all are."

"Seems you'd have difficulty reconciling the Convocation's more brutal and rapacious laws with your own vows to cause no harm," Jadren countered. "Don't you feel hypocritical?"

"*We*, those of us belonging to House Refoel, cause no harm," Chaim replied. "Seliah also brought up this argument. Directly causing harm is very different from being unable to prevent it. None of us can control all the world. The best we can do is live our own lives in accordance with our ethics, to change our small corner of the world." He gestured to the valley out the windows, an absurdly peaceful place from what Jadren had seen of it. It made him highly suspicious of what they were hiding here.

It warmed him to know that Seliah had been arguing with the guy. At least she hadn't been completely taken in by these serener-than-thou types. "What about being in a position to prevent harm and refusing to do so? That makes you complicit."

Chaim frowned. "I don't agree."

"You were in a position to keep Seliah from being injured," he persisted. "But you didn't. Instead, you and your people watched until I was forced to take dramatic measures to protect her."

"To protect yourself," Chaim shot back.

"The one requires the other. I am Seliah's wizard and as such bear a responsibility to protect her. I can't do that if I'm dead."

Chaim waved that off with some irritation. "As I told Seliah, these are questions for philosophers, which none of us are, least of all you. Our sole purpose here is to determine your guilt in murdering the El-Adrel wizard. For the record, I need to know her identity and yours."

Good luck with that, boy-o. Jadren smiled thinly. "I don't know her name and, as you've discovered, I don't have one."

Chaim drummed his fingers on the pristine stone surface. "I find both answers difficult to believe."

"Would I lie?"

"In a heartbeat," Chaim fired back. "What are you—a by-blow of Fyrdo's got on the wrong side of the blanket? Does Katica know about you? Why don't you carry your MP scorecard?"

"So many questions," Jadren marveled. He'd been perversely pleased when they'd searched him and his things, enjoying their frustration at being unable to find his scorecard. It was the first time he'd been happy he didn't have one. He grinned, then made a sad face. "And zero answers. How sad for you."

"With your life hanging in the balance, I'd think you'd want to take this conversation more seriously."

"Do you?" Jadren asked coolly. "*Think*, that is. I've received the distinct impression that you've already decided upon my guilt with your conveniently in-house eye-witnesses and no one to speak for me."

"The only person in a position to speak for you is your familiar," Chaim noted, "who is a prejudiced source, as well as not legally allowable."

"And your minions are not biased to favor your decisions?" Jadren swept a hand at Maya and Liat, who gazed back like serene statues. "Contractually obligated is the phrase that comes to mind."

"It's well known that familiars won't counter their wizards," Chaim said instead of answering.

Jadren laughed, a real one. "You clearly don't know Seliah." Sobering, he narrowed his eyes at Lord Chaim Refoel. "That's something for you to bear in mind as you're quite transparent in wanting her for your own familiar."

"Why wouldn't I be transparent about that? Seliah is an ideal choice for me," Chaim replied placidly. "She is intelligent, beautiful, scintillatingly powerful, her magic extraordinarily well-suited to a healer, especially one in my position. House Phel would no doubt be grateful for such a strong alliance with House Refoel." He paused, allowing the scathing silence to highlight how little he though of Jadren's wizardry. "The real puzzle is how you were able to bond her."

Jadren shrugged with feigned insouciance. "Just lucky I guess."

"Or you did it illegally."

"You clearly don't know Gabriel Phel, either, if you think he'd let a wizard live who illegally bonded his sister. Send him a courier, make an offer to bond Seliah, and just see what he says." A bit of a gamble there, but Phel had supported Seliah in her determination to seek out Jadren. He wouldn't throw Jadren to the wolves, if only for Seliah's sake.

Then, too, were Gabriel's parting words to him. *Everyone deserves a place of refuge, somewhere they can be safe. Seems to me you don't have one in your birth house, so I'm offering House Phel, should you ever want it.* Jadren didn't kid himself that Gabriel liked him, or remotely approved of him, but Gabriel also never said something he didn't mean. Part of that ridiculous integrity. With Phel's idealistic worldview, he'd consider saving Jadren part of that promise.

If only Refoel would contact House Phel. Jadren hated to be in the position of pleading for rescue, but he was up against a pretty hard wall here.

"If I were to send a courier to Katica El-Adrel, instead,"

Chaim asked cagily, "would she know who you are?"

"Lady El-Adrel is a busy woman," Jadren mused, considering the rather alarming potential consequences were his dear maman to receive *that* message. "I rather doubt she answers her correspondence personally."

"Oh, I think she'd be interested in one of her wizards being murdered," Chaim put in almost jovially.

"The victim was likely Ozana El-Adrel," Liat put in, watching Jadren closely for reaction. "According to the evidence," she added almost primly to Chaim.

Applying the word "victim" to Ozana nearly made Jadren choke. Besides that dramatic miscarriage of grammar, he wanted to point out that there were several El-Adrel daughters he could have cheerfully murdered, that Liat couldn't possibly have identified Ozana from the red mist he'd reduced her to. Although... evidence. *Shit.* Ozana probably had identification in the carriage, since she *did* possess an MP scorecard.

"Ozana El-Adrel," Chaim mused. "Katica's youngest daughter and rumored to be a favorite for her heir."

Jadren rolled his eyes at the obviously rehearsed proceedings—and at the absurdity of Ozana being a leading contender for becoming Lady El-Adrel. It was never going to happen, even before Ozana met her unfortunate demise. The only person who hadn't known that was Ozana. If there had been rumors to that effect, Ozana herself had no doubt started them.

"So, I ask myself," Chaim continued in the same falsely considering tone, "who would have the ability and the motivation to murder a scion of House El-Adrel, and I keep

325

coming up with another scion. But none of Katica and Fyrdo's acknowledged children match your description or... unusual abilities."

Jadren had no doubt of that. "Is there a question for me in there somewhere?"

"Yes." Chaim leaned forward, palms flat on the desk, almost as if he'd like to reach out to Jadren. Probably to strangle him. *Good luck with that.* "What wizardry did you use to murder Ozana El-Adrel that way?"

"You tell me." *Please,* he almost added.

Chaim cocked his head. "All right. I think you're a by-blow of Fyrdo El-Adrel and a powerful Refoel wizard who somehow disguised her pregnancy and birthed you in secret. You have an extraordinary amount of healing magic—that much is easy to sense—but it's perverted, twisted in upon itself in some way. I've never seen anything like it before."

"Aww," Jadren drawled. "A guy always likes to hear he's special."

"It's an abomination," Liat said, an almost gentle chiding, except for the sharpness of her wizard-black eyes. "You should have been put down as an infant."

Jadren couldn't argue that one, as he'd often had the same thought. Still. "That doesn't sound very 'all life is sacred.'"

"That is neither here nor there," Chaim said with more force, giving Liat a stern look that he transferred to Jadren. "Who was your mother?"

"Was?" he queried with lifted brows.

"I'm guessing she's gone from this world, or you would not have been abandoned. No Refoel wizard or familiar would willingly walk away from their child. It goes against all our principles. If your mother had lived, we'd have known about you."

Briefly he indulged in that fantasy—one he'd often had as a child—that his true mother was out there somewhere, missing him. Someone capable of love, as opposed to his Lady mother and tormentor. But no, Katica was his dear maman, for worse and worser. There was no denying that. Another reason that he recognized himself for the monster he was, having demonstrably come from those poisonous loins.

"I'm a little unclear on the trajectory of this inquisition," Jadren said. "The stated intent, and I believe I quote you accurately, Lord Chaim, is 'to determine my guilt in murdering the El-Adrel wizard.' How does my parentage have any bearing on that verdict?"

"You *are* guilty," Chaim shot back. "You will be remanded into the custody of the Convocation."

"Well, then, as entertaining as this little play has been, it feels like an immense waste of my time," Jadren noted. "May I be excused in that case? I could have a nice refreshing nap. Say farewell to my familiar. Taking me away from her will impact her sorely, you know. Attenuating the bond and all that. It might take a while for the Convocation to get around to executing me. The wheels of government turn slowly and so forth."

"We know how to care for her," Chaim retorted sharply. "Far better than you. And you will not be seeing Seliah again."

A surge of rage rolled through him in crimson heat. "You have no right to keep Seliah from me."

"Did someone say my name?" Seliah inquired cheerfully, her head appearing in one of the open windows that gave onto a precipitous drop.

Along with his own relieved delight at seeing Seliah alive and well, Jadren savored the exquisite pleasure of seeing Chaim at a total disadvantage, caught entirely flat-footed by the sight of Seliah nimbly climbing over the window ledge. "Hello, Seliah, darling," he murmured, something jagged in him settling back into place.

She flashed him a saucy grin. "Hello, wizard." Her jaunty demeanor went somber as she took in the proceedings, focusing a glare on Chaim. "Someone forgot to fetch me as promised, so I had to find my own way here."

Chaim opened his mouth, but nothing came out, he was so flabbergasted. The poor guy hadn't known to list "half-feral" and "uncannily agile" among Seliah's sterling qualities. "How—how did you get here?" he finally stammered.

Seliah glanced at Jadren with a theatrically confused expression, as if she thought Chaim might be dim-witted. "Through the window," she answered, pointing helpfully.

Maya had risen to her feet. "You... climbed off your terrace?"

"Oh, that—yes," Seliah replied. "Somehow my door got locked and funny about that lovely terrace—it's quite high, isn't it? But I managed. Then I had to wander around for some time, listening at windows for maundering voices who might be relevant to my interests. And here I am!" She went to Jadren's side. "So, murder verdict, is it?"

"Seemed to be a forgone conclusion," he replied in the

same confiding tone, setting a hand on the small of her back. "It's really good to see you."

"It will do you no good to touch her," Chaim cautioned. "With my restraints on you, you'll still be unable to access her magic."

Jadren gave him a bare glance. "Sometimes people touch for other reasons, you troglodyte." It felt divinely satisfying to be in contact with Seliah again, even with the bond muted. But then, they'd had this connection from almost the beginning. The first time he laid eyes on Seliah—mud-covered, wild hair tangled, in a spitting frenzy in the ropes that bound her—he'd felt a deep kinship with her. Something that went beyond compatible magic, which they had, despite Chaim's scorn. When she'd broken free and scrambled up the side of House Phel to escape, Jadren had wanted to cackle in sheer delight and had been hard-pressed to maintain his pose of jaded boredom.

Chaim barked out a disbelieving laugh. "Do you claim real affection?"

Jadren didn't bother to reply. Seliah touched light fingers to his cheek and he leaned into the caress, beyond tempted to kiss her right in front of them all. He didn't. Only because he couldn't discern how much of the impulse came from a desire to throw it in Chaim's face. Jadren wasn't noble—that had been multiply established—but it still seemed wrong to use Seliah's affection for him to punish someone else. She cared about him. She cared enough not only to disdain Chaim's interest, but to climb off her balcony to find him. To rescue him, yet again.

"Are you alright?" Seliah asked softly.

"Yes." He added a nod, immeasurably moved by the emotion in her eyes. "And you?"

"I've been treated well, aside from being locked in like a prisoner." She flicked a glance at the group of somewhat stunned wizards. "*And* prevented from communicating with my brother, Lord Phel, as I politely requested and as is my due."

Maya cast her eyes down and shifted slightly in her seat.

"Seliah," Chaim said soothingly, "we only wanted to protect you from undue influence."

"From my *brother*?" she asked in a scathing tone.

"You are absolutely welcome to contact Lord Phel," Chaim answered with exasperation. "In fact, I encourage it. We want only the best for you and simply held off until after this interview, in case you had been coerced or otherwise pressured."

"The only coercion and pressure here has come from House Refoel," Seliah snapped. "I admit I have little experience in Convocation ways, but I'm pretty sure holding me prisoner and forcibly separating me from my wizard counts as a hostile act against House Phel."

"House Refoel never commits hostile acts against other houses!" Liat burst out, clearly offended.

"I have news for you, honey," Seliah retorted. "That's what this is."

"Not if we determine that you are not mentally capable of acting in your own best interests," Chaim inserted, sounding kind, but with an unsettling firmness.

Seliah stiffened under Jadren's hand, tension firing through her body like a myriad of tiny lightning bolts. Even dampened to his senses, her magic went ice-cold and silver-sharp. *Uh-oh.*

"Are you questioning my mental stability?" Seliah asked, so quietly the words hissed like a cat's.

"Now, Seliah," Chaim said placatingly, a patronizing tone that put up Jadren's hackles and he wasn't even the intended recipient. Jadren was no lady-killer, but if this was how Chaim went about wooing women, or familiars, or both... well, no wonder the guy was unbonded. "We already had this conversation," Chaim continued, giving her a gentle smile better suited for small children or irascible patients. "I'm well able to sense the trauma you suffered from being an untapped familiar. We all can sense that and, while it's wonderful to see you doing so much better than rumor indicated, no one expects you to magically recover overnight. It takes time and patience. And care," he added darkly, throwing Jadren an accusing glare.

"*I* expect it—" Seliah began, then broke off, growling deep in her chest, tensing further.

Jadren was torn—should he attempt to talk her down or hold her bags while she taught Chaim a lesson?

Before Jadren could decide, Seliah stalked forward, planting palms on Chaim's desk. "You know, Lord Refoel," she ground out, "I was about to say that I expect it of myself. Something that I've said any number of times recently, to an array of people who care about me. I'll even be generous and include you in that group, because—despite your ugly enthusiasm for seeing my wizard dead—I don't believe you are actively malicious. Misguided and thick-headed, perhaps, and rather unpleasantly avaricious about acquiring me for your familiar."

Jadren couldn't help the possessive snarl at hearing Chaim had gone so far as to proposition Seliah while she was still bonded to him. Wizards had razed kingdoms for less.

Seliah glanced over her shoulder at him. "Yes, he asked. For the record, I said no. Give me some credit. I meant it when I said I love you. I know you think you're not worthy of love, but I do and I don't plan on stopping any time soon, so you can relax."

Chaim looked so stunned that Jadren was able to overcome his rage to shoot the wizard a smug grin. True, Jadren probably didn't deserve Seliah, but she was obstinately determined to keep him, so who was he to fight that?

Seliah turned back to Chaim. "Of course I know no one *magically recovers from trauma overnight*," she said, ruthlessly mimicking the man. "That's not how recovery works. But that doesn't mean that I can't have expectations for myself or that I'm some sort of walking invalid. Do you know what occurred to me just now, when you said no one expected me to magically recover overnight? There is one person who *has* expected me to get my shit together and deal. Him!" Seliah jerked her head Jadren. "My wizard is the one person who's always seen me for who I am, not my collection of wounds and inabilities. He challenges me to be a better person, to learn and grow and overcome."

"That's all lovely and heartfelt," Maya said, sounding sincere, though she flicked a glance at Jadren that showed how dubious she was. "Still, your devotion to your wizard and the reasons for it are not relevant to the matter at hand. You may believe you love him—and indeed you might, for good reasons—but none of that changes the fact that we all witnessed him murder Ozana El-Adrel on Refoel lands. Our laws and vows are crystal clear on this. He must be remanded into Convocation custody."

"Then so must I," Seliah said, not looking at Liat, but holding Chaim's gaze. "Because I'm equally guilty of murdering Ozana."

"Seliah, no!" *Dark arts curse him.* Jadren strode forward. "I'm the wizard. The guilt is mine."

"It was my idea," Seliah said flatly, turning to face him and folding her arms over her chest. "You would never have thought to reverse your healing ability that way if I hadn't suggested it."

He nearly choked on her casual dropping of that information, and on his terrible fear for her. "You need to stop talking right now."

Typical of her, instead of being even remotely cowed, she gave him a cheeky grin. "It's time to lay our cards on the table. We're between a rock and a hard place and have nothing to lose at this point."

"That was a dreadful mixing of metaphors," he growled.

She rolled her eyes. "The least of our problems. I won't tell them your name, since that's yours to share or not, but we came here so they could help you with your magic. It's time to ask for that help."

He nearly sputtered, pointing at Chaim. "Did you miss the part where he wants me *dead*?"

She glanced at Chaim consideringly. "I think he's new in his position as lord of a High House and is committed to following the rules and doing the right thing, so far as he understands it."

Chaim raised his brows. "I *am* sitting right here."

"Do you disagree with my assessment?" Seliah returned coolly.

"I'm not delighted by the implication that I don't understand my own mind," Chaim answered slowly. "But I think you are not wrong. You are also not quite who I thought."

Seliah smiled thinly. "Messed up in the head, yes. Stupid, no."

Chaim dipped his chin in acknowledgment, then focused his keen gaze on Jadren, looking *through* him as healing-wizards had an uncanny knack for doing, not unlike the Hanneil wizards and just as unsettling. "Explain what Seliah means by reversing your healing magic."

Jadren threw up his hands in resignation. Seliah had a point that they had little to lose. If the Convocation got their paws on him, things would only get worse, whether or not they figured out a way to kill him for good. Whereas if they could convince Refoel to help him instead of handing him over for execution... It was a long shot, but better than no shot at all.

"You already know I possess healing magic," he said. "I had a device—an El-Adrel widget—that enabled me to direct that healing outward. When Ozana hurt Seliah to force me to come with her, something I knew would be gravely dangerous for Seliah and me, I reversed the widget to use that magic to... Well, instead of knitting her tissues back together, I blew them apart."

"Abomination," Maya whispered, looking horrified.

"An easy stone for you to throw," Seliah said, "sitting here in your peaceful, beautiful valley. You have no idea what this man has endured at the hands of people like Ozana, who wanted to return him to a kind of torture you can't possibly imagine. You have no idea," she repeated, slanting Jadren a quirk of a smile.

He tried to frown at her but didn't quite get there, having to fight back a laugh. Funny girl.

"Why would you need a device to 'direct healing outward?'" Liat asked, a fascinated look on her face.

Though Jadren really hesitated to say—old habits of silence and secrecy die hard—Seliah gave him an encouraging nod. It was true, this was why they'd come to Refoel. "I've never been able to heal anyone else," he temporized. "I don't know why. Using this device, however, I was able to heal Seliah."

"Liat, why are we wasting time on this?" Chaim asked wearily. "So he's not a healing wizard. We knew that."

"You wondered why this wizard's—" Liat broke off with a sound of irritation. "It's annoying not to be able to call you by a name. Is there one you can give us?"

"Jadren," he supplied. Why not, at this point?

"Jadren," Chaim repeated. "I've still never heard of you."

"No, you wouldn't have."

"We asked why Jadren's healing magic feels so odd to us," Liat continued crisply. "Here is an opportunity to answer that question. In all my years of teaching, no wizard with healing magic that I've encountered, heard of, or studied in the annals, has demonstrated any difficulty healing someone. You know as well as I do that the challenge with young healing wizards, especially ones with high potentials as we sense in this one, is *preventing* them from unconsciously healing anyone with an injury or disease they come into proximity with."

"Unconsciously?" Seliah asked sharply.

"Yes," Liat answered, watching Seliah intently. "Arguably all magic works that way, though the Convocation closely monitors children with magical potentials above a certain level, so that they are trained to manage magic as a wizard in case they manifest as one. Convocation Academy contains new wizards quickly to prevent accidents. It's very rare in this day and age for a wizard to manifest without supervision, though I understand your brother did."

"Our family hadn't produced anyone with magic in generations," Seliah explained. "So, yes, when Gabriel manifested as a wizard, it was far from contained."

Liat nodded in sympathy. "With healing wizards, the danger is primarily to themselves." She turned that keen look on Jadren. "Have you experienced unconscious healing?"

Jadren exchanged a glance with Seliah who nodded encouragingly. This went so against the grain, but he set his teeth and plunged onward. "Yes, but not focused outward. I can only heal myself. That is, until I learned to use this device. Seliah was the first person I ever healed who wasn't me."

"Healing wizards are not able to heal themselves," Chaim put in with authority.

Jadren glared at him. "Well, I'm not a healing wizard, am I? I'm something else. A monster. Abomination," he added, flicking a look of disgust at a chagrined Maya.

"To what extent are you able to heal yourself?" Liat asked. Of them all, she seemed to be the one most interested in answers rather than judgments.

Jadren met her inquisitive gaze steadily. "Thus far, it seems to be unlimited."

"Unlimited?" Chaim repeated. "What severity of injuries have you recovered from?"

"Death." Jadren managed not to smirk at the man's discomfort. For once it was fun, acknowledging his monstrous nature.

"No wonder you weren't concerned about being executed," Chaim muttered after a pause. "If you can't be killed…"

"I really don't want the Convocation to become diligent in their efforts to find a way," Jadren replied.

"And this self-healing occurs unconsciously," Liat mused. "Have you tried to consciously control it?"

Jadren swallowed down the acid nausea that question provoked, a cold sweat beading on his skin, his throat tightening enough to make any answer impossible. How to explain?

Seliah edged closer, brushing her fingers against the back of his hand. "It's a long, involved, and intensely personal story," she answered for him. "Suffice to say, yes, he's tried for most of his life, with no success."

"You said you were coming to us for help—is this why?"

"Yes." Jadren gave in and took Seliah's hand, interlacing their fingers, the contact steadying. "I don't know how I came to be this way, or how to control it."

"Your mother was no Refoel healing wizard or familiar

337

who got you by Fyrdo," Liat said her gaze sharp.

"No, my mother is alive and well and not of Refoel," he admitted. "She's Katica, Lady El-Adrel herself."

~ 19 ~

I T TOOK SOME doing to calm the chaos that news elicited. Rather shocking, Jadren reflected, how much noise three supposedly serene healers could make.

Chaim, in particular, loudly proclaimed his disbelief—though Jadren suspected a lot of that came from denial. Any new lord of a High House would be alarmed at the news that the ostensibly houseless, rogue wizard he'd imprisoned and threatened with execution was in fact the scion of one of the most powerful High Houses and ruthlessly powerful high-house heads. No one deliberately crossed Katica El-Adrel and, as Chaim subsided into muttering at his desk, head in his hands, Jadren almost felt sorry for him.

Almost.

After her initial outburst, Maya had settled into silent tears, through which she glared at Jadren, as if he'd deliberately ruined her life. Of the three, Liat recovered from the shock the fastest, settling into quizzing Jadren on the particulars of his ability. With Chaim's weary permission, Liat soon took Seliah and him to the rooms where she practiced healing, so they could discuss in privacy, Liat drily commenting that the council chambers weren't nearly so inviolate as they'd assumed. Jadren complied willingly enough, happy to put some distance between Chaim and Seliah, and also beyond glad he didn't have to fight to keep Seliah with him.

With the way she still gripped his hand, or perhaps he was gripping hers that fiercely, it would've taken a pitched battle to separate them again.

Once in Liat's private treatment rooms, the door firmly closed, Liat first undid the binding Chaim had put on Jadren, smiling at his exhalation of gratitude. He hadn't realized how very constricting it had felt to have his magic bound against his skin like that, not unlike having his arms chained to his sides. Also, the sheer rush of the bond with Seliah flowing freely again nearly made him giddy. From the feel of her through the bond, and the glowing expression on her face, Seliah felt the same.

"Thank you," he said to Liat, meaning it sincerely.

She tipped her head in wry acknowledgement. "You're trusting us with this sensitive information. We can trust you to govern your behavior." She cast a thoughtful glance at Seliah. "I believe you have strong reasons to comply with our laws and eschew violence."

"Hey, I only murder people who try to murder me first," Jadren replied lightly, then winced as he realized how much of a lie that was and began rapid mental backpedaling to dig himself out of that inadvertent confession.

To his surprise, instead of pouncing on the error, Liat cocked her head at him, her face creasing in sympathy. "So much pain," she whispered. "What happened to you?"

A tremor rocked through his core self, an earthquake of

emotion he felt completely unequal to holding under control. "I—" he croaked, that cold slime of sweat breaking out over his body again. "I... I can't—"

"You don't have to," Seliah said calmly. She'd let go of his hand and held his face in her palms, standing between him and Liat, holding his gaze so all he could see were her compassionate amber eyes, thickly fringed in black, her oddly beautiful face full of solemn love. "Going to puke up your lunch?" she asked, the crisp question a contrast to the soft sympathy in her expression. He'd taught her this technique, he realized. It just figured she'd turn it around on him.

He narrowed his eyes and managed to extract a feeling of insulted indignation from the morass of emotion trying to drown him. "No," he answered, his voice only a bit tremulous, fuck him. "But I might just have to spank a certain insolent familiar later."

She fluttered those thick lashes. "Promises, promises." Patting his cheek, she turned to Liat. "My trauma is nothing compared to Jadren's. Tread carefully with your questions."

"We can help with that," Liat said, looking *through* him. "We have wizards here with Hanneil training in psychic healing. They can—"

"Let's stick to information exchange for now," Jadren interrupted. The thought of someone poking around in his head, seeing the things he'd done and that had been done to him, made him queasy. Well, queasier. "We don't have the time to linger here."

"No?" Liat raised her brows. "Did you have somewhere more important to be?"

Jadren opened his mouth to answer, then looked at Seliah. She met his gaze thoughtfully. "We have a number of interested parties chasing us," he said, in part to Seliah.

"You would be safe and protected here," Liat replied. "Earlier you asked about Lord Refoel, erm, 'trotting out to the border every time someone crosses,' is how I recall you phrased it. In truth, while our borders appear to be unguarded, we do have protections in place that detect when anyone with violent intentions sets foot on our lands." She produced a thin smile. "It doesn't happen often, so your concerns about Chaim's time may be laid to rest."

"I feel so much better now," Jadren replied in a dry tone, eliciting a slightly warmer version of Liat's smile.

"Something to bear in mind," Liat said with a verbal shrug. "Now, we must discuss your mother."

"Must we?"

"I'd heard, here and there," Liat continued, unbothered, "that Katica El-Adrel and some of her scions display unusually rapid healing, a resistance to disease, and perhaps slower aging than most.

Seliah looked startled. "You don't age?"

"Of course I age," he answered with irritation. "Do you think I was born with a beard and pubes?" Though he had to admit his mother looked far younger than her years. "How did you 'hear' this?" he asked Liat.

"We have Refoel healers contracted to House El-Adrel." Liat held up her palms. "All houses expect their wizards who go to work elsewhere to report back useful information. Healers are exceptionally well-positioned to discover what remains hidden to others."

"And I thought House Elal had the best spy network," he muttered.

"None of our people told us about *you*, however."

"I am—was—a well-kept secret."

"Why?"

A sarcastic reply hovering on his lips, Jadren pulled it back as Seliah caught his eye. She wasn't glaring or giving him any sort of *look*, but the very placidity of her expression spoke volumes. This was what he'd wanted: help with his extraordinary and awful talent. To get that assistance, he was going to have to open up a few cracks in the wall he'd carefully built around himself over all these years. Seliah had started the assault with her naïve tenacity and he'd failed to extract himself from her feral claws. She'd sunk her hold deep enough into his heart that there appeared to be nothing he wouldn't do to protect her. Including tearing that heart out of his rotten corpse and laying it bare on the table for the Refoel healers to dissect.

"Because I am my mother's greatest creation," he told Liat. "Here's what I know."

SELLY SOAKED NAKED in the hottest pool on the terrace of her now fully unlocked chambers. She'd checked, just to be sure. Not that they could keep her confined, as she'd demonstrated to her intense satisfaction, but the principle mattered. They were at least going through the motions of trusting each other. So much so that she'd finally agreed to wait in her rooms while Liat and a few others took turns poking at his magic.

She'd wanted to stay with Jadren, worried about how he'd hold up to an examination that could evoke memories of being an experimental subject, but he'd finally snarled at her to quit hovering like a momma cat with a wounded kitten and to find something else to do with herself.

The Jadren-code had been easy enough to decipher: they were digging into the aspects of himself that he feared were the most monstrous and he didn't want her to witness it.

That was fine. But it didn't mean she would let him off that easily.

She cocked her head at the sound of the outer door opening, then closing, and waited. Evening had deepened to night, fire elementals glowing with gentle light from cunningly placed lanterns amidst the flowers and flaming warmly from the tops of torches ringing the terrace.

"Nice digs," Jadren commented, sauntering onto the terrace, wizard-black eyes pits of shadow against his pale skin. He'd hooked his thumbs in his belt and stood hip-shot, conveying his trademark insouciance, but exhaustion tugged at her magic along the bond and he looked haunted, his face gaunt. "Glad to see how the favored children live around here. The room they gave me made that hut we shacked up in look like a palace."

"Good thing you can share these chambers with me then," she returned calmly, deciding that the care and feeding of her wizard in this case should not include sympathy. He looked brittle enough to shatter with a kind word.

"Share... with you?" He sounded so scornfully dubious that she might've responded in kind, if she hadn't known what he'd just been through.

"There's plenty of room," she said instead, making it nonchalant.

"Only one bed, I noticed."

"Yes."

A silence fell between them, not heavy, but as light as petals fluttering from the spring blossoms on the overhanging limbs.

"Liat wants us to stay a while," Jadren finally said. "It will take a while to figure out my innards, apparently. Seems there's quite a bit to untangle from what magic I was born with and what was... installed."

Oh. She wanted to reach for him, to offer him comfort, but he looked so tensely fragile. "Do you want to tell me about it?"

"Not really." He mock-shuddered, trying for a jaunty grin that fell short, then twisted into a grimace. "Not yet."

"You never did finish telling me what you're so afraid of becoming."

"A monster. You have no idea."

"Does Liat—have an idea?"

"Unfortunately, yes. That's part of why she wants us to stay. It might not be entirely optional at this point. Something something about the irresponsibility of unleashing me on an unsuspecting Convocation."

Selly took a breath. None of this was a surprise, in truth.

"Then it's good we came here for help," she replied calmly.

"Is that how it happened?" He snickered, then sobered, gazing off into the night. "If we stay, it will mean working together to sort out my magic. You'd be dragged into it, too, learning how to be a proper wizard–familiar team."

Team. The word filled her with all kinds of happiness. "Will that include me taking alternate form?"

"Do you want to?"

"Yes. I always wanted to be an animal."

"You *are* an animal, darling," he quipped, mostly out of reflex, she thought. His dark mood didn't quite allow for real humor.

"I'm willing to stay a while," she said. "It will be good to sort things out and this is a pleasant place."

"Except for Chaim," he said sourly.

"Don't worry about Chaim." She managed not to roll her eyes. "You are my bonded wizard."

"Yes. I suppose we might as well reconcile ourselves to that fact." Jadren hesitated. "I asked Liat if she knew of any way to sever the wizard–familiar bond. To set you free of me."

Selly's heart chilled and slowed. "What did she say?"

He shrugged. "Exactly what you'd expect. That we're stuck with each other. Sorry it's not better news."

She nodded, swallowing back the words. She should tell him about Alise's ability to sever the wizard–familiar bond. She *would* tell him. Eventually. Not tonight. They needed time together, to get to know each other when they weren't fighting for their lives. They deserved this opportunity. *She* deserved it, to live with him as her lover, just as she'd wanted.

Later, after they were easier with one another, she'd tell him and they could discuss their options rationally.

But for tonight, and for the next little while... "The water is lovely and warm," she said, coaxingly. "Relaxing. Join me?"

His lip curled. "Grooming imps are better for bathing."

"I'm already clean, but I can scrub your back, if you like." She allowed her gaze to drift over him, lean and dangerous looking in his own clothes again. "Or any other itch that needs scratching. I know you just got your clothes back, but I think it's safe to take them off."

His wicked lips quirked in a hint of a reluctant smile. "Trying to get me naked?"

"Absolutely," she purred. She stood, sensually aware of the water sheeting off of her in the flickering light, her nipples going taut as the cooler air teased them. His black gaze caressed her with almost palpable heat. "Come and soak with me, wizard."

"In that order?" he asked with a smirk that didn't bely the growing desire along their bond.

"Soak and come with me," she amended, giving him a saucy smile. "There's wine, too. I waited for you."

He considered for such a long moment that she feared he'd refuse. Then he came to some decision, methodically stripping off his clothes and leaving them in a heap on the stones. Naked, he walked to the carafe she'd indicated and poured two glasses of wine. Carrying them toward her, he looked so enticing that Selly shivered with anticipation. His cock hung heavy at his groin, already lengthening and growing thicker. Stepping into the pool, Jadren waded over to her, then handed her one glass.

She took it and paused, remembering. Jadren met her gaze somberly. "If anyone's wine is drugged this time, it would be mine," he noted. "You had control of the carafe and glasses."

"I thought I had control last time."

He dipped his chin in acknowledgment. "It would be too much to ask you to trust me."

"No, it wouldn't."

"No?"

"No." To prove it, she drank from her glass, more deeply than she had that night.

He watched her, black eyes glimmering, fraught emotion shimmering along the bond. Then he lifted his own glass, toasted her with it and drank. "Have I apologized for that?"

"You don't have to."

Taking the glass from her hand, he put both aside, then set his hands on her waist, smoothing those soft wizard's hands over her hips, sending little shocks of arousing sensation zinging through her. "I apologize," he whispered, holding her gaze. "I was a coward. Everything was so beautiful, the way you set it up, and I befouled it. I'm so very sorry I ruined that for you, Seliah."

"You didn't ruin anything." She ran her fingertips along his spine, scratching lightly with her nails. He shuddered, eyes half-closing. "But you can make it up to me."

"Oh?" He pressed a kiss to the hollow of her collarbone, sending shivers through her, his hands gliding over her as they sank deeper into the warm and welcoming water.

"Yes," she purred. "You have yet to fuck me senseless.

When will it ever happen?"

He laughed, a bare, low chuckle, but with real humor, at last. "I suspect you have far too much sense for me to exhaust you of it."

"Hmm. That could be. Still, if you're afraid of a challenge, then—"

He cut off her words with a deep kiss that made her dizzy, the draught of him more potent than any wine. "I'm done being a coward," he said against her lips, his clever fingers working erotic magic under the water. "With you with me, I'm afraid of nothing."

"Stronger together," she replied on a gasp, already losing her breath.

"For worse and worser," he predicted darkly.

She didn't care. They had this moment and that was enough.

It had to be.

Jadren and Selly's tale will continue in Twisted Magic!
Coming Fall 2023.

For the latest news on this and other releases, subscribe to
Jeffe's newsletter
or follow her on social media.

TITLES BY JEFFE KENNEDY

FANTASY ROMANCES

BONDS OF MAGIC
Dark Wizard
Bright Familiar
Grey Magic
Familiar Winter Magic
(Also Available in Fire of the Frost)

RENEGADES OF MAGIC
Shadow Wizard
Rogue Familiar
Twisted Magic

HEIRS OF MAGIC
The Long Night of the Crystalline Moon
(also available in *Under a Winter Sky*)
The Golden Gryphon and the Bear Prince
The Sorceress Queen and the Pirate Rogue
The Dragon's Daughter and the Winter Mage

FALLING UNDER
Going Under
Under His Touch
Under Contract

EROTIC PARANORMAL

MASTER OF THE OPERA E-SERIAL
Master of the Opera, Act 1: Passionate Overture
Master of the Opera, Act 2: Ghost Aria
Master of the Opera, Act 3: Phantom Serenade
Master of the Opera, Act 4: Dark Interlude
Master of the Opera, Act 5: A Haunting Duet
Master of the Opera, Act 6: Crescendo
Master of the Opera

BLOOD CURRENCY
Blood Currency

BDSM FAIRYTALE ROMANCE
Petals and Thorns

Thank you for reading!

ABOUT JEFFE KENNEDY

Jeffe Kennedy is a multi-award-winning and best-selling author of epic fantasy romance. She is the current president of the Science Fiction and Fantasy Writers Association (SFWA) and is a member of Romance Writers of America (RWA), and Novelists, Inc. (NINC). She is best known for her RITA® Award-winning novel, *The Pages of the Mind*, the recent trilogy, *The Forgotten Empires*, and the wildly popular, *Dark Wizard*. Jeffe lives in Santa Fe, New Mexico.

Jeffe can be found online at her website: JeffeKennedy.com, on her podcast First Cup of Coffee, every Sunday at the popular SFF Seven blog, on Facebook, on Goodreads, on BookBub, and pretty much constantly on Twitter @jeffekennedy. She is represented by Sarah Younger of Nancy Yost Literary Agency.

jeffekennedy.com
facebook.com/Author.Jeffe.Kennedy
twitter.com/jeffekennedy
goodreads.com/author/show/1014374.Jeffe_Kennedy
bookbub.com/profile/jeffe-kennedy

Sign up for her newsletter here.
jeffekennedy.com/sign-up-for-my-newsletter

Printed in the USA
CPSIA information can be obtained
at www.ICGtesting.com
LVHW091439270124
770083LV00043B/608

9 781958 679463